The Island of Doctor Moreau

An Interactive Adventure

By KJ Shadmand

Great Literature Gamebooks

Copyright © 2021 by Kurosh James (KJ) Shadmand

All rights reserved. This book or any portion thereof may not be reproduced or used in a manner whatsoever without the express written permission of publisher except for the use of brief quotations in a book review.

Cover by Pontus Unger
Interior Illustrations by Mays Thamer
Map by David Lowrie
Final Illustration by Leonardo D. Coleman
Copyediting by Deanna Bradford

Acknowledgements

Deanna Bradford, master of the technical arts of hyper-linking, formatting, and Amazon KDP.

Leonardo D. Coleman, for his brilliant sketch of Helmar and the sailor.

Samuel Isaacson, for his support, generosity of time and willingness to offer guidance in the art of gamebook creation.

Louise Lee, for her unfailing love of interactive fiction.

David Lowrie, for his excellent map.

James Spearing & Andy Redfern, gamebook enthusiasts and gentlemen whose sage and constructive feedback has been much appreciated.

Mays Thamer, for her hard work on the main internal illustrations.

Pontus Unger, for his splendid cover, GLG logo design and evocative secondary internal art.

Ryan from Brave Adventures, fellow Japanophile and friend whose early encouragement for my writing has meant much.

And of course, all members of the Gamebook Authors Guild!

The Island of Doctor Moreau

Adventure Sheet

PROWESS	BALLISTICS/RANGED DEFENCE
VITALITY	FATE
MEALS	TREASURE

EQUIPMENT LIST

NOTES

Creature Encounters

PROWESS: BALLISTICS: VITALITY: RANGED DEFENCE:	PROWESS: BALLISTICS: VITALITY: RANGED DEFENCE:	PROWESS: BALLISTICS: VITALITY: RANGED DEFENCE:
PROWESS: BALLISTICS: VITALITY: RANGED DEFENCE:	PROWESS: BALLISTICS: VITALITY: RANGED DEFENCE:	PROWESS: BALLISTICS: VITALITY: RANGED DEFENCE:
PROWESS: BALLISTICS: VITALITY: RANGED DEFENCE:	PROWESS: BALLISTICS: VITALITY: RANGED DEFENCE:	PROWESS: BALLISTICS: VITALITY: RANGED DEFENCE:
PROWESS: BALLISTICS: VITALITY: RANGED DEFENCE:	PROWESS: BALLISTICS: VITALITY: RANGED DEFENCE:	PROWESS: BALLISTICS: VITALITY: RANGED DEFENCE:

The Island of Doctor Moreau - An Interactive Adventure
By KJ Shadmand

Welcome to the World of Interactive Fiction!

The book you hold is a story with a difference. It is a re-imagining of a dark and ground-breaking science-fiction novel written by the British author H.G. Wells that places YOU at the heart of the story. By reading it, you will not only get a sense of a great work of 19th century adventure fiction, but you will also enter a thrilling and mysterious world in which YOU choose which direction to take, which dangers to risk and which enemies to fight. During your exploits you will gather weapons and items that may aid you in your quest, or you may fall victim to the many dangers that lie in wait…

The 19th century was an age in which humanity was truly beginning to tame the perils of the natural world, yet death still lurked around every corner. As such, you are unlikely to survive your first attempt to explore the Island of Doctor Moreau. With each attempt, however, you will be a little wiser and more experienced. Try a different path, make a different choice, or enjoy better fortune with your dice rolls. In the end, victory will almost certainly be yours if you do not give up!

To play this interactive gamebook, all you need are a pencil, some paper, and two six-sided dice.

STORY

In the latter part of the nineteenth century, Noble's Island was known as little more than an uninhabited volcanic outcropping set like an emerald in the middle of the tempestuous South Pacific Ocean. But in truth, it is home to a strange race of twisted and malformed creatures who are ruled over by their powerful and enigmatic master, the infamous vivisectionist Doctor Moreau, a scientist whose ambition and thirst for knowledge knows no bounds...

YOU are a passenger aboard the ill-fated ship *The Lady Vain*. When it sinks after colliding with a drifting derelict, you are thrown into a perilous adventure of survival, exploration, and dark discoveries. In this work of interactive fiction, YOU make the choices and decide your fate.

Will you escape the sinking ship and be able to defeat hunger and thirst while cast adrift upon a pitiless tropical ocean? Will you be rescued by the *Ipecacuanha*, a mysterious schooner that is ruled over by a delinquent captain and crammed with rare and exotic animals? If so, will you uncover the secrets and survive the perils of Noble's Island, the only land within a thousand leagues of anywhere?

The Island of Doctor Moreau - An Interactive Adventure is a re-imagining of the classic nineteenth century work of science fiction by H.G. Wells, presented as an exciting adventure gamebook.

YOU decide which paths to take, which enemies to fight, and which weapons to use. Whether you live to see England again to tell your extraordinary tale or fall foul of the many dangers you will face depend entirely on the choices that you make!

HOW TO SURVIVE THE ISLAND OF DOCTOR MOREAU

If you are a newcomer to interactive fiction and adventure gamebooks, then welcome! This is an exciting genre that you will surely love. Your experiences here may well encourage you to seek out similar books, such as those that form part of the Fighting Fantasy or Lone Wolf series, or the more recent Ace Gamebooks series.

You should know that you do not have to learn any rules or roll any dice at all in order to enjoy reading this book! If you would prefer to simply experience the story and explore Doctor Moreau's island, then feel free to pass every test you are asked to take and to win every battle you are told to fight. At a minimum, however, you should keep note of any weapons and items you acquire...

If on the other hand you are a gamebook veteran or would like to play *The Island of Doctor Moreau - An Interactive Adventure* with its full set of rules (this is arguably the best way to do it!), then you will find everything you need in the following 'Rules' section. Fear not, the rules are quite simple to master!

RULES OF PLAY

Before starting your interactive adventure, you need to establish your five main attributes by rolling one or two six-sided dice to determine your initial scores. These are PROWESS, BALLISTICS, VITALITY, RANGED DEFENCE and FATE. You can record these attributes in pencil on the character sheet at the front of the book or create your own character sheet on a piece of paper.

PROWESS

This is a representation of your hand-to-hand fighting ability and subsumes qualities such as coordination, balance and aggression. It is the attribute you will use in close combat encounters, and certain physical tests. The higher this score, the more skillful a fighter and survivor you will be!

To determine your initial PROWESS score, roll a dice, add 6 to this number and record this total on your character sheet. Your PROWESS score will not change much, unless you sustain a particularly nasty injury, or gain a powerful weapon. Note that your current PROWESS score cannot exceed your initial PROWESS score unless the text tells you so.

11

BALLISTICS

This is a representation of your shooting skill and is the attribute you will use whenever you are using a ranged weapon. Many of the creatures you will encounter on Doctor Moreau's island are extremely powerful. It makes sense to try to wound or kill them at a distance, if possible. The higher your BALLISTICS score, the more deadly you will be with missile weapons and firearms!

To determine your initial BALLISTICS score, roll a dice, add 6 to this number and record this total on your character sheet. Your BALLISTICS score will not change much, unless you sustain a particularly nasty injury, or gain a powerful weapon. Note that your current BALLISTICS score cannot exceed your initial BALLISTICS score unless the text tells you so.

VITALITY

This is a representation of your endurance, physical strength, and capacity to sustain injuries and wounds. You will deduct damage from this score if you are hurt and perform certain physical tests against it. If this score is ever reduced to zero, then you have died and will need to re-start the adventure. It is sensible to keep track of the previous section from which you have turned. Doing this will enable you to return to that section in the event that you suffer an unexpected end!

To determine your initial VITALITY score, roll two dice, add 12 to this number and record this total on your character sheet. Your VITALITY score will change a lot during your adventure as you sustain wounds, heal, rest and eat meals (see later for more on this). Note that your current VITALITY score cannot exceed your initial VITALITY score unless the text tells you so.

RANGED DEFENCE

This is a representation of you and your enemies' ability to evade and/or resist attacks from ranged weapons. Some small, agile creatures might have a high score in this attribute, as might creatures with tough, armoured hides. The higher this score, the better you will be able to resist the ranged attacks of your enemies!

To determine your initial RANGED DEFENCE score, roll a dice, add 6 to this number and record this total on your character sheet. Your RANGED DEFENCE score will not change much unless you gain some form of armour or shield. Note that your current RANGED DEFENCE score cannot exceed your initial RANGED DEFENCE score unless the text tells you so!

FATE

This is a representation of how cruelly or kindly the world will treat you. At times, you must trust to fate and face your destiny! The higher this score, the more fortunate you will be in your adventure.

To determine your initial FATE score, roll a dice, add 6 to this number and record this total on your character sheet. Your FATE score will change a lot during your adventure, especially if you rely on it to increase or decrease damage (see later for more on this). Note that your current FATE score cannot exceed your initial FATE score unless the text tells you so!

DAMAGE

Damage is not an attribute as such but will be decided by the weapon you are using. Whenever you find a weapon during your adventure, the text will tell you the damage it causes. If the text does not specify the damage caused by a ranged or close combat weapon, then you can assume that it causes 2 points of damage (this is the default damage for most weapons in the game). At the start of your adventure, however, you have only your bare hands for fighting that will cause 1 point of damage in close combat!

Some characters and creatures have a dual damage rating, such as 2/2. If so, then the first number refers to their *close combat* damage, while the second number refers to their *BALLISTICS* damage.

TESTING YOUR PROWESS AND VITALITY

At times, you will be asked to *test your PROWESS* or to *test your VITALITY*. When testing PROWESS or VITALITY the difficulty of the test will be indicated by the number of dice you must roll. If the total of your dice rolls is *lower than or equal to* your current attribute score, then you pass the test. If the total of your dice rolls is *higher than* your current attribute score, then you fail the test!

TESTING YOUR FATE

At times, you will be asked to *test your FATE*. This is always performed with two dice. If the total of your dice rolls is *lower than or equal to* your current FATE score, then you pass the test. If the total of your dice rolls is *higher than* your current FATE score, then you fail the test!

Each time you *test your FATE*, you must deduct 1 point from your current FATE score. Thus, fate is a finite blessing that will dwindle the more you rely on it!

SHOOTING AND CLOSE COMBAT

SHOOTING

During your adventure, you may come across a variety of ranged weapons such as slings, bows and arrows, and 19th century firearms. These will prove invaluable for fending off and killing the many fearsome enemies you will encounter!

Depending on several factors, the text will tell you how many shots you can fire before close combat is joined. Sometimes, you may be able to kill an opponent before they reach you, but often you will only be able to wound them before being forced to attempt to finish them off in close combat.

To resolve a shot, you should make a note of the target's RANGED DEFENCE and VITALITY scores. If you are facing more than one enemy, then you must choose which creature to target each round.

The sequence for shooting is then as follows:

1) Pick a target, then roll two dice before adding your current BALLISTICS score. This represents the accuracy of your shot and is your *ranged attack score*. Such is the power of gunpowder that if you are using a firearm and ever roll a double, then not only will your shot *automatically hit*, but it will also cause *double damage*! If this is the case, you may remove the damage from your enemy's VITALITY score before moving on to step 4. If you do not roll a double when using a firearm, then proceed to step 2.

Ranged weapons that do not rely on gunpowder (such as slings, bows, and crossbows) will also *automatically hit* on the roll of a double, but they will NOT cause *double damage*. Instead, they will cause the standard damage for the weapon (usually 2 points of damage, but sometimes higher or lower). If you roll a double when using a non-gunpowder ranged weapon, you may remove the damage from your enemy's VITALITY score before moving on to step 4. If you do not roll a double when using a non-gunpowder ranged weapon, then proceed to step 2.

As you may have deduced, non-gunpowder ranged weapons are potentially quite powerful, whilst firearms are potentially devastating!

15

2) Roll two dice before adding your target's RANGED DEFENCE score. This represents your opponent's evasive ability and/or resistance to ranged attacks and is their *ranged defence score*. Now proceed to step 3.

3) Compare the two results: if your *ranged attack score* is higher than your enemy's *ranged defence score*, then you have wounded your target. Remove the correct amount of damage from your enemy's VITALITY score (this will usually be 2 points of damage, but some ranged weapons cause lesser or greater damage). If however your target's *ranged defence score* is the same or higher than your *ranged attack score*, then your enemy has evaded or resisted the shot!

Now proceed to step 4 if your enemy has the means to shoot back. If not, then proceed to step 5.

4) If your enemy also has a ranged weapon, then they will attempt to shoot back, and you must repeat steps 1-3 on their behalf. If you are facing more than one enemy with a ranged weapon, then allow each of them to take shots at you in turn. As you can see, engaging multiple enemies in a shooting contest is a bad idea due to the risk of being outgunned! When your enemy's shots are resolved against you, proceed to step 5.

5) Return to step 1 until you have run out of ranged attack rounds, you or your enemy(s) is/are killed, or your ammunition is exhausted. Note that you may not switch ranged weapons midway through an engagement - there is simply no time to perform such a task!

Much of the time, your enemy will close the distance with you. If so, then you will be forced to fight hand-to-hand!

CLOSE COMBAT

During your adventure, you may come across a variety of close combat weapons such as knives and swords. These will prove invaluable for slaying the many fearsome enemies you are unable to slay at a distance! The sequence of close combat is similar to that for shooting:

1) Choose a target, then roll two dice before adding your current PROWESS score. This is your *close combat score* that represents the accuracy of your attack against a single opponent. Proceed to step 2.

2) Roll two dice before adding your opponent's PROWESS score. This is their *close combat score* that represents your opponent's attempt to dodge, block and strike back. Proceed to step 3.

3) Compare the two results: if your *close combat score* is higher, then you have wounded your target. Remove the correct amount of damage from your enemy's VITALITY score (this will usually be 2 points of damage, but some close combat weapons cause lesser or greater damage). If however your target's *close combat score* is higher than your *close combat score*, then your enemy has dodged or blocked the attack and managed to wound you instead! Remove the value of your opponent's DAMAGE attribute from your VITALITY score. If your *close combat score* is the same as your opponent's *close combat score*, then the round is a draw! Proceed to step 4.

4) If your enemy is still alive, then they will attempt to strike back. Repeat steps 1-3 on their behalf, then proceed to step 5.

4a) *Complete this step only if you are fighting more than one opponent.* If not, go to step 5:

17

Any further opponents you are fighting now get a chance to attack. Follow steps 1-3 on their behalf. As usual, if their *close combat score* is higher than yours, they will cause you damage. If your *close combat score* is higher, however, you do not cause your extra opponent(s) any damage but simply fend them off, as you are busy fighting your primary opponent! If your *close combat scores* are the same, you also avoid any damage. As you can see, fighting multiple opponents in close combat is a bad idea, due to the risk of being overwhelmed! Once multiple attacks have been resolved, proceed to step 5.

5) Return to step 1 and repeat the process until either you or your opponent is slain!

UNUSUAL COMBATS

At times, you may engage in ranged exchanges or close combats alongside allies. If so, the text will give you additional guidance on how to resolve these battles!

USING FATE IN SHOOTING AND CLOSE COMBAT

You may use your FATE to increase the amount of damage inflicted on an opponent or to decrease the amount of damage you sustain.

If you wound a creature and wish to increase the damage inflicted, then you may *test your FATE*. If you pass the test, then you may *double* the damage inflicted. If you fail the test, however, you must *half* the damage inflicted (rounding down). As you may have deduced, if you roll a double with a firearm and successfully *test your FATE*, then you have the potential to cause catastrophic wounds!

If you are wounded and wish to decrease the damage received, then you may *test your FATE*. If you pass the test, then you may *halve* the damage inflicted. If you fail the test, however, you must *double* the damage inflicted, so be careful when trusting to fortune!

18

Remember to deduct 1 point from your current FATE score, each time you *test your FATE!*

VITALITY AND MEALS

One of the main ways to restore your VITALITY score is to rest and eat meals. Though you commence your adventure with no meals, you may find them as you progress. When you do, record them in the *meals* section of your character sheet. You may eat a single meal at any time except when a battle is about to commence.

When you eat a meal, you may restore 4 VITALITY points, but remember that your current VITALITY cannot exceed your initial score, unless the text tells you otherwise.

HINTS FOR YOUR ADVENTURE

You will find that this is a story of adventure and exploration that permits you more than one way through the book. You will encounter all manner of perilous situations and meet many strange and dangerous creatures, some of which may be faster or stronger than you.

Seek out the deadliest weapons you can find and save your ammunition for the toughest enemies or most life-threatening situations. Gather meals and use them where you may - you never know what may lurk in the next patch of jungle or along a stretch of iron-grey beach.

Make notes and draw a map as you explore - these will be invaluable in any later adventures and will allow you to make more rapid progress. Most important of all: be brave, never give up, and you may survive the Island of Doctor Moreau!

NOW COMMENCE YOUR ADVENTURE!

Background

When you paid for passage on the sailing ship *The Lady Vain* at the bustling port-city of El Salvador, adventure was at the forefront of your mind. The three masted, square-sailed vessel was bound for the islands of Hawaii, where it would stop for several days to exchange its cargo of local textiles, grains and silver snuffboxes in return for as many bags of sugar it could carry. From there, it would press on through the Southern Ocean on towards Australia, that vast and parched continent of extraordinary indigenous life of which you have read so much.

You are an adventurer with an unquenchable thirst for knowledge and an innate curiosity that could not be satisfied by the interminable university classes, lectures and gruesome dissections which the more fortunate youths of England - such as you - were meant to attend. Instead, you wished only to study nature's vast creations *in vivo*, to observe and record their behaviours in sketches and in the written word.

Thus it is that (with your family's begrudging consent and financial support), you abandoned your formal studies and became an amateur scientist, becoming within five years something of an authority on the flora and fauna of south-west England. Gratifying though this achievement was, you longed for more and soon set your sights on the teeming expanses of the Americas. And so, with a pocket full of promissory notes, you bade farewell to your loved ones, took ship for New York and never looked back!

It took you five years to wander across the North American continent and come to the shores of the Pacific Ocean, from where you struck south to observe and record details of the extraordinary ecology of Mexico and Guatemala. In that time, you have become a tough and seasoned adventurer who has survived encounters with thieves, beggars and all manner of wild and dangerous beasts. You are adept in the fundamentals of boxing and wrestling, and are more than capable with knives, swords, and the sundry firearms made available to you in this free and untamed land. Aside from the means to defend yourself, all you need from life is sufficient coin for your next weeks' worth of meals, the means to procure sufficient game, notebooks, sketchpads, pencils and a couple of learned leather-bound treatises for your reference and enjoyment.

Early one morning, ten days out from El Salvador, you are resting in your cabin when *The Lady Vain* lurches with a violent crash and the deafening rending of wood. As you rush to your cabin window, you can see nothing but endless blue skies and a gently rippling sea, then you stagger as the ship starts to list. *The Lady Vain's* hull has been torn open and she is going down fast...!

Now turn to 1.

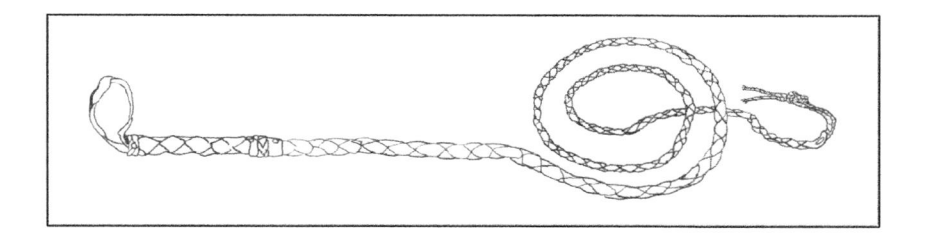

1

You rush out onto the deck to a scene of utter chaos and confusion. Everywhere, sailors and passengers are screaming, shouting and leaping into the glimmering blue waters. The cause of the collision seems to be a hulking, rag-sailed merchantman derelict that is drifting off starboard, while to the aft the ship's longboat is already pulling cleanly away from its mother, the dozen or so crew members

21

aboard it studiously ignoring the cries and pleas of those in the water around them.

To the port side you see a little dinghy with two men in it. One of them is a fellow passenger who is waving and beckoning for you to join him. It is Helmar, a young gentleman with whom you have held many a diverting conversation.

If you wish to dive overboard and swim towards the derelict merchantman, turn to **86**.

If you would rather swim towards the longboat, turn to **276**.

Alternatively, if you wish to strike out towards the dinghy, turn to **127**.

2

As you sprint into the jungle, you hear the Draconope crashing through undergrowth and snapping small trees as it gives chase. On open ground you could not hope to outpace it, but in the jungle, you at least have a chance...

Test your FATE!

If you are favoured, turn to **48**.

If you are unfavoured, turn to **352**.

3

If you murdered Helmar and the sailor, turn to 94.

If you killed them in self-defence, or they killed each other, turn to 182.

4

The island boat still rests beside the boathouse in its narrow channel, and you are pleased to find that it is stocked with sufficient crates of provisions and barrels of fresh water to last you for at least a month at sea. You trust that such a length of time will be sufficient for you to be picked up by a trader, or at least for you to land on an island uninhabited by unnatural beasts...

For a moment you hesitate and look back over the island. With its fine grey sand beaches, startlingly vivid flora, and smoking volcanic heart, it resembles some sort of primordial Eden, untouched and ripe with potential. You can well imagine the sense of excitement and possibility that Moreau must have felt arriving here more than ten years ago.

Then you hear a series of savage, hooting calls coming from the tree line, then a guttural roar followed by a terrified shriek...

Swiftly untying the boat, you unfurl the sails, watch them belly under the force of a decent offshore breeze and lurch towards the open sea.

Turn to 370.

5

The shark stoves in the barrel with a powerful bite, then - repelled by the unappetising nature of the object - glides back into the depths and swims away. Only then do you realise that you have sacrificed the one thing that was keeping you afloat!

This close encounter has reminded you of your love for life, and you make one last attempt to swim to the beach.

Roll a dice, modifying the roll for each point of FATE you are willing to spend!

If you roll 1-3, turn to **303**.

If you roll 4-6, turn to **240**.

6

You manage to cling to the rope long enough to reach the chasm floor, but try as you may, you cannot shake the rope free from the tree to which it is tied.

Remove the rope from your *equipment list*.

It is deadly silent in the chasm, and the walls down here seem to crowd together like the jaws of a crushing trap. There is a subtle declination to the floor of the chasm, running from the north to the south.

Uphill, the chasm widens and is better lit with moonlight, but downhill the walls narrow even further, and the air carries the faintly disagreeable odour of spoiling fruit, damp vegetation, and woodsmoke.

In which direction do you wish to go?

Uphill towards the moonlight? (Turn to **85**).

Or downhill towards the source of the unpleasant smells? (Turn to **300**).

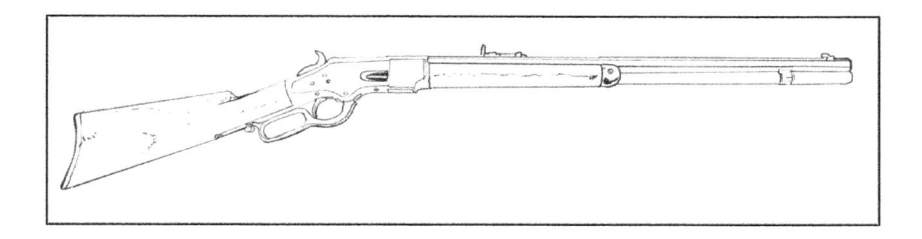

7

Now that you have proven your mettle by holding firm against the Pugnatyr's bluff, you suspect that you may be able to learn something from the beast.

To the Ape-man's surprise, you accompany him as he approaches the creature's den. As you do so, you take care to keep your head down and eyes averted so as not to be taken as a threat. The Pugnatyr glances at you sullenly, briefly bares its fangs, then looks away. You approach closer, patting the jungle floor with the back of hand and panting softly, before sitting sideways on to the creature. There you wait with your body pointing away from the beast, all the while casting furtive glances at the creature from over your shoulder. In the meantime, the Ape-man seems to be communicating with the Pugnatyr with a series of gestures, and gives a sudden, cackling laugh.

After what seems like an eternity, you hear heavy movement, and a brawny, black-furred arm encircles your shoulder and draws you into the den. You keep your gaze down, trying not to react too strongly to the numerous lice that are crawling through the Pugnatyr's dense black coat or the thick scars seaming its great body.

'Beast says...you have much courage for one so small,' the Ape-man reports, evidently proud of his interpreting skills. 'He has for you...a gift.'

The Pugnatyr reaches beneath a pile of branches and pulls out a small, worn, leather-bound book. It is a diary that seems to have been written either by a child, or an illiterate adult learning to read and write. It contains simple descriptions and drawings of the island and the sea, the weather, trees, birdlife and different sorts of fruit.

At first the writing and illustrations grow neater and more sophisticated, but about halfway through they start to degenerate, becoming little more than mindless scrawls and smears of pigment. The final dozen pages of the book have been ripped out, as if in a fit of sudden rage.

'Beast once made these,' the Ape-man tells you. 'Drew man-shapes and man-signs, before he could do so no longer. Master decides to make men of beasts; but without him, men once more become beasts!'

After these cryptic words, the Ape-man hands you a prickly pear from his pocket and follows the Pugnatyr as it moves off into the jungle, his broad silver back gleaming in the dappled light.

Add the **diary** and **prickly pear** to your *equipment list*.

Now, do you wish to head north through the jungle, down a gentle declination? If so, turn to **439**.

If you would rather head west through the jungle, turn to **459**.

8

The hunter looks up just as you are dashing between boulders. He immediately seizes his bow, leaps to his feet, notches an arrow and fires!

Roll a dice...

If you roll 1-4, the arrows slashes past you and buries itself in the soft soil!

If you roll 5-6, the shaft sinks into your shoulder (lose 2 VITALITY points!).

Now do you wish to charge the hunter? If so, turn to <u>55</u>.

If you would rather carry on towards the next boulder and take cover behind it, turn to <u>106</u>.

9

After dispatching the Hyena-swine you look over to see that Montgomery has shot his assailant through the head and is struggling to haul M'ling off his twitching opponent. Finally, the chimeric servant relinquishes his grip, and you are struck by the strange light in his eyes and the delight with which he licks the gore from his lips.

'My God!' exclaims Montgomery. 'These devils have gone mad! If the other beast-folk have done the same, then we are in trouble. It is even more vital that we find Moreau and get back to the enclosure.'

The three of you press on a little way, alert to the slightest sight or sound. The breeze shifts and M'ling raises his nose.

'Master is...close,' he mutters, pressing westward with sudden urgency. At last, you come upon the gnawed and mutilated body of the puma, its shoulder-bone smashed by a bullet. About twenty yards further down, near the base of a steep hill, you find what it is you seek.

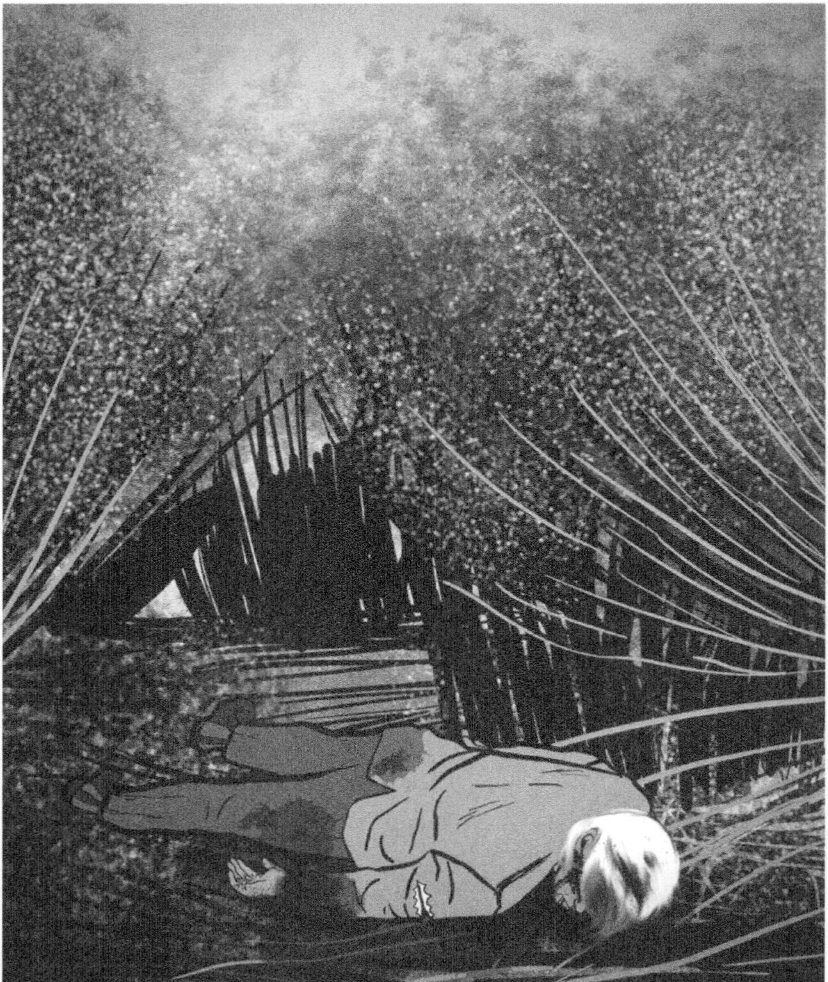

Doctor Moreau, lying face down in a trampled space in a cane brake...

One of his hands is almost severed at the wrist, and his silvery hair is dabbled in blood where his head has been battered in by the fetters of the puma. Of his revolver there is no sign. Montgomery turns him over and seems to stare at the body without seeing.

Suddenly, you become aware of dozens of creatures coming out of the foliage all around you, their faces eager and strangely animated. Your party is quickly surrounded, and M'ling makes a growling noise in his throat.

'He is dead!' they call out, a chorus of bestial voices. 'We saw, we saw!'

'The thing that bled and ran screaming and sobbing killed him!' rings a shrill voice. 'Is there a Law now?'

'Is there a Law?' repeat many voices in unison. 'Is there a Law??'

Your stomach twists and you look to Montgomery, but you see that he will be of no use here.

How will you reply to the beast-folk?

'The Master is dead, there is no Law, and all of you are free.' Turn to **354**.

'The Master is dead, but his Law lives on.' Turn to **524**.

'The Master is not dead, but he has changed his form.' Turn to **515**.

10

Heaving yourself from the quicksand is going to require an extraordinary feat of strength!

Roll five dice...

If the total is the same or less than your current VITALITY, turn to **44**.

If the total is greater than your current VITALITY, turn to **97**.

11

Your manoeuvres foil the aim of the hunter and you charge into the brake of trees just as an arrow hisses past your face. A shout from the north-west tells you that the second hunter is coming. Peering out from cover, you see him running towards you with a pair of long knives flashing in his hands.

The first hunter shoulders his bow and draws a similar pair of knives, the look on his face grim and stern.

Now that you have some cover, do you wish to make a stand in the tree line? If so, turn to **170**.

If you would rather keep running deeper into the trees and seek to escape the hunters, turn to **202**.

12

The Ape-man capers in delight at your acceptance, takes your arm and leads you into the jungle. You walk for several hours, all the time surrounded by towering beasts whose strange dimensions almost begin to seem normal to you after a time. As they progress, the fearsome mob grows increasingly pensive, until even the chattering Ape-man's spirits appear to decline.

Presently, you exit the jungle onto a hillside overlooking a steaming geothermic marsh fed by a number of boiling mineral pools. You then pass through a gap in a wall of blackened rubble and enter a bare clearing covered with a white sulphurous incrustation that leaks wisps of acrid smoke.

Without pausing, the group leads you into a narrow tunnel that plunges steeply into the earth before emerging into a narrow chasm some thirty to forty yards deep. After some time advancing along it, you discern the dim glow of burning torches lighting the narrow way and see two lines of crude, dark dens pressed against the chasm walls.

From them comes a disagreeable odour like that of a monkey's ill-cleaned cage, and you are appalled when the Ape-man guides you towards the largest of them.

'You must learn the Law, five-fingered man,' he jabbers. 'Only then can you become one of us!'

Your heart thumping in your chest, you allow yourself to be led inside and shown to a bench in a dim, dank corner. There you sit, staring at the shadows within shadows that are waiting in the hut...

Now turn to 350.

13

At your answer, a flicker of amusement crosses the MACAQUE-MAN's face, as if he knew all along that you had not intended to give away your things.

31

'My deepest apologies, lord,' he bows, before emptying the contents of the wicker box all over the ground. 'Perhaps then, you would prefer to...trade?'

Most of the weapons and baubles you see are either useless to you or heavily corroded, but you do spot a serviceable **cutlass**, **5 broad-headed battle arrows** and **6 hollow-tip revolver bullets** that have been stored in a watertight oilskin pouch. There is also a corked and wax-sealed **blue phial** that is filled with a mysterious liquid and labelled with the number *148* (make a note of this number if you acquire the phial!).

The **cutlass** is a sharp, heavy close combat weapon that (like a ranged weapon), will automatically cause *twice* the damage when you roll a double for your close combat score.

The **5 battle arrows** will only be of use if you have a bow but will cause 3 points of damage instead of 2.

The **6 hollow-tip revolver bullets** will only be of use if you have the revolver but have been designed to disintegrate on impact with flesh in order to cause maximum injury. They will also cause 3 points of damage, (and 6 points of damage on a double roll!).

The contents of the **blue phial** must remain a mystery, but the Macaque-man is able to tell you that such items are treasured by the Master.

Each of the above items can be traded for the following:

- 3 meals
- A pair of stone necklaces
- 2 leopard skins
- A pair of Toledo steel hunting knives
- A coil of rope

- 1 gold coin
- A bone knife
- A crossbow

Make your trades, if any, before carrying your possessions back to the side of the geothermic pool and getting dressed!

After doing so, you cast a final look at the oblivious bathers and their leader before making for the gap in the wall of volcanic rubble.

Turn to 349.

14

Your hand strays to your weapon as you stare into the gloom and try to discern the source of the sound. You exhale in relief when one of the rabbits that Montgomery released onto the island dashes past you towards the beach.

Have you killed the DRACONOPE? If so, turn to 52.

If not, turn to 139.

15

Just as you feel you can run no longer you hear a crash and a thump in the undergrowth just off the path. Forcing your way through a screen of vines you find the Ape-man laying stunned upon the soft jungle floor.

'You, you you...' he groans, his gaze now sorrowful and languid. Looking upon his prone form, you are certain now that he poses you no threat.

Do you wish to attack him anyway? If so, turn to <u>568</u>.

If you want to try to speak with him, turn to <u>151</u>.

16

When you demand to be taken to the House of Pain, the creature looks up at you in sudden fear, and you flinch at his pointed ears, lank hair, and his elongated lupine teeth set within an impossibly wide, grinning mouth.

It is a WOLF-MAN, one of the doctor's more malevolent creations!

'Yes, yesss,' the chimera whispers. 'To the House of Pain I will take you, lord. At the House of Pain I will leave you...'

He beckons with a swift movement and sets off into the jungle, one twisted hand still clutching at his wounded arm. Keeping your weapon at the ready, you follow the Wolf-man on a path that skirts the heights of the island's volcanic centre. You progress swiftly - south and then east - through the silent, moon-dappled jungle. Your guide's endurance seems inexhaustible, and just when you are at the point of commanding him to stop, he leads you onto a familiar silver-grey beach where you see the enclosure being warmed by the first light of dawn.

The silence is broken as the double gates of the outpost are flung wide, and a sudden frenzy of barking and growling breaks out. At this disturbance the Wolf-man takes fright and dashes into the forest before you have a chance to react. A moment later, the leashed staghounds come around the corner of the enclosure, closely followed by Doctor Moreau, Montgomery and M'ling.

Moreau restrains the dogs with a harsh command, stares at you for a few seconds, then leads the staghounds back into the enclosure, while Montgomery and M'ling advance towards you.

'Where the devil have you been?' Montgomery demands. 'We've been worried sick and were about to set out with the dogs to find you! Now get inside this instant, Moreau will want to have words!'

Your relief at being back among humans somewhat sullied by a flicker of dread, you do as Montgomery asks, enter the enclosure and let yourself in via the small door leading to the room. It does not take long before you hear the inner door to the courtyard being unlocked, and the doctor strides in...

Turn to 39.

17

While the Pugnatyr holds the Draconope's head away from his throat and fends off its wild attacks, you aim attack after attack into the monster's bloated body until grey-green ichor spurts darkly onto the sand. Finally, the Draconope gives a burbling shriek and falls limp and silent.

You sink to your knees, utterly exhausted. You have truly had a brush with death, and the sight and sound of the Draconope's shrieks of agonised hatred will stay with you as long as you live. Yet somehow, standing firm beside the Pugnatyr has filled you with confidence and pride.

Gain 2 FATE points!

While you are regaining your composure, the great ape drags the leaking corpse down to the surf, lifts it above his head and hurls it into the sea. He then comes to your side, gestures for you to wait and disappears into the jungle. After a short wait, the Pugnatyr reappears with a filthy oilskin bag that looks like it has just been dug up. He places it at your feet, nudges you affectionately with the back of his hand, and wanders off into the darkness of the jungle.

Your melancholy at the departure of the creature soon fades when you open the oilskin. Inside is a **breech-loading carbine** with a wax-sealed box containing a **magazine of 14 rounds**. You immediately attend to the weapon and find that it is in good working order. Also, you notice a silver strip soldered to the stock of the gun, on which is etched the number *367*. Be sure to make a note of this number!

Add the carbine to your *equipment list* and note that it does 3 points of ranged damage (6 on a double roll!). Additionally, the carbine has a rapid rate of fire which allows you to fire TWO bullets per shooting round.

Pleased with this deadly new weapon, you enter the jungle, find a comfortable spot and settle down to rest. Pillowing your pack under your head, you fall into a deep sleep.

Gain 4 VITALITY points.

When you awake, you realise that you have slept for several hours and that the dawn is not too far away. It is then that you notice an animal trail running away inland of where you have been resting.

Examining it closely, you see signs of the recent passage of what appears to be several people.

Intrigued, you decide to follow it.

Turn to **503**.

18

Helmar draws the shortest straw!

Eagerly, the sailor falls on him with his dagger, but he is too weak to kill the unfortunate passenger quickly. You watch in horror as Helmar tries to fight back, then the two men stumble over the gunwale, roll overboard together, and sink into the ocean like stones. In the terrible silence that follows you start to laugh, a dreadful mirth rising like a thing from without, before lapsing into bitter silence. Though you have been relieved of the temptation of committing the most horrible of crimes, it is just a matter of days now before you too, will perish...

As night falls, you slip into a morbid sleep, your mouth and throat a torment of thirst. When you awake the next morning, you are unsure whether you are alive or dead, for you see something you can scarcely believe - a set of sails dancing above the horizon!

For what seems like an endless period you lay with your head on the thwart, watching the schooner approach, lacking the strength to even cry out. You are dimly aware of being lifted up onto the gangway of a ship and perceive a large red-headed man with freckles staring down at you over the bulwarks. Then you gain the impression of a dark face with extraordinary eyes close to yours.

As some sort of metallic tasting liquid is forced between your teeth, you lose consciousness, unsure whether your rescue is a blessing or a curse...

Turn to **216**.

19

You are awoken in the night by a rhythmic chanting coming from the largest hut. Blinking away sleep, you recognise the Sayer's deep voice intoning a mad litany - line by line - which is repeated by a gathering of beast-folk and accompanied by the beating of hands on flesh:

'Not to go on all fours; *that* is the Law. Are we not men?'
'Not to suck up drink; *that* is the Law. Are we not men?'
'Not to eat flesh or fish; *that* is the Law. Are we not men?'
'Not to claw the bark of trees; *that* is the Law. Are we not men?'
'Not to chase other men; *that* is the Law. Are we not men?'

A kind of rhythmic fervour falls on the devotees, and the chant swings round to a new formula:

'*His* is the House of Pain.'
'*His* is the hand that makes.'
'*His* is the hand that wounds.'
'*His* is the hand that heals.'
'*His* is the lightning flash,'
'*His* is the deep salt sea...'
'*His* are the stars in the sky...'

At last the songs ends, and you drift back into a fitful sleep...

Now turn to **449**.

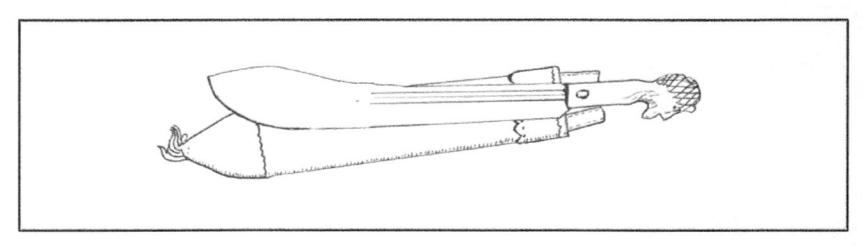

20

You press on into the jungle, the sounds of your passage masking those of your pursuers. Suddenly, something leaps onto your back from the darkness, and jaws clamp down on your shoulder. Your legs buckle under the sudden weight, and as you try to dislodge your assailant another ravening shape falls on you, this time seizing your arms and gashing your face with a snapping bite. Thrashing desperately, you give a single cry of terror before the creature on your back finds the side of your neck with its teeth.

As your blood pours onto the jungle floor, you are hauled to your back and catch sight of the leering WOLF-MEN who have brought you down. From them, there will be no mercy...

YOUR ADVENTURE ENDS HERE!

21

The ground becomes soft underfoot as you head towards the tree line to the south, but as the incline grows steeper the ground hardens. Before long you enter a dense brake of coconut palms.

Turn to **499**.

22

To your relief, the familiar figure of the Ape-man pushes his way to the front of the small crowd.

'Come with us now, five-fingered man,' he mutters, his darting gaze examining you as if for the first time. 'Come home...to the huts. To safety...to eat man's food!'

The other creatures crowd in, eager to hear your reply.

Do you wish to accept the invitation? If so, turn to **12**.

Or would you rather decline the invitation? (Turn to **57**).

As the figure draws to the edge of the quicksand, the moonlight reveals a creature unlike any you have ever seen. Dressed in rags like many of the other islanders, the newcomer has a large protuberant nose, liquid brown eyes, and extraordinarily large, wilting ears positioned high on his head. Everything about him - from the way he glances here and there with his nose held high, to the way he holds his arms awkwardly before him - is highly suggestive of a circus dog that has been taught to walk on its hind legs!

Indeed, he is a DOG-MAN, another of the doctor's bizarre experiments...

At your encouragement, the Dog-man throws you one end of the rope and pulls you out of the quicksand to the edge of the rocky shore.

'O Rider of the Sea, did I do well?' the creature begs, as you attempt to slap some life into your cold, aching legs. 'Did I pass the test?'

When you assure your benefactor that he has done well and passed the test, his eyes light up with delight, while his strangely jointed legs quiver with excitement.

'Men must sleep at night,' he grunts happily. 'That being so, I will show you a safe place to rest. Then, when light returns, I will guide you. To your home, to my home - my lord will choose!'

Feeling that you can trust this earnest little creature, you follow him through a mass of undergrowth on the southern side of the ravine (you may take the **rope** if you wish).

The vegetation here is so dense that it is as dark as a cave and seems well-nigh impassible, but the Dog-man grasps your sleeve and leads you through clinging leaves, creepers and grasping thorns until you emerge onto a tree-lined animal trail cutting from north to south. The pair of you follow the trail for perhaps a mile before your guide pauses, sniffs the air, then squeezes into a brake of tall, woody cane trees.

40

Shrugging off your pack and hugging it to your chest, you are only just able to follow him, until you emerge into a little den that is lined with ferns and leaves.

You lower yourself to the soft, dry ground, and watch as the Dog-man immediately sets to devouring some gruel he has wrapped up in banana leaves. When he has eaten his fill, he looks at you with sudden guilt, then offers you one of the meals.

You may eat it now to restore 4 VITALITY points or you may add the **meal** to your reserve.

With the Dog-man curled up contentedly at your feet, you fall into a deep sleep that ends with you being shaken awake. Though you have been woken prematurely, you still gain 3 VITALITY points from the rest.

'Master, it is time to leave,' whispers your guide. 'Bad men are close. Man-beasts. Savages. Not like you and I.'

Just as he finishes you hear a blood-curdling howl some distance away, then an answering call that is somewhat closer.

Where will you ask to be led?

To the Dog-man's home? If so, turn to <u>198</u>.

To 'your' home? (Turn to <u>475</u>).

24

The blunderbuss discharges with a flash of flame and a plume of smoke, but the lead shot fails to cause enough damage to dissuade the beast-folk from pressing home their attack. You fight bravely as you are seized, but your attackers are too strong and far too many. Pinned to the ground by gripping claws and tearing jaws, you begin to be eaten alive...

YOUR ADVENTURE IS OVER!

25

Even with the moonlight, it isn't easy to walk through the swishing reeds and tall grasses, and you find yourself plunging up to your knees in pools of stagnant water. Just as you sense you are reaching firmer ground, an animal burrow collapses under your weight and you sprain an ankle (lose 1 VITALITY point).

You limp on for another hour before the fatigue and frustration become overwhelming. You resolve to make camp, get some rest and await first light.

Pillowing your pack beneath your head, you drift into a fitful slumber...
Turn to **89**.

26

You leave your backpack and any weapons that might be damaged by the water on the bank before easing yourself into the swamp. Immediately, silt begins to rise from the bottom of the mire and - like boiling smoke - cloud the still waters.

Hurriedly, you dive towards the corpse, slide an arm around its chest and kick for the surface. As you strike out for the bank you find that the dead man's sodden head is almost side by side with yours, and you cannot help but glance at his features. Instead of the still face of death you expected, you perceive ice-blue eyes rolling towards you and a white-lipped mouth widening into a manic grin...

With a shout you attempt to thrust away the body, but ivory hands are now clutching at you with horrible strength as the corpse-thing sparks into sudden life and turns to face you. A series of pink gashes serrate either side of its throat; clean-edged incisions that pulse like the gills of a fish!

Your assailant is not some sort of undead horror, but a WATER WIGHT, the result of Doctor Moreau's ambition to equip a man with the ability to breathe fresh water. With lungs flooded with water and no longer able to draw air, this poor fellow has been deprived of speech and driven into madness. He will stop at nothing to drown you and make you his plaything!

You must engage in a contest of strength to see whether you are able to break free of the Water Wight's grip:

Roll a dice and add your opponent's VITALITY (8).

Then do the same and add your current VITALITY.

If your total score is less than the Wight's, then you must remove 2 VITALITY points and try again, until you are either drowned or your total is higher than your opponent's.

Once your total is higher, you are able to break free and haul yourself out onto the relative safety of the bank! The Water Wight is unable to leave the water but continues to claw at the bank and glare up at you through a few inches of water.

If you wish to use a ranged weapon to attempt to kill the Wight, turn to 136.

If you would rather leave the creature alone, you can continue to follow the edge of the swamp towards the west? (Turn to 184).

Or move away from the swamp and head north into the jungle (turn to 211).

43

27

When you indicate that you do not wish to fight, the creatures are upon you in a flash, restraining your arms and jostling you this way and that. They seize your weapons and remove your rucksack, ransacking your meagre possessions.

Do you possess the blood leaves? If so, turn to **84**.

If you do not possess the blood leaves but have the stone necklaces, turn to **125**.

If you possess neither of these items, turn to **76**.

28

You manage to negotiate your way across the warm, marshy ground and are relieved when the ground starts to become firmer and dryer underfoot. You approach the first of the huge boulders you saw from afar and press your back against it as you regain your breath.

Turn to **61**.

29

You follow a steady incline deeper into the island, where the atmosphere becomes humid and oppressive. After the best part of two hours' walk, you stumble upon a narrow, shaded path that appears fairly well trodden.

As you stand pondering which direction to take, you hear the approach of heavy footsteps coming from up ahead!

If you want to remain where you are to see what is coming, turn to **172**.

If you want to hide, turn to **148**.

30

'My destination is an island,' Montgomery replies. 'It's a beautiful, untamed place. At least, that's how it was when first I arrived there. One's perception of a place tends to turn sour the longer one lingers, haven't you found? I expect heaven itself would prove a tedium, given enough time. Hell, on the other hand...'

Montgomery's watery eyes become distant for a moment before he regains his focus.

'Anyway, my domicile is none of your concern,' he snaps. 'What *is* your concern is regaining your strength as quickly as you may. Now if you feel up to it, I suggest you accompany me onto the deck, to take some fresh air and gentle exercise. It will do you the world of good.'

You readily agree and follow Montgomery out of the cabin.

Now turn to **365**.

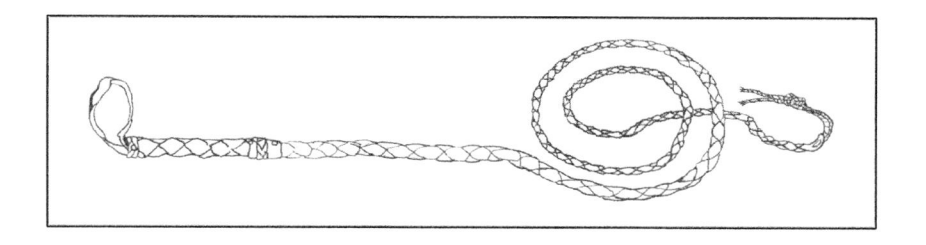

31

The books are old leather-bound works on surgery, or editions of the Latin and Greek classics which you cannot read with any comfort. As you leaf through them, a little buff-coloured pamphlet falls at your feet.

It is dated from more than ten years ago and is entitled 'The Moreau Horrors' in vivid red lettering.

Do you wish to read the pamphlet? If so, turn to <u>287</u>.

If you would prefer to investigate the inner door (if you have not already done so), turn to <u>109</u>.

32

As the last of the sunset fades from the horizon you guide the canoe onto the beach, drag it ashore and stretch yourself out on the sand. Overcome by the day's exertions, you fall into a healing sleep.

Gain 4 VITALITY points.

When you awake, you realise that you have slept through most of the night and that first light is not far away. Returning to the canoe, you set out on the water once more. Before long, you round a curve in the island and catch sight of a glimmer of light in the distance - it is the enclosure!

The creeping light of the new day is staining the horizon by the time you guide the canoe into the simple jetty alongside the island boat, and it is with some trepidation that you begin to walk towards the palisade. Suddenly, the double gates of the outpost are flung wide, and you see Doctor Moreau, Montgomery and M'ling leading the pack of staghounds out onto the beach. The dogs immediately catch your scent and lurch against their collars in a frenzy of barking and growling.

Moreau restrains the beasts with a harsh command, stares at you for a few seconds, then leads the staghounds back into the enclosure, while Montgomery and M'ling advance towards you.

'Where the devil have you been?' Montgomery demands. 'We've been worried sick and were about to set out with the dogs to find you! Now get inside this instant, Moreau will want to have words!'

Your relief at being back among humans sullied by a flicker of dread, you enter the enclosure and let yourself in via the small door leading to the room. It does not take long before you hear the inner door to the courtyard being unlocked, and the doctor strides in...

Turn to <u>39</u>.

33

You will need to dash between three boulders before you are behind the hunter. This involves two sprints, the first of which will pass dangerously close to his line of sight.

Test your FATE twice, adding +1 to your first roll to reflect the difficulty of evading detection.

If you pass both tests, turn to <u>79</u>.

If you fail either of the tests, turn to <u>8</u>.

34

You call on reserves of endurance and determination that you did not know you possessed, eventually emerging out of the jungle onto the scrubby hillside you saw from the rocky clearing.

The Dog-man leads you past pockets of volcanic soil that have been sown with a wide variety of exotic flowers, plants and fruits, and you are startled to arrive at the edge of a steep chasm cutting through the hillside and extending into the dense jungle on either side. Your guide rushes to a rough hemp ladder that descends some thirty yards to the chasm floor which is illuminated by the soft flicker of torchlight and lined with a number of makeshift dwellings that rest against both sides of the rock face.

'Do not be afraid, my lord,' your guide mutters, clambering down the ladder and staring up at you with his large brown eyes. 'Follow me down now, safe to the huts!'

Your hesitation is banished by the sight of two tall, hunched creatures with glowing eyes stalking out onto the hillside. Thus encouraged, you begin your descent into the darkness. Though crude, the ladder is solid enough and you are soon on the floor of the chasm, where you are struck by an odour that reminds you of a monkey's ill-cleaned cage.

The Dog-man grins at your arrival, then ushers you towards the largest of the huts.

'Even men must learn the Law,' he mumbles apologetically, following you inside the dwelling and guiding you to a bench in a dark, dank corner. As he does so, he hands you a small, brass key which you slip into a pocket (add the **brass key** to your *equipment list*).

Your heart thumping in your chest, you sit and stare at the shadows within shadows that are waiting in the hut...

Now turn to **350**.

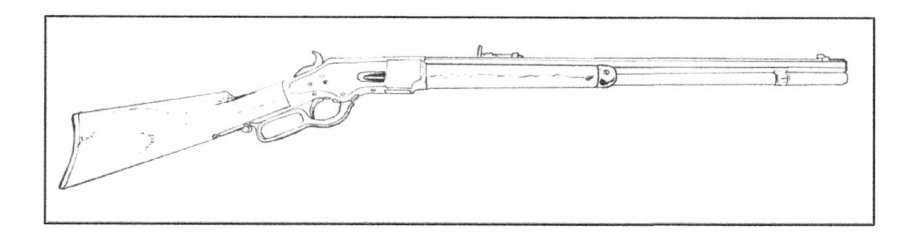

35

The oar strikes you hard on the temple, knocking you unconscious. You slip beneath the waves, just another victim of the sinking of *The Lady Vain*...

YOUR STRUGGLE IS OVER!

36

You jump over the brook and ascend the steps into the jungle. Using the occasional breaks in the canopy to navigate your way by the light of the moon, you press on away from the ravine in a southerly direction.

After several hours of painstaking progress, you begin to consider bedding down for a few hours' sleep when you hear a blood-curdling howl. It appears to be some distance away, but then you hear an answering call that is somewhat closer. All thoughts of rest set aside, you push on as fast as you dare through the dense vegetation.

Just when you think that you are going to be left in peace, you see a pair of luminous green eyes staring at you from the dense undergrowth. Then you hear a rustle to your right, followed by the flash of a second set of eyes.

You are being stalked!

If you wish to press on at a steady pace, in the hope that the creatures will leave you alone, turn to <u>20</u>.

Alternatively, you can throw down your rucksack, prepare your weapons and wait? (Turn to <u>54</u>).

37

You put an arm around the captain's neck and try to drag him off Montgomery! As you do so, you hear more sailors running up onto the deck. Blows start to rain down from all sides, and before you know it you are being forced face down on the deck and having your wrists tied painfully behind your back…

Lose 2 VITALITY points from the beating!

You see Montgomery and the misshapen man being treated in a similar way, and the three of you are soon lashed to the rear railings of the ship, bleeding and bruised.

Note, however, that you have *won Montgomery's trust*.

'This treatment of us will not stand, captain,' Montgomery spits. 'When the law hears of this, you'll never be permitted to sail again.'

'I'm already forbidden from taking to sea, you damn fool!' Davis leers. 'Why else do you think that my rates are so low? Now, let's see how the three of you like spending the night up here with the beasts. Then, come the morning, I'll have decided what to do with you all!'

With that, the captain and his crew return below deck.

Turn to **461**.

38

As you walk along the beach, you feel the strong tropical sun beating down on your head and shoulders. A rabbit emerges from the line of jungle to your left, hops around in a circle on the hot sand, then retreats back into the shade of the straight-stemmed trees.

Do you wish to get out of the sun and proceed north-west through the jungle? If so, turn to **566**.

If you would rather continue following the beach north, turn to **206**.

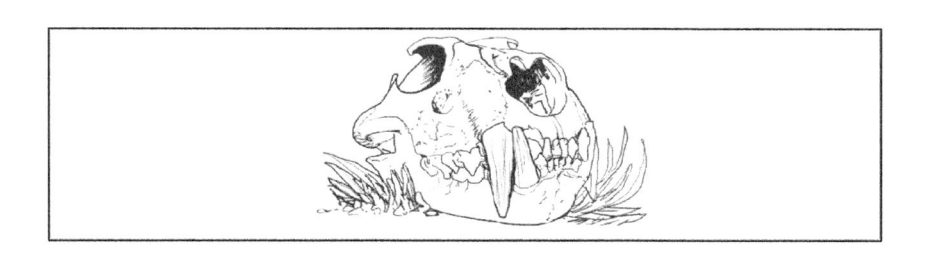

39

You sit very still as the doctor strides over to the bookcase, retrieves a cigar from a small wooden box, strikes a match and savours the first mouthfuls of dense, blue-grey smoke. Only then does he cast his dark, deep-set eyes in your direction.

'I must confess you are the most trying guest I ever entertained,' he says very deliberately. 'Here is my warning, sir. Listen closely, for I shall not repeat it: the next time you resolve to strike out into the island alone, alone you shall remain. The only reason that I came searching for you this time is due to a sense of responsibility I felt for your ignorance. I wished to keep my work from you until I could fathom your disposition and capacities, you see. Well, now I am satisfied in those regards, for very few could survive for a day and a night upon the island. You have proven your toughness, wit and resolve. In return, I will shed some light on my activities here.'

Forthwith, beginning in the tone of a man supremely bored but presently warming a little, Moreau begins to explain his work to you.

'First and foremost, you must be very clear that none of the creatures you have met upon the island are at all human, nor have they ever been,' the doctor explains.

'Rather, they are animals that have been humanised through *vivisection*, a discipline to which I have dedicated the best part of my life. Over the years, I have refined techniques of surgery, grafts, transplants and the transfusion of blood that have allowed me to create reflections of humanity from the beasts of the fields, forests and mountains.'

Moreau draws on his cigar, his inscrutable gaze piercing the fog of smoke that curls about him.

52

'But the changes I have wrought are not merely aesthetic,' he continues. 'My interventions go deep, transplanting one part of an animal to another part, or even moving parts between animals. I have altered my subjects' chemical reactions and methods of growth, modified the articulations of their limbs, and refined their most intimate structures, even shaping and sculpting the tissue of the brain. As I am sure you have noticed, this has gifted the majority of my creations with the gifts of speech, rudimentary thought and some sense of a moral code. Indeed, the more recent of my experiments have become astonishingly advanced. More advanced than you can imagine, indeed...'

'What of your decision to take the human form as your model?' you ask, growing uncomfortable under the doctor's keen stare. 'Would it not have been safer to form llamas into sheep, or some such thing?'

'I did not set out to imitate men,' Moreau shrugs. 'Once or twice I tested the plasticity of flesh and bone to its utter limits, creating masterpieces of design that were terribly dangerous and utterly inimical to other life. Purely experiments, you understand? Creatures that were never meant to get away. After some early accidents, I confined myself to emulating men and women. In time, I discovered that there is something in the human form that appeals to the artistic turn of mind more powerfully than any animal shape can.'

The doctor smiles faintly as this, as if recalling a distant love affair. But as swiftly as it came, the sentiment fades.

'But this choice has brought difficulties,' he says. 'Difficulties that I have grappled with for these past eleven years. Trouble with altering claws into hands, for example, or the challenges presented when grafting and re-shaping animal brains. Until recently, my creations suffered low intelligence with unaccountable blank ends. Least satisfactory of all was something that I could not touch, somewhere in the seat of the emotions. Cravings, instincts, desires that harm humanity, a strange hidden reservoir that bursts suddenly and inundates the whole being of the creature with anger, hate or fear. These challenges I am close to overcoming, but one more yet remains...'

The next word uttered by the doctor carries with it a note of bitterness and frustration.

'*Reversion,*' Moreau says, staring at you darkly. 'No matter what changes I make, the beast begins to creep back, begins to assert itself again. First one animal trait, then another creeps to the surface and stares out at me. Can you imagine creating a great work of art or literature that simply faded before your eyes? The erosive effect this might have on a man's resolve? Long ago I learned that resilience is but one of the demands placed by science on its agents. Thus, instead of lamenting, I have applied myself to the problem by asking questions, then devising some method of getting an answer, then facing fresh questions. You cannot imagine what this means to an investigator, what an intellectual passion grows upon him.'

Moreau takes a final puff of his cigar and grinds it out on the sole of his boot.

'In this spirit, you will be glad to hear that I have perfected enzymatic elixirs that either hasten or inhibit this process of reversion,' he tells you. 'There was a break-in to my lab a little while ago by some of the more daring of my creatures that saw a collection of these substances stolen. It was a dire nuisance and significantly set back my work. But the recent arrival of the *Ipecacuanha* has seen to it that I once again have what I need to resume manufacture. I will conquer yet!'

'In the meantime, you have simply taken the things you have made and set them free on the island?' you ask, after a long silence.

'They live short, brutish lives, I know,' Moreau nods. 'Torn this way and that by base drives that conflict with a sort of upward striving -

54

in some of them at least. They do have their hovels, which offers them a sanctuary of sorts. Fortunately, they retain an instinctive dread of the enclosure and a superstitious fear of me, a fact that has kept Montgomery and I safe all these years. As for their travesty of a moral code...well, it serves my purposes if they wish to view me as a God. Its existence also saves the weaker among them from a violent and gruesome death. At least, it has until now, though I fear those restraints are slipping. In truth, all of my attention rests for now on the puma. I have worked hard on her head and brain and expect her to turn out very well once her cuts and grafts have fully healed.'

After a second long silence, Moreau stands up and gives a thin smile.

'Well, what do you think?' he asks. 'Are you in fear of me still?'

You are about to reply when a scream comes through the inner door, the very same sound that drove you from the enclosure in the first place...

Turn to 154.

40

The blunderbuss discharges with a flash of flame and a plume of smoke, blasting a number of beast-folk to the ground and causing their charge to falter. You sweep your now empty Dragon back and forth in the hope that it will keep your enemies at bay while you reach for another weapon, then there is the sharp crack of a revolver.

Montgomery has freed his upper body from beneath the slain monster and is firing wildly at the beast-folk! Eagerly you join in the shooting with your own revolver before all the creatures have fled into the jungle.

Remove 1 blunderbuss charge, 3 revolver rounds but gain 1 FATE point!

In the dead silence that follows, M'ling staggers to his feet, shakes his head groggily, and surveys the carnage around him. At your urging, he helps you drag Montgomery free.

'It's a fine thing all three of us made it through in one piece,' Montgomery mutters, as he brushes himself down and reloads his revolver with trembling hands. 'After all, it's going to take a grand effort to drag poor old Moreau back to the enclosure. We can't rightly leave him here to have his bones picked, can we...?'

Do you wish to agree that you have to try to return Moreau's body to the enclosure? If so, turn to **223**.

If you would rather counsel that you must leave Moreau's body where it lays and return to the enclosure as quickly as possible, turn to **520**.

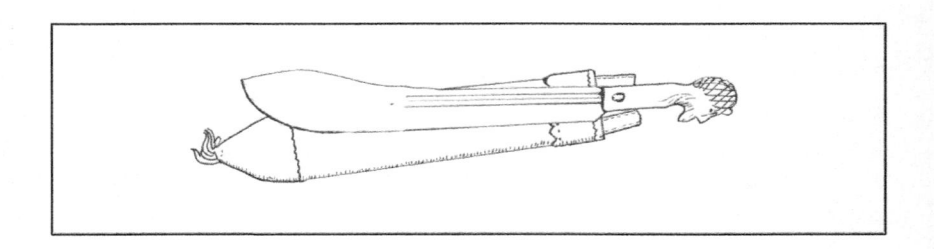

41

You step forward and try to persuade Montgomery that the captain is too drunk to know what he is saying, reminding him that it would be better not to quarrel with the owner of a ship while out of sight of land...

Test your FATE, deducting 2 from your roll if you have *explained your survival*.

If you are favoured, turn to **107**.

If you are unfavoured, turn to **251**.

42

The MACAQUE-MAN's sly smile widens at your response.

'Excellent, my lord, excellent!' he chuckles. 'We must share this delightful news with the others!'

Before you can stop him, he calls out to the bathers, telling them that the time has come to make offerings to the Heart of the Island. Emerging from their soporific state with alacrity, the creatures clamber from the geothermic pool, pull on their ragged garments and crowd around you in curiosity.

'To the Heart of the Island, to the sacred Heart!' they chant, leading you towards the highest point of the geothermic system, a superheated pool that wells up from deep beneath the earth. For a moment you fear that the creatures intend to hurl you to your death, but instead they begin to recite a primal dirge as their leader lays out your possessions with great ceremony. Then he proceeds to toss each item into the boiling water!

With the exception of any items that can fit into your pockets (such as keys, coins, or phials) and TWO ranged weapons and ONE close combat weapon of your choosing (the Macaques do not wish to disarm you entirely) you must remove all your weapons and possessions from your *equipment list*!

When the infuriating ceremony is done, the creatures embrace one another and take turns patting you on the back, before ambling off into the jungle. Their leader is the last to leave, but before doing so, he offers you a length of slender cord that was wrapped around his waist. Only then do you see that it has a large knot tied in the end. It is a **wind-cutter**, a simple device that is spun through the air to send whirring sound messages over great distances.

'You have sacrificed much to our divinity, my lord; it is only fair that you receive something in return,' he tells you. 'If you are the agent of change for whom we have prayed, then go forth with our blessing. Bridge the gap between beast-folk and Other, as only you know how. And if you are ever in dire need of help, then we will come.'

With that, the Macaque-man follows his kin into the night. Immediately, you return to your clothes and dress, grateful that they (and any armour you were wearing) were not destroyed. You then give the wind-cutter an experimental whirl before noticed the **iron dagger** (2 points of *close combat damage*) laying forgotten by one of the pools.

Take the weapon if you wish, before making your way over to the gap in the wall of volcanic rubble.

Turn to <u>349</u>.

43

In the face of your stiff defence, the Humboldts relinquish their attack and plunge into the deep as swiftly as they appeared. Grateful to be alive, you paddle the scratched and scored canoe towards the beach, vowing never to be caught out on the water so close to nightfall again...

Now turn to 82.

44

Your arms and shoulders trembling, you somehow manage to drag yourself from the quicksand and tumble gratefully into the canoe. You are utterly exhausted by your efforts and must lose 2 VITALITY points!

Once you come to your senses, you realise that although you are out of immediate danger, you are still stranded upon the delta with no way of reaching the ravine other than by attempting a different path across the mire...

You must *test your FATE* and run the gauntlet of the quicksand yet again!

If you are favoured, turn to 293.

If you are unfavoured, turn to 382.

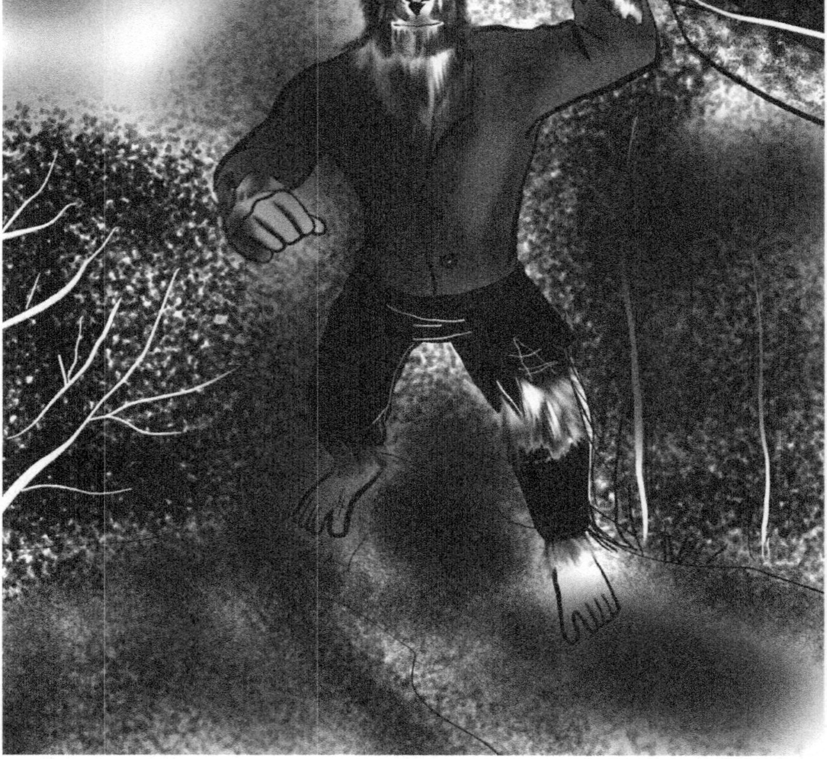

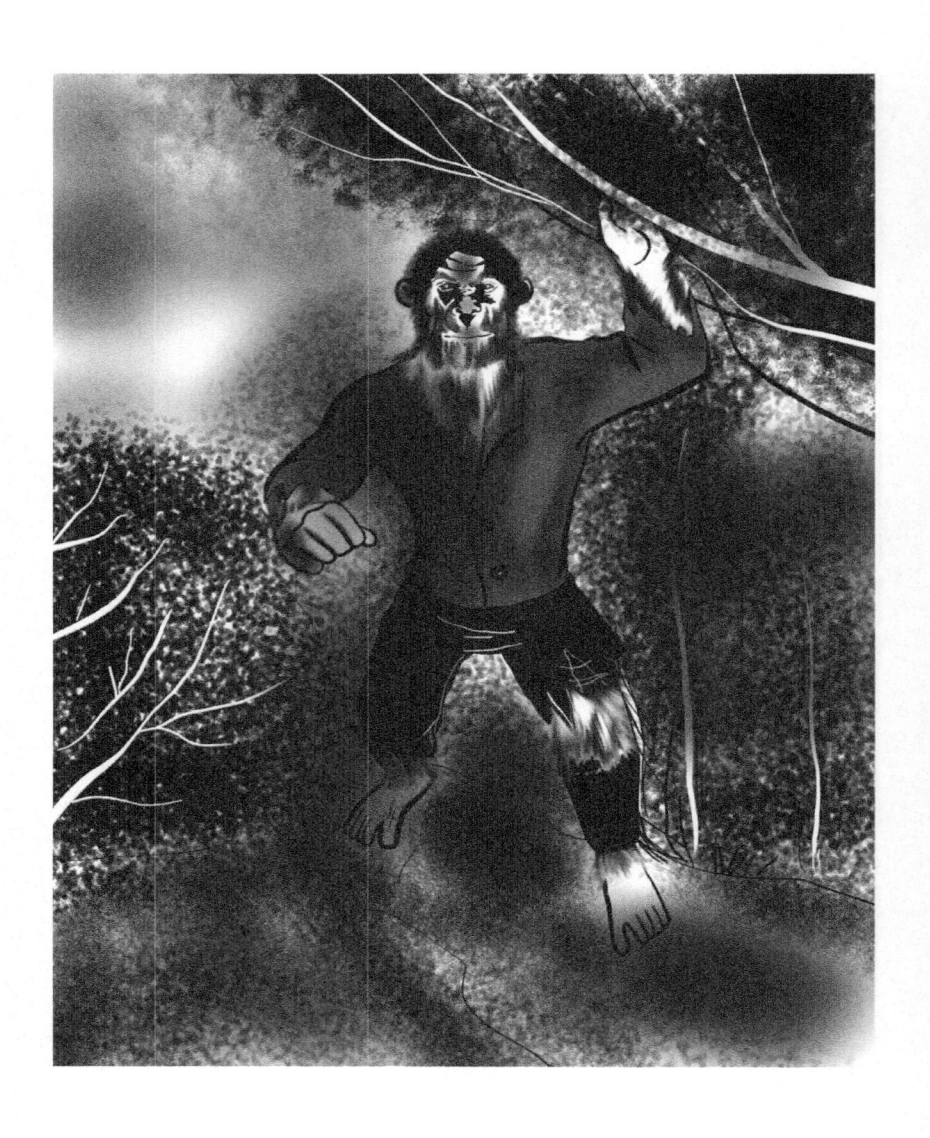

45

As you approach the man, his gestures grow even more animated, and you see that he rivals the manservant M'ling in his strangeness. He is of medium size, with lank arms, long thin feet and bow legs. His bright, restless eyes travel all over you, to your hands, feet, and the tattered places in your coat. Suddenly, he retreats into the undergrowth before his heavy face reappears between some fronds he is holding apart with his long, dexterous hands.

'You, you you...!' he chatters excitedly.

You do not feel the same repugnance towards this creature as you did with the bandaged boatmen or with M'ling. Still, you are unsure of this APE-MAN's intentions.

Do you wish to attack him? If so, turn to **96**.

Would you prefer to speak with him? If so, turn to **151**.

If you would prefer to avoid him and press on north along the beach, turn to **38**.

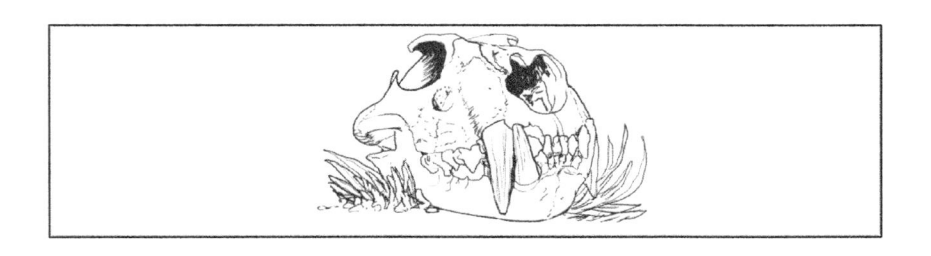

46

You aim attack after attack at the Draconope's leathery neck until its burbling roars cease and its thrashing form falls limp. You have truly had a brush with death; the sight and sound of the Draconope's shrieks of agonised hatred will stay with you as long as you live...

Lose 1 FATE point!

When you have regained your composure, you continue to walk along the beach. Just as you are beginning to fall asleep on your feet, you round a rocky headland by means of a frill of rock hidden just beneath the surface of the ocean and catch sight of a glimmer of light in the distance - it is the enclosure!

The creeping light of the new day is staining the sky by the time you pass the simple jetty harbouring the island boat, and it is with some trepidation that you begin to walk towards the enclosure. Suddenly, the double gates of the outpost are flung wide, and you see Doctor Moreau, Montgomery and M'ling leading the pack of staghounds out onto the beach. The dogs immediately catch your scent and lurch against their collars in a frenzy of barking and growling.

Moreau restrains the beasts with a harsh command, stares at you for a few seconds, then leads the staghounds back into the enclosure, while Montgomery and M'ling advance towards you.

'Where the devil have you been?' Montgomery demands. 'We've been worried sick and were about to set out with the dogs to find you! Now get inside this instant, Moreau will want to have words!'

Your relief at being back among humans somewhat sullied by a flicker of dread, you enter the enclosure and let yourself in via the small door leading to the room. It does not take long before you hear the inner door to the courtyard being unlocked, and the doctor strides in...

Turn to 39.

47

The creatures overpower you, seize your arms and legs and begin dragging you across the rocks. At first you think yourself taken captive, but then you see that you are being hauled towards a boiling pool at the highest point of the geothermic system. You resist with all your strength, but are unceremoniously hurled into the water where you are swiftly boiled alive...

YOUR STRUGGLES ARE AT AN END!

48

You manage to keep from falling and tear uphill through the jungle, your breath ragged and your heart thumping!

Eventually, the Draconope gives an enraged shriek and turns back in the direction of the beach, the sounds of its clumsy passage swiftly fading. It is now almost dark, so you decide to make a camp for the night.

Piling leaves and branches around you so that any creature will wake you with the noise of its approach, you pillow your pack under your head and fall into an exhausted sleep. When you awake, you realise that you have slept for several hours and that the dawn is not far away.

Gain 4 VITALITY points.

It is then that you notice a jungle path just in front of you, bearing on an east-west axis. You are quite sure that heading east will take you in the direction of Doctor Moreau's enclosure, whereas west will take you in the direction of the volcanic spring you saw from the beach.

If you wish to head east towards the enclosure, turn to 60.

If you would rather head west, turn to 450.

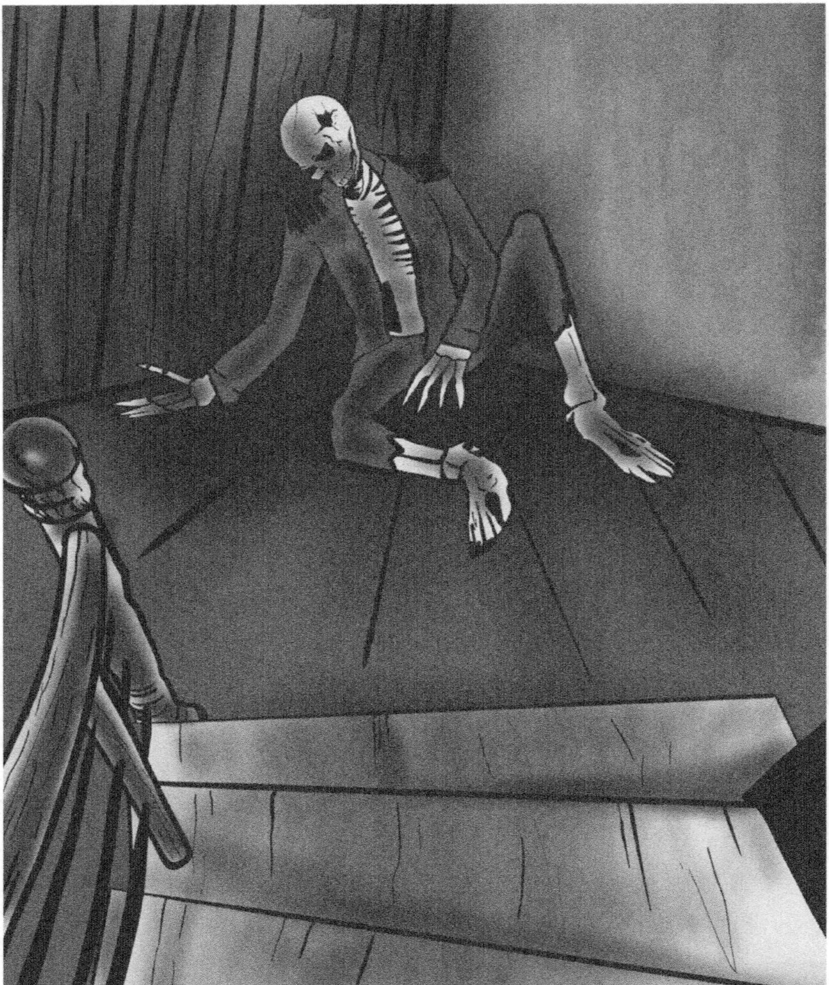

49

The sunlight illuminates enough of the staircase to reveal another skeleton slumped at the base of the steps. It is dressed in an officer's uniform and has a jagged hole in the side of its skull. There is no sign of the firearm used to inflict the wound, although a quick search of this unfortunate reveals a **large handkerchief**.

Add this item to your *equipment list* before hurrying back up onto the deck.

Now, if you wish to search the deck (if you have not already done so), turn to 308.

If you would prefer to climb back down the rigging and strike out for the dinghy, turn to 95.

50

You secure the rope around a sturdy tree and begin to lower yourself into the chasm. The sides of the rock wall are smoother and glassier than you had expected, and your feet keep slipping out from beneath you. When you are about halfway down the face, your arms begin to tremble with fatigue and your hands start to lose their grip.

You fight the feeling of panic as you realise that you might not be able to hold on!

Roll four dice...

If the result is less than or equal to your current VITALITY, turn to 6.

If the result is greater than your current VITALITY, turn to 339.

51

'Probably for the best, if I'm being honest,' Montgomery says, when you offer to accompany him on his search for Moreau.

If you do not possess a **revolver**, then Montgomery will give you a spare from the belt of his trousers. If you do possess a revolver, then he will give you an extra **6 rounds** of ammunition.

The pair of you set off along the beach, following Moreau's boot prints towards the bushes where he vanished from sight. The morning is as still as death. Not a whisper of wind is stirring, the sea is like polished glass, the sky empty, the beach desolate. You find yourself in a half-excited, half-feverish state where the stillness of your surroundings is oppressive.

You are swallowed up by the tree line and press inland as Montgomery leads the way through the jungle and begins to call out: 'Coo-ee...Mor-eau! Coo-eeee!'

The trail is plain enough on account of the crushed and broken bushes, white rags torn from the puma's bandages, and occasional smears of blood on the leaves of the shrubs and undergrowth. As you press on north-west, you reach a more open area of stony ground with a stream running through it, and here the trail goes cold. For some time you ramble this way and that, until you hear a single pistol shot echo through the jungle.

'Let's hope he's brought down the devil!' Montgomery mutters, angling towards the sound of the shot. You have gone less than half a mile when you see a figure ambling towards you, but you relax when you see that it is M'ling, Montgomery's deformed manservant who you now recognise is some complex trophy of Moreau's skill in blending a bear with a dog and an ox.

66

'I was gathering wood, Masters,' M'ling explains grovellingly, pointing to the hatchet tucked into his belt. 'Then I heard your calls, and the other thing...'

Montgomery quickly explains the situation, before the three of you advance westward, shouting Moreau's name. M'ling takes the lead, his shoulders hunched, his strange head moving with quick starts as he peers this way and that. His hatchet remains tucked into his belt, and you realise that *teeth* are his weapons when it comes to fighting.

Your strange party presses on for a good while through the wild luxuriance of the island, until M'ling stops, his body rigid with watchfulness. Moments later, three grunting, hunched shapes come crashing through the ferns. They are unlike any beast-folk you have seen thus far - short, squat creatures with glittering black eyes, quivering snouts, and fang-filled, dribbling mouths that look to be blood-stained.
They come to a halt before you, their fierce, excited faces lit with a strange, menacing light.

'Beggars...!' Montgomery says sharply, cracking his whip. 'Stay back, I tell you! You have no business approaching us without summons!'

Heedless of the order, one of the creatures charges at M'ling, who meets it halfway so that the pair fall rolling and snarling in the soil. Montgomery's face pales as he realises what is happening, then he raises his revolver as a second creature charges him.

The third beast-man leaps towards you!

You may perform TWO ranged attacks before close combat is joined.

HYENA-SWINE: Prowess - 7; Vitality - 6; Ranged Defence - 6.

If you win, turn to 9.

67

52

Moments after the rabbit disappears, you hear the violent scuffing of sand and a brief squeal. Alarmed, you move in the direction of the beach and peer through the trees. Standing halfway up the beach are a pair of male AFRICAN LIONS, one of which has the kicking rabbit dangling from its jaws!

The great felids are gangly and underfed, and you can only surmise that they are test animals which have managed to escape the clutches of the doctor. They sniff the air, fix their flashing green eyes upon you and advance with their bodies low to the sand...

The tree line will slow these predators down, allowing you to perform TWO ranged attacks before entering close combat!

First LION: Prowess - 8; Vitality - 8; Damage - 2; Ranged Defence - 7.

Second LION: Prowess - 7; Vitality - 7; Damage - 2; Ranged Defence - 7.

If you win, turn to **378**.

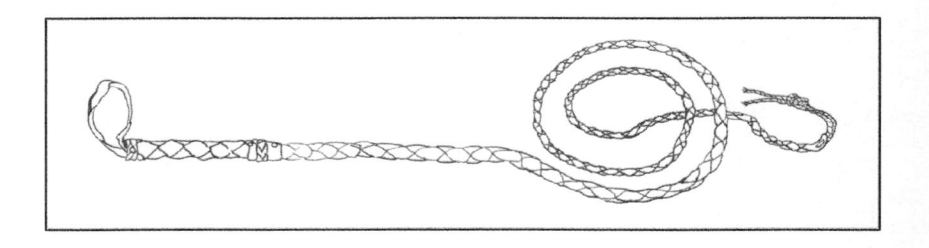

53

Montgomery reaches the outer door, unlocks it and flings it open. He stands half-facing you, between the yellow lamplight and the pallid glare of the moon.

'You're a solemn, silly ass!' he declares. 'Always fearing and fancying. Trying to make sense of things when we are nothing more than bubbles blown by a baby. We're on the edge of things here, you know. Tomorrow, I'm bound to cut my throat. But tonight, I'm going to have a damned good bank holiday!'

He turns and strides out into the moonlight, shouting at the top of his lungs for M'ling. You follow as far as the doorway and see three figures come along the edge of the beach, one a white-wrapped creature, the other two blotches of blackness following it. They halt, staring. Then you see M'ling's hunched shoulders as he comes around the corner of the house.

'Drink!' cries Montgomery. 'Drink, ye brutes! Drink and be men!'

Waving the bottle in his hand, Montgomery heads off at a quick trot to the westward, M'ling ranging himself between him and the three dim creatures who follow. Before their figures become indistinct in the mist, you see Montgomery administer a dose of the raw brandy to M'ling, then the five figures melt into one indistinct patch.

Reluctantly, you close the door and lock it.

Is Moreau's body in the courtyard with you?

If so, turn to **425**.

If not, turn to **543**.

54

You shrug off your rucksack and raise your guard, eyes straining to penetrate the darkness, ears intent on the slightest sounds. You catch a rustle to your flank and swivel towards it...

Do you possess a ranged weapon which you wish to use? If so, turn to **126**.

If you do not wish to use a ranged weapon, or if all you have are close combat weapons, turn to **145**.

55

The hunter's eyes widen, then harden as you charge in. Calmly, he reaches for an arrow and notches it to his bow.

Your opponent has time to fire off TWO arrows before you can engage him in close combat.

VAI THE HUNTER: Prowess - 8; Ballistics - 8; Vitality - 9. Damage - 2/2.

Deduct 2 points from your *close combat strength* if you are unarmed, deduct 1 if you are wielding a rock.

If you win, turn to **310**.

56

As soon as you leave the path you seem to enter another world - one of dappled light, muffled sounds, and rampant vegetation. Taking this route means that progress will be slow, but at least you have the benefit of concealment, and you doubt that even the finest

70

bloodhound could track you through the rich earthen and decomposition scents that permeate the air.

Wide-eyed at this rich and unfamiliar environment, you press on towards the south, alert for any of the many dangers that might lurk in the humid gloom. After expending a good deal of effort weaving your way through the jungle, you catch the sound of excited yips and growls coming from ahead.

Not wishing to retrace your hard-won steps, you press on determinedly and break through a screen of vines into a dank clearing.

Turn to 173.

57

When you decline his invitation, the Ape-man steps back in surprise, shakes his head and makes a rapid panting sound.

'Then you, you, you, must return to the Master,' he jabbers. 'You must return to the House of Pain!' He points east, in the direction of the dense interior of the island. 'That way to the Master; that way to the House of Pain. Go now!'

Not wanting to provoke the group, you pick up your rucksack and prepare to leave.

Did you choose to spend the night inland? If so, turn to 121.

If you chose to stay on the beach, turn to 215.

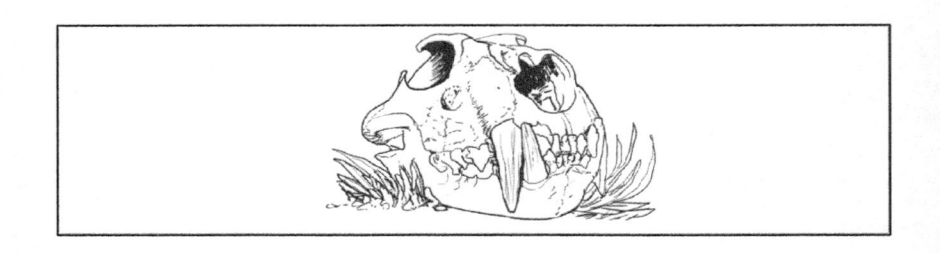

58

Before you can awaken fully, you are seized by many pairs of strong hands and subjected to a flurry of heavy blows!

Roll a dice, divide it by 2 (rounding up) and deduct the result from your VITALITY.

Thus subdued, you are marched into the jungle at the centre of a pack of polymorphic brutes. Since none of your captors seem inclined to dignify your objections, you take the opportunity to gather as much visual information about them as you may. As they move through shafts of moonlight, you ascertain that the creatures' variations in height and shape are unified by a common feature - that of steady domesticity and mob identity.

It is as if these creations of Doctor Moreau are based on the sorts of powerful yet docile beasts one might find in the fields of England, rather than the fierce predators of Africa or the Americas. The throb and ache of your bruises, however, remind you of your captors' capacity for violence. Furthermore, you cannot help but wonder to what purpose they are leading you...

After a few stumbling hours, your captors push you into a tunnel that carves through the side of a hill. It terminates in a large boulder which the leader of the party pushes forward with a heave and a grunt, allowing you access a slightly broader chasm that affords a glimpse of the starry night sky. After the brute returns the boulder into place, the mob escorts you deeper into the chasm until you discern the glow of torches and a series of crude, dark dens huddled on either side of the rock face. From the shelters comes a disagreeable odour like that of a monkey's ill-cleaned cage, and beyond them you see the chasm disappear into darkness once more.

Suddenly, a towering brute pushes you towards the largest of the malodorous huts, shoves you inside and escorts you to a bench in a dim, dank corner.

Your heart thumping in your chest, you stare at the shadows within shadows that are waiting in the hut...

Now turn to **350**.

59

Roll one dice!

If you roll 1-4, turn to **523**.

If you roll 5 or 6, turn to **208**.

60

You walk briskly along the jungle path. Just as you are beginning to think you have lost your bearings, you find yourself emerging onto the small sandbank overlooking the beach where you first set out on your exploration of the island.

The dawn has begun to touch the eastern sky, and by the strengthening light you catch sight of the enclosure in the distance. As you trudge wearily towards it, you are surprised to see the figures of Doctor Moreau, Montgomery and M'ling leading the pack of staghounds out onto the beach. The dogs immediately catch your scent and lurch against their collars in a frenzy of barking and growling.

Moreau restrains the beasts with a harsh command, stares at you for a few seconds, then leads the staghounds back into the enclosure, while Montgomery and M'ling advance towards you.

'Where the devil have you been?' Montgomery demands. 'We've been worried sick and were about to set out with the dogs to find you! Now get inside this instant, Moreau will want to have words!'

Your relief at being back among humans somewhat sullied by a flicker of dread, you do as Montgomery asks, enter the enclosure and let yourself in via the small door leading to the room. It does not take long before you hear the inner door to the courtyard being unlocked, and the doctor strides in...

Turn to 39.

61

Peering around the edge of the boulder, you see that it is indeed the hunters' camp. It is an excellent location for men not wanting to be discovered, for not only is it well-screened by the steaming streams to the south-east and a fringe of dense jungle to the south-west, but it is protected to the north and west by the sea itself.

Though the camp is surrounded by boggy ground on three sides, a steady onshore breeze keeps the air clear of insects, steam and smoke, and in the direction of the beach there is an ample copse of swaying palm trees. The huge boulders strewn about this part of the island seem to you like ancient moss-covered sentinels, and lend the site a sacred, mysterious air.

You absorb these details quickly, before your eyes are drawn to the hunter who is knelt in the middle of the camp, about fifty paces away. His is facing you but engrossed in the act of sharpening a knife on a whetstone. Before him is a small campfire while behind him are two simple lean-tos built from large leaves and branches. The man's bow and quiver are by his side.

As you ease back behind the boulder, you hear the sound of chopping coming from the copse of palm trees. For now, the hunters are apart - you could not have hoped for a better chance to overcome them!

Do you wish to risk dashing from boulder to boulder to get behind the hunter from where you might creep up on him? If so, turn to **33**.

If you would prefer to launch a direct charge at the man before his friend returns to the camp, turn to **55**.

62

The sailor holds out the three splinters and offers you the first pick, his weary eyes fixed on yours. With bated breath, you must make your choice...

Roll a dice!

If you roll 1-2, turn to **131**.

If you roll 3-4, turn to **249**.

If you roll 5-6, turn to **527**.

63

At your request, the Dog-man nods eagerly and whisks off down the ravine before returning with a coil of rope, which he hurls up to you. A little while later, you have climbed down the rope and are shaking it loose of the tree to which it is tied (you may keep the **rope** if you wish).

'Master, did I do well?' the Dog-man asks, sidling towards you. 'Did I pass the test?'

When you assure your benefactor that he has done well, his eyes light up with delight, while his strangely jointed legs quiver with excitement.

'Men must sleep at night,' he grunts happily. 'That being so, I will show you a safe place to rest. Then, when light returns, I will guide you. To your home, to my home - my lord will choose!'

Feeling that you can trust this earnest little creature, you follow him down the ravine. By the time you enter the mass of undergrowth on its southern side, dusk has given way to night.

The foliage appears impossible in the dark, but your guide leads you through it until you emerge onto a tree-lined animal trail. The pair of you follow it for about a mile, before the Dog-man turns aside and squeezes into a brake of tall, woody cane trees. You follow and emerge into a little den that has been cleared of trees and is comfortably lined with ferns and leaves.

You lower yourself to the soft, dry ground while your guide immediately sets to devouring some gruel he has wrapped up in banana leaves. When he has eaten his fill, he looks at you with sudden guilt, then offers you one of the meals.

You may eat it now to restore 4 VITALITY points or add the **meal** to your reserve.

With the Dog-man curled up contentedly at your feet, you fall into a deep sleep that ends when you are shaken awake. Though you have been woken prematurely, you still gain a further 3 VITALITY points from the rest.

'Master, it is time to leave,' whispers your guide. 'Bad men are close. Man-beasts. Savages. Not like you and I.'

Just as he finishes speaking you hear a blood-curdling howl some distance away, then an answering call that is somewhat closer.

Where will you ask to be led?

To the Dog-man's home? If so, turn to 198.

To 'your' home? (Turn to 475).

64

Though you have been exposed to dangerous species-leaping infections and your chimeric body is the perfect breeding ground for new diseases, you have avoided bringing any contagion to the North American mainland!

Now turn to 570.

65

Your desperate cries carry into the jungle, and it is not long before you see a shadowy figure emerge from the gloom of the ravine. You call out that you are stranded and need help, but the figure slinks away.

Darkness has fallen by the time the figure reappears, only this time it appears to be carrying a coil of rope!

Roll a dice.

If you roll 1-3, turn to 23.

If you roll 4-6, turn to 375.

66

The man's deep-set eyes gleam with interest when you mention that you are a scientist of the natural world. He asks you one or two questions relating to biology and ethology until he is satisfied that you are telling the truth.

'Well, this information alters the case a little,' the man says. 'Montgomery did not mention you were an educated man. You may cross the gangplank and rest in our boat, if you wish, while we bring aboard our stock.'

Not wishing to spend a moment longer aboard the *Ipecacuanha* and her bully of a captain, you thank the white-haired man and cross over into the island boat.

Turn to **468**.

67

Your manoeuvres foil the aims of the hunters and you reach the brake of trees with heaving lungs and burning legs. Glancing out from cover, you see both hunters shoulder their bows and draw pairs of long, shining hunting knives, the expressions on their faces grim and stern.

Now that you have some cover, do you wish to make a stand in the tree line? If so, turn to **170**.

If you would rather continue running deeper into the trees to escape the hunters, turn to **202**.

68

After the first day adrift, you and your companions speak little with one another, instead staring at the horizon with eyes that grow larger and more haggard with every passing hour. On the fourth day the water runs out, and on the sixth Helmar suggests in a dry, parched voice that the three of you draw straws.

'Why would we do such a thing?' you croak.

'So that he with the shortest straw will have his throat cut, so that the other two may live,' comes his grief-stricken reply.

'If it means that I have a chance of a drink, then count me in,' the stocky sailor grimaces, prying the first of the splinters from the dinghy that he plans to use in this dreadful game of chance.

If you wish to agree with the plan to draw straws, turn to 62.

If you wish to refuse the idea, turn to 156.

69

Unfortunately, the python has pinned both of your arms to your sides, leaving you helpless! As you begin to lose consciousness, the last thing you feel is the cold, moist touch of its jaws upon your scalp as it begins to devour you, headfirst...

YOUR DAYS HAVE COME TO A GRUESOME END!

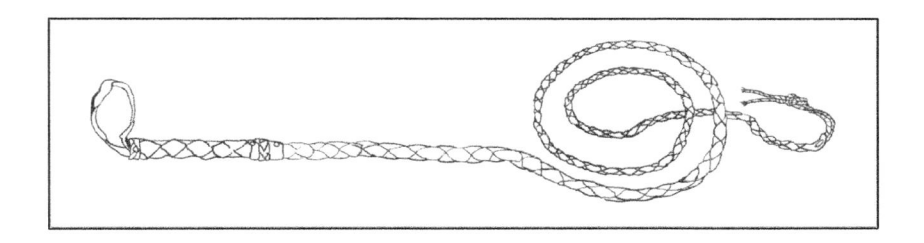

70

Save for the whimpers of the creature before you, the forest has fallen still and silent; you guess that the noise of your firearm must have frightened off the other stalker.

'Please...' hisses the injured creature, his face downcast so that it is difficult to discern his features. 'You are an Other...an Other with the Fire that Burns. This I did not know, believe me! Even the Master does not walk these places at night. Spare me, and I will take you to the House of Pain, or to the huts. I will lead you anywhere you choose, great lord!'

Where will your demand the man take you?

To the House of Pain? If so, turn to <u>16</u>.

Or to the huts? (Turn to <u>110</u>).

71

Test your FATE!

If you are favoured, turn to <u>347</u>.

If you are unfavoured, turn to <u>274</u>.

72

Murmurs of wonder and whispers of admiration ripple through the crowd when you agree to fight!

The Elephant-man relieves you of your rucksack and weapons, takes you firmly by the shoulder, leads you into the arena and waves the astonished Goat-man away. He then hands you the rusted falchion, slaps you on the shoulder and leaves you to face your opponent.

Though less than five and a half feet tall and slightly built, the Ocelot-man seems unperturbed by the impending duel. Quite to the contrary, he stares at you intensely and gives a low, menacing growl.

Grimly, you heft the **falchion**. It is a clumsy but brutal weapon that will reduce your *close combat score* by 2 but causes 3 points of damage on a successful hit.

The moment the order to begin is given, the Ocelot-man springs in and aims a vicious cut at you head. You can expect no mercy from this natural predator!

OCELOT-MAN: Prowess - 10; Vitality - 7; Damage - 3.

Note: reduce the Ocelot-man's *close combat score* by 2 due to the falchion he too is using.

If you reduce your opponent's vitality to 1, turn to <u>247</u>.

73

Test your FATE to see how you fare picking your way through the sulphurous swamp!

If you are favoured, turn to <u>28</u>.

If you are unfavoured, turn to <u>116</u>.

74

Many in the mob remain unpersuaded, but your allies have raised enough of a doubt to prevent your party from being torn to shreds. With a quick glance and nod in your direction, your saviours mingle with the other beast-folk, urging them to return to their dens.

They also single out a pair of strong Bull-men to help you carry Moreau's body back to the enclosure. The powerful creatures are evidently still afraid of the doctor, but they lift him gingerly and follow you back to the enclosure. Progress is slow, for Moreau was a heavy man, and there are still flurries of sudden movement on the edges of sight and nearby roars that have you reaching for your weapon. Montgomery says nothing the entire journey back, while M'ling ranges around your group, his eyes and ears alert.

Finally, as dusk is falling, you make it back to the enclosure, where the Bull-men eagerly depart. Montgomery opens the double gates and the three of you lay Moreau's body upon a pile of brushwood in the courtyard. Seeming to be drawn by something, M'ling then ventures out into the deepening darkness, while you and Montgomery lock yourselves in, then slump to the floor in grief.

Gain 1 FATE point for retrieving Moreau's body, then turn to <u>525</u>.

75

Relieved to be out of the water, you take a moment to study the approaching island. It is relatively low, covered in abundant vegetation, and from deep in its interior comes a thin white thread of vapour that rises slantingly to a great height, before fraying out like a downy feather. The boat is advancing into the embrace of a broad bay fronted by a strip of dull grey sand that slopes up to a ridge set with trees and vegetation. Halfway up the slope is a piebald stone enclosure out of which you discern two thatched roofs.

Three tall, strange men await you at the water's edge. They are swathed from head to toe in grubby white linen, have lank black hair, elfin faces, and twisted legs that seem jointed in the wrong place. As you come alongside them, they grow uncomfortable under your curious stare, and you turn your attention elsewhere so as not to offend them. But then the staghounds catch sight of them and begin to bark furiously and strain at their chains.

'Come, help me with the hutches!' Montgomery tells you, as the boat settles into a narrow channel that acts as the island's dock and the strange men set about unloading the cargo under the white-haired man's brisk orders.

Together, and with the help of the crook-backed man, you carry several hutches of rabbits onto the beach. There, to your surprise, Montgomery upends them, turning their living, wriggling contents onto the grey sand. He claps his hands, and the little creatures go hopping off up the beach.

'Increase and multiply, my friends,' Montgomery calls. 'Replenish the island! Hitherto we've had a lack of meat here...'

Your stomach grumbles at the thought of a rabbit on a spit, and Montgomery nods in understanding.

'All this manual work and we have not even breakfasted,' he smiles. 'Let's go inside and see if we can remedy that.'

After affirming this fine sentiment, you follow Montgomery and his strange attendant up the beach towards the enclosure.

Now turn to 465.

76

Once your rucksack is empty, the Macaque-folk escort you to the highest point of the geothermic system, a super-heated pool surging from deep beneath the earth. For a moment you fear that the creatures intend to hurl you to a horrible death, but instead they begin to recite a primal dirge as their leader lays out your possessions with great ceremony. Then, he proceeds to toss each item one by one into the boiling water!

Except for any items that can fit into your pockets (such as keys, coins, or phials) as well as TWO ranged weapons and ONE close combat weapon (the Macaque-folk do not wish to disarm you entirely) you must remove all your weapons and possessions from your *equipment list*!

When the infuriating ceremony is done, the Macaque-folk shove you towards the gap in the wall of rubble. Fearful of sharing the fate of your equipment, you have little choice but to comply.

Now turn to **349**.

77

You are unable to keep up with the tree-leaping Ape-man and come to a halt, your lungs heaving and your legs burning. As the sounds of your quarry fade into the distance, you are faced with a choice:

Do you want to continue along the path to see where it leads? If so, turn to **115**.

Or return to the beach and follow it north? (Turn to **38**).

78

The last of the Hyena-men fall with a defiant snarl, and you turn your attention to the creatures' weapons.

You are most drawn to the **crossbow**. It is a powerful ranged weapon that inflicts 3 points of damage but is slow to reload. So, if the text says you have 2 ranged attack rounds available, then you have only 1 ranged attack round if using the crossbow. You may round up odd numbers. For example, 3 ranged attack rounds would permit you 2 ranged attack rounds with the crossbow (rounded up from 1.5). 5 ranged attacks would permit you 3 with the crossbow, and so on. The crossbow comes with **7 quarrels**.

There is also a **bone knife** and **2 wooden clubs**, any of which causes 2 points of close combat damage. Remember to make any additions to your *equipment list*.

Pleased with your new weapons, you decide to head away from the spongy ground and explore the line of trees from where the Hyena-men came.

Turn to **499**.

79

You successfully work your way around the back of the hunter, your heart pounding and the sweat trickling from your brow (gain 1 FATE point!). You also notice a **large rock** lying at the base of the megalith you are hiding behind. It is not much, but it is better than proceeding unarmed.

Now, do you wish to charge towards the man and try to overwhelm him? If so, turn to **157**.

If you would prefer to sneak up on the man and take him by surprise, turn to **130**.

80

Just as you feel you are going to find cover in the brake of trees, something hits you hard in the back and your legs give out from beneath you. Pushing your face and chest out of the dirt you are horrified to see an iron arrowhead protruding from between your ribs. Then the blood rises in your throat and you begin to choke...

YOUR ADVENTURE IS OVER!

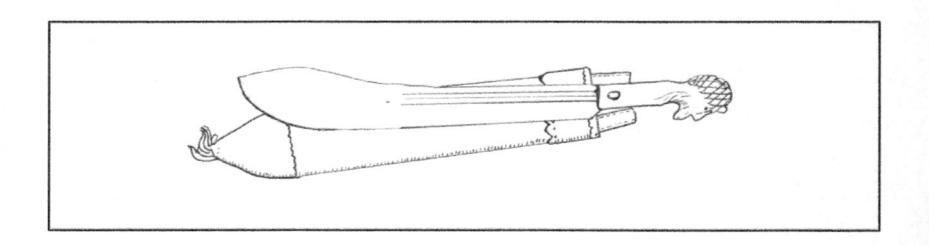

81

You try to time your blow to hit the shark on the tip of its snout, while trying to keep the barrel between you and its jaws!

Test your PROWESS!

If you succeed, turn to 140.

If you fail, turn to 233.

82

When your canoe grounds on the sand, you leap out and pull the craft high onto the beach. Scanning inland for a suitable campsite, you see a broad expanse of cone-shaped reeds leading into a strip of lush jungle. Above this is a distant hillside covered with pockets of rich volcanic soil. In daylight, you estimate that it would take you around three hours to reach the hill, assuming the ground through the reeds is solid underfoot. It will be a difficult walk by moonlight, but once on the hill you could take several hours' rest, then be in a good position to explore the interior of the island in the morning.

Then again, the beach appears comfortable enough, and you could embark on the walk inland in the morning...

Do you wish to hike inland through part of the night in order to reach the hillside? If so, turn to 25.

If you would rather simply spend the night on the beach, turn to 137.

83

You shove your way through the crowd and begin to sprint up the chasm, immediately spotting a hemp ladder resting against the rock face to your left. At the same time, you hear the Sayer bellowing orders and his followers scrambling after you!

Do you wish to attempt to climb the ladder to escape your pursuers? If so, turn to 364.

If you would rather ignore the ladder and run on, turn to 509.

84

When the Macaque-man leader sees the blood leaves, he looks at you with a new-found respect and orders his group to return your possessions.

'Any ally of the brothers is an ally of mine,' he says, opening the wicker box and pushing it towards you. 'If anything we possess is of use to you, then it is yours to take.'

Within the box are an assortment of heavily corroded weapons and baubles that can serve no practical use, but you do spot a serviceable **cutlass, 5 broad-headed battle arrows** and **6 hollow-tip revolver bullets** that have been stored in a watertight oilskin pouch. You also find a corked and wax-sealed **blue phial** that is filled with a mysterious liquid and labelled with the number *148* (make a note of this number if you choose to take it!).

The **cutlass** is a sharp, heavy weapon of close combat that (like a firearm), will automatically cause *twice* the damage when you roll a double for your attack dice.

The **5 battle arrows** will only be of use if you have a bow but will cause 3 points of damage.

The **6 hollow-tip revolver bullets** will only be of use if you have the revolver, but they have been designed to disintegrate on impact with flesh in order to cause maximum injuries. They will also cause 3 points of ranged damage, and 6 points of damage on a double roll!

The Macaque-man knows nothing of the contents of the **blue phial**, but he tells you that coloured phials are of great importance to the Master.

Take all of these items if you wish and make the necessary additions to your *equipment list*.

Thanking the Macaque-man for his aid, you cast a final curious glance at the bathers before making for the gap in the wall of volcanic rubble.

Turn to **349**.

85

The chasm curves upwards in a bend until it becomes a tunnel of volcanic rock that leads out onto a clearing covered with a pale encrustation through which wisps of acrid smoke leak. At the edge of the clearing the charcoaled trunks and twisted limbs of trees poke through heaps of blackened rubble that rise to the height of your head.

To the left of the clearing is a ragged gap in the rocks, through which you can see plumes of billowing steam, while ahead of you is a path leading through the jungle.

Orienting yourself by the light of the sinking moon, you realise that the jungle path will take you towards the eastward beach and Doctor Moreau's enclosure, so you decide to follow it.

Turn to 60.

86

As you bump into the side of the derelict merchantman, you realise that its hull is covered in green slime and sharp barnacles. Worse still, there are no ropes or ladders visible that will enable you to climb aboard...

If you wish to swim around the derelict to see if there are any ways aboard, turn to 334.

If you would rather turn away from the derelict and swim towards the longboat (if you have not already done so), turn to 276.

Otherwise, you may turn away from the derelict and strike out towards the dinghy? (Turn to 127).

87

The animal-folk have left little behind except for a few rusted axes and badly corroded farming implements that look to have been abandoned at the edges of the arena for some time.

In the long grass of the meadow, however, you discover that one of the spectators has left behind a primitive **short-bow** (1 point of ranged damage) with a **quiver of 8 copper-headed arrows**.

Add the weapon to your *equipment list* if you wish.

If you now wish to enter the jungle to the west, turn to **199**.

If you would rather try the jungle to the east, turn to **265**.

88

Unfortunately, the white-haired man is unmoved by your appeal.

'I am sorry, but I cannot have you upon my island,' he reiterates sternly.

Now, if you have not already done so, you may appeal to the captain? (Turn to **59**).

If you have already appealed to the captain, then you must accept your fate and turn to **427**.

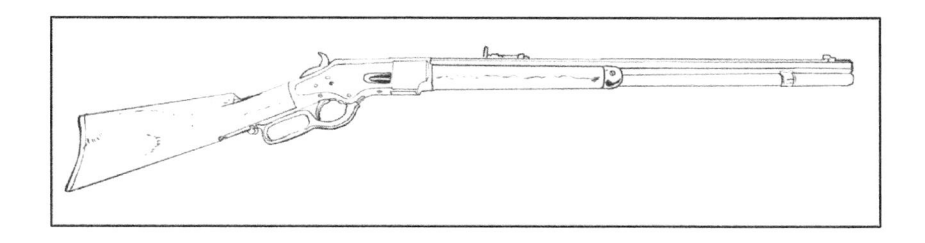

89

You awake suddenly in the depths of the night to what you think can only be a terrible dream. Clustered around you are a dozen misshapen forms, powerful brutes who are thickly boned and rippling with sinew.

Instinctively, your hand strays to your weapon, before you realise the futility of doing so.

Do you have the prickly pear? If so, turn to 22.

If not, turn to 58.

90

At your order, the Dog-man sets off into the jungle at a rapid pace. Shafts of moonlight allow you to avoid blundering blindly into the trunks of trees, but your progress is slower than you might have hoped and soon you are bathed in sweat and gasping for breath. All the while, the sound of the howling echoes through the jungle.

You are utterly disorientated and have no idea from which direction the predators might come.

Roll five dice!

If the total is less than or equal to your current VITALITY, turn to 34.

If the total is greater than your current VITALITY, turn to 400.

91

As you throw open the hatch you come face to face with a large SHIP-RAT. It seems stunned by the sunlight, but as its eyes begin to adjust, two more of the odious creatures clamber up a set of timber steps and hiss at you menacingly.

Will you:

Slam the hatch back down and search the deck (if you have not already done so)? (Turn to **308**).

Make for the dinghy? (Turn to **127**).

Or fight the rats? (Turn to **446**).

92

This part of the island is spongy underfoot, riven by steaming hot streams, and colonised by stubby reeds and tenacious, twisted little trees. Every now and then you sink up to your knees in squelching, sulphurophagous mosses and fungi, and stumble over rocks and boulders that have sunk into the mire.

It is exhausting work, so you must lose 1 VITALITY point!

It dawns on you that the hunters chose this route precisely because of the dangers it would pose to you if you chose to follow them. At the same time, you can now see that upon the north-west corner of the island is sited a rocky plateau strewn with immense boulders that must have been blown out by a violent eruption in ages past. There is also a single geothermic stream running around the base of the plateau that appears to drain out onto a beach of slate-grey sand. Upon the plateau are a pair of shelters that must be the hunters' camp.

If you wish to press on towards this area, turn to **73**.

If you would prefer to give up the chase and head towards the interior of the island where the geothermic streams have their source, turn to **261**.

93

As you follow the chasm north, it curls around to the east as the jungle begins to thin. You catch the acrid smell of sulphur and see before you a gently curving wall of rubble about three yards high. To your right the chasm tunnels beneath the rocks, no doubt emerging on the other side of the wall, while to your left the wall curves out of sight.

Do you wish to attempt to climb the wall of rubble to see where the chasm emerges? If so, turn to **552**.

If you would rather try to work your way around the wall towards the left, turn to **230**.

94

Montgomery nods calmly as you tell him of the murder of your fellow survivors.

'You did what you felt you needed to do, I am sure,' he says. 'There are few fates worse than being cast adrift and dying of thirst. Speaking of which, please allow me to fetch you something else to drink. You are badly dehydrated and still not entirely out of danger.'

But when Montgomery returns, he is not alone. Behind him shuffles a misshapen man with a crooked back, powerful arms, and a bestial head sunk between hulking shoulders. Without a word, the newcomer seizes you about the middle and drags you up onto the deck, where you see a tall, red-haired man leering at you from beside a pack of huge, barking staghounds. Before you can say a word, the dogs fall on you, their sharp teeth tearing at your flesh.

As if from a great distance, you hear Montgomery remonstrating with the red-headed man, but it will make no difference to your fate. You are still alive and struggling weakly by the time the dogs are brought under control, but you cannot prevent yourself being dragged to the rail of the ship by a pair of strong ship hands and cast overboard to join Helmar and the sailor...

YOUR ADVENTURE ENDS HERE!

95

Do you have both the mariner's knife and the handkerchief? If so, turn to 292.

If you have only one of these objects, turn to 149.

If you have neither of these objects, turn to 127.

96

At the first sign of aggression, the Ape-man jumps up into the tree with remarkable dexterity and goes crashing from bough to bough deeper into the jungle, gibbering in a loud, plaintive voice. Suddenly, you become aware of the possibility that there may be others of his kind lurking nearby...

Do you wish to give chase? If so, turn to 535.

If you would prefer to leave the Ape-man alone and continue heading north along the beach, turn to 38.

97

Try as you may, you simply do not have the strength to overcome the suction of the quicksand. Your futile efforts rapidly exhaust you, and the muscles in your hands and arms cease up and cramp. Groaning helplessly, you slide back into the quicksand, which receives you with an eager, smothering embrace...

YOUR ADVENTURE ENDS HERE!

98

You strike again and again at the Draconope's leathery neck, kicking for the shore as the abomination slides beneath the waves for the last time. You have truly had a brush with death, and the sight and sound of the Draconope's shrieks of agonised hatred will stay with you as long as you live.

Lose 1 FATE point!

Once safely back on the beach you hurry on, encountering nothing other than some furtive, scurrying shapes that resemble large rabbits.

Just as you are beginning to fall asleep on your feet, you catch sight of a glimmer of light in the distance - it is the enclosure! The creeping light of the new day is staining the horizon by the time you can see the individual stonework of the outer wall. Suddenly, the double gates of the outpost are flung wide, and you see Doctor Moreau, Montgomery and M'ling leading the pack of staghounds out onto the beach. The dogs immediately catch your scent and lurch against their collars in a frenzy of barking and growling.

Moreau restrains the beasts with a harsh command, stares at you for a few seconds, then leads the staghounds back into the enclosure, while Montgomery and M'ling advance towards you.

'Where the devil have you been?' Montgomery demands. 'We've been worried sick and were about to set out with the dogs to find you! Now get inside this instant, Moreau will want to have words!'

Your relief at being back among humans somewhat sullied by a flicker of dread, you do as Montgomery asks, enter the enclosure and let yourself in via the small door leading to the room. It does not take long before you hear the inner door to the courtyard being unlocked, and the doctor strides in...

Turn to <u>39</u>.

99

'This is the *Ipecacuanha*, a trading ship out of the Peruvian port-city of Callao,' Montgomery tells you. 'That is at least where I boarded her. I never bothered asking where she came from in the beginning - out of the land of born fools, I guess. The silly ass who owns the ship is her captain, too. He's named Davis, a drunkard who's lost his certificate, or something. Fortunately, our ways will soon part. He is destined for Hawaii, you see, while myself and my cargo will be landed first.'

Next, do you wish to ask Montgomery about his cargo? If so, turn to <u>284</u>.

If you elect to ask more about the captain, turn to <u>200</u>.

Alternatively, if you wish to ask more about Montgomery's destination, turn to <u>30</u>.

100

At this, the Sayer demands that you recite your Commandments so that he may judge their quality. You are very aware of sharp, white teeth and strong claws pressing in, so you do as he asks.

At first the Sayer and his followers seem to approve of the prohibitions you recite, but they grow confused at the exhortation to 'Honour thy father and mother...'

Test your FATE!

If you are favoured, turn to **398**.

If you are unfavoured, turn to **418**.

101

You haul yourself out of the pool and charge towards the thief without heed of your nudity! When the retreating figure sees you coming, his eyes go wide with shock and he drops your rucksack and weapons, as well as the wicker box he has tucked under an arm. Now that you are closer, you see that he is dressed in a simple belted habit made from coarse brown wool that makes him resemble one of the monks of France you have seen on your travels.

With his thick white hair, bushy mutton chops, long arms and crooked bow legs, he makes a singularly curious sight! Even more surprising is his voice, which is astonishingly smooth and cultured.

'There is no need for such savagery, my lord!' he complains, as you lay your hands on him. 'Did you not leave these things as an offering to the Heart of the Island?'

Do you wish to reply that you did not leave your possessions to the Heart of the Island? If so, turn to **13**.

Otherwise, you can reply that you did leave your possessions to the Heart of the Island by turning to **42**.

102

As you walk along the beach, the sighing of the palm trees in the breeze and the rhythmic crash and roar of the surf breaking upon hidden reefs quickly banishes any sense of unease. The soothing air and warmth of the sun raises your spirits and tames your aches and pains.

Gain 2 VITALITY points.

After walking for a little while you look back and see that the enclosure is almost hidden from view behind the curve of the island's shore. Just as you are considering the wisdom of continuing you see a figure in the tree line to your left. He is wearing the same blue serge jacket and trousers favoured by Moreau and is waving at you with energetic but strangely grotesque motions.

If you wish to approach him, turn to <u>45</u>.

If you would prefer to ignore him and press on along the beach, turn to <u>38</u>.

103

Unfortunately, your encounters on the Island of Doctor Moreau have exposed you to animal infections that cannot ordinarily be transmitted to humans. In your chimeric blood, however, these infections have found a home and grown accustomed to your variegated constitution.

You sneeze violently, becoming aware of a chill and a soreness in your throat. Stopping a promenading couple, you ask for directions to a cheap hotel. By the time you close the door to a private room behind you, you have infected at least five other people, one of whom is a merchant sailor on his way to a packed ship bound for Japan, as well as another traveller heading inland on a stage coach.

Even your hybrid immune system will struggle to fend off this novel virus, which – being both virulent and highly contagious - poses a genuine threat to humanity. If you do survive, the world will be a vastly different place...

YOUR ADVENTURE ENDS HERE!

104

As you shove your way through the onlookers, you hear the Sayer roaring orders and his followers giving chase. A few of the animal-folk stretch their arms out towards you, but you duck beneath them and are soon clear of the crowd. The chasm walls open up into tangled jungle, at which point you realise your mistake.

It is still the dead of night, and you have yet to explore this part of the island. You stumble on gamely but cannot hope to compete with the beast-men's night vision and sense of smell. Soon you are apprehended, beaten, and dragged back into the chasm where the Sayer of the Law awaits...

Lose 2 VITALITY points, then turn to **307**.

105

You stare down in shock at the dead bodies before you, then feel the alluring wetness of their blood on your hands...

Do you wish to try drinking the corpses' blood? If so, turn to **373**.

If you would rather cast aside the thought and throw the bodies over the side, turn to **161**.

106

You manage to dive behind a boulder just as another arrow slices through the air behind you. The hunter is now shouting at the top of his voice, and you know his friend will soon appear on your flank.

Now do you wish to risk a charge on the hunter? If so, turn to <u>55</u>.

If you would rather remain where you are and call out that you are not a threat, turn to <u>177</u>.

Alternatively, you can try to escape by sprinting uphill across a stretch of reed-infested ground towards a brake of trees to the south. To try this, turn to <u>144</u>.

107

At your words, Montgomery takes a deep, calming breath and turns away from the ranting captain.

'You are right, of course,' he says. 'It is just that I cannot stand to see drunkenness used to excuse such vile conduct.'

He turns on his heel, returns to the companionway ladder and disappears below deck. After a moment's hesitation, the misshapen man follows him. Noticing the hostile glares of the captain and sailors, you decide it is best to retire for the evening.

Gain 1 FATE point for successfully intervening in the quarrel!

Then turn to <u>406</u>.

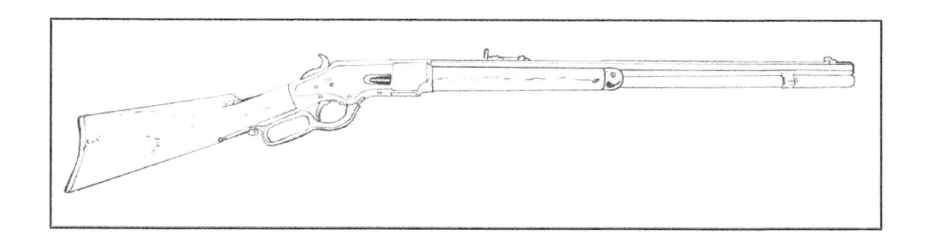

108

As soon as you have caught your breath after the colossal battle, you begin to sort through the heap of weapons and the contents of the wicker box for which you have shed so much blood (if you have sustained any wounds from the Macaque-folk, note that you have been *exposed to zoonotic infection*).

You find an assortment of heavily corroded weapons and scraps of primitive wicker armour that can serve no practical use, but you do spot a serviceable **cutlass**, **5 broad-headed battle arrows** and **6 hollow-tip revolver bullets** that have been stored in a watertight oilskin pouch. In addition to these items, you also discover a corked and wax-sealed **blue phial** that is filled with a mysterious liquid and labelled with the number *148* (be sure to make a note of this number if you choose to take this item!).

The **cutlass** is a sharp, heavy weapon of close combat that (like a firearm), will automatically cause *twice* the damage when you roll a double for your *close combat* score.

The **5 battle arrows** will only be of use if you have a bow but will cause 3 points of damage with each successful hit.

If you possess a revolver, the **6 hollow-tips** are extremely effective against flesh and bone. They will cause 3 points of damage, but 6 points of damage on a double roll!

The contents of the **blue phial** must remain a mystery until you can gain more information about it.

Make the necessary additions to your *equipment list*.

You linger at the geothermic pools only long enough to conceal the bodies of the Macaque-folk in the edges of the jungle, before making for the gap in the wall of volcanic rubble.

Turn to **349**.

109

The door is made of solid wood fitted snugly into its frame. You put an ear to it but hear nothing. Then, just as you are about to turn the brass handle you hear a gentle scrape and click and remember that Montgomery said that he intended to lock the door from the other side!

Now, do you wish to examine the pile of books (if you have not already done so)? If so, turn to **31**.

If you have already looked at the books, then it is not long before you hear Montgomery and M'ling returning. Turn to **301**.

110

When you demand to be taken to the huts, the man peers up at you curiously, and you cannot help but flinch at his pointed ears, long, lank hair and grinning mouth that is marred by elongated canine teeth. The WOLF-MAN looks you up and down, glances at your weapon, then instantaneously fawns like a chastened hound.

'Yes, yesss,' he whispers. 'To the huts I will take you. At the huts there are other men like you, like I...'

He beckons with a swift movement and sets off swiftly into the jungle, one clumsy hand still clutching at his wounded arm. Keeping your weapon at the ready, you follow the creature on a path that seems to run parallel to the westward coast but inclines steeply upwards. Between keeping your eyes on your guide's back, staying alert for possible ambush and avoiding a broken ankle, you are unable to memorise the route you take, but the moon is low in the night sky when you emerge onto a scrubby hillside indented with pockets of rich volcanic soil out of which grow all manner of exotic flowers and plants.

The Wolf-man runs across the hillside, then stops abruptly before a steep chasm that cuts through the hillside and extends into the moonlight on either side. Using only one arm and displaying remarkable strength and dexterity, the creature eases himself over the edge of the chasm and descends into the darkness via a rough hemp ladder. Some thirty yards down you can make out the soft flicker of torchlight illuminating the chasm floor, where rows of makeshift dens line the length of the chasm on both sides of the rock face.

'Yesss, we are here,' the Wolf-man grins up at you, the pale-green glitter of his eyes ghastly in the gloom. 'Follow me, Other with a gun. Do not be afraid.'

Reluctantly, you do as the creature says. Though crudely made, the hemp ladder is solid enough, the rough material offering a reassuring purchase for hand and foot. The deep darkness that envelops you as you begin your descent soon retreats before the glow of the torches below, and a disagreeable odour - like that of a monkey's ill-cleaned cage - assails you. You feel a thrill of fear as the walls press in on one another like the jaws of a crushing trap…

Your guide averts his gaze as you arrive on the chasm floor, then ushers you towards the largest of the malodorous huts.

'You must learn the Law,' he mutters nervously, suddenly shoving you inside. Before you can protest, something towering and black seizes your arm in a grip of iron and forces you into a dank corner of the abode.

Your heart thumping in your chest, you stare at the shadows within shadows that are lurking in the hut...

Now turn to <u>350</u>.

111

After you deal M'ling a mortal wound he crawls to Montgomery's side, lays a brawny arm across his master's chest, and quietly dies.

Lose 2 FATE points for being forced to kill such a loyal servant!

Suddenly, you hear the disordered shouts of many beast-folk approaching the enclosure and realise that they must have been drawn by the gunshots and the smell of Montgomery's blood.

Peering through the barred window, you see a mob of black shadows roiling hither and thither upon the beach. As you watch, they hurl firewood into a pile and set it ablaze with flaming torches...

Now turn to <u>528</u>.

112

Wary of ambush, you cautiously follow the path through the coconut palms until you come out onto a raised circular plateau strewn with immense boulders that must once have been ejected by an ancient volcanic eruption.

To the south of this clearing is a line of trees upon a low ridge, while inland to the south-east is a broad swathe of reed-infested fenland through which meander a number of smoking geothermic streams.

But of far more immediate interest are the pair of lean-tos standing in the middle of the plateau. This is some sort of camp, and there are objects lying in the shade of the shelters.

Do you wish to risk searching the lean-tos? If so, turn to **220**.

If you would rather retrace your steps and take a canoe towards the south, turn to **353**.

Or you can retrace your steps, ignore the canoes and continue walking south? (Turn to **285**).

113

Your worse fears are realised when you hear the swirl of water and see something large angling towards the beach. At first you think it might be a whale, for it is a mottled grey colour and swims with a vertical rolling motion, but then you see a hideously twisted human face gasping for air before disappearing beneath the surf.

Within moments a creature resembling a gigantic maggot fused with the hideously twisted head of a giant man surges out of the shallows. It fixes you with streaming eyes, licks its lips, then lurches up the beach with an ear-piercing shriek of agony and rage.

The DRACONOPE is one of Doctor Moreau's earliest and most reprehensible experiments. Tormented by unrelenting pain, it is a gibbering, shrieking monstrosity that lives only to unleash its rage upon the world. It is deadliest within the water but is also a terrible adversary upon the land.

For a moment you are transfixed by the sight and sound of this abomination, but then you scramble to your feet and prepare your weapons!

You may perform THREE ranged attacks before entering close combat!

DRACONOPE: Prowess - 10; Vitality - 12; Damage - 3; Ranged Defence - 12.

If the Draconope wins three rounds in succession, turn to <u>456</u>.

If you are able to defeat the Draconope without losing three successive attack rounds, turn to <u>46</u>.

114

Although it is extremely dark within the ravine, you follow it a good way inland until you are able to find a shallow alcove at the base of the southward face that is both dry and defensible. You gather some broken branches that have fallen from the overhanging trees and scatter them in front of your simple lay-by, trusting that any intruders will wake you with the noise of their approach. Bone-weary now, you pillow your head upon your pack and soon fall into a deep sleep.

Gain 3 VITALITY points.

When you awake, it is still dark. In alarm you sense something crouched together close beside you. Whatever it is, it must have either been extremely stealthy, or the noise it made was insufficient to wake you. Hardly daring to breathe, you keep very still and the intruder begins to move slowly, interminably.

Then something soft, warm and moist passes across your hand, so that it takes all of your restraint not to react!

Do you wish to attack the intruder? If so, turn to 262.

If you would prefer to demand to know who is there, turn to 377.

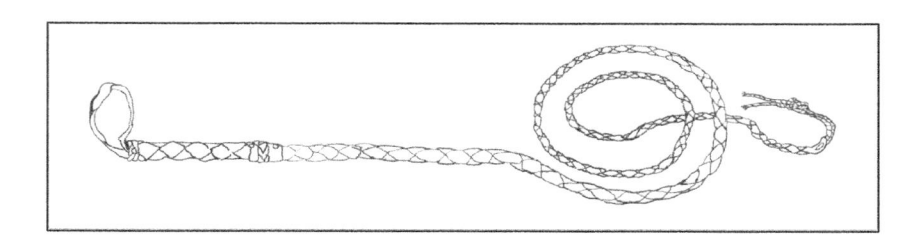

115

After a few minutes on the path, you hear the heavy approach of someone - or something - coming straight towards you!

If you want to remain where you are to see what is coming, turn to 172.

If you want to hide, turn to 148.

116

As you struggle across the warm marsh, one of your boots sinks deeper than you expect, and you pitch forwards. As you fall you thrust out your hands, submerging one of them in a pool of scalding hot water!

Roll a dice...

If you roll 1-3, you have burned your off-hand. Lose 1 PROWESS point and 2 VITALITY points.

If you roll 4-6, it is your dexterous hand you have burned! Lose 2 PROWESS points, 2 VITALITY points and 1 BALLISTICS point.

Feeling very much at odds with the island, you grit your teeth and press on until you finally reach firmer and dryer ground. You approach the first of the huge boulders you saw from across the marsh, press your back against it and regain your breath.

Now turn to **61**.

117

Retreating a little way back down the path, you tug a mouldering branch out of the mire and begin to beat the surface of the water to draw the predator away from the stretch you wish to cross. After several minutes, you see a tell-tale shape gliding towards you. Waiting until the alligator is almost upon you, you hurl the branch into its snapping jaws and sprint back towards the section you need to cross.

Do you still wish to risk the swim? If so, turn to **518**.

If you would rather abandon the idea, you will have to leave your possessions where they lay (make a note of this loss!) and retrace your steps along the path...

Once you return to the entrance of the swamp, do you wish to follow its boundary north? If so, turn to **155**.

Or south? (Turn to **279**).

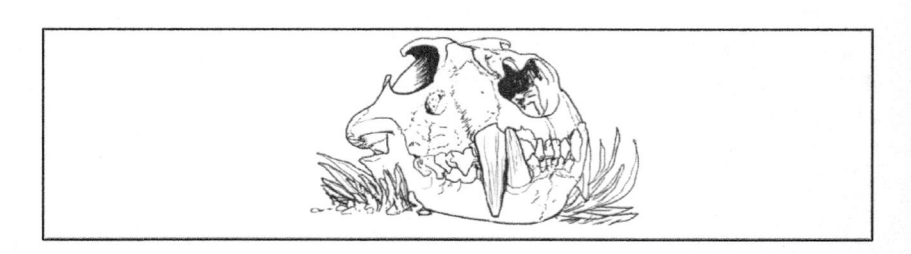

118

Montgomery sighs sadly. 'Well, we can't have you running around the island all half-cocked, my man,' he says, nodding at M'ling.

Suddenly, the servant seizes you by the arms and begins to force you to your knees. As you struggle against the creature's tremendous strength, Montgomery calmly sets down his tray, circles behind you and strikes you over the head with the butt of one of his revolvers...

Turn to 165.

119

By the time you slay the Hyena-man leader, his kinsfolk have been overcome by the poison gas and lay sprawled upon the ground behind you. Giving a sigh of relief at your narrow escape, you turn your attention to the **crossbow**, which comes with **7 quarrels.**

The crossbow is a powerful ranged weapon that inflicts 3 points of damage, but it is slow to reload. Therefore, if the text says you have TWO ranged attack rounds available, then you have only ONE ranged attack round when using the crossbow. You may round up odd numbers. For example, THREE ranged attack rounds would permit you TWO ranged attack rounds with the crossbow (rounded up from 1.5). FIVE ranged attacks would permit you THREE with the crossbow, and so on).

The **bone knife** is a simple weapon that may be used in close combat for 2 points of damage.

Pleased with your new weapons, you decide to head away from the spongy ground and explore the line of trees from where the Hyena-men came.

Turn to 499.

120

The rigging fails to hold and you plunge back into the water, the cordage landing on top of you. There is a very real risk that you may become entangled and dragged into the deep!

Test your FATE...

If you are favoured, you manage to swim through a gap in the rigging and return to the surface. You see that the longboat has pulled too far away from you to reach, so you have no choice but to strike out for the two men in the dinghy. Turn immediately to **127**.

If you are unfavoured, the rigging wraps around you like a shroud and you are swiftly drowned, yet another victim of the sinking of *The Lady Vain*...

YOUR DOOM HAS COME!

121

Even though you are sure that it would be easier to reach the enclosure by following the unimpeded beach towards the south, the creatures around you seem tense and you suspect that it is only the presence of the Ape-man that is preventing them from ripping you apart. Not wanting to offend you protector by ignoring his directions, you shoulder your pack and continue to press inland through the jungle.

The gang of creatures watch you leave, and you give a sigh of relief when they are lost to sight. After several hours of painstaking progress, you are entirely lost, and resolve to wait for first light before going on. Just as you are thinking about removing your rucksack and bedding down for a few hours' sleep, you see a pair of luminous green eyes staring at you from the dense undergrowth. Then you hear a rustle to your right, then the flash of a second pair of eyes.

You are being stalked!

If you wish to press on into the jungle, in the hope that the creatures leave you alone, turn to **20**.

Alternatively, you can throw down your rucksack, prepare your weapon(s) and wait? (Turn to **54**).

122

The gap in the north part of the wall leads out onto a rocky hillside overlooking a steaming expanse of reeds and marshland. Laid out before you are a dozen or so geothermic pools from which a number of heated streams gurgle energetically down a steep decline until they become sluggish and serpentine as they approach sea level. In the distance, you can see a distant ribbon of beach and silver surf delineating the northernmost limits of the island.

The billowing steam in your immediate area reflects the moonlight in a silver haze, but you are able to discern some indistinct shapes floating in one of the lower pools.

If you wish to investigate the shapes in the water, turn to **402**.

If you would rather not linger on this rocky hillside, then return to **517** and make a different choice.

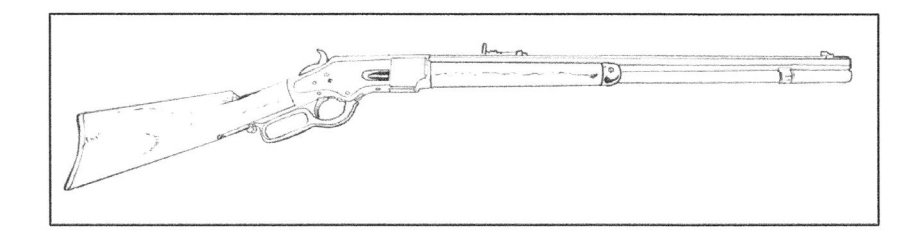

123

'That way, young scrounger!' the captain roars, gesturing once more to the gangway. 'We're cleaning the ship out and seeing as you've not a penny to your name, you'd best be alighting with the others.'

Pleased by the notion of avoiding a journey as the sole passenger of this quarrelsome sot, you approach Montgomery, but it is the large newcomer who speaks.

'We can't have you, sir!' he says concisely, his square face stern and resolute. 'You'll have to find your own way, either with Captain Davis here, or in the little rowboat I see lashed over there...'

He nods towards the back of the *Ipecacuanha*, where the dinghy of *The Lady Vain* - now languishing with several inches of seawater in her hold - has been towed behind the schooner since your rescue.

The thought of being put back into the dinghy in which you almost perished fills you with dread. You appeal to Montgomery in desperation, but he only shakes his head coldly and looks away.

'Well, well, well, looks like you're going overboard once more, my little proud-pike!' the captain yells with relish. 'From ashes to ashes, dust to dust, looks like you're destined to occupy a watery grave!'

If you wish to try appealing to the captain to allow you to stay on board the *Ipecacuanha*, turn to **59**.

If you would rather beseech the large, white-haired man, turn to **453**.

Alternatively, you can simply accept your fate and do nothing? If so, turn to **427**.

124

'It was chance,' Montgomery says. 'Pure chance. Just as it was chance my coming across you when I did. If I had been jaded that day or hadn't liked your face...well it's an interesting question where you might be right now.'

He shakes his head doubtfully. 'You asked why I left London? Well, the truth is that I lost my head for ten minutes on a foggy night, and now I can never return.'

Montgomery lapses into a brooding silence. It would be unwise to inquire further on this point!

If you would prefer to ask him about the ship you are on, turn to 99.

Otherwise, you can inquire about the wild animal sounds from overhead by turning to 176.

125

When the leader of the creatures sees the stone necklaces, he looks at you with a new-found respect and orders his group to return your possessions.

'The fiends who presume such affectations may only be parted from them by death,' he says. 'You have done us a great service, my lord, and I give thanks that we did not come to blows. We will trade with you if you are willing?'

He then throws open the wicker box and tips out its contents. Most of the weapons and baubles you see are either useless to you or heavily corroded, but you do spot a serviceable **cutlass, 5 broad-headed battle arrows** and **6 hollow-tip revolver bullets** that have been stored in a watertight oilskin pouch. There is also a wax-sealed **blue phial** that is filled with a mysterious liquid and labelled with the number *148* (be sure to make a note of this number if you acquire this item!).

113

The **cutlass** is a sharp, heavy close combat weapon that (like a firearm), will automatically cause *twice* the damage when you roll a double for your close combat score.

The **5 battle arrows** will only be of use if you have a bow but will cause 3 points of damage instead of 2.

The **6 hollow-tip revolver bullets** will only be of use if you have the revolver but have been designed to disintegrate on impact with flesh in order to cause maximum injury. They will also cause 3 points of damage, (and 6 points of damage on a double!).

The Macaque-man knows nothing of the contents of the **blue phial**, but he tells you that coloured phials are of great importance to the Master.

Each of the above items can be traded for the following:

- 3 meals
- A pair of stone necklaces
- 2 leopard skins
- A pair of Toledo steel hunting knives
- A coil of rope
- 1 gold coin
- A bone knife
- A cross-bow

Make your trades, if any, remembering to make any changes to your *equipment list*.

You thank the Macaque-man, cast a final look at the oblivious bathers, then make your way to the gap in the wall of the volcanic rubble.

Turn to <u>349</u>.

126

You fire in the direction of the sound and hear a yelp of pain. Pushing aside ferns and creepers you stride towards whatever it was you hit. Vaguely illuminated by shafts of moonlight you discern a rangy, hunched figure clutching a wound in its arm.

If you used a firearm to hurt this creature, turn to 70.

If you used a non-gunpowder ranged weapon, turn to 217.

127

You make it to the side of the dinghy and are relieved when Helmar and the stocky sailor drag you aboard. After you have muttered your thanks, the three of you watch in silent horror as *The Lady Vain* overturns and vanishes beneath the swell. Helmar almost tips the dinghy as he tries to hail the distant longboat, but the sailor pulls him back to his seat.

'Save your breath,' the seaman advises. 'They'll be eager to conserve whatever rations and water they've aboard. Last thing they need is another mouth to feed. Chances are they're even worse off than us. We at least have a good-sized beaker of water and a box of sodden ship's biscuit to keep us fed a while. 'Twas all I was able to grab, so quickly did the poor Lady go down.'

'But how long will these provisions last?' Helmar stammers.

'The water...four days if we ration it,' the sailor replies. 'The food a little longer, though that will not matter much once the water's gone.' He grins blackly. 'There's nothing to do now but hope and pray. Aye, pray for rescue, lads, before we dry out like old leather and our bones bleach beneath the sun.'

Helmar falls silent and there is nothing to be heard beyond the lapping of the sea against the dinghy's side. You are in a desperate strait and have, in all probability, merely deferred the certainty of your death by a week or so!

If you wish to try to kill the two men in order to conserve the supplies for yourself, turn to **540**.

If you would rather refrain from murder and instead place your hope in rescue, turn to **68**.

128

'Then you must remain our enemy!' the hunter says coldly. You hold out your hands in an attempt to ward off the arrows you think must come, but instead the two men lower their bows and haul you to your feet.

'Even between enemies, there may be respect,' the hunter explains. 'I am Lazalo and this my brother Vai.'

Vai proceeds to inspect your hands, face and neck, grunts in satisfaction and steps away.

'He checks you do not carry the marks of one of Soul-stealer's minions,' Lazalo explains, as he beckons you to walk with him. 'This is what we call your famous doctor, the cast of man you white-eyes admire above all others. You love strength and the mastery of numbers and letters far more than you despise domination and enslavement. My brother and I, however, we are not so lost. We see Moreau for what he is - a demon cloaked in the skin of a man; one who makes thralls of all those who feel the bite of his knives. He will never know peace; he will never feel the simple love of the Earth's creations. This is why he must die; this is why we have sworn to kill him!'

Lazalo explains that he and his brother are cousins of a man who once served the doctor as a labourer. When their kinsman learned of Moreau's experiments, he and several other Pacific Islanders in the doctor's pay sought to escape the island.

'But Moreau will do anything to protect his secrets,' Lazalo says. 'If you try to leave the island without his blessing, your life is forfeit. Soulstealer's minions killed our cousin and his companions, all save one. The survivor found his way to our island home and told us of his ordeal. It took us many moons to find this place, and we have been waiting for a good omen to launch our attack. The killing of the snake-demon is such a sign. Soon, we will seek out the doctor himself and avenge our fallen.'

When you ask the hunter how the animal-folk and monsters of the island came to be made, both of the brothers shake their heads darkly.

'Somehow, Moreau breaks borders between men and beasts,' Lazalo tells you. 'He throws the Mother's perfect order into chaos and disarray. It is the darkest sort of magic!'

Suddenly, the hunter grins wildly and holds up his hands. 'I have talked enough, man from the West - we are enemies, remember? Even so, we will return the things we took from you in recognition of your reckless courage, then we will eat together. After that, you must go on your way and think deeply about your association with the doctor.'

The men lead you into their makeshift camp, tend your wounds and offer you a meal of some sun-dried fish, fresh fruit and a bowl of some sort of soaked grain.

Restore 6 VITALITY points and reclaim any equipment that was lost to the brothers!

Next, the men gift you a **bow** just like their own, a **quiver (10)** of brightly-fletched **arrows** (this ranged weapon causes 2 points of damage), a coil of **rope**, enough food for 4 **meals** and a pouch of crimson **blood leaves**.

Make these additions to your *equipment list*.

'If you find yourself in need, then cast these leaves upon a fire,' Lazalo says of the blood leaves. 'The red smoke that results is distinct in sight and scent – such a signal will summon us to your side!'

Thanking the brothers for the gifts, you prepare to be on your way.

'You may walk south-east towards the heart of the island or take one of our canoes to explore the island's coast,' Lazalo says. 'The choice is yours.'

If you wish to head south-east towards the heart of the island, turn to **261**.

If you would prefer to take a canoe and explore the island's coast, turn to **396**.

129

Even in your best condition you would struggle to fight off five sea-toughened sailors. Try as you may, you are soon beaten into submission!

Roll one dice and deduct this number of VITALITY points!

If you are still alive, the crew tie a rope around you, secure the other end to a boom spar, swing you out into the water-logged dinghy, then cut you adrift. You swirl away from the schooner, watching in a stupor as all hands take to the rigging and bring the ship around to the wind. The sails flutter, belly out with a whoosh, and the ship's weather-beaten prow heels steeply towards you!

Roll a dice...

If you roll 1-3, turn to <u>255</u>.

If you roll 4-6, turn to <u>316</u>.

130

You creep up on the hunter, expecting him to notice you at any moment...

Test your PROWESS with a -1 adjustment, due to the soft and uneven nature of the ground.

If you pass, turn to <u>207</u>.

If you fail, turn to <u>195</u>.

131

Your heart sinks when you realise that you have drawn the shortest straw!

'Do not fight!' the sailor whispers, pulling out his dagger and inching closer. 'We'll put an end to your suffering as swiftly as we may.'

'Yes, lay back and close your eyes,' Helmar pleads weakly. 'It is only fair, after all!'

You have no choice now but to fight the men simultaneously for your life! (If you are unarmed, remember to reduce your *close combat score* by 2).

SAILOR: Prowess - 6; Vitality - 3; Damage - 2.

HELMAR: Prowess - 5; Vitality - 2; Damage - 1.

If you win, turn to **105**.

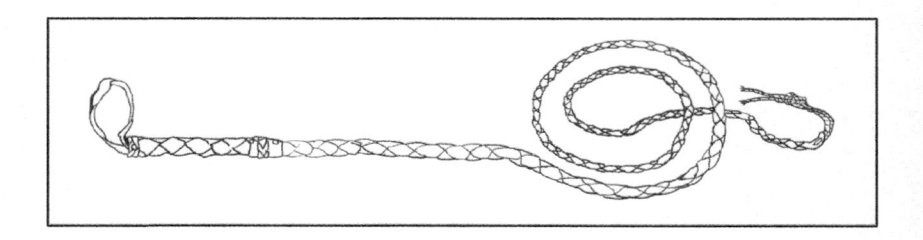

132

The Thylacine-men rush to your side. At first you think that they are going to help you to your feet, but they simply press their large noses into your pockets, huffing and lapping at the areas of your shirt and pockets where the eggs you collected have been smashed. Grimacing, you pick bits of broken shell and scoop yolk from your garments, flinching as the excited creatures snap at the air around you and lick the unctuous slime from the jungle floor.

Suddenly, the Thylacine-men give a series of yelps, and you see the python slithering rapidly down the trunk of the mahogany tree. Fearlessly, the hybrid creatures start to worry it with darting lunges before one of them is seized in the serpent's jaws and rapidly smothered in a coiling embrace. The captured beast thrashes wildly while its companion gives a savage snarl and sinks jaws like a mantrap into the snake's scaly side!

Do you wish to aid the Thylacine-men in their fight? If so, turn to **327**.

If you would rather leave these creatures to their primal battle and escape to the south while you can, turn to **171**.

133

As you grapple with your opponent, you become aware of two heavy shapes crashing through the jungle toward you, no doubt alerted by the Ape-man's cries. Unable to break free of your opponent's grip, you are helpless to resist as a pair of huge, twisted hands with fingernails like claws sink into your shoulders and haul you backwards with tremendous strength. Swift to take advantage of this intervention, the Ape-man delivers a painful bite to your leg!

Lose 2 VITALITY points and note that you have been *exposed to zoonotic infection*.

Then the second of the newcomers appears before you, a towering brute more than six and a half feet tall, dressed in ragged trousers and a soiled cotton shirt. He, like the Ape-man, seems a hideous mix of man and some sort of towering, predatory beast.

'He, he, he, broke the Law!' the Ape-man tells him. 'He made war upon me! One five-fingered man against another!! We must take him to the...the...the...Master! We must take him to the House of Pain!'

'It must die now,' the brute beside him says in a rumbling baritone, his huge eyes shining.

'For such crimes, none escape,' comes the voice of your captor, his rough claws moving up to your neck.

You must act quickly!

If you want to attempt to break free of the monster's grip, turn to **169**.

If you demand to be taken to the House of Pain, turn to **205**.

If you would rather proclaim ignorance of the law, turn to **246**.

134

The keen edge of your weapon slices through the soft flesh of the squids and sends spurts of blue blood into the water, whipping the Humboldts into a cannabalistic feeding frenzy!

As the creatures thrash and tear at one another, you row towards the beach, vowing never to be caught out on the water so close to nightfall again. As your canoe grounds on the sand, you notice part of a **severed tentacle** has landed in the foot of your vessel. It is about the length of a human arm and sports a row of retractable, venomous claws.

Add it to your *equipment list* if you wish, then turn to **82**.

135

At the mention of a reward, the man's resolute face remains unmoved. He is clearly unmotivated by money!

Now, if you have not already done so, you may appeal to the captain? (Turn to **59**).

If you have already appealed to the captain, or wish to simply accept your fate, turn to **427**.

136

The Water Wight will attempt to swim deeper into the swamp as soon as you start shooting. You must kill it within FOUR rounds, or it will escape!

WATER WIGHT: Prowess - 7; Vitality - 8; Ranged Defence - 6.

If you are able to kill it within four rounds, turn immediately to **519**.

If you are unable to kill it in time, then there is nothing you can do as the creature vanishes into the depths of the swamp...

You must now continue on your way!

To do so by following the edge of the swamp towards the west, turn to **184**.

Alternatively, you can head away from the swamp northward into the jungle by turning to **211**.

137

The gentle breeze, soft sand and breath-like murmur of the water reassures you that the beach should be a fine place to spend the night. You pick a spot upon the sand, pillow your head beneath your pack, and lay back to watch the last of a crimson sunset retreat before the night. Marvelling at the beauty of the constellations above, you drift off into a deep and welcome sleep.

Turn to **89**.

138

You inflict grievous casualties upon your attackers, sending one after another tumbling from the roof until the predatory roars and angry shouts of the beast-folk transmute into the hoarse cries and shrieks of the wounded and dying. You see several individuals fleeing into the jungle, or tearing along the beach like mad dogs, before the remainder of the mob scatters in all directions.

As the beast-folk disappear from sight, a sudden gust of black smoke causes you to choke, followed by the sight of numerous threads of flame boiling up out of the thatch of the roof and crackling towards you. Whether by accident or design, a fire has caught in the tinder-dry roof of the enclosure!

Knowing that you have not the means to save the structure, you drop to the ground. With nowhere else to go, you make for the boathouse by the ocean's edge, sit with your back to its wall and watch the enclosure burn long into the night...

Turn to **409**.

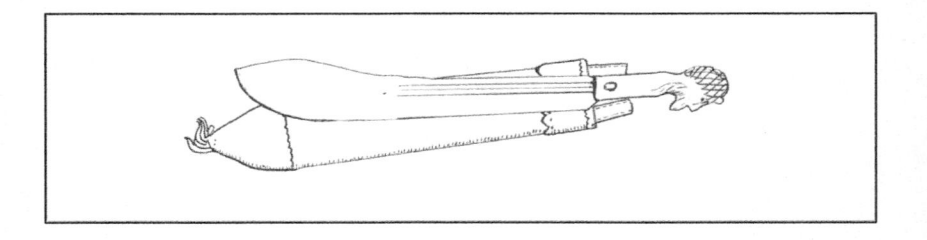

139

Moments after the rabbit disappears, you hear the violent scuffing of sand, a brief squeal and a snapping, gulping sound. Alarmed, you move in the direction of the beach and peer through the trees. Poised upon the sand is a nightmare vision; a gigantic grey maggot eight feet long and as wide around its middle as four wine barrels lashed together. But instead of a blind, tapering head, the bloated body is somehow fused with the hideously twisted head of a giant man that is dripping with mucus. As the trembling hind-legs of the unfortunate rabbit slide down the apparition's throat, the thing fixes you with streaming eyes and smacks its lips gleefully.

The DRACONOPE is one of Doctor Moreau's earliest and most reprehensible experiments. Tormented by unrelenting hunger and pain, it is a gibbering, shrieking monstrosity that lives only to unleash its rage upon the world. It is deadliest within the water but is also a terrible adversary upon the land.

As you stand transfixed, the monster screeches and jerks towards you with a pulsing, undulating charge!

If you wish to attempt to escape this horror by fleeing deeper into the jungle, turn immediately to **2**.

If you would rather stand your ground and fight, then the tree line will slow the monster down. You may perform FOUR ranged attacks before entering close combat!

DRACONOPE: Prowess - 10; Vitality - 12; Damage - 3; Ranged Defence - 12.

If the Draconope wins three rounds in succession, turn to 456.

If you are able to defeat the Draconope without losing three rounds in succession, turn to 168.

140

You strike the shark hard on the nose and manage to avoid its serrated teeth. Repelled by your resistance, the shark glides into the depths and swims away. Weary though you are, the close encounter with the shark has reminded you of your love for life, so you make one last attempt to swim to the beach.

Roll a dice, modifying the roll for each point of FATE you are willing to spend!

If you roll 1-3, turn to **303**.

If you roll 4-6, turn to **240**.

141

When you decline his invitation, the Ape-man steps back, shakes his head and pants rapidly.

'Then you, you, you, must return to the Master!' he jabbers. 'Stay at the huts or stay at the House of Pain.' He points east along the beach. 'That way to the Master; that way to the House of Pain. Go there...now!'

Not wanting the to provoke the mob into violence, you pick up your rucksack and head east. You walk until the dawn touches the sky, and by the growing light catch sight of the enclosure in the distance! As you draw closer, you see the figures of Doctor Moreau, Montgomery and M'ling leading the pack of staghounds out onto the beach. The dogs immediately catch your scent and lurch against their collars in a frenzy of barking and growling.

Moreau restrains the beasts with a harsh command, stares at you for a few seconds, then leads the staghounds back into the enclosure, while Montgomery and M'ling advance towards you.

'Where the devil have you been?' Montgomery demands. 'We've been worried sick and were about to set out with the dogs to find you! Now get inside this instant, Moreau will want to have words!'

Your relief at being back among humans somewhat sullied by a flicker of dread, you enter the enclosure and let yourself in via the small door leading to the room. It does not take long before you hear the inner door to the courtyard being unlocked, and the doctor strides in...

Turn to 39.

142

The serenity of the evening is interrupted when you see an immense creature angling through the water towards you. At first you think it might be a whale, for it is a mottled grey colour and swims with a vertical rolling motion, but then you see a hideously twisted human face gasping for air before plunging into a deep dive. As it does so, you catch sight of a bloated maggot-like tail lashing in powerful propulsion. Moments later, the creature smashes into your canoe and sends you spinning through the air!

The DRACONOPE is one of Doctor Moreau's earliest and most reprehensible experiments. Tormented by unrelenting pain, it is a gibbering, shrieking monstrosity that lives only to unleash its rage upon the world. Upon land it is dangerous enough, but in the water it is deadly.

Remove all of your equipment and weapons as they are lost to the sea, with the exception of any knives or daggers that are belted around your waist...

Next you must fight for your life!

DRACONOPE: Prowess - 10; Vitality - 12; Damage - 3.

If you are unarmed, subtract 2 from your *close combat score*. Even if you possess a weapon, you must subtract a further 2 from your *close combat score* while fighting an amphibious enemy in the water!

If the Draconope wins two rounds in succession, turn to **456**.

If you are able to defeat the Draconope without losing two successive rounds, turn to **98**.

143

Without the correct elixirs, there is nothing you can do to prevent the reversion from completing. Within an hour the agony becomes unbearable, and you unleash a bestial roar that wakes the entire ship!

Within moments, armed sailors storm into your cabin, their faces twisting in horror when they see what you have become. The last thing you see is the barrel of a gun, then a merciful flash...

YOUR LIFE IS OVER!

144

The ground between you and the brake of trees is soft underfoot, but it becomes firmer with each stride. Daring to hope, you swerve this way and that, but you have a highly skilled hunter taking aim at your back at only a modest range...

Roll a dice!

If you roll 1-4, turn to **11**.

If you roll 5-6, turn to **80**.

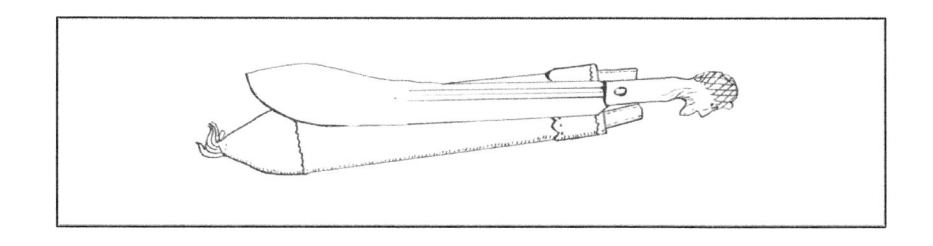

145

Suddenly two tall, lithe figures come hurtling toward you out of the gloom! Your immediate impression is that of hunch-shouldered madmen, but then you catch sight of their baleful green eyes, impossibly wide jaws and elongated killing fangs.

They are WOLF-MEN which you must fight simultaneously!

First WOLF-MAN: Prowess - 7; Vitality - 7; Damage - 2.

Second WOLF-MAN: Prowess - 6; Vitality - 7; Damage - 2.

If you win, you find nothing of use upon the creatures other than small stones with holes through them that are hung around their necks on leather cords.

Take the **stone necklaces** if you wish, then turn to 181.

146

Test your FATE!

If you are favoured, turn to 347.

If you are unfavoured, turn to 495.

147

You may engage in a ranged battle with the Hyena-man leader for as long as your ammunition lasts!

HYENA-MAN LEADER: Prowess - 9; Ballistics - 8; Vitality - 10; Ranged Defence - 8; Damage - 2/3.

Note that the Hyena-man leader has **7 quarrels** for his crossbow (keep a record of how many bolts he has remaining), and that each hit will cause 3 points of damage. After these are exhausted the Hyena-men will retreat to the north. If the Hyena-man leader is killed, then his friends will retreat, taking all of their leader's equipment with them.

If this happens, turn immediately to 186.

If you run out of ammunition first or tire of shooting, then you may charge into close combat anytime! Remember to take into account any damage you have caused, then turn to 322.

148

You crouch in the thick foliage at the side of the path as two huge creatures with feral, snarling faces come lumbering past. From the closeness of your position, you can see that their arms and exposed chests are seamed with scars and covered with a fine dark fur, while beneath their tattered trousers their unshod feet are splayed and alien. You also see that their hands are huge and clumsy, with long, blunt claws in place of where fingernails should be.

Suddenly it dawns on you...these creatures are some sort of BEAR-MAN hybrid!

To your relief, the brutes fail to notice you and quickly pass out of sight. This close encounter has persuaded you that you are too exposed upon the path...

This being so, do you wish to press north into the jungle? If you want to head this direction, turn to 514.

If you would rather head south into the jungle, turn to 56.

149

The dinghy has drifted some way from the derelict, and you are now faced with a difficult and dangerous swim!

Roll four dice and *test your VITALITY*...

If the total is the same as or less than your current vitality, turn to 127.

If the total exceeds your current vitality, turn to 564.

150

Just when you feel that the Draconope is weakening, it breaks free of the Pugnatyr's grip and tears a mortal wound in his throat with its gnashing teeth. The great ape fights on for several seconds, but suddenly slumps to one side with blood pouring down his chest.

Enraged, you launch attack after attack into the Draconope's bloated body until grey-green ichor spurts and spills darkly onto the sand. Finally, the monster gives a burbling shriek, thrashes desperately, then flops dead to the ground.

You sink to your knees, utterly exhausted. You have truly had a brush with death, and the sight and sound of the Draconope's shrieks of agonised hatred will stay with you as long as you live. Worse still, you have lost a powerful ally who has given his life to save you. Yet above the grief rises another sensation - a sense of pride at having stood firm beside the Pugnatyr in the face of such horror.

Gain 1 FATE point!

After you have regained your composure, you try to drag the body of the great ape into the jungle where he may be laid to rest, but the beast is too heavy for you to move. So, you leave him beside the leaking corpse of the Draconope, hopeful that he would have been glad to know that his death did not go unavenged.

You walk back into the jungle and settle down to rest. Pillowing your pack beneath your head, you soon fall into a troubled sleep.

Gain 3 VITALITY points.

When you awake, you realise that you have slept for several hours and that the dawn is not too far away. It is then that you notice an animal trail running away inland of where you have been resting. Examining it closely, you see signs of the recent passage of many creatures.

Intrigued, you decide to investigate.

Turn to **503**.

151

'Yes, me,' you reply, feeling faintly ridiculous. 'I came in the boat. From the ship?'

'From the ship...' the Ape-man says, pulling back his large, lipless mouth in a broad, ugly grin. His roving eyes go back to your hands, at which point he seems suddenly puzzled. He holds a hand out, counting the digits slowly.

'One, two, three, four, five, eh?' he queries.

Assuming that this is some sort of greeting, you repeat the same thing by way of reply, and the creature grins again with immense satisfaction. In an attempt to follow up on this success, you ask him who he is, and where he is from.

'I am a five-fingered man,' he replies proudly. 'Home is at the huts...where we eat man's food. It is...over there!' He waves vaguely over his shoulder. 'Do you wish to see?'

If you wish to reply that you would like to see the huts, turn to **236**.

If you would rather make your excuses and reply that you do not wish to see the huts, turn to **269**.

152

You must trust to chance to see if you can slip by the men unseen!

Roll a dice...

If you roll an even number, turn to **557**.

If you roll an odd number, turn to **479**.

153

You find a small notebook in the doctor's breast pocket. As you leaf through it, your attention is arrested by a page entitled 'Antidotes to Reversion', and an especially interesting passage that reads:

'Stubborn beast-flesh! I cannot prevent it from reverting...

'In some of my coarser experiments the original forms make their presence known rather slowly. With my finer specimens, however, bestial reemergence appears with alarming alacrity. I simply do not know why this should be the case!

'There seems to be some fundamental essence that is possessed by all living things. It is apparent from birth, largely immutable and transmitted from generation to generation. I must devise an elixir that compels this essence to forget its natural lineage and rather to respect the altered forms I have spent so many years refining...'

Then a much later entry that reads:

'It is done!

'The red elixir now achieves what the blue, green and purple elixirs accomplished when taken together: it prevents reversion, reverses early-stage reversion, and permanently preserves the altered form. It must not fall into the hands of any of the beast-folk!

'I am less concerned about the theft of my earlier formulas, for it is unlikely that any of my creatures will have the intelligence or daring to imbibe all three liquids simultaneously. If they did achieve this and were to somehow escape the island...well, the inconvenience of having my activities reported to the scientific communities in England, America or Europe does not bear thinking about.

'I plan to hide the red elixir in an inaccessible part of the island, for I may need it if my distillation equipment fails, or my notes are somehow lost. Perhaps one of my creations will eventually prove worthy of permanence? For now, I lament the loss of the days when all the beast-folk were mortally afraid of the enclosure.

'Truly, nothing stands still with science...'

Add **Moreau's pocketbook** to your *equipment list*.

Now, do you wish to search Montgomery and Moreau's private quarters? If so, turn to <u>407</u>.

If not, turn to <u>185</u>.

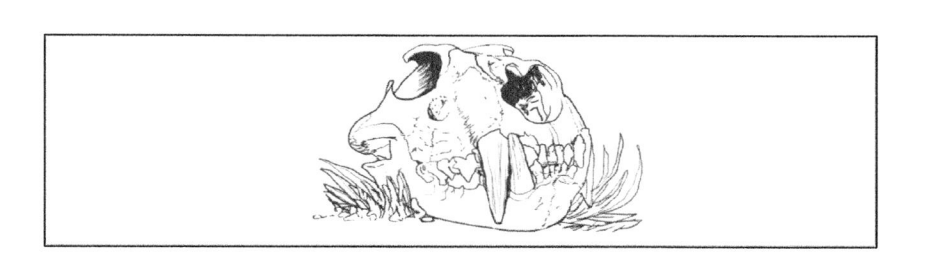

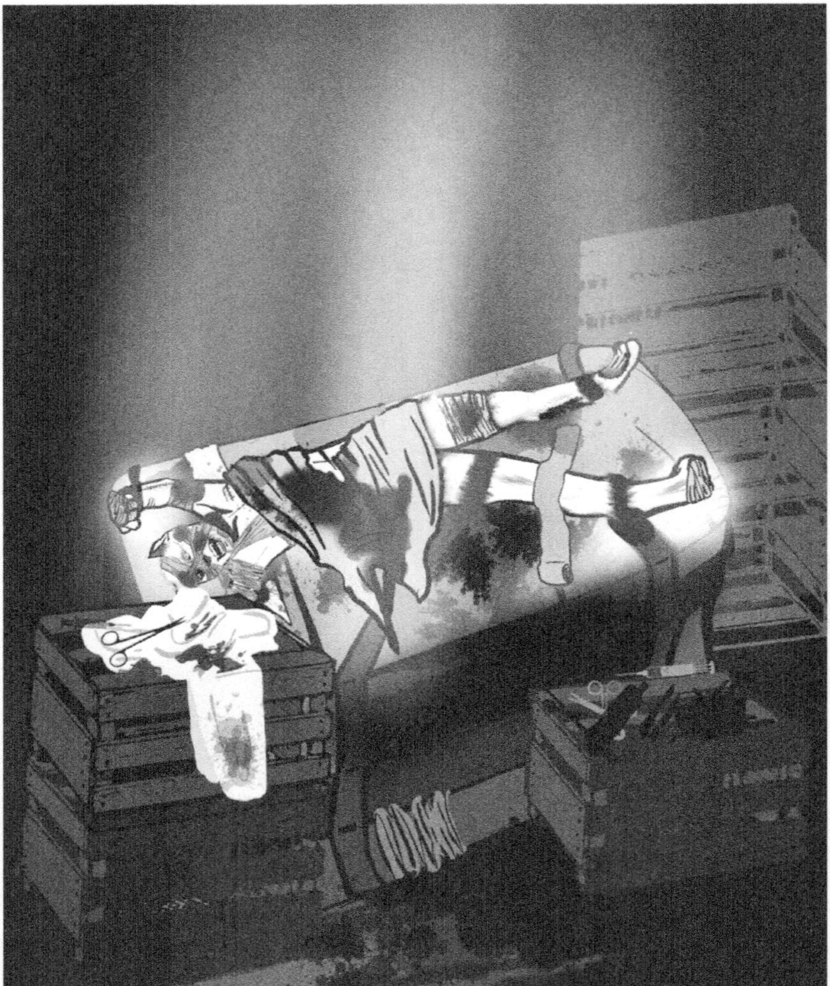

'It is the perfect time for you to inspect my present study!' Moreau says, smiling faintly at your discomfort. 'The sight of it is not pleasant, but you will see that it is not any worse than what you have imagined.'

Leaving the remains of his cigar upon the table, the doctor throws open the inner door and beckons you through. Immediately you are struck by a cloying antiseptic odour and gain the vague impression of wooden medicine cabinets and tables set against the walls of a rectangular room which has a second door leading into an open air courtyard. The laboratory is strewn with medical and surgical apparatus of all kinds, but it is to the middle of the room that your attention is drawn.

There, tightly lashed to a metal operating table and starkly lit by sunlight that is streaming through an open skylight is a living thing so cut and mutilated that you feel sick to your soul. Between blood-soaked bandages you discern patches of matted golden fur and meet a pair of maddened feline eyes that leave no doubt in your mind as to what it is you are seeing.

'You would not be the first visitor to take fright at the thought that I was vivisecting human beings,' Moreau explains. 'Frankly, I am not opposed to the idea when it comes to the most hardened and fiendish criminals, or those who are hopelessly deranged. But will you now admit that the subject you see before you is, after all, only the puma you saw us transport from the *Ipecacuanha*?'

You nod mutely, the disgust etched on your face.

'You can spare me your youthful consternation, by the way,' Moreau says. 'Montgomery used to be just the same until he grew a little more...calloused. For now, you admit it is the puma, at least, and not a poor tormented man being made into a monster. This is progress! Now, let us return to the other room so that I may deliver my physiological lecture to you. First, I will secure for us a little peace and quiet.'

The doctor strides to a medicine cabinet, douses a yellowed handkerchief in chloroform, then clamps the rag over the puma's mouth and nose. Enraged, the creature bucks furiously against its bonds so that the surgical table rattles and dances. To your horror, there is the sound of wrenching metal, and one of the creature's powerful forelimbs breaks free, slamming into Moreau's broad chest and knocking him to the floor! Terror has made the great cat even more formidable, and you realise that it is only a matter of moments before it frees itself entirely from its bonds...

'Help me restrain the beast, for heaven's sake!' roars the doctor, picking himself off the floor and struggling with the hissing, spitting abomination. 'If it escapes, it'll kill us both!'

Do you wish to help Moreau restrain the puma? If so, turn to **512**.

If you wish to help the puma by striking the doctor over the head with one of your weapons, turn to **413**.

155

As you progress along the northern edge of the swamp, a fetid mist begins to rise from the stagnant waters to drift ghost-like among the cypress trees crowding the hillside to the north. The silence is oppressive, broken by little more than the dull pop of bubbles or subtle liquid sounds. Just as you are beginning to consider abandoning the water's edge, you catch sight of something that makes your heart skip a beat. There is the body of a man lying face down on the bottom of the mire a few yards from the shore!

He is wearing a billowing white shirt, dark trews and well-made knee-high boots. His long hair has settled around the sides of his face like a blonde funerary shroud, but you can see that his fish-white hands are remarkably well preserved. Either this unfortunate drowned very recently, or the low oxygen environment of the swamp has slowed the processes of decomposition. It is then you notice that the corpse is wearing a short-sword and has a small leather purse fastened to its belt.

The thought of sharing the stagnant waters with a dead body makes you shudder, but pulling the man from the swamp should be straightforward enough. Doing so would allow you to offer the man a decent burial, and his trappings might prove useful...

Do you wish to enter the swamp and retrieve the drowned man? If so, turn to 26.

If you would rather leave the body where it is and continue to follow the edge of the marsh towards the west, turn to 184.

Alternatively, you could abandon the edge of the marsh and strike north through the cypress trees. To try this, turn to 211.

156

Your refusal to participate in the drawing of straws seems to bring the other two men to their senses, but during the thirst-torment of the night, you hear Helmar and the sailor whispering urgently to one another. In the morning you find them sat next to one another and staring at you intently.

You are desperately thirsty and must lose 2 VITALITY points!

If you now wish to agree to draws straws, turn to 62.

If you continue to refuse, turn to 273.

157

You come running out from behind the megalith, your eyes fixed on the back of the hunter!

Roll a dice...

If you roll 1-2, turn to 266.

If you roll 3-4, turn to 195.

If you roll 5-6, turn to 278.

158

You unsheathe your weapon and begin a desperate fight for your life!

GIANT PYTHON: Prowess - 9; Vitality - 12; Damage - 2.

After each combat round, you must deduct 2 VITALITY points due to the snake's constricting coils.

If you are able to win two combat rounds, the Python will release you, sending you plummeting to the ground.

Turn to **484**.

159

You empty your bullets into the thrashing limbs, but the heavy slugs of the revolver pass through the flesh of the squid without causing much damage! Worst still, the sound of the gun seems to excite the predators even more, and they buffet the canoe wildly as you desperately try to keep your balance.

Note that you have exhausted all ammunition for your revolver, then *test your PROWESS*!

If you pass, you are able to stop the canoe from tipping over for now and have little choice but to battle the oceanic predators with your oar! Turn to **166**.

If you fail, you cannot stop yourself from plunging into the water and must turn to **380**.

160

Helmar draws the middle straw, but before either of you can react, the sailor - unwilling to accept his fate - leaps at the passenger with his dagger held high! Weakened from hunger and thirst, the sailor fails to make a quick kill and Helmar gamely seizes his attacker's knife-hand.

You step in to help your fellow passenger, but before you can intervene the two men stumble over the gunwale and roll overboard into the ocean where they sink like stones. In the terrible calm that follows you start to laugh, a dreadful mirth rising like a thing from without, then you lapse into bitter silence. It is just a matter of days now before you too are dead...

As night falls, you slip into a morbid sleep, your mouth and throat a torment of thirst. When you awake the next morning, you are unsure whether you are alive or dead, for you see something you can scarcely believe - a set of sails dancing above the horizon! For what seems like an endless period you lay with your head on the thwart, watching the little ship approach, lacking the strength to even cry out.

You are dimly aware of being lifted up onto the schooner's gangway and perceive a large red-headed man with freckles staring down at you over the bulwarks. Then you gain the impression of a dark face with extraordinary eyes close to yours. As some sort of metallic-tasting liquid is forced between your teeth, you lose consciousness, unsure whether your rescue is a blessing or a curse...

Turn to **216**.

161

Cursing your desperate situation, you heave the men's bodies over the side of the dinghy and watch dully as the patient sharks move in to feed. Then you spot the sailor's **dagger** lying before you, which you may keep if you wish (this simple weapon will cause 2 points of close combat damage).

Lying back beneath the plank seats, there is nothing to do but listen to the motion of the water and the whisper of the wind.

Lose 2 VITALITY points from hunger, thirst and sunstroke!

As night falls, you slip into a morbid sleep, your mouth and throat a torment of thirst. When you awake the next morning, you are unsure whether you are alive or dead, for you see something you can scarcely believe - a set of sails dancing above the horizon! For what seems like an eternity you lay with your head on the thwart, watching the schooner approach, lacking the strength to even cry out.

Finally, you slip into a state of semi-consciousness, and are only dimly aware of being lifted up onto a ship's gangway, where you perceive a large red-headed man with freckles staring down at you over the bulwarks. Then you gain the impression of a dark face with extraordinary eyes close to yours. As some sort of metallic-tasting liquid is forced between your teeth, you lose consciousness, unsure whether your rescue is a blessing or a curse...

Turn to **216**.

162

You stare down at the malnourished bodies of the lions, angry that the doctor would allow such animals to roam the island unchecked.

You are proud, however, of standing firm beside the Pugnatyr, and feel the intoxicating flush of victory.

Gain 2 FATE points!

The great ape comes to your side, gestures for you to wait and disappears into the jungle. After a short wait, he reappears with a filthy oilskin bag that looks like it has just been dug up. Placing it at your feet, the Pugnatyr nudges you affectionately with the back of his hand and wanders off into the darkness of the jungle.

Your melancholy at the departure of your ally soon fades when you open the oilskin. Inside is a **breech-loading carbine** with a wax-sealed box containing a **magazine of 14 rounds**. You immediately attend to the weapon and find that it is in good working order. Add the carbine to your *equipment list* and note that it does 3 points of ranged damage (6 on a double roll). Also, you notice a silver strip soldered to the stock of the gun, on which is etched the number *367*. Be sure to make a note of this number!

Pleased with this deadly weapon, you enter the jungle, find a comfortable spot and settle down to rest. Pillowing your pack beneath your head, you fall into a deep sleep.

Gain 4 VITALITY points.

When you awake, you realise that you have slept for several hours and that the dawn is not too far away. It is then that you notice an animal trail running away inland of where you have been resting. Examining it closely, you see signs of the recent passage of what appears to be several people.

Intrigued, you decide to follow it.

Turn to 503.

163

As you float despondently and try to regain some strength, you feel something large pass under you. Your worse fears are realised when you see a sleek, iron-grey fin cutting through the water towards you. All your kicking has attracted the attentions of a shark!

Do you wish to escape the shark by quickly swimming closer to the beach? If so, turn to **385**.

If you would rather tread water and prepare to fight, turn to **469**.

164

As you work your way down towards the sea, the steaming brook becomes cooler, and the steep sides of the ravine become infested with livid mosses, fungi and small, twisted trees with claw-like branches.

Ahead, you see that a small delta has formed where the flow of water joins a strip of silver-white sand. Though the beach is serene and enticing, the delta is composed of slurrilous minerals and volcanic sediment that have a reddish-brown hue and emit an unpleasant stink.

Fortunately, it is not too difficult to pick a path over some rocks onto the beach, but first you must decide whether you wish to head north or south…

If you wish to head north along the beach, turn to **197**.

If you would rather head south along the beach, turn to **191**.

165

When you wake you find yourself lashed to a cold operating table, your arms and legs spreadeagled. Beside you stands Doctor Moreau, now dressed in a physician's gown with a surgical mask covering his nose and mouth. He turns towards you, a dark green bottle and stained handkerchief held before him.

He drenches the handkerchief with chloroform and clamps it over your nose and mouth. Unconsciousness comes mercifully fast, a nothingness from which you never rise...

YOUR ADVENTURE ENDS HERE!

166

If you can fight off the Humboldts for long enough without falling into the water, they may leave you alone in favour of easier prey! Fight the shoal of squid as a single enemy:

HUMBOLDT SQUID: Prowess - 10; Vitality - 10; Damage - 2.

If you ever roll a 'double one' for your *close combat score*, then you are unable to prevent yourself from being tipped into the water. If this happens, turn immediately to **380**.

If you are able to keep out of the water and fend off these aquatic predators, turn to **43**.

167

The white-haired man fixes his dark, glittering eyes upon you, and you sense his indomitable power and resolve.

'Montgomery tells me that you are a man of science,' he says. 'I can make use of such a man. If you wish to accompany us back to the island, then you may cross the gangplank and rest in our boat, while we bring aboard our stock.'

Not wishing to spend a moment longer aboard the *Ipecacuanha* and her bully of a captain, you thank the white-haired man, give Montgomery an appreciative nod, and cross over into the island boat.

Turn to **468**.

168

You aim attack after attack into the Draconope's leathery neck until its burbling roars cease, then fall to your knees in exhaustion and shock. You have truly had a brush with death, and the sight and sound of the Draconope's shrieks of agonised hatred will stay with you as long as you live...

Lose 1 FATE point!

When you have regained your composure, you move back into the jungle before choosing a place to rest. Pillowing your pack beneath your head, you fall into a deep sleep.

Gain 4 VITALITY points.

When you awake, you realise that you have slept for several hours and that the dawn is not too far away. It is then that you notice an animal trail running away inland of where you have been resting. Examining it closely, you see signs of the recent passage of what appears to be several people.

Intrigued, you decide to investigate...

Turn to **503**.

169

At the first signs of struggle, the great hands seize your head and wrench it to the side, breaking your neck instantly...

YOUR ADVENTURE IS OVER!

170

Seeing as you possess no ranged weapons, all you can do is fight the hunters simultaneously once they enter the forest!

LAZALO THE HUNTER: Prowess - 7; Ballistics - N/A; Vitality - 8; Damage - 2.

VAI THE HUNTER: Prowess - 8; Ballistics - N/A; Vitality - 8; Damage - 2.

Note: Both men wield pairs of **Toledo steel hunting knives** that add +1 to their *close combat score*.

If you win, you may take one of the hunters' **bows** (2 points of ranged damage) and **quivers** (they have **12 arrows** between them), as well as two pairs of **Toledo steel hunting knives** (+1 to your *close combat score*).

After you have made any adjustments to your *equipment list*, you may investigate the hunters' camp (if you have not already done so) by turning to <u>241</u>.

If you have already visited the hunters' camp, then you may explore the brake of trees by turning to <u>499</u>.

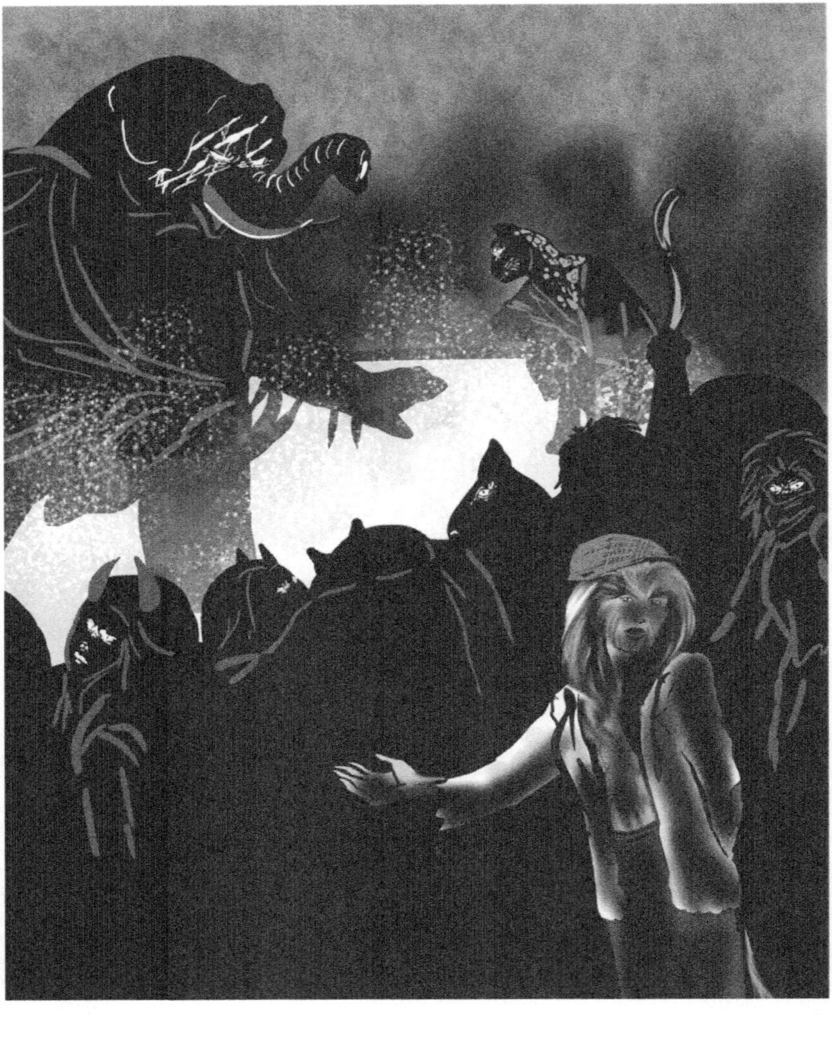

171

As you pick your way towards the south the land begins to rise towards the island's centre on an east-west axis. The jungle is so dense towards the island's centre, however, that you decide to continue heading south in the hope that there will be an easier route inland.

In time, the forest opens out onto a wide bowl of verdant sun-drenched meadow at the base of which is a small sand-covered arena in which two fighters are engaged in a bout of unarmed combat!

One of the participants is of a sleek felid extraction, while the other is a lumbering, grey-skinned giant sporting a pair of smooth, white tusks curving from his lower jaw. Both fighters are clad in scraps of crude leather armour and are circling one another warily.

Some two dozen creatures of bizarre hybrid physiologies are standing around the edges of the circle and cheering the fighters on, their inhuman voices ugly and harsh.

As you look on in astonishment, the ELEPHANT-MAN initiates a sudden charge. His opponent darts to one side and launches a series of lashing, open-handed hooks to the giant's head and neck. Bellowing in rage, the Elephant-man performs a ponderous turn and charges once again, but the JAGUAR-MAN evades him, unleashing more strikes until the grey-skinned fighter's face becomes a mask of blood.

As the brawl rages, a red-haired, thin-faced creature in the crowd beckons you over. From her grubby, long skirt and frayed bonnet, you infer that she is female, but you cannot place her animal origin. Then you catch wind of her powerful, vulpine body odour and deduce that she is some sort of FOX-WOMAN hybrid!

'Which champion do you favour, my lord?' she calls eagerly. 'The grey giant, or the shadow-stalker?'

Several other bestial creatures tear their attention from the fight and glare at you, waiting for your answer...

Write down your choice, then turn to **221**.

172

Two towering creatures with inordinately long torsos, shambling legs and enormous, brutish faces come lumbering down the path toward you. They are dressed in tattered trousers and filthy cotton shirts but are unlike any human you have ever seen. They possess huge, glaring eyes and toothy muzzles that growl a word so guttural and ill-formed that you are only just able to comprehend their accusation...

'*LAWBREAKER!*'

They then charge you with a speed that belies their awkwardness. If you possess a ranged weapon, then you have time for TWO shots before fighting these powerful creatures simultaneously!

First BEAR-MAN: Prowess - 8; Vitality - 10; Damage - 2; Ranged defence - 7.

Second BEAR-MAN: Prowess - 7; Vitality - 9; Damage - 2; Ranged defence - 7.

If you win, turn to **314**.

173

In the middle of the clearing you see two lean, rangy creatures trying to scramble up the trunk of a twisting, moss-infested mahogany tree. High above, in the crook of a gnarled branch, you see what interests them: a large bird's nest formed from a mass of twigs and leaves.

The creatures have their backs to you, and you take a moment to appraise them. The only clothing they possess are the ragged remains of grubby white breeches that flutter about their knees, but you are most arrested by the faint, dark stripes that cover the grimy skin of their backs.

Such patterning is highly reminiscent of jungle cats, yet the creatures seem to lack the felid affinity for climbing. Indeed, they possess disproportionately small hands and feet that are so twisted and malformed as to be next to useless in their present endeavour. With each failed leap, the creatures' snarls and grunts grow increasingly frustrated…

Furthermore, the pair are so obsessed with the object of their desire that they have failed to notice you!

Do you wish to take advantage of the element of surprise and attack the creatures? If so, turn immediately to **194**.

If you would rather clear your throat to announce your arrival, then the creatures spin around, their eyes widening in excitement and surprise. Turn to **238**.

Otherwise, you can try to sneak past the creatures and head south? Turn to **539**.

174

The two men glance at each other, clearly unimpressed. 'What make you of this Moreau?' the one nearest you demands.

How will you answer?

Do you wish to say that Moreau has been kind to you and that you owe him your life? If so, turn to **218**.

If you would rather say that you fear for your life at Moreau's hands, turn to **320**.

175

As you set off along the beach, you cannot help but cast your gaze over your shoulder to see if the group of creatures are following. When you are sure that they are not, you cast anxious glances toward the inland jungle, where every moon-cast shadow looks as though it might be a lurking, watching shape.

But the sea offers a share of dangers that are at least the equal of the land...

Have you killed the Draconope?

If so, turn to **306**.

If not, turn to **113**.

176

'Staghounds and pumas never did keep good company,' Montgomery tells you. 'Honestly, I lament ever being so bold as to bring two ancient enemies aboard the same ship. If you feel you have the strength, then I suggest you come up on deck and see for yourself.'

You readily agree and follow Montgomery out of the cabin.

Now turn to 365.

177

The hunter comes around the side of the boulder, his bow trained on your chest. You hold up your hands and explain that you are simply a stranded explorer seeking to recover your lost possessions, but the man's face remains hard and suspicious. Soon, his friend comes running up from the copse of palm trees to the north-west, but instead of putting an arrow to his bow, he stares at you curiously.

'Without weapons of war, you are either very stupid or very brave to follow us here,' he says. 'We are enemies of Moreau, yet you tell us you owe him your life. So tell me: will you turn against him or not? If so, we can talk. Refuse, and you too are our enemy.'

Having spoken these words, the hunter also notches an arrow to his bow and aims it at your heart.

How will you reply?

If you wish to say that you are willing to turn against Moreau, turn to 213.

If you would prefer to say that you will not turn against a man who has saved your life, turn to 128.

178

As you reel from the blow, you trip over a seating plank and crash head first into the sea!

When you surface, you see the sailor rowing the dinghy hard and Helmar staring at you in horror and shock. Desperately you swim after the little boat, incoherent apologies frothing at your lips, but it pulls away and vanishes into a thick bank of sea fog that quickly surrounds you. It is all you can do to tread water for as long as your strength holds out, which is not for long...

YOUR ADVENTURE ENDS HERE!

179

You follow the narrow path with no small degree of trepidation, stepping carefully around clumps of yellow grass and keeping as far away from the water's edge as possible. Just as you are beginning to think that the swamp may not be as bad as it appears, the path ends abruptly at a stretch of still, turgid water before continuing about fifteen yards ahead. The only reason you can imagine that anyone would have dredged the waterlogged soil to create this barrier is to make the centre of the swamp as inaccessible as possible.

Still, the stretch of water should be fairly straightforward to swim, if you are able to throw your rucksack and any ranged weapons in your possession ahead of you before venturing into the water...

Do you wish to attempt this? If so, turn to **329**.

If you would rather not risk losing any of your items to the swamp, nor risking entry into the murky water, then you must re-trace your steps and follow the edges of the mire towards the north (turn to **155**), or towards the south (turn to **279**).

180

In the face of your disdainful courage the creatures rush at you, a mass of shrieking faces, grasping hands and gnashing teeth. There is no time to bring a ranged weapon to bear, so you must fight them all simultaneously in close combat!

MACAQUE-MAN LEADER: Prowess - 7; Vitality - 5; Damage - 2.

First MACAQUE-MAN: Prowess - 5; Vitality - 6; Damage - 2.

Second MACAQUE-MAN: Prowess - 6; Vitality - 6; Damage - 2.

Third MACAQUE-MAN: Prowess - 5; Vitality - 6; Damage - 2.

Fourth MACAQUE-WOMAN: Prowess - 5; Vitality - 8; Damage - 2.

Fifth MACAQUE-MAN: Prowess - 5; Vitality - 6; Damage - 2.

Sixth MACAQUE-WOMAN: Prowess - 4; Vitality - 6; Damage - 2.

Seventh MACAQUE-MAN: Prowess - 5; Vitality - 6; Damage - 2.

If you lose two consecutive rounds, turn immediately to 47.

If you win against these appalling odds, turn to 108.

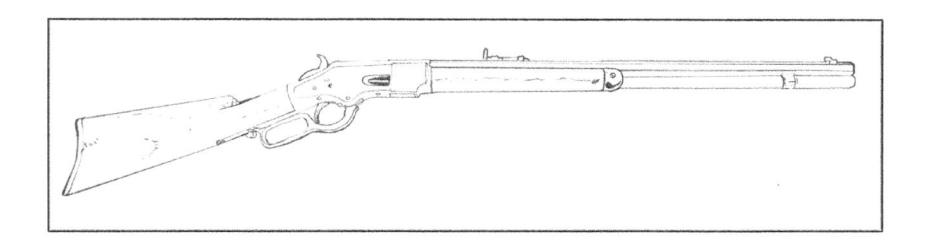

181

Not wanting to linger so close to the bodies of the Wolf-men, you resolve to advance uphill towards the interior of the island until first light. After a few hours, the incline levels out and you come to a halt at the edge of a chasm that slices through the jungle on a north-south bearing.

It is too wide to jump and too steep to safely descend, though the quick cast of a pebble tells you that it is no more than thirty to forty yards deep.

If you possess a **rope** and wish to use it to reach the bottom of the chasm, then turn to <u>50</u>.

If you do not have a rope, or do not wish to use it, then you may follow the chasm to the north? (Turn to <u>93</u>).

Or you may follow the chasm to the south? (Turn to **<u>286</u>**).

182

Montgomery nods at your account, evidently satisfied with the frankness of your story. When you tell him that you have taken to the study of natural history as an escape from a life of comfortable dependence, his face brightens.

'I've done some scholarship myself,' he says. 'Studied biology at University College, London. But that was ten years ago now - more than a lifetime away, it seems!'

Note that you have *explained your survival* to Montgomery.

Next, do you want to ask about the ship you are on? If so, turn to <u>99</u>.

If you would rather ask Montgomery why he left London, turn to <u>124</u>.

Otherwise, you can inquire about the wild animal sounds from overhead by turning to <u>176</u>.

183

Helmar draws the longest straw, but before either of you can react, the sailor - unwilling to accept his fate - leaps at the passenger with his dagger held high! Weakened from hunger and thirst, the sailor fails to make a quick kill and Helmar gamely seizes his attacker's knife-hand.

You step in to help your fellow passenger, but before you can intervene the two men stumble over the gunwale and roll overboard into the ocean where they sink like stones. In the terrible calm that follows you start to laugh, a dreadful mirth rising like a thing from without, then lapse into bitter silence. It is just a matter of days now before you too, are dead...

As night falls, you slip into a morbid sleep, your mouth and throat a torment of thirst. When you awake the next morning, you are unsure whether you are alive or dead, for you see something you can scarcely believe - a set of sails dancing above the horizon! For what seems like an endless period you lay with your head on the thwart, watching the schooner approach, lacking the strength to even cry out.

You are dimly aware of being lifted up onto the gangway of a ship and perceive a large red-headed man with freckles staring down at you over the bulwarks. Then you gain the impression of a singular face with extraordinary eyes close to yours. As some sort of metallic-tasting liquid is forced between your teeth, you lose consciousness, unsure whether your rescue is a blessing or a curse...

Turn to **216**.

184

You follow the northern edge of the swamp towards the west until you spy a ridge of jungle that seems to demarcate the western-most limits of the swamp.

Cutting up through the jungle is a red-soiled, weed-choked trail. It appears to be the best way to advance into the heart of the island, so you elect to follow it.

Turn to **395**.

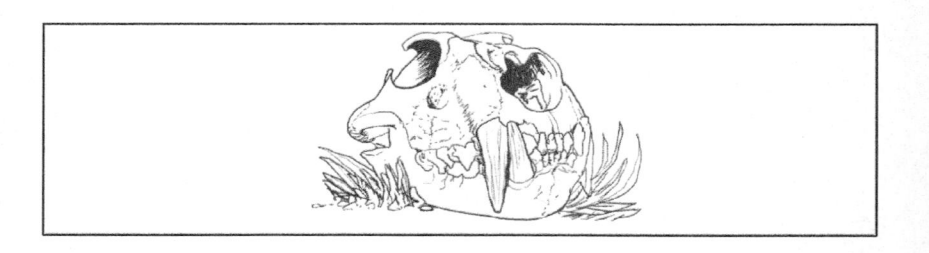

185

The courtyard is now bathed in a silvery light and recessed with ominous shadows. You begin to search through the various crates, boxes and barrels, gathering together anything that will be useful for your escape from the island.

About an hour into this activity, the return of Montgomery to your neighbourhood is marked by a commotion of exultant cries passing down towards the beach - whooping and howling and excited shrieks - which seem to come to a stop at the water's edge. The riot rises and falls, then you hear heavy blows and the splintering and smashing of wood, to which you pay little heed.

Then a discordant chanting begins...

You ignore the distraction and go on rummaging through the stores. For quite some time you become interested in the contents of some biscuit tins as you estimate how long they might last on a two-month voyage. Then you find a crate of fine brandy, and a box of fine cigars.

Suddenly, the chanting dies down and is replaced by the sound of quarrelling. You hear cries of 'More, more!' that precede a startling, wild shriek. Then, cutting like a knife across the confusion comes the crack of a revolver - Montgomery is in trouble!

Do you wish to rush outside to help Montgomery? If so, turn to **551**.

If you would rather not risk it, but simply wish to go to the small window in your room to try and see what is happening, turn to **521**.

186

Aware that the hideous creatures could return at any time, you decide to risk escaping the pocket of gas on which you are standing. Fortunately, much of the hydrogen sulphide has been liberated, and you escape without harm.

Gain 1 FATE point!

Relieved to be free of the natural hazard, you decide to head away from the spongy ground and explore the line of trees from where the Hyena-men came.

Turn to **499**.

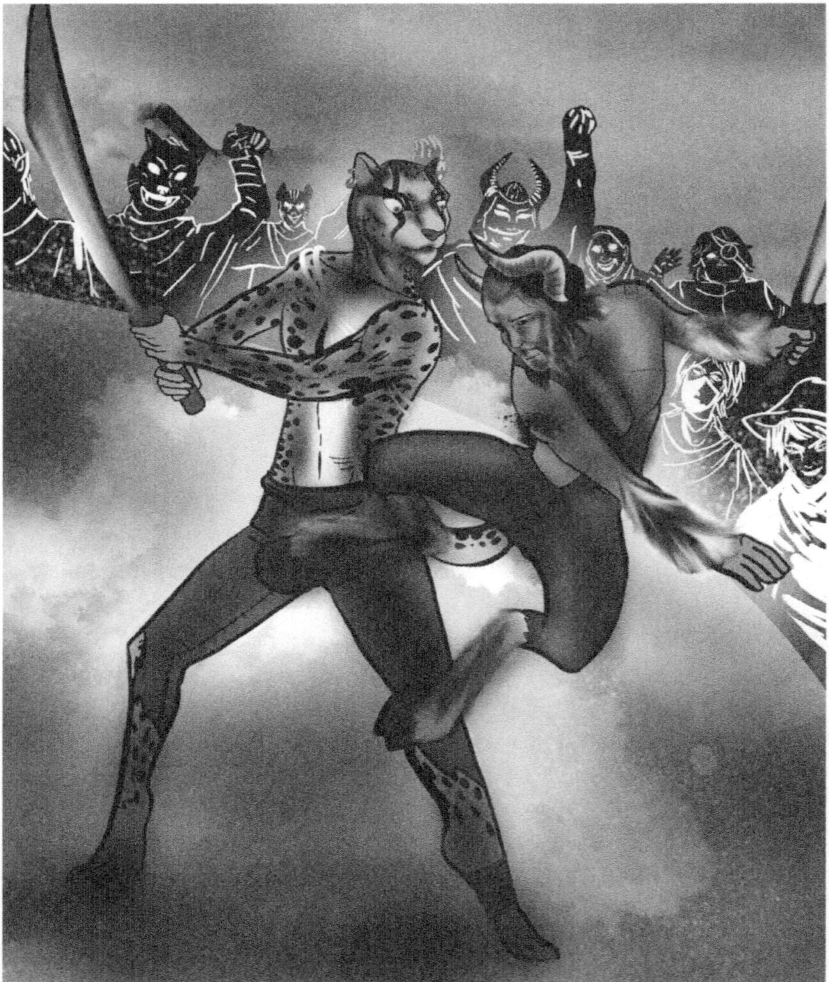

187

The mob returns to the edges of the circle and at an order from the Elephant-man, the fight begins. At first, the little Satyr does a fine job of keeping his distance from his opponent and is able to fend off the swift, slicing cuts of the Ocelot-man, but after a few minutes he suffers a nasty gash to his sword-arm and is forced to drop his blade. The predator stalks in for the kill, chasing his quarry around the circle until the crowd hoots and jeers with contempt.

As the Goat-man staggers past, his desperate eyes meet yours.

'Please, my lord, help me!' he begs, before facing his opponent, ducking a savage cut, and tackling the Ocelot-man to the ground. The crowd roars in delight as the combatants roll around in the sand, a confused tangle of hirsute arms and legs.

If you wish to shout out that the fight be stopped, turn to 229.

If you would rather ignore the Satyr's appeal and allow the fight to reach its natural conclusion, turn to 323.

188

You scramble up the sandy bank onto the scrub-covered ridge, wincing in the bright sunlight. Looking around, you see that to the south is a jutting headland that forms an impassible ridge leading inland, which leaves you with two directions to explore:

If you wish to head north along a stretch of golden beach fringed by deep jungle, turn to 102.

If you would prefer to head into the jungle along the path of a narrow streamlet, turn to 451.

189

Not wanting to disturb the flying foxes, you continue to pick your way through the guano, consoled by the knowledge that mammalian urine - though unpleasant - is generally harmless.

Despite feeling the occasional stream of warm, odiferous fluid wetting your head and shoulders, you fix your eyes on the items and press on stoically towards the prow of the vessel.

Turn to **420**.

190

Concealing yourself behind one of the boulders, you wait until the men draw near, prepare your ranged weapon, then lean out and shoot!

You may perform TWO ranged attacks against the men before they are able to return fire with their bows but add +2 to your *ranged attack score* due to the element of surprise.

LAZALO THE HUNTER: Prowess - 7; Ballistics - 8; Vitality - 8; Ranged Defence - 8; Damage - 2/2

VAI THE HUNTER: Prowess - 8; Ballistics - 8; Vitality - 8; Ranged Defence - 8; Damage - 2/2.

After your bonus attack rounds, the hunters will shoot back as they close in on your position. Engage in a ranged combat for TWO more rounds but add +2 to your *Ranged Defence* due to the cover of the boulder. After this (if at least one of the hunters is still alive), you must finish the fight in close combat!

Note: Lazalo and Vai both wield pairs of **Toledo steel hunting knives** that give them +1 to their *close combat score*.

If you win, turn to <u>317</u>.

191

Glad to feel sand under your boots once more, you make good progress along the beach towards the south as darkness falls. Scanning inland for a suitable campsite, you see a broad expanse of cone-shaped reeds leading into a strip of lush jungle. Above this is a distant hillside covered with pockets of rich volcanic soil.

In daylight, you estimate that it would take you around three hours to reach the hill, assuming the ground through the reeds is solid underfoot. It will be a difficult walk by moonlight, but once on the hill you could take several hours' rest, then be in a good position to explore the interior of the island in the morning.

Then again, the beach appears comfortable enough, and you could embark on the walk inland in the morning...

Do you wish to hike inland through part of the night in order to reach the hillside? If so, turn to <u>25</u>.

If you would rather simply spend the night on the beach, turn to <u>137</u>.

192

The force of the blast catches you full in the chest and hurls you onto your back. Spasming in shock, you look down at your smoking, tattered body and dully register several splinters of twisted silver jutting from your torso. Your trembling hands pluck at the slippery metal, but they are too burned to be of any use. Indeed, even the finest surgeon could not save you now. As you slip towards unconsciousness and death, you cannot help but marvel at the ingenuity of the trap to which you have fallen foul...

YOUR ADVENTURE IS OVER!

193

Fortunately, one of your arms is still free, and you might just be able to reach a knife or dagger before the python crushes the life out of you!
If you possess a knife or dagger, turn to <u>158</u>.

If not, then there is nothing you can do to escape this doom. Your adventure has come to a gruesome and untimely end...

194

You may perform a single ranged attack against one of the creatures that hits automatically and causes double damage. Or, if you do not have a ranged weapon (or do not wish to use it), then you may claim an automatic hit with a single close combat attack!

When the creatures spin around with surprised snarls, you are taken aback. Despite the stripes across their backs, your opponents appear more canid than felid. They possess broad, snarling, fang-lined mouths that gape wider than any mammalian that you have ever seen. In addition to the dark stripes across their backs and wolf-like vocalisations, this feature alone betrays their lineage.

These creatures are THYLACINE-MEN, crafted from the rare marsupial tigers of Tasmania about which you have read so much. Usually shy and disinclined to fight, such creatures are deadly when threatened.

You must fight these formidable predators simultaneously!

First THYLACINE-MAN: Prowess - 8; Vitality - 10; Damage - 2; Ranged Defence - 7.

Second THYLACINE-MAN: Prowess - 8; Vitality - 11; Damage - 2; Ranged Defence - 8.

If you win, a quick search of the bodies reveals nothing of use. If you received any wounds from the Thylacine-men, note that you have been *exposed to zoonotic infection.*

Next, do you wish to attempt to climb the tree in order to reach the nest in which the Thylacine-men were so interested? If so, turn to **277**.

If you would prefer to ignore the nest and immediately press on towards the south, turn to **171**.

195

You cover half of the open ground towards the hunter before he seizes his bow, leaps to his feet and turns to face you. Your opponent has time to fire off a single arrow before you can engage him in single combat! Resolve the outcome of the one ranged round against you, before continuing the fight:

VAI THE HUNTER: Prowess - 8; Ballistics - 8; Vitality - 9; Ranged Defence - 8; Damage - 2/2.

Deduct 2 points from your *close combat score* if you are unarmed, deduct 1 point if you are using a rock.

Note: Vai wields a pair of knives that add +1 to his *close combat score*.

If you win, turn to **310**.

196

'Moreau...' you say. 'I know that name. It was associated with a masterful and pre-eminent scientist who was howled out of England, was it not?'

'The devil it was!' Montgomery retorts, the irritation evident in his voice. 'The doctor is a remarkable man, but I thought his revealing his name to you was a mistake. Still, your deduction will give you an inkling of our mysteriousness, no? Above all, remember that you and I alike owe the doctor more than we can know. Leave it at that, my man!'

He pours himself another generous dram of whisky, and you are about to reply when you hear a commotion coming from the other side of the inner door…

Now turn to **227**.

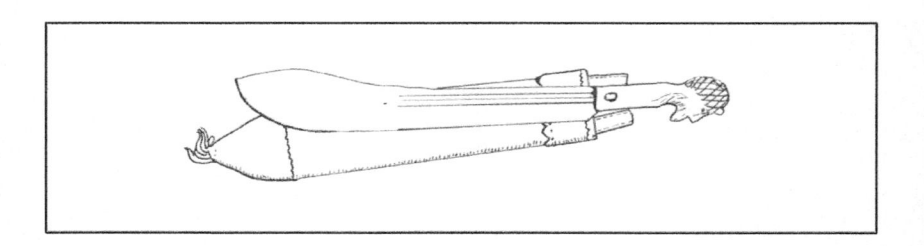

197

Glad to feel sand under your boots once more, you make good progress along the beach until you reach the north-west extremity of the island, where you find four canoes drawn up high on the beach.

They are beautifully carved from a chestnut-coloured wood, and each canoe has a single, double-sided oar cast within. Though you do not have the seamanship to handle one of them out on the open sea, you feel confident that you could paddle along the island's coast for a fair way and spare your legs a considerable amount of work.

Do you wish to continue your journey in one of the canoes? If so, turn to **410**.

If you would rather continue along the beach on foot, turn to **498**.

198

At your request, the Dog-man nods eagerly and leads you back out onto the trail, whisking along it at great speed. You race after him, then redouble your efforts when you hear the howls again, one to either side.

After about a mile, the tall cane trees give way to a patch of rocky ground that precedes the beginnings of the island's deep inland jungle. In the middle of the open space your guide is waiting for you, his nose quivering as he sniffs the air.

'Home is up on high,' he says, pointing up towards a distant moon-lit hillside. He then gestures to the north and south. 'But enemies draw close, murderers and blood-claws. They will fall on us if they can. But from where or when, I cannot say...'

The howls are drawing nearer, and the Dog-man gazes at you steadily, awaiting your instructions.

Do you wish to tell the Dog-man to continue to lead you through the jungle to his home in the hope that you can out-run your pursuers? If so, turn to **90**.

Or would you prefer to tell the Dog-man that the two of you will make a stand here in the rocky clearing? To try this, turn to **492**.

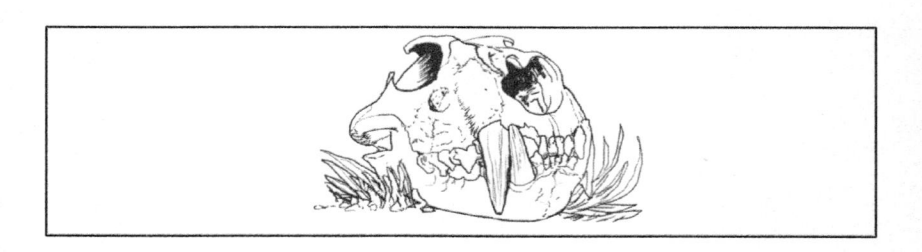

199

You advance westward into the jungle, mindful of encountering any more of Moreau's creations. After less than an hour's walking, the rainforest begins to descend towards a broad area of stinking, festering mire that gleams with flashes of sunlight and is flecked by spots of livid, bilious green. As you draw nearer, you see that the stagnant, scum-coated waters are festooned with immense water lilies of an unknown type, and that the mire has a number of little islands to which cling clumps of arrow-headed reeds and jaundiced grasses. The entire area is wreathed in a squatting miasma that reeks of dankness, disease and slow vegetative decay.

Upon reaching the edge of the mire, you notice a single muddy path leading into its depths. Deep tracks that belong to some sort of large, bipedal creature with three-toed, clawed feet proceed along it. Such signs alone are a reason to avoid the path, but a detour will add miles to your journey...

If you wish to follow the footprints into the centre of the swamp, turn to 179.

If you wish to avoid venturing into the mire, you will need to detour around its edges:

Do you wish to do so along the northern edge of the swamp? If so, turn to 155.

If you would rather do so along the southern edge of the swamp, turn to 279.

200

'As I say, he's a drunkard and an ass,' Montgomery tells you with sudden heat. 'If you've any sense, you'll keep your distance from that fool! Having said that, I think it's important that you take some fresh air on deck, if you feel up to it. It will assist your recovery, even if it does mean rubbing shoulders with the captain and his crew. Whatever gets said, leave the talking to me!'

You readily agree and follow Montgomery out of the cabin.

Now turn to 365.

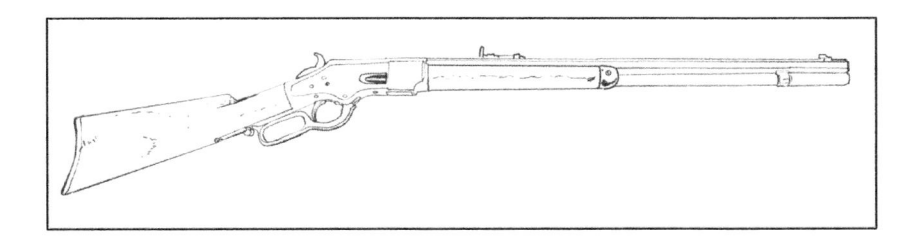

The skill with which you slay these aggressors sends the gang of remaining beast-folk into a panicked rout up the beach. No longer immediately threatened, you turn to the black heaps upon the ground...

Montgomery lays on his back, a hairy grey beast-man sprawled across him. The brute is dead but still gripping Montgomery's throat with its curving claws. Nearby lays M'ling on his face and quite still, his neck bitten open and the upper part of the smashed brandy bottle in his hand. Two other chimeric corpses lay beside the fire.

You haul the grey creature from Montgomery and pillow the man's head under your rolled-up coat, noting with concern the bloody rents in his shirt. His face is dark, and he is barely breathing. The fire settles with a crackle and you consider adding more fuel to keep it going. It is then you notice - with a sinking heart - where Montgomery got his wood. The island boat and dinghy that had been drawn up on the beach beside the boathouse have vanished. All that remains of them are some chips and splinters that lay beside a pair of axes, and the waning embers of the fire.

Montgomery has burnt the boats to spite you and prevent your return to humanity! The stirrings of a blinding anger are stifled by the sounds of a thud and hiss behind you. Spinning about, you vent a cry of horror. Against the night sky great tumultuous masses of black smoke are boiling up out of the enclosure, and through their stormy darkness shoot flickering threads of blood-red flame. Then the thatched roof goes up with a whoosh. You remember the crash you heard when rushing to Montgomery's aid; in your haste, you must have overturned your oil-lamp...

Montgomery groans, stirs feebly, and opens his eyes a little. For a moment he stares up at the bright stars, then his gaze meets yours. His heavy eyelids fall.

'Sorry...' he says presently, with an effort. 'The last of this silly universe. What a mess...'

Then his head falls helplessly to one side.

You lay the dead man's head gently upon the rough pillow you have made before carrying M'ling's body into the water and giving him to the black desolation of the sea. Then you do the same for Montgomery. As for the slain beast-folk, you leave them where they lay, settle with your back to the boathouse, and watch the enclosure - with all its provisions and ammunition - burn long and noisily into the night.

Turn to 409.

202

Doubtful of whether you can defeat both men at once, you rush deeper into the trees, ignoring the tearing thorns and lashing creepers. You crash through a screen of undergrowth and run at full tilt over the edge of a narrow ravine that slices through the jungle!

Roll a dice - this is the amount of damage you take to your VITALITY as you crash to the ravine floor and are knocked unconscious...

If you survive the fall, you come to your senses not within the ravine, but in a little den formed in the hollow of a dense press of cane trees. It appears to be the dead of night, a small candle shedding enough light for you to see a most peculiar face staring down at you - one with a large and protuberant nose, liquid brown eyes, and extraordinarily large and mobile ears located high on its head.

It is a DOG-MAN, another of the doctor's bizarre experiments!

Startled, you reach for the weapons at your belt, only to see them lying across the den in a pile beside your rucksack.

'Master, did I do well?' the Dog-man inquires eagerly, leaning in. 'Did I pass the test?'

171

Realising that this creature may well have saved you from the hunters, you thank him and assure him that he has done well. At these words, the Dog-man's eyes light up with delight, while his strangely jointed legs quiver with excitement.

'When light returns, I will guide you,' he grunts. 'To your home, to my home - Master must decide!'

With that, the creature lowers himself to his haunches and sets to devouring some gruel he has wrapped up in banana leaves. When he has eaten his fill, he looks at you with sudden guilt, then offers you one of the meals. You may eat it now to restore 4 VITALITY points or add the **meal** to your *equipment list*.

Moments later, you hear a blood-curdling howl some distance away, then an answering call that is somewhat closer.

'Master, it is time to leave,' whispers your guide. 'Bad men are close. Man-beasts. Savages. Not like you and I.'

Where will you ask to be led?

To the Dog-man's home? If so, turn to 198.

Or to 'your' home? (Turn to 475).

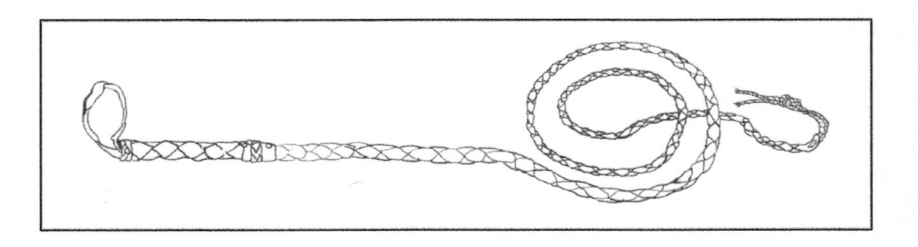

203

The man's resolute face remains unmoved, but as you describe the suffering you have endured and how you could not survive being set adrift again, you see his expression begin to soften.

Test your FATE but add 2 to your roll to reflect the difficulty of persuading the white-haired man.

If you are favoured, turn to 553.

If you are unfavoured, turn to 88.

204

You are so focussed on trying to keep up with the Dog-man and staying out of the reach of your pursuers, that it is only at the last moment that you catch sight of a mob of creatures charging out of a fringe of palm trees towards you. Some are small and stunted, others are huge and musclebound, but all have in common the baleful green-fire stare of the nocturnal hunter, and the unmistakable mark of the beast!

They are upon you before you can react, and you are knocked head over heels in the sand before being dragged upright by many pairs of strong, calloused hands.

'LAWBREAKER!' come the howls of outrage.

In the background you hear the yelping protestations of the Dog-man. By the time that he has explained to the mob that you were following him rather than chasing him, the Wolf-men have slipped away into the jungle…

Angry at the escape of the true lawbreakers and eager for some sort of justice, a glowering creature tells you that you must accompany them to their village to meet an individual they refer to as The Sayer.

You are then marched into the island's interior, led this way and that until you are utterly disorientated. In time you find yourself entering a steep-sided chasm lined with oily torches that illuminate lines of crude dens huddled against the granite walls. The air is thick with the smell of smoke, the malodour of the creatures all around you, and the miasma of slow vegetable decay.

Suddenly, the Dog-man appears by your side once more. He is carrying a small brass key, which he presses into your hand with a wink. (Add the **brass key** to your equipment list).

'Apologies, my lord,' he croons, guiding you to the largest of the huts and pushing you inside. 'Despite this misunderstanding, all will be well if you learn the Law...'

Your heart thumping in your chest, you are led to a seat in a dim, dank corner and stare at the shadows within shadows that are waiting in the hut...

Now turn to <u>350</u>.

205

You realise that the House of Pain must be the enclosure where Moreau performs his experiments, and that he must be the Master of whom the Ape-man speaks. When you tell the towering brutes that you are guest of the doctor and that he will be furious if anything happens to you, they are swiftly persuaded.

The Ape-man leads the way through the jungle until you emerge onto the beach once more. At the sight of the human habitation, however, your captors grow hesitant and fearful. Clearly, the enclosure is a place of vague and terrible memory for them.

'Leave him here!' Ape-man chatters. 'The Master will know of his crime! He will find him and punish him with pain!'

With that the creatures melt back into the tree line, leaving you alone once more.

Now, do you wish to head north once more, past the place where you encountered the Ape-man? If so, turn to **38**.

If you would rather head inland along the path of the narrow streamlet you saw earlier, turn to **451**.

206

You walk along the beach for more than an hour, your attention drawn to a line of roaring breakers that topple onto underwater reefs that lay half a mile out to sea. Upon the beach lie countless smooth stones that you realise would make excellent projectiles.

Do you possess the large handkerchief? If so, turn to **239**.

If not, turn to **270**.

207

The hunter is oblivious to your presence as you come to within striking range. You notice that he is singing a soft, gentle melody as he hones the sharpness of his knife.

Do you wish to hit him over the head with the rock? If so, turn to **245**.

If you would rather strike him across his neck with your hand, put him in a wrestling choke and try to subdue him that way, turn to **282**.

208

A cunning look creeps through the slack drunkenness of the captain's face.

'Seeing as you asked so nicely you can stay, my lad,' he leers. 'But you'll be the most junior member of the crew and will have to earn your keep. A lot of the boys don't trust you on account of your surviving so many days at sea and the blood that was found on your boat. Call you a cannibal, they do...ha! With all that to take in, are you sure that you still desire sanctuary on my lovely ship?'

If you wish to accept the captain's offer, turn to **351**.

If you would rather decline the captain's offer and simply accept your fate, turn to **427**.

If you wish to decline the captain's offer and appeal to the white-haired man instead, turn to **453**.

209

The Lizard-man and monitor lizards hardly spare you a glance but adjust their formation to allow you room to fight by their side. Due to their presence, there are no opportunities for ranged attacks, so you will have to engage the Crocodile-man in close combat. In doing so, at least you are not alone!

Resolve the combat for all the participants in this battle in the order presented, before rolling for yourself. Remember that your side are able to attack the enemy simultaneously, and that the Crocodile-man will focus all of its attacks against the Lizard-man.

First MONITOR LIZARD: Prowess - 7; Vitality - 8; Damage - 2.

LIZARD-MAN HUNTER: Prowess - 10; Vitality - 10; Damage - 4. (Note: the Lizard-man wears armour that will reduce any damage received by 1 point on a dice roll of 5-6).

Second MONITOR LIZARD: Prowess - 6; Vitality - 5; Damage - 2.

CROCODILE-MAN: Prowess - 9; Vitality - 16; Damage - 4.

If the Lizard-man is killed, take note of the Crocodile-man's remaining VITALITY, then turn immediately to 556.

If the Crocodile-man is killed first, turn to 260.

210

The Hyena-men seem to find your account highly amusing and break out in fits of mewling giggles.

'Quite a fix you are in!' the one with the crossbow cackles. 'It is a rare thing indeed to find a target that dare not move...!'

With that, he fires a bolt that sinks into your shoulder (lose 3 VITALITY points)!

Gritting your teeth against the pain, you see the creature load another bolt and grin at his friends, whose laughter has reached a fever pitch.

If you have a ranged weapon and wish to return fire, turn to 147.

If you do not have a ranged weapon, or do not wish to use it, then you have no choice but to charge your tormentors! (Turn to 322).

211

The cypress trees on the edge of the swamp are so tightly packed that you are forced to squeeze between them, but as the ground rises, they are gradually replaced by tall palm trees the trunks of which are festooned with vicious, barbed thorns as long as your index fingers.

Interwoven among them are a type of plant with green and crimson stems, ragged leaves the size of dinner plates, and crowns of white blossom the height of your head that exude a strong, sweet perfume…

Do you wish to continue walking through the thorny palm trees and blossoming plants? If so, turn to **299**.

If you would rather return to the edge of the swamp and follow it west, turn to **184**.

212

As soon as the python succumbs to the onslaught, the Thylacine-men set to tearing it apart with their powerful jaws and razor-sharp teeth. Wearily, you lower yourself to the jungle floor and watch the creatures feed until their bellies are distended with raw flesh.

You then notice an object sticking out of a gaping hole in the serpent's flank. When you investigate, you discover a gore-covered **Blunderbuss pistol**, also known as a **Dragon** due to the flame that belches from its muzzle when fired.

The firearm must have gotten lodged in the python's digestive system after a previous victim was devoured, and a quick examination tells you that it is still loaded with balls of lead shot that will discharge in a devastating blast when fired. If you can dry out the flintlock mechanism, clean the gun, and procure fresh powder, then the powerful weapon may be salvaged!

If you can find these items, then you will possess the **Restored Dragon**, which is unusual insofar that it will allow you to cause one dice worth of damage to one dice worth of enemies in any close combat round (thus it is possible to cause 6 points of damage to 6 close combat enemies!). Remember that a successful FATE test can double the amount of damage caused!

Make this addition to your *equipment list*.

You show your find to the Thylacine-men, who sniff at it diffidently before curling up on the floor to sleep off the effects of their huge meal.

'Eggs and fresh meat for a thunder-maker, a good trade...' one of them growls, glancing contentedly at the huge quantity of snake-flesh remaining that will provide them with many meals to come. 'Also, check the base of the tree, lord,' he adds, before closing his eyes.

Do you wish to search the base of the mahogany tree as the creature suggested? If so, turn to 504.

If you would rather press on through the jungle towards the south, turn to 171.

213

'Then you are not to be trusted and already dead!' the hunter says coldly. The beginnings of your scream are cut short as the arrows transfix your heart in a rapid double beat...

YOUR TROUBLES ARE OVER!

214

Try as you may, you simply do not have the strength to reach the island. Overcome by exhaustion and agonising cramps, it is all you can do to keep hold of the barrel to prevent yourself from slipping under.

You are roughly back at the point where the *Ipecacuanha* unloaded Montgomery's cargo onto the island boat, and you can see figures on the grey sandy beach moving crates and cages of animals to a pair of thatch-roofed buildings nestled in a piebald stone enclosure.

Do you wish to try and attract the attention of the figures on the beach?

If so, turn to __71__.

If you would prefer to rest in the water awhile to regain your strength, turn to __163__.

215

While the Ape-man is correct that the most direct route back to the enclosure is across the island, the fastest and safest way to that destination is by simply following the beach southward. It is still the dead of night, but you should be able to return to Moreau and Montgomery before the dawn if you leave immediately.

If you possess a canoe, then you may continue paddling along the shore towards the south? To do this, turn to __263__.

If you do not possess a canoe, or would rather walk south on foot instead, turn to __175__.

216

You awake in a small, untidy cabin to find a youngish man holding your wrist and watching you with watery grey eyes that are oddly void of expression. He is large and long in the limb, with flaxen hair and a straw-coloured mustache.

'You were lucky to be picked up by a ship with a medical man aboard,' he says with a faint lisp. 'My name is Montgomery. Here, drink some of this.'

He hands you a cup of iced scarlet liquid which tastes revolting, but immediately makes you feel stronger.

Gain 4 VITALITY points.

'We found you in a dinghy attached to a ship named *The Lady Vain*,' the man continues. 'Frankly, I could not help but notice that there were scuffles and even a spot of blood on the gunwale...'

Suddenly you hear a sound like an iron bedstead being knocked about, and the angry growling of some large wild beast coming from overhead. Montgomery glances towards the ceiling and takes the empty cup from you.

'I'm dying to know how you ended up in that little boat all alone and on the verge of death,' he says, recovering from the distraction and fixing you with a questioning look.

Do you wish to tell Montgomery the truth of what happened? If so, turn to 3.

If you would rather evade the question and ask him about the ship you are on, turn to 99.

Alternatively, you can evade the question by asking about the wild animal sounds from overhead. To do this, turn to 176.

217

Suddenly there is another rustle to your left and you see a second tall, lithe figure hurtling out of the gloom towards you! Your immediate impression is that of a hunch-shouldered madman, but then you catch sight of the creature's baleful green eyes and impossibly wide, protruding jaws that are drawn back in a fang-filled snarl.

While you are distracted, the creature you have injured surges to its feet and lunges at you with a growl!

You must defend yourself against these WOLF-MEN!

Due to the proximity of the ambush, you are permitted only ONE ranged attack before close combat is joined.

Wounded WOLF-MAN: Prowess - 7; Vitality - 5; Damage - 2; Ranged Defence - 8.

Second WOLF-MAN: Prowess - 6; Vitality - 7; Damage - 2; Ranged Defence - 8.

If you win, you find nothing of use upon the creatures other than a pair of small stones hung upon leather cords.
Take the **stone necklaces** if you wish, then turn to **181**.

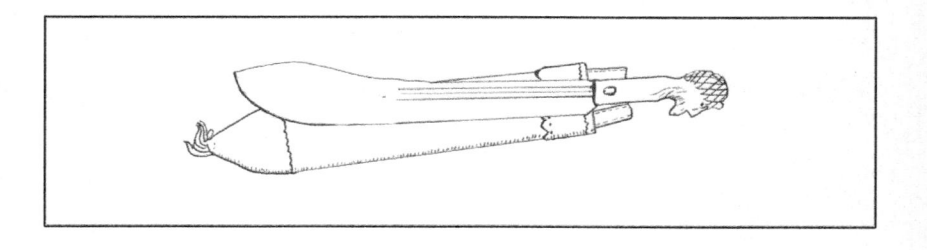

218

The men nod thoughtfully before ordering you to turn around. Faced with two drawn bows, you do as they ask, tensing for the arrows that you are sure must come. Instead, something hits you hard over the head and you crumple to the ground, unconscious…

Lose 2 VITALITY points, then turn to **544**.

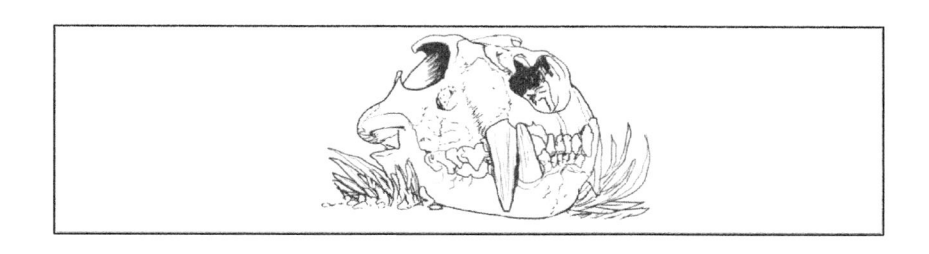

219

What item or weapon do you want to use against the Humboldt Squid?

A knife or dagger? Turn to 134.

A revolver? Turn to 159.

A bow and arrow? Turn to 256.

A spear? Turn to 330.

A meal? Turn to 361.

220

A quick search of the camp uncovers a beautiful **bow** of indigenous craftsmanship (2 points of ranged damage), a **quiver** of **10 brightly-fletched arrows**, and enough sun-dried fish, fresh fruit, and a sort of multi-hued seed-like grain sufficient for **5 meals**. There is also a coil of **rope**. Add these items to your *equipment list*.

Just as you are finishing your search, you see two figures emerging from the fenland to the south-east. Peering closely, you see that they are minimally clad copper-skinned men who are handsomely proportioned, covered in savage tattoos and wielding hunting bows like the one you have just stolen.

It is also clear that they are the occupants of the camp, for they are striding toward you with the eagerness of returning wanderers, their deep voices high spirited and glad.

If you wish to launch a surprise attack on the men, turn to **190**.

If you would rather surrender to the men, turn to **386**.

Alternatively, you can try to escape by making a run for the line of trees to the south (turn to **435**).

Otherwise, you can slip back along the path through the palm trees and take one of the canoes towards the south. To do this, turn to **353**.

Or you can slip back along the path through the palm trees, ignore the canoes and head south along the beach on foot by turning to **285**.

221

After you deliver your prediction, the Fox-woman smiles wickedly, takes you by the arm, and leads you into the baying crowd to watch the rest of the fight.

By now the Elephant-man's face and upper body have been badly cut by his opponent's flashing claws, but you see that his thick hide has protected him from deep or dangerous wounds. He also seems less tired than his rival, whose smooth evasions and blistering attacks appear to have slowed.

The grey giant continues to close the distance, his great arms raised. Suddenly, he catches one of his opponent's strikes and hauls him into a vicious headbutt. The shadow-stalker twists violently to evade the main force of the blow, breaks the clinch, and circles behind his opponent. From this advantageous position he leaps onto the Elephant-man's broad back, kicking and scratching with his powerful hind legs. Unperturbed, the grey giant hurls his tormentor over a broad shoulder, promptly pinning him beneath his bulk.

The Jaguar-man thrashes gamely for a few seconds, then falls limp as the Elephant-man wraps a great hand around his throat and renders him insensible. The fight is over!

If you predicted that the Elephant-man (the grey giant) would win, gain 1 FATE point. If, on the other hand, you predicted that the Jaguar-man (the shadow stalker) would win, you must lose 1 FATE point.

Now turn to 283.

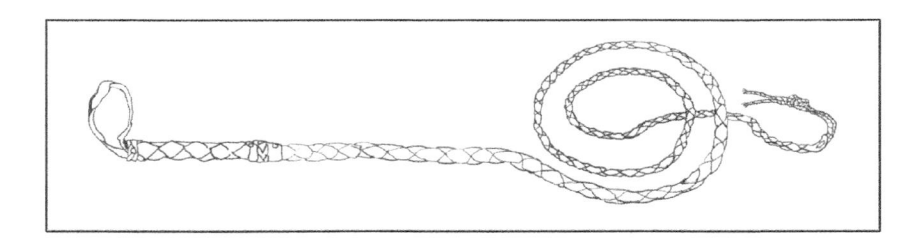

222

The rigging holds and you climb onto the deck of the derelict. To you horror, you see more than twenty human skeletons propped against the railings of the ship, all clad in the torn and faded livery of the British merchant navy. Whether thirst or disease killed these men is uncertain, but it appears that the ship's rats have picked the bodies clean of flesh before going to war with their own kind, for alongside the human remains are countless tiny bones that crunch beneath your boots.

From your viewpoint you notice that the longboat has pulled away too far for you to swim. The dinghy, however, is still within range, though it is drifting more distant with each moment...

If you wish to leave the derelict immediately, then you may climb back down the rigging and make for the dinghy (turn to **127**).

If you wish to risk staying aboard, then you can perform a quick search of the skeletons on the deck (turn to **308**).

Or you may open a nearby hatch to perform a quick search below decks (turn to **91**).

223

You know that carrying Moreau's body through the jungle is an enormous risk, but the thought of leaving him behind as mere carrion for the creatures he once ruled revolts you. Thus, you and Montgomery - being of similar height - each drape one of the doctor's arms over your shoulders, while M'ling - facing away from the body and leading the way - supports Moreau's long legs. Your party is forced to stop for breaks and to stand at guard as creatures rush howling and shrieking nearby, but you are not attacked again.

Finally, as dusk is falling, you make it back to the enclosure, open the double gates and lay Moreau's body upon a pile of brushwood in the courtyard. Seeming to be drawn by something, M'ling then ventures out into the deepening darkness, while you and Montgomery lock yourselves in, before slumping to the floor in exhaustion and grief...

Lose 2 VITALITY points but gain 1 FATE point for retrieving Moreau's body, then turn to **525**.

224

Remembering what you were told by the hunters, you hurry to the enclosure and throw the blood leaves onto some glowing embers. Immediately, red smoke starts to rise into the air, becoming a substantial plume as the leaves smoulder and catch.

In the presence of the smoke, the advancing beast-folk freeze, sniff the air uncertainly and slink back into the jungle. Despite their new-found boldness, the creatures are clearly no strangers to the fighting skills of Lazalo and Vai.

Gain 1 FATE point!

It is around noon when the hunters arrive, and they grin when they see the state of the enclosure.

'It is true then, Soul-stealer is dead!' Lazalo laughs. 'What of his follower, the straw-haired one?'

When you disclose that Montgomery too is dead, the hunter embraces you and lifts you briefly from your feet. Vai also strides in, slaps you on the shoulder and begins to pick through the wreckage of the enclosure.

'The abominations that remain have gone insane,' Lazalo tells you, scanning the bushes with an eagle eye. 'It has become too dangerous here even for us. Soon, we will return to our island home. It is not far for us, and canoes will serve.'

The hunter seems amused at your obvious discomfort.

'Fear not, my friend. We will not abandon you!' He says something to his brother in their own tongue, and the two of them roar with good-natured laughter.

'We will gift you a raft with which to ride the trade winds, as well as food and water to last a full cycle of the moon,' Lazalo tells you. 'If the sea spirit is kind, you will be seen by a trader, or carried to an island free from monsters. If the spirit is angry, you will die of thirst, or sink into the deep...'

Lazalo shrugs. 'Either way, it is better than being eaten alive, no?' he says.

After concluding that there is nothing of any value to be scavenged in the ruins of the enclosure, the brothers lead you back to their camp and to the copse of palm trees that borders the western beach. Within the tangle of undergrowth is concealed a good-sized raft equipped with wicker baskets that are threaded to the logs that form the hull. The three of you drag the raft down to the beach where the brothers insert the mast into a central recess and begin to load the wicker baskets with dried provisions, fruits and water-skins. Finally, to the mast they attach a large, canvas sail.

'Go now, while the wind is with you,' they insist. 'And do not be afraid. The ocean is a finer mistress than this island could ever be.'

You shake hands with the brothers, load your equipment and weapons onto the raft and push out into the surf. Leaping aboard, you unfurl the sail and steady yourself as the raft lurches towards the open sea. After a harrowing episode of navigating the sizeable offshore breakers, you reach a stretch of calmer water and look back towards the island. With its fine sand beaches, startlingly vivid flora, and smoking volcanic heart, it resembles some sort of primordial Eden, untouched and ripe with potential. For a moment, you share some sense of the excitement that Doctor Moreau must have felt arriving here more than ten years ago...

Then you hear a series of hooting, savage calls coming from the tree line and watch as the distant figures of Lazalo and Vai notch arrows to their bows and jog out of sight.

Softly wishing them well, you return you attention to the sea.

Turn to 370.

225

You do not resist as the crew tie a rope around you, secure the other end to a boom spar, swing you out into the water-logged dinghy, then cut you adrift! The little craft spins away from the schooner, and you stare blankly as all hands take to the ship's rigging and bring her around to the wind.

The sails flutter and belly out with a whoosh, before the *Ipecacuanha's* weather-beaten hull heels steeply towards you...

Test your FATE!

If you are favoured, turn to 255.

If you are unfavoured, turn to 316.

226

When you repeat the formula, the insanest ceremony begins. The grey thing intones a mad litany, line by line, and the beast-folk repeat it. As they do so, they sway from side to side and beat their hands on their knees, leaving you little choice but to follow. Suddenly, you gain the sense that you are already dead and in another world: the gloomy hut with its dim orange light and dancing shadows, the grotesque figures, all swaying in unison and chanting...

'Not to go on all fours; *that* is the Law. Are we not men?'
'Not to suck up drink; *that* is the Law. Are we not men?'
'Not to eat flesh or fish; *that* is the Law. Are we not men?'
'Not to claw the bark of trees; *that* is the Law. Are we not men?'
'Not to chase other men; *that* is the Law. Are we not men?'

A kind of rhythmic fervour falls on you, and you gabble along with these creatures, swaying faster and faster, repeating this amazing Law. Superficially, the contagion of these brutes is upon you, but deep down within laughter and disgust struggle together in revulsion at this barbaric ritual!

Then the chant swings round to a new formula:

'*His* is the House of Pain.'
'*His* is the hand that makes.'
'*His* is the hand that wounds.'
'*His* is the hand that heals.'
'*His* is the lightning flash,' you sing. '*His* is the deep salt sea...'

A horrible fancy comes into your head that Moreau - after crafting these creatures - has infected their dwarfed brains with a kind of deification of himself. However, you are too keenly aware of sharp, white teeth and strong claws about you to stop your chanting on that account.

'*His* are the stars in the sky...'

At last the songs ends, and the creatures - with faces rapt and shining with perspiration - start to file outside until you are left alone with the Sloth-man and the Sayer of the Law.

'Take the rest of this night and think on what you have learnt!' the grey-haired beast-man tells you. 'And remember that the punishment is swift and sure for breakers of the Law...!'

190

With that, the Sloth-man leads you to a smaller hut that has a fire burning near its entrance, then leaves without a word. Entering the hut, you see that it contains several rush-woven mattresses, a jug of water and a mound of fruit piled against the inner rock wall.

You take some time to eat from the store of food (restore 4 VITALITY points), before stretching out on one of the beds and falling into a troubled sleep.

Now turn to <u>449</u>.

227

The sounds from beyond the inner door grow louder; the rapid pattering of paws and the sounds of sniffing and growling, followed by Moreau's deep voice muttering reassurances - it is the staghounds being brought in from the beach.

A moment later you hear a grinding, rolling sound, the clang of a cage door being opened, then a sharp cry of animal pain that is deep and hoarse - it is the sound of the puma being struck!

Montgomery winces at this disturbance. Then the puma howls again, louder and more painfully this time. Then it gives vent to a series of short, sharp screams.

'So it has begun...' Montgomery mutters, rising abruptly from the reading chair. 'The doctor has seen to you, his special guest. Now without pause, he hurls himself into a novel project. If you'll excuse me, I cannot abide that sound.'

Montgomery makes for the outer door, then pauses.

'I do not expect you to endure the sound of...*experimentation* any more than I,' he says. 'Especially in light of your recent ordeals. You may leave the enclosure and explore a little of the island if you wish, but only on the condition that you do so at your own risk. There are dangers you cannot imagine, and malarial swamps to the south and west of the island that will see you dead as sure as any animals with

191

fangs and claws. Still, you have many questions which I either cannot or will not answer. My loyalties lay with the doctor, first and foremost, for he has done more for me than any other in my life. But that does not prevent you from seeking those answers for yourself...'

He glances about the little room, and on an impulse turns over the deck chair, places his foot on it, and tears off one of its legs.

'We have plenty of these spare,' he mutters, handing you the makeshift club. 'Use it like you would with stray dogs back in England. There are also stones and rocks scattered about the island that can be useful in deterring unwanted attention.'

Add the **chair-leg** to your *equipment list* and note that it causes 2 points of close combat damage.

To your surprise, Montgomery also hands you one of the revolvers.

'For life-or-death emergencies, do you understand?' he urges, before leaving the room.

Add the **revolver** to your equipment list and note that it is loaded with **6 rounds** that cause 2 points of damage (4 points on a double roll!).

Nonplussed, you sit down to finish the breakfast, trying to ignore the screams of the puma. Soon, the sounds of torment become intolerable, so you twist what remains of the breakfast into a piece of cloth you find draped over the back of the deck chair (the leftovers will provide **2 meals**). You then exit the enclosure into the bright sunlight.

Looking around, you see a jutting headland to the south that forms an impassible ridge leading inland, which leaves you with two directions to explore:

You may head north along a stretch of golden beach fringed by deep jungle? To do this, turn to 102.

Or you can head inland along the path of a narrow streamlet, by turning to 451.

192

228

With a strong current threatening to pull you further off course and a dinghy half-filled with water, making headway through the ocean is going to require all that remains of your strength and determination!

Roll three dice and compare the total to your current VITALITY score.

If the result is less than your current vitality, then you are able to paddle close to the beach before the dinghy is swamped by a wave. Turn to **240**.

If the result is equal or greater than your current vitality, then you are still a long way from the beach when the dinghy is swamped. Turn to **303**.

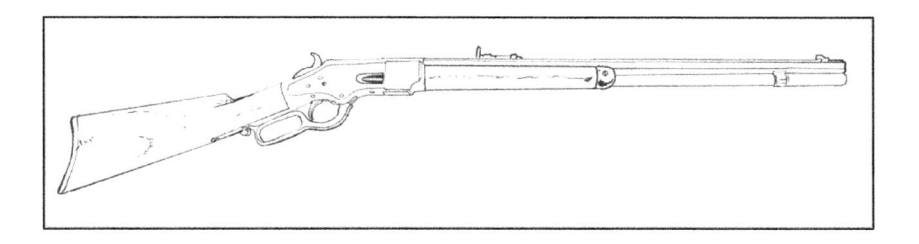

229

It is rarely wise to get between a mob and their bloodlust, and this crowd is more bestial than most. At your sudden protestations, incensed howls split the air and about half of the mob come snarling toward you, their fangs bared and claws outstretched!

'Foolish young lord, sentimental human!' the Fox-woman shrieks, her feral face ablaze with righteous rage. 'You will pay the price for daring to forestall our sacred rite!'

You begin to panic when you see the Elephant-man also thundering towards you, and a number of fleet-footed hybrids running to cut off your escape. You are trapped and within moments of being torn to pieces...

If you possess a firearm with at least one round of ammunition, you must discharge it into the mob in the hope of breaking the charge. To attempt this, turn to **376**.

If you do not possess a firearm and ammunition, turn to **414**.

230

You follow the wall as it curves towards the north-east and comes out of the thinning jungle onto a rocky hillside overlooking a steaming expanse of reeds and marsh. Laid out before you are a series of geothermic pools surging up from deep beneath the earth before overflowing in cascades of heated waterfalls. These energetic waterways rush down the steep inland heights, then grow sluggish and indistinct as they wander over more level ground toward a distant ribbon of sand and silver surf to the north.

The billowing steam in this area reflects the moonlight in a misty haze, but you are able to discern a number of indistinct shapes that seem to be floating in one of the lower pools. There is also a curving wall of rubble to your right that appears to offer entry via a jagged gap in its north face.

Do you wish to make straight for the gap in the northern face of the wall? If so, turn to **349**.

If you would rather take a closer look at the shapes in the water, turn to **402**.

'Montgomery,' you say. 'There is something unnatural about your man-servant. He gives me a nasty sensation whenever he draws near. And it is not only me. The crew of the *Ipecacuanha* seemed similarly disposed, though their reaction was unacceptably coarse. Do you realise that M'ling has pointed ears that are covered by fur?'

'Pointed ears?' Montgomery says over his first mouthfuls of food. 'I was under the impression that M'ling's hair covered his ears. What were they like?'

'Pointed, small and furry. Distinctly so,' you repeat. 'In fact, the whole man is one of the strangest beings I ever set eyes on. He has a touch of the diabolical, I fear.'

'Rum!' Montgomery shrugs. 'Don't each and every one of us have a small measure of that? Better not to cast aspersions on others while we live by whatever animal urges command us. Besides, I have known M'ling for so long that any oddities in his countenance will have become normalised for me by now. I at least cannot see that there is anything wrong with him!'

Montgomery pours himself another generous dram of whisky. You are about to press the point further when you hear a commotion coming from the courtyard on the other side of the inner door.

Now turn to 227.

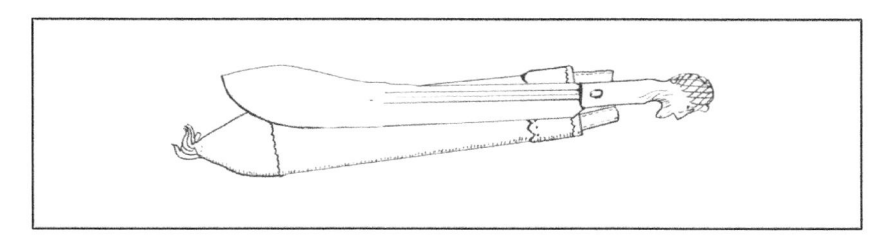

232

The Goat-man's knowledge of the thorn-tangled jungle is faultless, and you are soon led back into the open air of the meadow and arena.

'My village is not very far from here,' the Satyr says as he is bidding you farewell. 'But it is well defended by cliffs and can only be accessed from two directions - from the north via a ravine or from the west via a hemp ladder. To reach the nearer rope ladder, head west from here. You will encounter a swamp that is rumoured to have something of great importance hidden within its depths. Unfortunately, it is also a most unpleasant place! Regardless of whether you choose to pass through the swamp or go around it, you must reach its westernmost point before turning north into the jungle. Once you have done so, ascend for a steady three hours until you can see the ocean. Then, head east. Sooner or later, you will encounter the ravine in which my village is located. Follow it and you will find the ladder I mentioned. But be diligent and cautious, good sir! As you have already learned, not all of my kind are as docile as I...'

The Goat-man gives a deep bow, then trots off towards the north. You watch him disappear into the jungle, then set off into the tree line towards the west.

Turn to **199**.

233

You mistime your strike and the shark clamps down on your arm, tearing through flesh and biting down on bone. It releases you and swims away, but you know that it is only biding its time before you lose consciousness from blood loss and pain. The world swirls before you, then fades as you sink below the crimson waters.

YOUR ADVENTURE ENDS HERE!

234

By some stroke of chance, you avoid cannoning into any of the thorny trunks and collapse near the edge of the swamp, your skin blistered and your breathing laboured.

Do you wish to kneel by the swamp and relieve you face and arms with water? If so, turn immediately to 505.

If not, such is the potency of the Bloodroot toxin that you must roll two dice and deduct the total from your VITALITY score!

If you are still alive, you allow your lungs to recover and the irritation to your skin to subside before following the edge of the swamp towards the west.

Turn to 184.

235

To your relief the waters remain undisturbed, and you see nothing on the beach other than some furtive, scurrying shapes that you take to be large rabbits.

Just as your arms and shoulders are beginning to burn with fatigue, you round a rocky headland and catch sight of a glimmer of light in the distance - it is the enclosure! The creeping light of the new day is staining the horizon by the time you guide the canoe into the simple jetty alongside the island boat, and it is with some trepidation that you begin to walk towards the enclosure. Suddenly, the double gates of the outpost are flung wide, and you see Doctor Moreau, Montgomery and M'ling leading the pack of staghounds out onto the beach. The dogs immediately catch your scent and lurch against their collars in a frenzy of barking and growling.

Moreau restrains the beasts with a harsh command, stares at you for a few seconds, then leads the staghounds back into the enclosure, while Montgomery and M'ling advance toward you.

'Where the devil have you been?' Montgomery demands. 'We've been worried sick and were about to set out with the dogs to find you! Now get inside this instant, Moreau will want to have words!'

Your relief at being back among humans somewhat sullied by a flicker of dread, you enter the enclosure and let yourself in via the small door leading to the room. It does not take long before you hear the inner door to the courtyard being unlocked, and the doctor strides in...

Turn to <u>39</u>.

236

The Ape-man chortles at your acceptance and swiftly vanishes between a pair of giant fern fronds. You push through the brake after him and are astonished to find him swinging cheerfully by one long arm from a rope of creepers that loop down from the foliage overhead. His back is to you, so you reach up to tap him on the shoulder. In response, he comes down to face you with a twisting jump.

'We go to my home now,' he says, his eyes straying from you to the gently swinging ropes. 'Go back to my home and eat...man's food! At the huts...come along!'

He turns and sets off into the jungle at a quick walk, and you see that he is following a vague jungle path that ascends quite steeply the further you advance inland. You try to make conversation with your companion, but his chattering responses are quite often at cross purposes with your questions. When you persevere, the Ape-man seems to grow bored, and springs up at some fruit that is hanging from a tree. He brings down several prickly husks and goes on with eating their contents.

'Man's food!' the creature says, through a mouth thick with pulp and seeds. 'But also beast's food. He lives near here. My friend...but friend to no others!'

This appears to set off a train of thought in your guide's mind, and without warning he veers off the trail into the thick jungle to the north.

'For beast, five fingers are good!' he mumbles. 'Five fingers with which to groom and feed and carry...'

Despite your rising trepidation at these words, you already seem to have lost your bearings and decide to accompany your new-found companion for the time being.

Now turn to <u>324</u>.

237

You swim madly for the opposite bank as the alligator thrashes its tail and puts on a spurt of speed, its jaws gaping in anticipation!

Test your VITALITY with four dice:

If the total is less than or equal to your current vitality, turn to **275**.

If the total is greater than your current vitality, turn to **309**.

238

The creatures stalk towards you with a fluid, animal grace, their wide nostrils quivering as they suck in your scent. As they draw close, one of them emits a creaking yowl, his jaw hinging at close to 180 degrees to reveal a long, curling tongue and a row of sharp, canid teeth. This remarkable articulation of the mandible clinches the conclusion that was growing in your mind: these creatures seem to be a blend of men and the rare marsupial tigers of Tasmania that are something of an enigma to British ethologists.

'Stranger...help us,' one of the THYLACINE-MEN murmurs, his muzzle struggling to form the shape of words. 'Help us by using your hands and feet...to climb?' His eyes flicker toward the nest, then he and his companion stare at you expectantly.

Clearly, the creatures want you to climb the tree and retrieve whatever eggs or hatchlings lay within. You do not as yet sense any danger from them, but if they are hungry, then it may be wise to do as they ask. Then again, the climb to the nest will not be easy. One slip and you could break a leg and be left at the mercy of these strange creations...

Will you agree to attempt to climb the tree and retrieve whatever food is in the nest? If so, turn to **277**.

If you wish to refuse the request, then you can offer the creatures a **meal** instead (if you have one)? Turn to **454**.

If you do not wish to attempt to climb the tree and do not have any meals (or do not want to give one away) then you have no choice but to make your excuses and attempt to press on through the jungle towards the south. Turn to **397**.

239

You realise that you might make a primitive yet passable sling from the handkerchief. Slipping one of the stones into the fabric and twisting it around your wrist, you whirl the weapon around your head and send the missile hurling far out to sea. After a little practice, you are able to unleash the stones with a fair degree of accuracy and power.

Note that you now possess a **sling** with **10 shots**. Its inaccuracy is such that it will reduce your BALLISTICS skill by 2, but it will still cause 2 points of ranged damage on a successful hit.

Pleased by this addition to your arsenal, you continue walking along the beach to the west. As you proceed, you begin to feel the exposed areas of your skin burn and a mild nausea brought on from the beginnings of sunstroke…

Lose 1 VITALITY point, then turn to **485**.

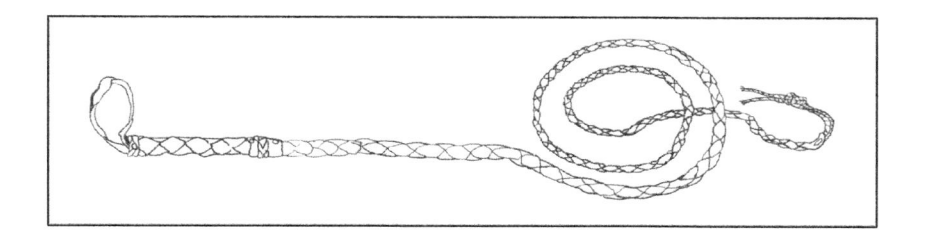

201

240

Just as your strength is failing, you feel the welcome touch of sand beneath your feet. With a final effort, you struggle out of the water and collapse onto the beach!

Lose 2 VITALITY points due to sheer exhaustion!

You are not sure how long you lay there, but when you come to your senses Montgomery and his crook-backed attendant are staring down at you in amazement.

'First, I find you in the dinghy of *The Lady Vain*, and now this!' Montgomery remarks. 'Well, I am not one to stand in the way of a man of such good fortune. You had better follow me, so that I can introduce you properly to the master of this island.'

With that, Montgomery turns on his heel and strides along the dull grey sand of the broad bay towards a piebald stone enclosure out of which you discern two thatched roofs. The buildings lay about halfway up a gentle slope from the beach that ends at a ridge set with trees and dense vegetation.

The crook-backed man follows Montgomery, ranging ahead to the left and right and sniffing the air like a dog being taken for a stroll.

You climb to your feet and follow them as swiftly as you are able, glad to be back on solid ground. As you walk, you see a number of rabbits nibbling at the foliage at the edges of the ridge where several of the hutches you had seen aboard the *Ipecacuanha* are upturned nearby.

'We brought them here in the hope that they would colonise the island and multiply,' Montgomery calls over his shoulder. 'Hitherto, we've had a lack of meat on the island, you see.'

Your stomach grumbles at the thought of a rabbit on a spit, but your hunger is forgotten when you catch sight of three tall, strange men moving the last of the crates from the island boat into the enclosure. They are swathed from head to toe in grubby white linen, have lank black hair, elfin faces, and twisted legs that seem jointed in the wrong place. They seem to be having particular trouble on the sandy uphill walk and seem especially uncomfortable under your curious stare.

Not wanting to offend them, you turn your attention to the walls of the enclosure where Montgomery is waiting.

Turn to 465.

241

Your search of the hunters' lean-tos uncovers some sun-dried fish, fresh fruit and a large earthenware bowl of some sort of soaked grain. You may eat this and gain 4 VITALITY points and take enough food with you for **5 meals**. You also find a wooden snuff-box full of a thick **pungent paste** that is for the treatment of wounds (you may use the paste twice to restore 2 VITALITY points at any time other than in combat), as well as a coil of **rope**.

Make a note of all these additions to your *equipment list*, before deciding where to go next:

If you want to head towards the sea through the copse of trees towards the west, turn to 348.

If you would rather head back inland towards the source of the hot springs, turn to 261.

Alternatively, you can explore deeper into the brake of trees where you killed the hunters, by turning to 499.

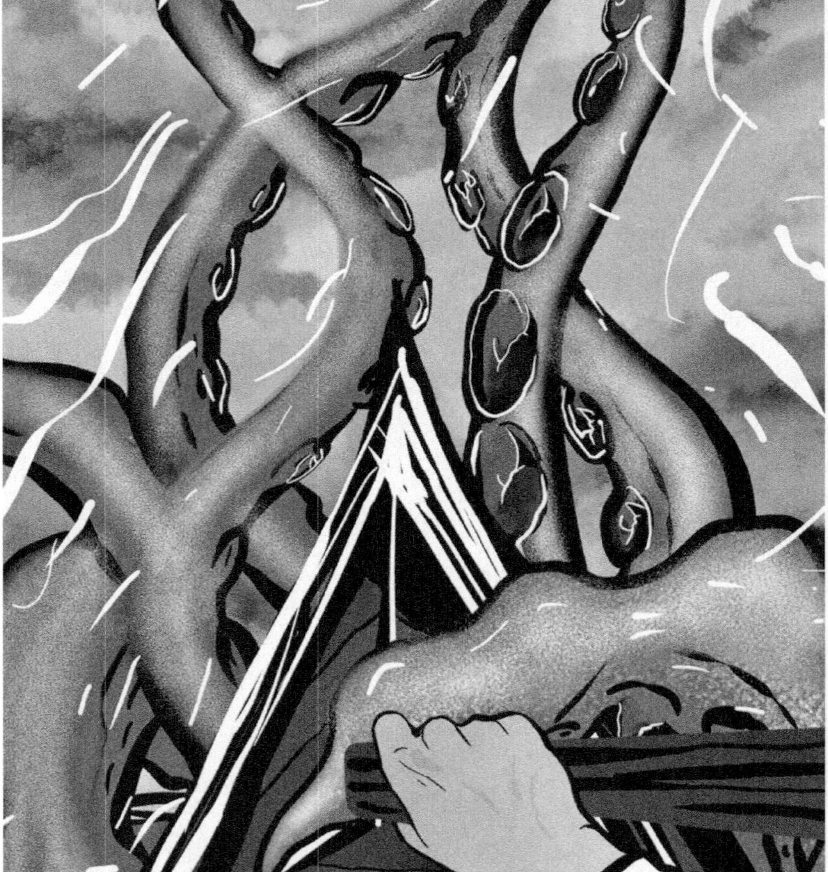

242

You paddle into the dying day at a steady pace and are just about to turn in towards the beach when something bumps against the bottom of the canoe. You stare over the side, but the reflecting light of the setting sun makes it impossible to see beneath the surface. Then there is another thump, then another, before an arrhythmic succession of heavy blows rocks the vessel and causes the water around you to ripple and seethe...

Suddenly, a double pair of gleaming tentacles whip out of the sea and clamp around the sides of your canoe. You hear a scraping sound as something sharp scores the underside of the hull. Frantically, you slam your oar into the clinging limbs with a ferocious, panic-fuelled strength. The tentacles relinquish their hold, there is a moment's calm, then chaos as dozens of the muscular appendages slash out of the water from all directions. One of them catches you across the cheek, lacerating the flesh there with a row of claws that are as sharp as a panther's!

Lose 2 VITALITY points!

You have read about the aggressive nocturnal cephalopods known as HUMBOLDT SQUID. Related to octopus and cuttlefish, each is similar in size and weight to a man. More worryingly, they are known to hunt in packs. If fishermen's lore is to be given any credit, then these creatures are opportunistic predators that are unafraid to take human prey...

You are in grave danger and must decide your next move with care!

Do you wish to continue to lay about you with you oar? If so, turn to **166**.

If you would prefer to stow your oar and attempt to use another weapon or item, turn to **219**.

Alternatively, if you wish to abandon the canoe and try to swim back to the beach, turn to **380**.

243

Mercifully, you are able to stay on your feet and reach the prow of the frigate unsoiled! After spending a few moments scraping the worse of the muck from your boots on the timbers of the hull, you turn your attention to the box and the leather bag.

Turn to **420**.

244

As you reach up to grab the railing of the longboat, the sailor who turned you away takes a full-blooded swing at you with his oar!

Roll one dice...

If you roll 1-2, turn to **35**.

If you roll 3-4, turn to **359**.

If you roll 5-6, turn to **312**.

245

The rock strikes the hunter's skull with a sickening crack, and he crumples sideways to the ground.

Quickly, you pick up the man's pair of **Toledo steel hunting knives**. These handsome weapons are forged from the finest Spanish steel and will add +1 to your *close combat score*. You may also take the man's **bow** and **quiver of 7 arrows** (2 points of ranged damage).

You then head to the lean-tos, where you may retrieve any items previously lost to the hunters. In addition, the camp contains some sun-dried fish, fresh fruit and a large earthenware bowl of some sort of soaked grain. You may eat this and gain 4 VITALITY points and take enough food with you for **5 meals**. You also find a wooden snuffbox full of a **thick pungent paste** that is for the treatment of wounds, and a coil of **rope**. You may use the paste twice to restore 2 VITALITY points at any time other than in combat.

Make a note of all these additions to your *equipment list*.

Next, if you want to head towards the sea through the copse of trees where the sounds of wood chopping can still be heard, turn to **313**.

If you would rather head back inland towards the source of the hot springs, turn to **261**.

246

When you proclaim your ignorance of the Law, the Ape-man and the brutes look at each other in horror, before quickly agreeing that you should be taken for an audience with someone they call The Sayer. You are hauled to your feet and - with each of the Bear-men guarding you to either side - are escorted west along the trail.

After less than an hour of walking, a piercing shriek carries eerily through the jungle. The Ape-man freezes in terror, then hauls himself high into the branches of a tall coconut palm. At first you think he has done so to get a superior perspective on the origin of the sound, but then you see him extend a long arm to an adjacent tree and disappear from view. The Bear-men stare hard into the canopy, utter disapproving growls, then advance along the path, their heads lowered and claw-like hands outstretched.

They appear to have entirely forgotten about you, and there will be no better opportunity to escape!

Will you rush into the jungle to the north? If so, turn to **514**.

If you would rather try the jungle to the south, turn to **56**.

247

Do you wish to spare the Ocelot-man's life?

If so, turn to **271**.

If not, turn to **360**.

248

The captain and mate offer their condolences for the hardships you have endured, then show you to a small cabin where the sailors have stowed your equipment. You spend your days wandering the deck and enjoying the sweep of the wind and the warmth of the sun upon your skin. The captain even lends you one or two of his books when he learns that you are disposed towards science and literature.

Thus, the weeks pass easily enough, and you begin to think about what you will do when you reach San Francisco...

Turn to **319**.

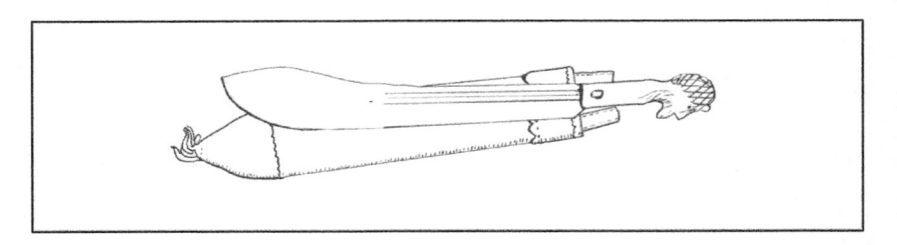

249

You have drawn the middle straw! Now Helmar must take his turn. Roll one dice for him:

If you roll 1-3, turn to **18**.

If you roll 4-6, turn to **183**.

250

The hunter is as strong as a bull and manages to throw you over his shoulder into the fire! Lose 3 VITALITY points from the impact and the burns you sustain.

Rolling to your feet, you now have no choice but to fight!

VAI THE HUNTER: Prowess - 8; Vitality - 8; Damage - 2.

Deduct 2 points from your *close combat score* if you are unarmed, deduct 1 point if you are using a rock. Note: Vai fights with a pair of knives that add +1 to his *close combat score*.

If you win, turn to **310**.

251

Montgomery ignores you, his temper warming to a white heat, while a continuous stream of vile language pours from Captain Davis' mouth.

'If that ugly devil of yours comes to the aft of the ship one more time, I'll cut his blasted insides out!' the drunkard rages. 'Yours as well, Sawbones, if you dare stand in my way!'

At this, Montgomery seizes the captain, and the two men go down on the deck in a tangle of limbs. Seeing his master in danger, the misshapen man finds a sudden wild courage and leaps into the fight, only to be dragged off by two sailors, who he turns on with animal swiftness.

A vicious brawl erupts, and you must decide your place in it!

Will you:

Dive in to Montgomery's aid? (Turn to **37**).

Try and help the captain and the sailors? (Turn to **280**).

Stay out of it and hope for the best? (Turn to **326**).

252

The last of your enemies yowls mournfully as you strike it down. To your surprise, the Leopard-folk handlers simply stare at you for a moment before melting back into the jungle. They have witnessed your fighting skills and have no stomach for further conflict.

Gain 2 FATE points for surviving an encounter with these dangerous creatures!

You take to one knee to regain your breath and consider your predicament. It seems that M'ling and the white-swathed servants you have seen are milder instances of whatever bizarre phenomenon is at work on Doctor Moreau's island. Quite how that eminent scientist has created such entities is beyond your understanding, and it is questionable whether what he has done should be condoned or censured. More to the point, you are clearly in no small amount of danger!

Even so, you feel a steely determination to explore the island as thoroughly as possible. In doing so, you may find some answers, make some allies or even find a way to ensure that you are not the doctor's next test subject...

A quick search of the Leopard-man you killed reveals nothing of use, but your eyes are drawn to the leopards' beautiful pelts. If you possess a dagger or knife, then you may spend some time skinning the cats. If so, then add **2 leopard skins** to your *equipment list*.

If you do not possess a bladed tool, then there is no way for you to remove the pelts and you will have to leave the carcasses where they lay.

Now, do you wish to head back to the beach and follow it west? If so, turn to **485**.

If you would rather press on south-west into the jungle, turn to **29**.

253

The dusk presses in as you hurry along the beach and scan for a safe place to camp. Inland, you see a broad expanse of cone-shaped reeds leading into a strip of lush jungle. Above this is a distant hillside covered with pockets of rich volcanic soil. In daylight, you estimate that it would take you around three hours to reach the hill, assuming the ground through the reeds is solid underfoot. It will be a difficult walk by moonlight, but once on the hill you could take several hours' rest, then be in a good position to explore the interior of the island in the morning.

Then again, the beach appears comfortable enough, and you could embark on the walk inland in the morning...

Do you wish to hike inland through part of the night in order to reach the hillside? If so, turn to 25.

If you would rather simply spend the night on the beach, turn to 137.

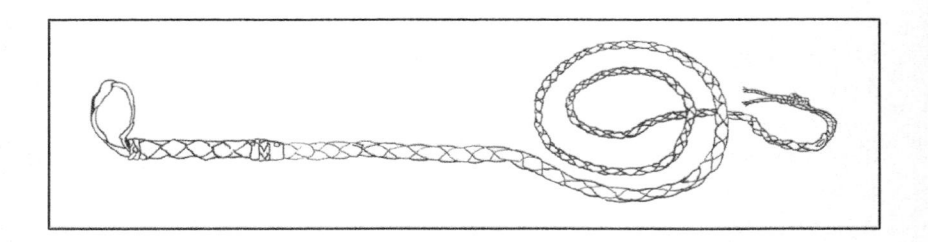

254

You decide to make the most of what remains of the light and paddle on as the sunset begins to turn the surface of the ocean the colour of blood...

Have you killed the Draconope?

If so, turn to 32.

If not, turn to 142.

255

The schooner cuts past without colliding with the dinghy, but leaves you rocking sickeningly in her wake. Looking back over the gunwale you see Captain Davis mocking you from his ship's taffrail, then he and the *Ipecacuanha* dwindle into the distance. Turning back towards the island, you see the island boat growing smaller as she approaches the beach. There upon the line of sand are a number of figures awaiting her arrival.

Suddenly, you feel the acute cruelty of this desertion. It is unlikely that you will drift to the island by chance, and you are still weak from your original ordeal. You must fight the rising tide of despair and decide what to do!

Do you wish to stand in the dinghy and try to attract the attention of the figures on the beach? If so, turn to 146.

If you would rather try to paddle the dinghy closer to the island, turn to 228.

256

A bow and arrow is a cumbersome weapon to attempt to use from within a rocking canoe, and as you put the first arrow to the string and draw, a large squid flops onto the front of the canoe and flails its arms towards you!

Instinctively, you fire the arrow at the underside of the beast, spitting it through and through. The Humboldt thrashes wildly, rips the bow from your hands, then slides back into the water...

Remove the bow from your *equipment list*.

The other squid are all around you now, and you have little choice but to battle the oceanic predators with your oar!

Turn to 166.

257

The Boar-men tear up the forest floor as they lunge and wrestle, their hoarse cries replete with frustration and rage. After a number of clashes, the larger of the two sends his opponent fleeing past you in a head-long, panicked flight.

The victor now fixes his baleful stare upon you, then comes on with a series of belligerent grunts. It is obvious that his blood is up and that he wishes to do battle with a second foe!

Do you wish to engage this brute in a contest of strength? If so, turn to **338**.

If you would prefer to attempt to mollify the Boar-man with an offering of food, turn to **405**.

Alternatively, if you simply wish to raise your hands and slowly back away out of the clearing, turn to **483**.

258

As you try to remonstrate with the captain, he strikes you in the face without warning!

Lose 2 VITALITY points.

At this, Montgomery seizes the captain, and the two men go down on the deck in a tangle of limbs and outpouring of insults. Seeing his master in danger, the misshapen man finds a sudden wild courage and leaps into the fight, only to be dragged off by a pair of sailors, who he turns on with animal swiftness.

A vicious brawl erupts, and you must decide your place in it!

Will you:

Dive in to Montgomery's aid? (Turn to **37**).

Try and help the captain and the sailors? (Turn to **280**).

Stay out of it and hope for the best? (Turn to **326**).

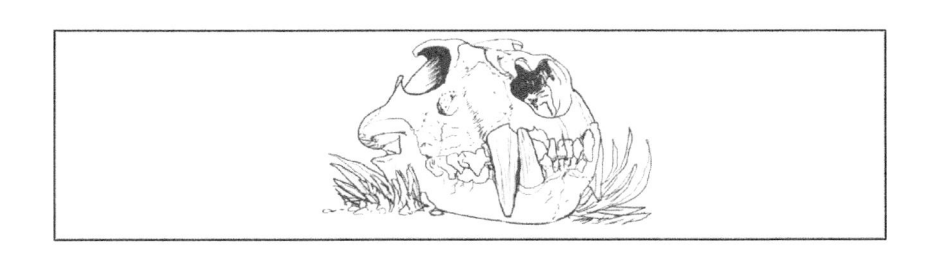

259

You stagger like a drunkard into the sunlight and spy the muffled figure of the puma running in great leaping strides along the beach with Moreau in hot pursuit. The puma turns her head, sees the doctor, and doubles for the line of bushes, gaining on her tormentor with every stride. Running slantingly to intercept her, Moreau fires wildly and misses as the creature plunges into the foliage. Undeterred, the doctor continues the chase until he too vanishes in the green confusion.

Gradually, your feelings of nausea begin to fade, just as Montgomery appears around a corner of the enclosure with the staghounds. Upon seeing you, he lets the dogs loose into the jungle, pulls out his revolver and rushes past you to inspect the laboratory. Moments later, you hear his wordless exclamations.

'Great God, that brute's loose!' Montgomery says, returning to your side and giving your injuries a cursory examination. 'Tore its fetters clear out of the steel of the chair. You're damned lucky it didn't take your head clean off! Now tell me, what happened to Moreau?'

When you tell him that Moreau set off in pursuit of the puma, Montgomery pulls at his lower lip, straightens up and stares into the tree line.

'I can neither see nor hear any sign of him,' he mutters. 'He may want our help, you know.'

Standing lost in thought for a few moments, Montgomery seems to reach a decision.

'Yes, I will go after him,' he says. 'To tell you the truth, I feel anxious somehow. That puma was an unfinished subject and will be in a continual state of pain. Such a creature will make for dangerous quarry. Are you in a fit enough state to come with me? If so, you are very welcome. If not, it may be just as useful for you to keep a lookout from the enclosure. It is entirely up to you.'

Montgomery stares at you with his expressionless grey eyes, awaiting your answer...

Will you say that you will accompany Montgomery in his search for Moreau? If so, turn to **51**.

If you prefer to tell Montgomery that you will keep a lookout from the enclosure, turn to **513**.

260

As soon as the Crocodile-man falls, the Lizard-man seizes its enemy's upper and lower jaws, forcing them apart until they break with a horrid crack! Then, the creature turns its small, slanted eyes upon you.

'With your aid, the most hated one is slain,' it hisses, the words coming with difficulty from its lipless slash of a mouth. 'My pride tells me to resent your assistance, but I choose to heed my reason. Without you, I might have died. Had that occurred, the many friends

I have lost to the Maw-kin would have lain unavenged. That being so, adventurer, what would you ask of me in return?'

The Lizard-man then falls silent, as still as an effigy that has sprung from the imagination of a mad but gifted sculptor.

What will you ask as a reward?

Will you ask to be given the Lizard-man's halberd? If so, turn to **346**.

If you would prefer to ask to be given the Lizard-man's peculiar armour, turn to **545**.

If you would rather ask to receive one of the Lizard-man's pets as your own, turn to **431**.

Alternatively, if you wish to reply that you require nothing other than the Lizard-man's thanks, turn to **481**.

261

As you trudge uphill towards the island's centre, you pass clusters of stunted trees and patches of sickly scrub, before entering an area of spongy ground soaked by steaming geothermic spring water. With each step you are alarmed to see bubbles of gas effervescing through a thin layer of surface water and freeze when you are struck by a distinctive rotten-egg odour - the smell is quite clearly that of hydrogen sulphide!

This toxic gas is produced by subterranean chemical reactions and sometimes accumulates in underground pockets. It can be deadly in high enough concentrations; so much so, that a number of well-known geologists and volcanologists have been asphyxiated by it in recent years.

Indeed, your head is already swimming from the exposure, and you can feel an acrid burning in the back of your throat...

If you wish to attempt to escape the poison gas by running uphill, turn to **423**.

If you would rather remain very still in the hope that the bubbles will subside, turn to **561**.

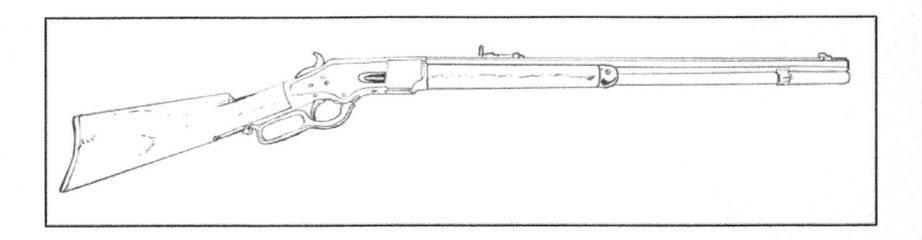

262

Taking the intruder by complete surprise you strike it a vicious blow to the head and send it staggering out of the alcove. You wait for several minutes, but when the creature does not return you venture out into the moon-lit night. A hundred yards up the ravine you find the body of a creature unlike any you have ever seen. Dressed in rags like many of the other islanders, it has a large protuberant nose, liquid brown eyes, and extraordinarily large, wilting ears positioned high on its head.

It is some sort of DOG-MAN, no doubt another of the doctor's bizarre experiments...

Ashamed of having killed such an apparently benevolent creature and disturbed by the amount of blood that has flowed from the wound on its head, you elect to retrieve your rucksack, take advantage of the brightness of the moon and press on up the ravine towards the source of the geothermic stream.

Now turn to **496**.

263

Under the baleful watch of the island creatures, you set off in the canoe once more, nervously scanning for movements in the ocean that may betray the presence of nocturnal oceanic predators...

Have you killed the Draconope? If so, turn to **235**.

If not, turn to **315**.

264

'Soul-stealer!' the man spits. Before you can react two arrows transfix your chest with a rapid double beat. Your legs give out and you die face down in the dirt...

YOUR TROUBLES ARE AT AN END!

265

The jungle to the east of the arena is particularly dark, dense and choked with a species of thorny vine that snags your clothing and makes progress extremely labourious. After an hour or so of toil, you mop your brow, glance at the shallow cuts covering your arms and prepare to abandon this direction in preference for a westerly bearing.

Did you save the Satyr [Goat-man] from the arena?

If so, turn to **291**.

If not, turn to **342**.

266

The hunter seems to have a sixth sense, because almost as soon as you begin your charge, he seizes his bow, leaps to his feet and turns to face you. Your opponent has time to fire off two arrows before you can engage him in close combat!

Resolve the outcome of the TWO ranged attacks against you, before continuing the fight (if you are still alive).

VAI THE HUNTER: Prowess - 8; Ballistics - 8; Vitality - 9; Damage 2/2.

Deduct 2 points from your *close combat score* if you are unarmed, deduct 1 if you are using a rock. Note: Vai wields a pair of **Toledo steel hunting knives** that add +1 to his *close combat score*.

If you win, turn to <u>310</u>.

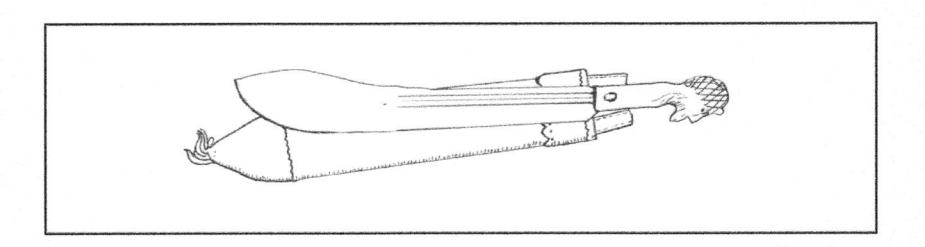

267

In which direction do you wish to run?

Up the chasm? Turn to <u>83</u>.

Down the chasm? Turn to <u>104</u>.

268

Using the momentum of the Boar-man's charge, you grip hard to his shrunken arms, roll to your back upon the soft jungle floor and send your opponent flying over your head with a solid double kick to the midriff!

The creature's enraged squeals are cut short as it impacts with the truck of a tree with a sickening thud. Scrambling to your feet, you see the female fleeing into the jungle. Urgently, you examine your attacker. The Boar-man has been knocked unconscious but is already beginning to snore and snort.

It could come around at any moment...

Do you wish to perform a quick search of the clearing? If so, turn to **392**.

If you would rather leave the clearing immediately, turn to **436**.

269

Fortunately, the Ape-man does not seem insulted by your lack of interest but turns around and disappears into the jungle at a quick walk. You hear the swish of branches as he hauls himself into the trees, followed by the receding rustle of his treetop progress.

Alone once again, you press on north along the beach.

Turn to **38**.

270

As you proceed along the beach, you begin to feel the exposed areas of your skin burn and a rising nausea brought on from the beginnings of sunstroke.

Lose 1 VITALITY point!

Ignoring the discomfort, you continue walking towards the west. Turn to **485**.

271

You inflict a nasty gash on the Ocelot-man's arm, send his weapon spinning through the air, and force him to his knees with the edge of your weapon resting against the side of his neck.

'It is over!' you yell to the crowd. 'I have no desire to take this creature's life!'

For a moment a stunned silence descends, followed by a ripple of angry whispers.

'No mercy!' bray a number of spectators, before the crowd is repeating the phrase with a single diabolical voice. 'NO MERCY!!'

As one, the beast-people rush into the arena, a roiling mass of outrage and unsated bloodlust. Helpless, you are jostled this way and that, and forced to look on in horror as the yowling Ocelot-man is torn apart.

Appalled, you lay into the mob with the flat of your blade and fists, disgusted by this display of pointless barbarity. But as swiftly as it arose, the fury of the mob subsides. The beast-folk begin to return to the jungle, several knots of killers parading pieces of your erstwhile opponent above their heads in glee.

The sight is so ghastly that you double over in retching spasms, the sight of the contents of your stomach mingling with the lifeblood of the ocelot only driving you into greater paroxysms of revulsion.

Lose 1 VITALITY point!

'Brutal, isn't it?' says a sly voice, and you look up to see the Fox-woman standing over you. 'But then what can men expect when beasts such as we are given human form?'

She passes you your rucksack and the Elephant-man hands back your weapons.

'You should have killed him while you had the chance,' the grey giant rumbles. 'It is nothing more than he would have done to you, and it would have been cleaner. Still, blood is blood, and our rites are satisfied this day. Go home, friend of the Master, leave here while you may. This is no place for you!'

With that, the unlikely pair follow the hooting mob into the jungle. They do not seem concerned about the **falchion**, which you may keep if you wish.

Do you now wish to perform a quick search of the area? If so, turn to **87**

If you would rather leave this place immediately, then you see two directions open to you:

Into the jungle towards the west? Turn to **199**.

Or into the jungle towards the east? Turn to **265**.

272

With extraordinary dexterity, you slide around the flank of the cane toad and seize the base of its head, holding its toothless mouth away from you. The squirming creature discharges a few more puffs of venom, then begins to swell into a hard, warty ball, its stumpy legs sticking out at absurd angles, its golden eyes bulging as if they are about to pop...!

If you wish to release the cane toad and continue your journey, turn to **493**.

If you would rather keep hold of the cane toad, turn to **506**.

273

You find yourself drifting in a delirium and are aroused to wakefulness only when Helmar and the sailor leap on you in a coordinated attack!

All of you are terribly weak, but you are able to seize the sailor's knife-arm after he gashes your ribs (lose 2 VITALITY points), while Helmar doggedly attempts to pull your legs out from under you!

You must fight these desperate opponents simultaneously! Remember to reduce your close combat score by 2 points if you are unarmed.

SAILOR: Prowess - 6; Vitality - 3; Damage - 2.

HELMAR: Prowess - 5; Vitality - 3; Damage - 1.

If you win, turn to **105**.

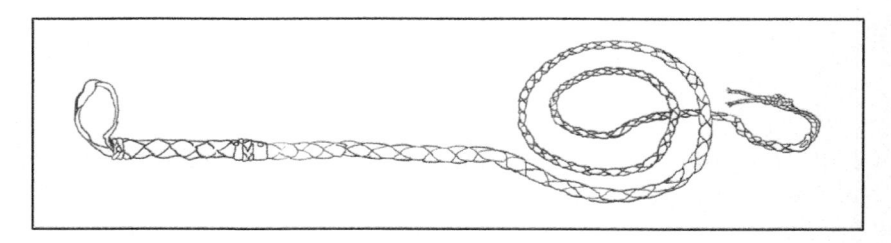

274

Try as you may, none of the figures on the beach seem to notice you and you begin to feel the effects of the intensity of the sun…

Lose 1 VITALITY point!

As you float despondently, you feel something large pass under you. Your worse fears are realised when you see a sleek, iron-grey fin cutting through the water towards you.

All your thrashing and shouting has attracted a shark!

Will you:

Try to swim quickly for the beach? If so, turn to 385.

Or prepare to fight?! Turn to 469.

275

You reach the opposite bank and haul yourself out of the water moments before the alligator's jaws snap shut a few inches behind you! Scrambling further up onto the path, you scan the surface of the swamp, but see nothing apart from the rippling disturbance left by the predator's lunge. Within seconds the waters are still and placid once more, giving no indication of the danger that lurks there.

Hoping that the risk you took proves worthwhile, you retrieve your rucksack and any ranged weapons you previously threw across the gap and press on into the middle of the swamp.

Turn to 331.

276

The swim towards the longboat is tiring and you are forced to fight off a number of drowning passengers who try to seize a hold of you.

Though you succeed in fending them off, you sustain a number of scratches and bruises and swallow several mouthfuls of sea water…

Lose 2 VITALITY points!

As you draw close to the longboat, one of the sailors aboard it shoves you away with an oar. 'No room onboard for ye, landlubber!' he shouts. 'Look elsewhere for salvation or better still, commend your soul to the Lord!'

To your dismay, a chorus of lusty cheers come from his shipmates…

If you wish to attempt to climb aboard the longboat despite this opposition, turn to **244**.

If you would rather give up on the longboat, then you may swim towards the derelict merchantman (if you have not already done so). If so, turn to **86**.

Alternatively, if you wish to strike out towards the dinghy with the two men, turn to **127**.

277

Climbing the slippery, moss-covered mahogany tree is far from easy. You must *test your PROWESS* to see if you are able to reach the nest!

If you succeed, turn to **569**.

If you fail, then you slip and fall! Roll a dice, divide it by 2 (rounding up) and deduct the total from your VITALITY as you crash to the ground. You may attempt the climb as many times as you wish by repeating the test but must stop if your VITALITY falls to 5 for fear of killing yourself in this endeavour.

If you wish (or are forced) to give up trying to reach the nest, then you may do the following:

If the Thylacine-men are still alive, you can offer them a meal (if you have one) by turning to 454.

If you do not have a meal, or do not wish to give one away, then you have little choice but to mutter your apologies to the Thylacine-men and attempt to press on through the jungle towards the south. Turn to 397.

If you have killed the Thylacine-men, there is little to do but press on towards the south. Turn to 171.

278

The hunter seems lost in thought, and you are able to strike him a telling blow over the head before he is able to offer any resistance.

Resolve your desperate close combat struggle!

VAI THE HUNTER: Prowess - 8; Vitality - 4; Damage 2/2.

Deduct 2 points from your *close combat score* if you are unarmed, deduct 1 if you are using a rock. Note: Vai wields a pair of **Toledo steel hunting knives** that add +1 to his *close combat score*.

If you win, turn to 310.

279

As you progress, a fetid mist begins to rise from the stagnant waters and the oppressive silence begins to be broken by the occasional

227

chirping of frogs that swiftly swells into a steady chorus. This rising symphony is punctuated by the louder, ruder calls of what you guess to be enormous toads. Your suspicion is confirmed when you see a specimen standing at the edge of the swamp. It is larger than any toad you have ever seen and looks capable of devouring a small dog whole! As you draw closer, it unleashes a revolting burping croak, adjusts its position and glares at you with horizontally-slitted eyes the colour of amber.

It is some sort of GIANT CANE TOAD. If you remember rightly, this species has such a voracious appetite that it is being considered for introduction into Australia, where it might prove helpful in controlling the continent's excessive rodent population. Cane toads are also well known for exuding a toxin from their backs, one that can be fatal if ingested by humans or introduced into open wounds…

Do you wish to try rubbing any arrows (if you have them) and close combat weapons against the back of the cane toad in the hope of making your attacks poisonous? If so, turn to **336**.

If you would rather leave the creature alone and press on past it towards the west, turn to **493**.

280

You put an arm around Montgomery's throat and try to drag him from the captain! As you do so, you see him stare up at you with a look of betrayal.

Note that you have *gained Montgomery's resentment.*

More sailors rush up onto the deck. In the confusion of the struggle, they do not realise that you are trying to help them, and you go down under a hail of blows. Within moments, you find yourself forced face down on the deck and having your wrists tied painfully behind your back.

Lose 2 VITALITY points from the beating!

You see Montgomery and the misshapen man being treated in a similar way. Soon, the three of you are being lashed to the rear railings of the ship, bleeding and bruised.

'This treatment of us will not stand, captain,' Montgomery spits. 'When the law hears of this, you'll never be permitted to sail again!'

'I'm already forbidden from taking to sea, you damn fool!' Davis leers. 'Why else do you think that my rates are so low? Now, let's see how the three of you like spending the night up here with the beasts. Then, come the morning, I'll have decided what to do with you all.'

With that, the captain and his crew return below deck.

Turn to **461**.

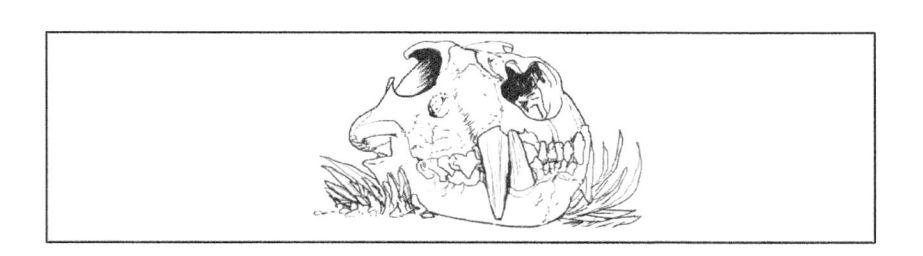

281

Just as you are attempting to sidestep around the cane toad it spits a glob of venom that hits you squarely in the face! You stagger away gagging and coughing (lose 2 VITALITY points), and by the time you have recovered the warty creature is nowhere to be seen.

Swearing under your breath, there is little now to do but continue following the edge of the swamp to the west.

Turn to **493**.

282

With a sharp chop across the neck, you manage to stun the hunter before wrapping your left arm around his throat and seizing his knife-hand. But the man is young and strong; he is not going to give up without a fight!

Test the hunter's VITALITY by rolling three dice…

If the result is greater than 8, turn to **355**.

If the result is equal or less than 8, turn to **250**.

283

The crowd of animal-folk roar their approval at the Elephant-man's victory while the Jaguar-man climbs to his feet and slinks off into the jungle. The victor of the bout comes towards you, wiping the blood away from his face with the back of his huge hands. Up close, you see that he is at least seven feet tall and looks to weigh the same as three large men. Under your gaze, the Elephant-man flaps his inordinately large ears, cleans his tusks with a rag proffered by one of the crowd and harrumphs in annoyance.

'It's unwise having strangers here, Madam, you know that,' the Elephant-man rumbles, studiously ignoring you and directing his question towards the Fox-woman. 'He may report back to the Master about our activities, then it'll be the House of Pain for us all. Now I know you have some unusual tastes in entertainment, but I'd have thought that having your soul cut away was a step too far even for you!'

'The young lord would never tell,' the red-haired creature retorts. 'He's here for the entertainment, just the same as everyone else. You did well beating the young stalker, my love. He is undefeated no more! Where on earth did that cat-legged loser creep off to anyway?'

'Some dank hole where he can spend the next few days sulking?' the Elephant-man shrugs. 'What do I care with the main event coming up?'

He seems to notice you for the first time and leans forward conspiratorially.

'It's likely to be quite the show, fella,' he sneers. 'Let's make it a fight to the death in honour of you, our very special *manling* guest!'

He jabs a malformed thumb towards a commotion where two small creatures are being forced into the arena by a bestial mob, gives a hooting laugh and returns to the centre of the circle where a pair of rusty falchions have been cast at the feet of each of the contestants.

One of them, a slender GOAT-MAN with wide-set eyes, stares down in horror at the blades. The other - a sleek yet diminutive OCELOT-MAN with a fierce face and lithe, finely muscled limbs - seizes a weapon and slices it through the air with a casual, preternatural grace.

'Well, my lovely, what are your thoughts on the winner of *this* bout?' asks the Fox-woman with a malevolent, sharp-toothed grin. 'Guess correctly and you'll win a blessing from us. Choose poorly, and the blessing will be ours to take...'

Will you go along with this cruel gladiatorial game?

If so, make a note once again of which contestant you favour, then turn to <u>187</u>.

If you would prefer to speak out against the contest, turn to <u>497</u>.

284

'My cargo is nothing more than a collection of live and exotic specimens for biological study,' Montgomery shrugs. 'Now, if you feel up to it, I suggest you take some fresh air up on deck with me. Doing so will allow you to get a sense of your surroundings for yourself.'

You readily agree and follow Montgomery out of the cabin.

Now turn to **365**.

285

As you walk along the beach, you notice that the day is growing old and that you will need to make camp in the next few hours.

Not too far ahead, you notice a small delta exiting onto the beach. The sediment has accumulated at the mouth of a steep, narrow ravine with banks that are infested with livid mosses, fungi, and small, twisted trees with claw-like branches. Washing out of the ravine is a channel of water that steams with remnants of geothermic heat.

Beyond the ravine the island ascends from a strip of silver-white sand through layers of lush lowland reeds and deep jungle that is crowned by a rounded summit of fertile meadow punctuated by occasional outcroppings of glassy black rock and jagged iron-grey stone.

Do you wish to search for a campsite in the ravine? If so, turn to **114**.

Alternatively, you can press on past the delta and look for somewhere else to camp? (Turn to **253**).

As you follow the chasm towards the south, the jungle emerges onto a scrubby moon-silvered hillside indented with pockets of rich volcanic soil out of which grow all manner of exotic flowers and plants. Yet there is a sight more arresting still - rows of makeshift dens huddled against either side of the walls of the chasm that are dimly illuminated by a series of flickering torches. Furthermore, there is a rough hemp ladder leading down into the gloom.

Reluctant though you are to meet the inhabitants of the huts, you reason that it would be more dangerous to spend the night in the jungle alone. Thus resolved, you lower yourself onto the ladder and begin your descent, reassured by the fact that the hemp fibres offer a reassuring grip for hand and foot.

The deep darkness that envelops you soon retreats before the glow of the torches below, and a disagreeable odour - like that of a monkey's ill-cleaned cage - becomes overpowering. You try to ignore the way that the walls of the chasm seem to close in on you like the jaws of a crushing trap and are relieved when your boots finally touch the ground.

Too late, you notice a child-like figure squatting at one of the entrances of the huts. Before you can react, the creature emits a sudden, high-pitched shriek that causes you to fall back in alarm! Within moments, sundry bestial forms burst out of the huts, an amorphous, shadowy mass of monsters that defies rational explanation. The creatures press in on all sides, twisted hands pulling you this way and that. The double insult of fetid breath and malodorous flesh causes you to swoon...

'An Other, an Other...!' moan many voices, some deep chested and resonant, others high pitched and childlike. 'Take it to the Sayer, the Sayer! The Sayer of the Law!'

233

You are dragged into the largest of the huts and thrust onto a bench in a dim, dank corner. Your heart thumping in your chest, you stare at the shadows within shadows that are waiting in the hut...

Now turn to **350**.

287

The pamphlet is a mawkish and sensationalist account of a great man's fall from grace, but as you read you remember where you have heard the name of Doctor Moreau before. The man you have just met was one of England's most prominent scientists. Your father used to read reports on his breakthroughs in the fields of blood transfusions, restorative surgery, and the excision of malignant growths.

But as the pamphlet reports, Doctor Moreau was disgraced after an undercover journalist posing as a research assistant gained access to his laboratory in order to expose an abundance of cruel and inhumane vivisectionist experiments. Worse among the 'Moreau Horrors' (as they came to be known) was a flayed dog that had run amok in the streets of London after the reporter had set it free.

According to the article, the doctor had been forced to purchase his social peace by abandoning his investigations in England and paying an enormous fine. Having done so, he disappeared into obscurity with none knowing where he went. Until now...

What a chance it is that you have discovered that Doctor Moreau has not abandoned his controversial research after all! Quite to the contrary, he appears to have been pressing on with it here, on this remote and little-known island...

As you read the pamphlet, the fate of the puma and the other animals you have seen becomes apparent, and for the first time you catch an odour that had been in the background of your consciousness

234

hitherto: the anti-septic odour of the operating room, seeping from the laboratory that lies beyond the inner door.

You feel a sudden twist of fear as you realise that there is nothing so horrible in vivisection to explain Montgomery's and Moreau's secrecy. Why then, do they insist on such subtleties? Suddenly, you remember the crippled and distorted servants you have seen thus far, the crook-backed M'ling with his shining eyes, the tall and ungainly men shrouded in white bandages...

Is it possible that Moreau has devolved into experimenting on men during his decade away from civilisation? Worse still, are you intended to be his next subject?

Your thoughts are interrupted when you hear voices coming from outside. Through the barred window you see Montgomery and M'ling approaching the enclosure from about fifty yards away. The manservant is carrying a tray of vittles, while you notice that Montgomery has a pair of revolvers tucked into his belt.

Do you wish to take no chances and try to escape via the outside door? If so, turn to 152.

If you would prefer to wait for Montgomery and M'ling to arrive, turn to 301.

288

Your desperate flight comes to an end when you trip over a root and slam head first into the trunk of a devil-palm. Though the ragged lacerations to your skull would not ordinarily have been fatal, this is no place to lose consciousness. Soon, your lungs will succumb to the venom of the Bloodroot plants, and within a week your liberated nutrients will begin to sustain many generations of this deadly floral killer...

YOUR STRUGGLES ARE AT AN END!

289

You strike again and again at the Draconope's leathery neck, kicking for the shore as the abomination slides beneath the waves for the last time. You have truly had a brush with death, and the sight and sound of the Draconope's shrieks of agonised hatred will stay with you as long as you live...

Lose 1 FATE point!

Once safely on the beach you have no choice now but to walk back to the enclosure. To your relief, nothing else comes out of the water and the moonlit beach shows no signs of life other than some furtive, scurrying shapes that you take to be large rabbits.

Just as you are beginning to fall asleep on your feet, you round a rocky headland by means of a frill of rock just below the surface of the sea and catch sight of a glimmer of light in the distance - it is the enclosure! The light of the new day is soaking the horizon by the time you pass the simple jetty harbouring the island boat, and it is with some trepidation that you begin to walk towards the buildings. Suddenly, the double gates of the outpost are flung wide, and you see Doctor Moreau, Montgomery and M'ling leading the pack of staghounds out onto the beach. The dogs immediately catch your scent and lurch against their collars in a frenzy of barking and growling.

Moreau restrains the beasts with a harsh command, stares at you for a few seconds, then leads the staghounds back into the enclosure, while Montgomery and M'ling advance towards you.

'Where the devil have you been?' Montgomery demands. 'We've been worried sick and were about to set out with the dogs to find you! Now get inside this instant, Moreau will want to have words!'

Your relief at being back among humans somewhat sullied by a flicker of dread, you enter the enclosure and let yourself in via the small door leading to the room. It does not take long before you hear the inner door to the courtyard being unlocked, and the doctor strides in...

Turn to 39.

290

You charge through the bushes with a fierce shout, fully expecting the furtive creature to flee. Instead, it meets you with a savage snarl and engages you a vicious wrestling match!

Your opponent is tremendously strong for its size, and you are startled by its backward-jointed legs that kick up into your midriff with raking, claw-tipped strikes.

But this is not the time for curiosity. You are in a battle to overpower your writhing opponent before its kinsfolk come to its aid...

LEOPARD-MAN: Prowess - 8; Vitality - 7; Damage - 2.

If you lose or draw two attack rounds, turn immediately to 372.

If you win without losing or drawing two attack rounds, turn to 416.

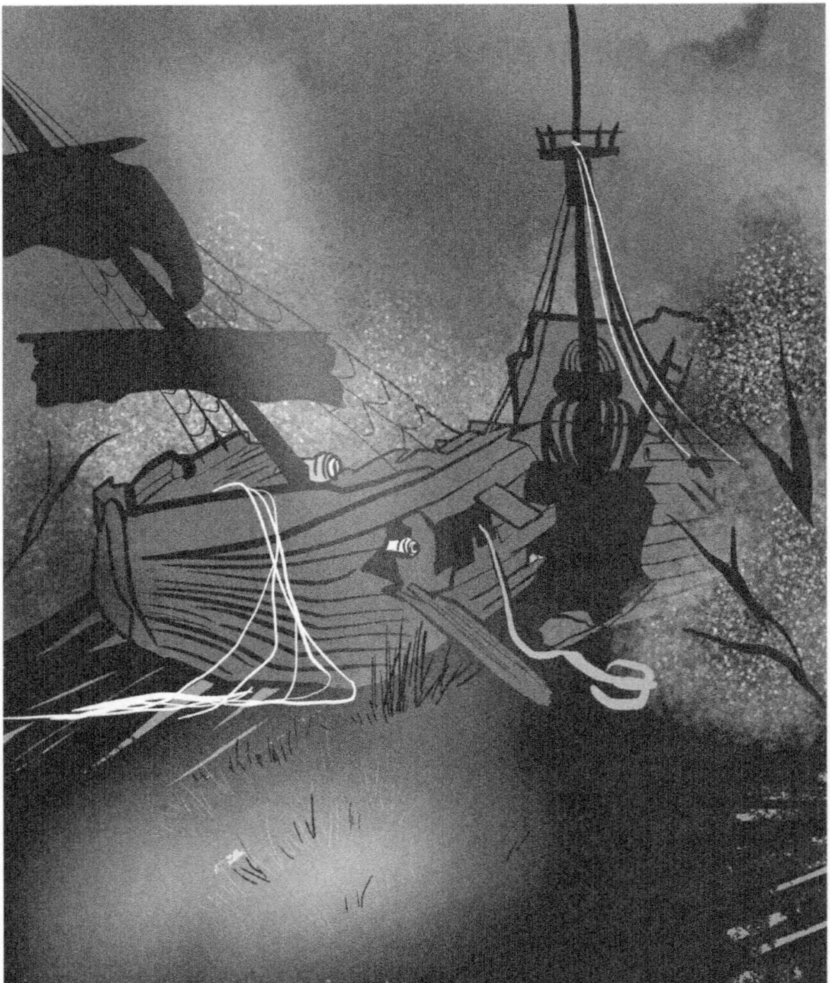

As you are pondering your predicament, you hear a tell-tale rustle in the dense vegetation and see the wide-eyed Satyr picking his way towards you, his injured arm bound up in a rudimentary, blood-stained sling. He represents a gleam of classical memory on the part of Doctor Moreau, being graced with a placid, bearded and intelligently ovine face, while his legs and hooves are bestial and satanic in form.

'Thank-you, lord, for helping me,' the Satyr bows, his voice straining at a pitch somewhere between the refined tones of a gentleman of Kent and a goat-like bleat. 'In return for your aid, I will guide you to a location in these woods that you may find of interest, if you will suffer my company for a little while?'

Seeing no reason to distrust the earnest little creature, you are led by a circumspect route through the tangle of thorns and gnarled branches to the tip of a v-shaped, tree-choked gully that widens like an inverted funnel as it descends towards the southern extremities of the island.

Lodged against the narrowing sides of the fissure are the rotting remains of an eighteenth-century frigate. Its bow looks to have been shattered in two by a tremendous impact and its mouldering masts lay flat across its partially collapsed deck like the limp antennae of a dead insect. You estimate the sea to be a mile away and in excess of a hundred yards of declination from this point...

'The earth heaves from time to time and the seas rise up in accord,' the Satyr comments listlessly. 'I myself have once seen such phenomenon, though nothing of the power that must have destroyed this vessel. Still, there may be one or two things of use within for one such as you. The broken ship is something of a known secret around here; humans have used it as a hideaway and meeting place multiple times over the years, or so I've heard.'

With that the Satyr wanders a little way off and begins to nibble at an outgrowth of tender leaves growing out of the gully.

239

Do you wish to take some time to search the shattered hull of the frigate? If so, turn to **536**.

If you would rather ask the Satyr to lead you away from the wreck and back towards the arena, turn to **489**.

292

When you look over the side of the derelict, you see that the dinghy has drifted too far away for you to reach. You have tarried too long aboard this ship of death! Desperately, you try to manoeuvre the merchantman, but its rudder is gone, and its sails are in tatters. As night falls, you hear the scratching of more ship rats, then perceive countless pairs of hungry eyes staring at you through the gloom. Whether you perish from thirst, or under a surge of furry bodies, there will soon be one more skeleton to grace the deck...

YOUR ADVENTURE ENDS HERE!

293

You sink no deeper than your knees and are strong enough to drive your way through the sand to the rocky shore of the ravine.

Gain 2 FATE points!

You see now that the delta is formed by the decelerating wash of an energetic geothermic stream that rushes down the deep, narrow ravine, the sides of which are thickly lined with trees and creepers. A little way up the ravine you locate a shallow alcove on the southern side of the stream that is both dry and defensible. You gather some rotting branches and scatter them in front of the alcove, trusting that any intruders will wake you with the noise of their approach. With the dark closing in, you pillow your head upon your pack and soon fall asleep.

Gain 3 VITALITY points.

When you awake it is still dark, but you sense something crouched beside you. Whatever it is, it must have been extremely stealthy to breach your makeshift barricade. Hardly daring to breathe, you keep very still, and the intruder begins to stir.

Then something soft, warm and moist passes across your hand, so that it takes all of your restraint not to react!

Do you wish to lash out at the intruder with your hand weapon? If so, turn to **262**.

If you would prefer to demand to know who is there, turn to **377**.

294

You haul yourself back out onto the path and watch as the alligator comes to a halt in the middle of the stretch of water, its unblinking eyes fixed upon you. While you have escaped danger, the items you threw remain on the opposite bank!

Unmoved by your curses, the great reptile sinks beneath the surface of the murky water. But you are not fooled. Now that it knows you are there, the alligator is unlikely to leave the area until it is sure that you have gone.

Do you wish to attempt to draw the alligator away from the stretch of water, then risk everything on a fast swim to the other side of the path? If so, turn to **117**.

If this sounds too risky, then you have little choice but to abandon your possessions and retrace your steps along the path (be sure to make a note of the loss of your equipment!).

Once you return to the entrance of the swamp, do you wish to follow its boundary north? (Turn to **155**).

Or south? (Turn to **279**).

295

Without access to your equipment, there is nothing you can do to prevent the reversion from completing. Within an hour the agony becomes unbearable, and you unleash a bestial roar that wakes the entire ship.

Within moments, armed sailors storm into your cabin, their faces twisting in horror when they see what you have become. The last thing you see is the barrel of a gun, then a merciful flash...

YOUR LIFE IS OVER!

296

When the MACAQUE-MAN hears that you are lost, he points towards the gap in the wall of rubble.

'Once you are in the clearing you may head east or west,' he explains. 'East will take you along a forest path to the beach where the Master's stronghold is located. West will take you through a tunnel down to the huts. It really is that simple!'

Now, if you wish to ask whether the Macaque-man wishes to trade, turn to **371**.

Alternatively, you can head straight for the gap in the wall of rubble by turning to **349**.

297

Alarmed, you move in the direction of the beach and peer through the trees. Standing halfway up the sand are a pair of male AFRICAN LIONS, one of which has the trembling body of the rabbit in its jaws!

The great felids are gangly and underfed, and you can only surmise that they are test animals which have managed to escape the clutches of the doctor. They sniff the air, fix their flashing green eyes upon you and advance with their bodies low to the ground...

Immediately, the Pugnatyr thunders past you with a deafening roar, seizes a lion in each arm and smashes them together. Startled, the cats scramble away, then circle the Pugnatyr on either side. The great ape is incredibly strong and possesses fangs the size of daggers, but you fear that the lions are hungry enough to try to bring him down.

If you wish to leave the creatures to their battle and flee deeper into the jungle, turn immediately to 507.

If you wish to help the Pugnatyr, then you may fire at the lions for as many combat rounds as you possess ammunition (and in this instance you may switch ranged weapons at any time) before engaging in close combat. If you cannot or do not wish to use a ranged weapon, then simply join the fight in close combat!

PUGNATYR: Prowess - 9; Vitality - 12; Damage - 3.

First LION: Prowess - 8; Vitality - 7; Damage - 2; Ranged Defence - 7.

Second LION: Prowess - 7; Vitality - 6; Damage - 2; Ranged Defence - 7.

Note: the lions will focus entirely on the Pugnatyr in this fight and will attack him simultaneously. You will be able to attack them, but if they roll a higher *close combat score*, then they have simply fended off your blows.

If the Pugnatyr is killed, then you must continue to fight the lions in close combat, unto death!

If you win, and the Pugnatyr is still alive, turn to 162.

If you win, but the Pugnatyr has been killed, turn to 462.

298

You recall reading that Silverbacks are naturally peaceful creatures, and that their charges against rivals are usually bluffs. Despite the terrifying sight of the great ape's glaring eyes, gleaming fangs and immense rippling shoulders, you manage to hold your ground. Just when you think you are doomed, the Pugnatyr veers away from you and thunders through the jungle, smashing small trees and hurling branches this way and that.

The furious beast makes several more half-hearted rushes at you, then looks you up and down before retreating to its den. The next thing you know, the Ape-man emerges from the bushes and tugs at your sleeve.

'This is good, good, good,' he chatters. 'You have shown your courage, five-fingered man! You may go north to the sea. Or west, towards the marshes. But I must stay with beast-friend. I must soothe his anger!'

Before moving over to the creature's den, the Ape-man reaches into a pocket and gives you a **prickly pear**. Add it to your *equipment list*.

Now, do you wish to head north through the jungle towards the sea? If so, turn to **439**.

If you would prefer to head west through the jungle towards the marshes, turn to **459**.

Alternatively, if you wish to join the Ape-man in approaching the Pugnatyr, turn to **7**.

299

You begin to push your way past the leaves of the flowering plants, careful to avoid the thorny trunks of the DEVIL PALMS. The scent of the blossoms soon becomes cloying, and you begin to feel the back of your throat itch and your breathing becoming laboured. The exposed skin of your face and arms is also beginning to redden and smart, and you realise that the leaves and flowers must be discharging some sort of poison...

Lose 2 VITALITY points!

Indeed, these innocent-looking BLOODROOT plants are notorious among the indigenous people of the south Pacific. In low densities, they induce respiratory and dermal irritation as a deterrent against animals that might eat them. But in over-colonised patches like the one into which you have wandered, the plants have evolved a way to kill unwary victims so that they might feed off the nutrients liberated by their decomposition...

As you feel your skin blister and lungs begin to burn, you must decide which way to run in order to escape this Bloodroot trap!

Do you wish to run back towards the swamp? If so, turn to 443.

If you would prefer to run in the direction you have been going, turn to 487.

300

As you walk deeper into the gorge the smell gets stronger, reminding you of the disagreeable odour of a monkey's ill-cleaned cage. Further on, you catch sight of the faint orange glow of burning torches, then the indistinct shapes of a series of crude, dark dens huddled against either side of the chasm walls. Beyond, you see the rock walls opening up again into dense, tangled jungle.

You hear a whisper of movement behind you and turn to see a small group of creatures following in your wake. The pair at the front are bent double with hunched and crooked backs; they appear to be tracking you in the manner of bloodhounds! The trio standing behind them have eyes of flashing green fire that are fixed on you with terrifying avidity.

And that is not all, for other shapes have begun to emerge from the makeshift dens. They are forming an amorphous, shadowy mass from which comes low grunts, growls and squawks; a hideous mob of inhumanity that defies clear identification. You are hopelessly trapped! The creatures press in on all sides, twisted hands pulling you this way and that. The double insult of fetid breath and malodorous flesh causes you to swoon...

'An Other, an Other...!' moan many voices, some deep chested and resonant, others high pitched and childlike. 'Take it to the Sayer, the Sayer! The Sayer of the Law!'

You are dragged into the largest of the huts and thrust onto a bench in a dim, dank corner. Your heart thumping in your chest, you stare at the shadows within shadows that are waiting in the hut...

Now turn to **350**.

301

After the men have entered the room, Montgomery throws himself into the reading chair while M'ling lays out the breakfast. It is a simple repast of bread, vegetables and coffee, but you notice a flask of whisky standing beside the pitcher of water. You also cannot help but stare at the manservant, noticing in surprise that his ears are small, pointed, and covered with a fine brown fur! Under your appraisal, M'ling becomes uneasy, his restless eyes darting this way and that.

'I will breakfast with you,' Montgomery says, staring at you closely and adding a healthy slug of whisky to his coffee. 'Moreau is too preoccupied with his work to join us, sadly, but he insisted that I see that you are well and without pain. He has been utterly pre-occupied of late, more so than you can know, engaged in truly heroic work. Anyway, you must eat. Help yourself, dear guest!'

You join Montgomery in the meal, enjoying the seep of energy into your weakened frame and the awakening of your senses to an intensity you cannot recall. Such acute sensations of sight, smell and sound leave you rather puzzled…

Is this the fresh appreciation of life that those who have come close to death oftentimes report? If so, then your ordeal upon the ocean may not have been in vain!

Gain 1 PROWESS point, 1 BALLISTICS point and 4 VITALITY points, even if these bonuses take you beyond your *initial* scores.

Once M'ling is satisfied that you need nothing else, he leaves you alone with Montgomery. You smile pleasantly, your eyes straying to the two large revolvers tucked into his belt.

What will you talk about?

If you have seen the pamphlet and wish to ask Montgomery about 'The Moreau Horrors', turn to 196.

If you wish to ask Montgomery about M'ling's ears, turn to 231.

If you wish to ask Montgomery what brought him to the island, turn to 318.

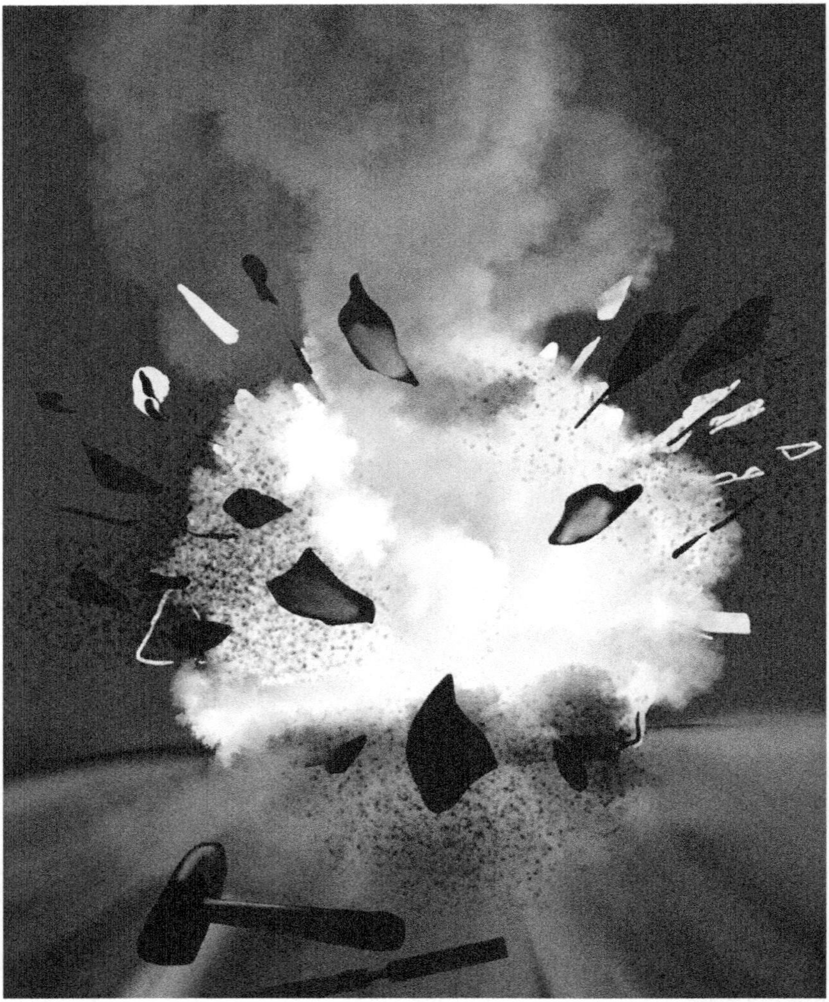

302

You set the coffer upon the ground, rest the point of the chisel on the faint line where the silver lid meets the tray, and strike down hard with the hammer. The tool pierces deep into the fine metalwork, springing the lid wide open and - to your astonishment - setting off a shower of bright red sparks!

The coffer has been lined with a fine layer of flint...but why? Then you see the fiendish intention: the coffer is not only crammed with a collection of silver coins and a single velvet bag, but also contains a deep bed of fine, black powder that is beginning to smoulder and catch...

Black powder?!

Too late, you hurl the coffer away from you as it disintegrates in an explosion of red flame, white smoke, and glittering shrapnel!

Roll a dice...

If you roll 1-4, turn to 529.

If you roll 5-6, turn to 192.

303

Try as you may, you do not have the strength to swim all the way to the beach. As you sink beneath the water, you wonder if your lifeless body will be washed up onto the beach, or if the creatures of the sea will devour you...

YOUR ADVENTURE ENDS HERE!

304

The moment you attempt to interfere in the fight, the Boar-men turn upon you in savage fury. They are utterly heedless of your pleas, and you have no choice but to fight them simultaneously!

First BOAR-MAN: Prowess - 7; Vitality - 9; Damage - 2.

Second BOAR-MAN: Prowess - 7; Vitality - 7; Damage - 2.

Note: whenever an opponent hits you, roll a dice. On the roll of a 6 you suffer 4 points of damage from the Boar-men's flashing tusks!

If you win, turn to **457**.

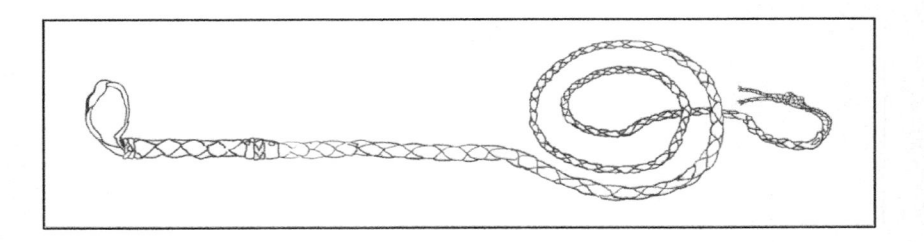

305

Try as you may, you find it impossible to keep your balance. With a shout of dismay, you slide rump first into the reeking guano!

Immediately, you scramble to your feet and stagger to the prow of the frigate, but you can already feel a hot throbbing in the many cuts and scrapes you have sustained.

Make a note that you have been *exposed to zoonotic infection*.

250

Cursing your misfortune and scraping the worst of the muck off on the timbers of the hull, you turn your attention to the items.

Turn to **420**.

306

To your relief, the water remains undisturbed and the moonlit beach shows no signs of life other than some furtive, scurrying shapes that you take to be large rabbits.

Just as you are beginning to fall asleep on your feet, you round a rocky headland by means of a frill of rock just below the surface of the ocean and catch sight of a glimmer of light in the distance - it is the enclosure!

The creeping light of the new day is soaking the sky by the time you pass the simple jetty harbouring the island boat, and it is with some trepidation that you begin to walk towards the buildings. Suddenly, the double gates of the outpost are flung wide, and you see Doctor Moreau, Montgomery and M'ling leading the pack of staghounds out onto the beach. The dogs immediately catch your scent and lurch against their collars in a frenzy of barking and growling.

Moreau restrains the beasts with a harsh command, stares at you for a few seconds, then leads the staghounds back into the enclosure, while Montgomery and M'ling advance toward you.

'Where the devil have you been?' Montgomery demands. 'We've been worried sick and were about to set out with the dogs to find you! Now get inside this instant, Moreau will want to have words!'

Your relief at being back among humans somewhat sullied by a flicker of dread, you enter the enclosure and let yourself in via the

251

small door leading to the room. It does not take long before you hear the inner door to the courtyard being unlocked, and the doctor strides in...

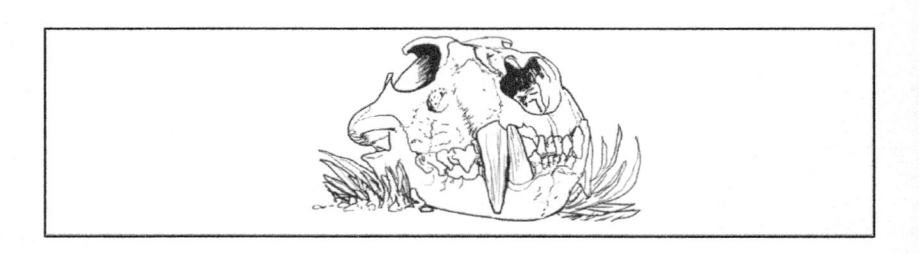

Turn to <u>39</u>.

307

You are forced onto your knees in front of the Sayer, who glares down at you through his veil of thick, grey hair.

'Evil are the punishments for those who do not say the Law,' he announces. 'Worst still are they for those who would tempt others into chasing or fighting them!'

'Are we not men?!' comes the dutiful chorus.

'Punishment is sharp and sure,' the Sayer nods, holding his shaggy arms out to his followers. 'Thus, what should I do with this Lawbreaker?'

'Use the brand, the brand!' the beast-folk chant. 'Let him be burned! Sear away the want that is bad! Purify him with pain!'

At these words you begin to struggle and protest, but the Sayer has one of his followers lash a gag across your mouth. Mumbling incoherently, all you can do is watch in mute horror as the Sayer disappears into one of the huts and re-emerges with a glowing iron held aloft in a cloth-bound claw.

Two strong brutes hold you fast while another stamps on your wrist to hold the back of your hand in position. Powerless to prevent this torture, you grit your teeth as the Sayer plunges the burning brand into your flesh...

Test your FATE!

If you are favoured, then the Sayer has selected your offhand to burn. Lose 2 VITALITY points and 1 PROWESS point.

If you are unfavoured, then it is your dominant hand that has been burned! You must lose 2 VITALITY points, 2 PROWESS points and 1 BALLISTICS point.

Your punishment complete, you are thrown into one of the smaller huts. It contains several rush-woven mattresses, a jug of water and a pile of fruit piled against the inner rock wall.

You take some time to eat and bath your burned hand (restore 4 VITALITY points), before stretching out on one of the beds and falling into a troubled sleep.

Now turn to 19.

308

The skeletons seem to have been stripped of all valuables, but you do find a serviceable **mariner's knife** tucked into one of the skeleton's waistbands. Keep the knife if you wish and note that it will cause 2 points of *close combat* damage.

Now, if you wish to swim for the dinghy, turn to 95.

If you wish to search below decks (if you have not already done so), turn to 91.

309

Try as you may, you simply do not have the speed to out-swim the alligator. The great predator clamps its jaws around your mid-section and drags you beneath the water in a froth of bubbles and a spurt of blood...

YOUR STRUGGLE IS AT AN END!

310

Your opponent has barely fallen when another arrow slashes by your face! The second hunter has heard the sounds of your combat and is striding towards you from the direction of the sea-side copse of palm trees, another shaft already poised to fire.

You must scoop up the dead man's **bow** (2 points of ranged damage), **quiver** (**5 arrows**) and **Toledo steel hunting knives** (these handsome weapons are forged from the finest Spanish steel and will add +1 to your *close combat score*) and defeat this second opponent!

Due to the hunter's steady advance from afar, each of you may perform FOUR ranged attacks, before close combat is joined (if both of you are still alive). Roll for both yourself and the hunter, with you going first.

LAZALO THE HUNTER: Prowess - 7; Ballistics - 8; Vitality - 8. Damage - 2/2; Ranged Defence - 7.

Note: Lazalo also possesses hunting knives that give him +1 to his *close combat score*.

If you win, turn to **343**.

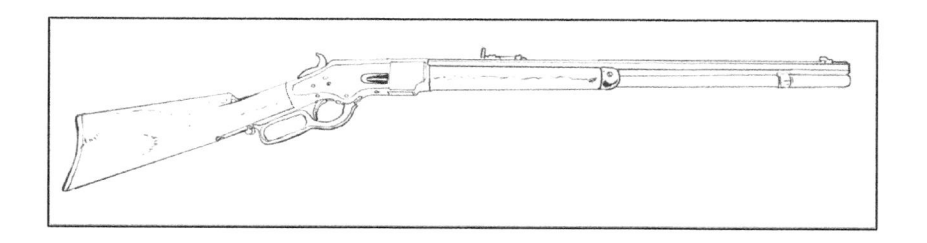

311

You roar at the thief to stop, shattering the tranquility of the pools and causing the bathers to erupt into chaos and confusion. Water froths and foams as the creatures shriek, yell and beat the surface of the pool in agitation. Then they turn on you, seizing your arms and forcing your head beneath the mineral soup!

You manage to break free and haul yourself out of the pool, but your adversaries surround you, beat you senseless and begin to drag you across the rocks. At first, you think yourself taken prisoner, but then you see that your captors are hauling you towards a boiling pool located at the highest point of the geothermic system. Scarcely able to believe what is happening, you give an indignant shout before you are hurled into the water and swiftly boiled alive...

YOUR ADVENTURE ENDS HERE!

312

The sailor slips as he swings the oar, unbalances and topples into the water!

Do you wish to attack the sailor in the water? If so, turn to **401**.

If you would rather attempt to swim past the sailor and take his place in the longboat, turn to **388**.

Alternatively, you can turn away from the longboat and make for the derelict merchantman (if you have not already done so)? Turn to **86**.

Otherwise you can strike out for the dinghy, by turning to **127**.

313

As you approach the trees, you catch glimpses of the glittering blue sea beyond, and a stretch of slate-grey beach washed by a gentle surf. The sounds of chopping grow louder, and when their steady rhythm stops you crouch low, fearful of discovery. To your relief, the sounds resume, and you work your way into the copse until you see the second hunter hacking at the trunk of a tall palm tree with a small hand axe.

If you want to get close to the hunter and attempt to kill him with a single, well-aimed ranged attack, turn to **363**.

If you would prefer to sneak past the man and take a look at the beach, turn to **437**.

Alternatively, you can retrace your steps and head back inland towards the source of the hot springs? (Turn to **261**).

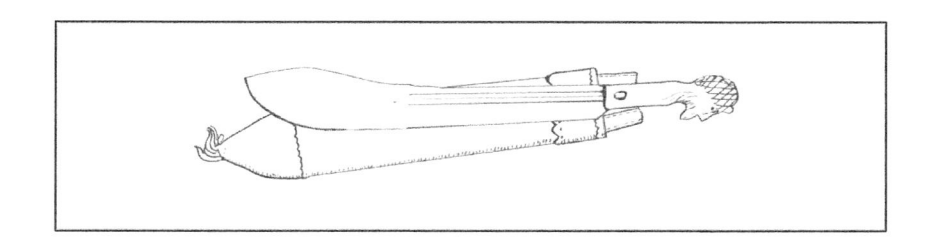

314

After you have killed the Bear-men, you take a moment to examine the thick, seam-like scars that mark areas of their anatomy and stand in pale contrast to the dense, dark pelts that adorn much of their flesh. The creatures' hands are huge and clumsy, with long, blunt claws in place of fingernails, while their feet are splayed and atavistic. A quick search reveals that they possess nothing of use.

It seems that M'ling and the white-swathed servants you have already seen are milder instances of whatever bizarre phenomenon is at work on Doctor Moreau's island. Quite how that eminent scientist has been able to provoke such bestial traits in living men is beyond your understanding, but you have a natural suspicion about the utility of such experimentation, as well as a dawning appreciation of how much danger you may be in.

Even so, you feel a steely determination kindle within your breast. If you are able to explore the island as thoroughly as possible, you may find some of the answers Montgomery felt it was your prerogative to seek. At the least, you can take steps to ensure that you are not the doctor's next test subject...

For now, you are concerned that more beast-men might have heard the sounds of the fight. As such, you decide that it would be wise to abandon the path.

With this in mind, do you wish to press north into the jungle? If so, turn to **514**.

If you would rather head south into the jungle, turn to **56**.

315

Your worse fears are realised when you hear the swirl of water and see an immense shape angling through the water towards you. At first you think it might be a whale, for it is a mottled grey colour and swims with a vertical rolling motion. Then you see a hideously twisted human face gasping for air.

Thinking it is a drowning man you cry out, but then you see that the face is somehow fused with a bloated maggot-like body that thrashes up and down in powerful propulsion. The monster glares at you with streaming eyes, then dives. Moments later, your canoe is smashed out of the water and you are sent cartwheeling through the air!

The DRACONOPE is one of Doctor Moreau's earliest and most reprehensible experiments. Tormented by unrelenting pain, it is a gibbering, shrieking monstrosity that lives only to unleash its rage upon the world. Upon land it is dangerous enough, but in the water it is deadly.

Remove all of your equipment and weapons as they are lost to the sea, with the exception of any knives or daggers that are belted around you waist, and any items that might fit into your pockets (such as keys, coins or phials).

Then, you must fight for your life!

DRACONOPE: Prowess - 10; Vitality - 12; Damage - 3.

If you are unarmed, subtract 2 from your *close combat score*. Even if you possess a weapon, you must subtract 2 from your *close combat score* while fighting in the water!

If the Draconope wins two rounds in succession, turn immediately to **456**.

If you are able to defeat the Draconope without losing two successive combat rounds, turn to **289**.

316

The keel of the *Ipecacuanha* stoves in the side of the dinghy and hurls you into the sea! You are caught in the churning wake of the vessel and are sucked into the depths. Ordinarily, you would have the strength and resolve to survive such an ordeal, but in your weakened state you drown amidst the debris of the little boat that offered you sanctuary for so many days...

YOUR TROUBLES ARE AT AN END!

317

You stare down at the bodies of the two men, scarcely able to believe the ends to which this island has led you.

You may take 8 more **arrows** from the dead men, as well as both pairs of **Toledo steel hunting knives** that will add +1 to your *close combat score*. One of the hunters also carries a wooden snuffbox full of a thick **pungent paste** that is for the treatment of wounds (you may use the paste twice to restore 2 VITALITY points at any time other than in combat).

Make a note of these additions to your *equipment list*, before deciding where to go next.

If you wish to head inland in the direction from which the hunters came, turn to **261**.

If you would rather head towards the line of trees to the south, turn to **21**.

Instead, you can return along the path through the coconut palms and take a canoe south (turn to **353**).

Or you can return along the path through the coconut palms, ignore the canoes and head south on foot, by turning to **285**.

318

Montgomery looks morose when you ask him about the circumstances of his arrival to the island.

'It was chance, pure chance,' he mutters. 'I have been blown here and there by forces beyond my reckoning. Just as you were at the mercy of the fates when you were set adrift in that rowing boat!'

Montgomery smiles humourlessly, his lower lip drooping.

'The difference is: while the vast infinite smiled on you when I pulled you from the water, so it has frowned on me for most of my life. Moreau, though, he is a gentleman and has always treated me well. He had the good grace to take me in when England offered me nothing but condemnation. How is it possible for a life to be ruined by a single hot-headed, ill-considered act? Can you tell me that?'

You are about to reply when you hear a commotion coming from the courtyard on the other side of the inner door.

Now turn to <u>227</u>.

319

After your twentieth day aboard the brig, you awake in the depths of night contorted with pain. With shaking hands, you light an oil lamp and stare in horror at the backs of your hands - they are sprouting with a silken down like that of an animal pelt, and your fingernails are becoming split with the tips of keen, keratinous claws...!

Surely, this is a nightmare?!

Yet the sense that your bones are about to crack is real, as is the inhuman groan you utter. Elongating canines cut your unaccustomed lip, and you clutch your head in your hands.

'*Hypnosis...*' you hear Moreau's deep, cultured voice within the depths of your mind. '*It is another branch of science in which I have gained a certain mastery. It allows me to lock the secret of your origin in a chamber in your mind, a secret that none other than you and I will ever know...*'

Ice-cold dread chills you to the core, for a moment distracting you from the pain.

Then the voice goes on:

'*The memory of my words will return only if you are to undergo REVERSION. Such shocking physiological alteration alone will unlock this knowledge, which you should regard as my parting gift, for if you are recalling this then I shall be dead or hopelessly* indisposed. No other explanation can have kept me from you. Only oblivion can have stopped me from preventing the onset of this unseemly stage...'

Your spine arches, then whiplashes convexly, forcing you to hunch like a demon. You see your legs are thickening, your bare feet curling over like claws. Remorseless, the subconscious utterings persist like a lecture given in a crypt.

'*Splendidly, you do not know what it is you are. This is accounted for by the fact that your brain is - with the exceptions of certain autonomic nervous regions that I saw fit to replace with more courageous feline and ursine extractions - that of a man.*'

Moreau sounds momentarily smug, a voice from the grave that is delighted with the transgressions it has wrought. But it swiftly regains its accustomed gravity:

'*Your mind belonged to a certain Mr. Edward Prendick, an amateur scientist cast adrift by the sinking of The Lady Vain. The memories you possess are his memories, real enough in their way: Prendick WAS rescued by Montgomery and taken aboard the Ipecacuanha; he DID meet Captain Davis and M'ling, and he DID find himself upon my island. But you are NOT Mr. Prendick. That unfortunate young man nearly died shortly after his arrival at the enclosure. His heart gave out, you see, a catastrophic failure precipitated by starvation, dehydration, and trauma, though I discovered massive scarring upon his cardiac tissue that likely came about as a result of scarlet fever suffered during adolescence...*'

'*Naturally, I was dismayed by the sudden demise of my guest, and Montgomery took it especially hard. Upon rushing Mr. Prendick into my laboratory, I saw that the only way to save him was to push the very limits of science and morality. Suffice to say, I viewed it as an excellent opportunity to test my hard-won expertise.*'

As was his way, you can hear that the doctor was warming to his subject the longer he spoke. His confession proceeds apace, shredding your equanimity with the harshness of unadulterated truth...

'*For a day and a night I worked ceaselessly, employing daring techniques of transplant, transfusion and resuscitation. I plundered my live specimens, grafting and cross-linking disparate parts of a cheetah, a black bear, a stag and a lion into Prendick's body, so that much of what he had been lived and breathed again. To Montgomery I disclosed little, maintaining the fiction that our guest had been revived and was simply convalescing. He had the good grace not to ask too many questions...*'

You can well believe that Montgomery – desperate for companionship – would not have wanted to know the truth of what Moreau had done to save Prendick's life. For years, Montgomery had had his choice of chimeric associates, but he had come to desire the company of a fully human friend; one who could acclimate him to decent society; one who could make him feel more like a man; one who might encourage him to return to the London he had loved so much. Alas that such hopes had been founded on a grievously ironic deception!

'*It has now been two months since Mr. Prendick came so close to death, and I am about to return you to the chair in which you were found unconscious. After I administer powerful restoratives, you will have no knowledge of your death or the changes I have wrought. You will be unaware of the passage of time, and Montgomery has agreed to conform to the pantomime that will not confound that impression.*'

'*I am confident that you will think you are a man, a guest upon my island. You will think that you are Mr. Edward Prendick, when you are in fact a subtle and beautiful BEAST-MAN, the crowning achievement of my life's work; a perfection of surgery, transfusions, splicings and grafts. Unscarred and indistinguishable from a true man, you are my magnum opus, my gift to the world...!'*

You thrash in a multiplicity of suffering, knowing in your soul that the voice you are recalling is a true echo of the past. If you revert, there is no knowing what influence the beasts that are a part of you will exert. Regardless, you are sure that what remains of who you thought you were will be no more...

Did the captain of the brig lock you up? If so, turn to **295**.

If you have remained free upon the brig, turn to **563**.

320

At these words, the men lower their bows and exchange glances.

'That is good,' says the hunter. 'It means that you can help us destroy the doctor as we destroyed this...*Aitu*.' He spits out this final word and kicks the reeking corpse of the Draconope with his foot. 'I am Lazalo, and this is my brother Vai.'

Wordlessly, Vai proceeds to inspect your hands, face and neck. Apparently satisfied, the hunter steps away.

'He checks you do not carry the marks of one of Soul-stealer's minions,' Lazalo explains, as he beckons you to walk with him. 'This is what we call your famous doctor, the cast of man your white-eyes admire above all others. You love strength and the mastery of numbers and letters far more than you despise domination and enslavement. My brother and I, however, we are not so lost. We see Moreau for what he is - a demon cloaked in the skin of a man; one who makes thralls of all those who feel the edge of his knives. He will never know peace; he will never feel the simple love of the

Earth's creations. That is why he must die; that is why we have sworn to kill him.'

Lazalo proceeds to explain that he and his brother are cousins of a man who once served the doctor as a labourer. When their kinsman learned of Moreau's experiments, he and several other Pacific Islanders in the doctor's pay sought to escape the island.

'But Moreau will do anything to protect his secrets,' Lazalo says. 'If you try to leave the island without his blessing, your life is forfeit. Soulstealer's minions killed our cousin and his companions, all save one. The survivor found his way to our island and told us of his ordeal. It took us many moons to find this place, and we have been waiting for a good omen to launch our attack. The killing of the Aitu is such a sign. Soon, we will seek out the doctor himself and avenge our kin.'

When you ask the hunters how the animal-folk and monsters of the island came to be made, both of them shake their heads darkly.

'Somehow, Moreau breaks borders between men and beasts,' they tell you. 'He throws the Mother's perfect order into chaos and disarray. It is the darkest sort of flesh-craft!'

The hunters then fall stubbornly silent, and you content yourself with following them back to their camp. After you have traversed a broad area of steaming fenland, you spy a large circle of raised ground that is strewn with immense boulders and set with a pair of lean-tos and several fire pits. It is a good location for a camp, benefiting from a steady onshore breeze that keeps the air clear of insects and geothermic fumes, as well as affording a fine view of the sea.

Once in the camp, the hunters offer you some medicinal paste for your wounds, a meal of some sun-dried fish, fresh fruit and a bowl of some sort of soaked grain.

Regain 6 VITALITY points.

Next, the men gift you a **bow** just like their own (2 points of ranged damage), a **quiver (10)** of brightly-fletched **arrows**, a coil of **rope**, enough food for **4 meals** and a pouch of crimson **blood leaves**.

Make these additions to your *equipment list*.

'If you need aid, the blood leaves will create red smoke when cast upon a fire,' Lazalo tells you. 'When we see the signal, we will come. It is our way of repaying the aid you have given us!'

Thanking the brothers for the gifts, you prepare to be on your way.

'You may walk south-east towards the heart of the island or take one of our canoes to explore the island's coast,' Lazalo says. 'The choice is yours.'

If you wish to head south-east towards the heart of the island, turn to **261**.

If you would prefer to take a canoe and explore the island's coast, turn to **396**.

321

The alligator is a fearsome foe, but at least you have a few moments to position yourself to strike at its eyes with your weapon!

ALLIGATOR: Prowess - 9; Vitality - 10; Damage - 2.

Note: you must deduct 2 from your *close combat score* while fighting in the water!

266

If you roll any doubles, you have found one of the creature's eyes and it will release you. Otherwise, you will be forced to fight to the death!

If you are released or win, turn to 356.

322

Throwing caution to the wind, you hold your breath and charge your enemies! There is still a considerable amount of hydrogen sulphide beneath you, and though it stings your eyes as it bubbles forth, much less of the poison is released by the pounding of your feet than you had feared.

Suddenly, there is the thwack of the crossbow discharging! Resolve the outcome of the attack against you, using the BALLISTICS skill of the Hyena-man leader (note that crossbow bolts will cause 3 points of damage if they hit).

After shooting, the creature pulls a bone knife from its waistband, while its friends brandish crude wooden clubs. You must fight these three opponents simultaneously!

HYENA-MAN LEADER: Prowess - 9; Ballistics - 8; Vitality - 10; Damage - 2/3.

First HYENA-MAN WARRIOR: Prowess - 8; Vitality - 8; Damage - 2.

Second HYENA-MAN WARRIOR: Prowess - 7; Vitality - 6; Damage - 2.

If you win, turn to 78.

323

You feel the mocking eyes of the Fox-woman upon you as you allow the ghastly contest to reach its end, averting your eyes when the bleating Satyr has his throat torn open in a gory spurt.

Lose 1 FATE point for leaving the harmless creature to his doom!

The crowd roars its approval and storms into the middle of the arena. There, they lift the blood-drenched Ocelot-man into the air and carry him into the jungle, their raucous hymns of victory receding into the distance. Meanwhile, the body of the Goat-man is kicked and spit upon by a few stragglers in a most pitiable and revolting fashion.

'Brutal, isn't it?' smiles the Fox-woman. 'But then what can men expect, when beasts such as we are given human form?'

She cackles maliciously as the Elephant-man drives away the last of the mob and hoists the body of the Satyr onto a shoulder. Then, the unlikely pair follow the hooting mob into the jungle.

Do you now wish to perform a quick search of the area? If so, turn to **87**.

If you would rather leave this place immediately, then you see two directions open to you:

Into the jungle towards the west? Turn to **199**.

Or into the jungle towards the east? Turn to **265**.

324

The pair of you press on north-west, where a canopy layer of palm leaves admits a dappled light that glitters on a profusion of immense fronds, choking creepers and flowering plants heavy with sweetly-scented blossom that buzzes and crawls with insects. Except for the incessant drone of countless gossamer wings, the pressing stillness beneath the canopy is broken only by the snap of twigs beneath your boots, or the occasional warbling cries of iridescent birds of paradise.

You walk for the best part of an hour, first ascending then following a gentle declination back towards the sea, before your companion picks up a faintly marked animal trail. After another hundred yards or so he freezes and points a drooping hand in the direction of a shadowy tangle of creepers and ferns.

At first you see nothing, but when your guide pulls a piece of fruit from his pocket and ambles towards a thicket, you see a black shadow resolve into an outline of hulking shoulders and a great domed head set with the close-set glimmer of jet-black, smouldering eyes. Then you hear a deep-throated grunt unlike any sound a man could make, and a huge, furry black hand enters a sunbeam as it takes the fruit from your guide. All the while, your Ape-man is making a series of propitiatory cackles and sycophantic gibes, his head bowed and shoulders dropped.

Suddenly, the grunts assume an interrogative huff, and the shining eyes fix on you with fierce intensity. Below the stare, a snarling muzzle draws back to reveal a pair of fangs the size of daggers. Then the undergrowth erupts as a raging mountain of muscle comes roaring towards you!

Though you have yet to travel to Africa, you have read enough illustrated books and visited a sufficient number of zoos and private menageries to recognise that the beast seems to be a cross between a man and a silverback gorilla in its prime.

The creature before you is a PUGNATYR, one of Doctor Moreau's earliest experiments!

Do you wish to fight the Pugnatyr? If so, turn to 542.

If you would rather attempt to flee the creature's wrath, turn to 549.

Otherwise you can simply stand your ground, by turning to 298.

325

Just as you are nearly at the top of the wall, a section of rubble gives way beneath your feet. As you fall, your hands and knees are dashed against the rocks, causing painful lacerations!

Lose 2 VITALITY points.

Cursing your misfortune and casting a filthy look at the wall, you decide to try to work your way around it. Just as you are about to do so, you see that the dislodged rocks have revealed a cavity in the wall in which you find a wax-sealed **purple phial** that is filled with a mysterious liquid and labelled with the number *83* (be sure to make a note of this number!).

Add the phial to your *equipment list*, then turn to **230**.

326

At the sound of the commotion, more sailors rush onto the deck and beat Montgomery and his assistant into submission until they are bleeding and bruised. As the defeated pair have their faces forced to the deck and their hands tied behind their backs, Montgomery shoots you a contemptuous look.

Note that you have *gained Montgomery's resentment*.

The two passengers are tied to the rear railings of the ship as Captain Davis lords it over them.

'This treatment of us will not stand, captain,' Montgomery spits. 'When the law hears of this, you'll never be permitted to sail again.'

'I'm already forbidden from taking to sea, you damn fool!' Davis leers. 'Why else do you think my rates are so low? Now, let's see how the two of you like spending the night up here with the beasts. Then, come the morning, I'll have decided what's next for you both, Sawbones and pet alike.'

The captain then spares you a bleary look and a wicked grin. 'Make friends, make enemies, but live like a man, my boy,' he sneers. 'Now, best scurry below deck, lest one of my men frightens you.'

Lose 1 FATE point for failing to help Montgomery!

Disheartened, you return to your cabin.

Turn to **406**.

327

As soon as you intervene, the snake releases its victim and lunges at you!

You and your allies must battle the python simultaneously (if you have already wounded the snake, make any adjustment to its VITALITY score). Note that the snake will focus its attention on you and that the Thylacine-men will get bonus attacks in which the python will simply fend them off if it rolls the higher *close combat score*:

GIANT PYTHON: Prowess - 9; Vitality - 15; Damage - 3.

First THYLACINE-MAN: Prowess - 8; Vitality - 8; Damage - 2.

Second THYLACINE-MAN: Prowess - 8; Vitality - 11; Damage - 2.

If you win, turn to **212**.

328

You stand still as Montgomery seizes the captain by his upper arms.

'I tell you for the last time, that man of mine is not to be ill-treated,' he insists.

'He's not a man, he's an ugly devil!' Davis spits, shrugging off Montgomery's hold. 'I can't stand him, and neither can my crew. Not you neither!'

The captain jabs Montgomery in the chest and the two men go down on the deck in a tangle of limbs and outpouring of invective. Seeing his master in danger, the misshapen man finds a sudden wild courage and leaps into the fight, only to be dragged off by two sailors, who he turns on with animal swiftness.

A vicious brawl erupts, and you must decide your place in it!

Will you:

Dive in to Montgomery's aid? (Turn to **37**).

Try and help the captain and the sailors? (Turn to **280**).

Stay out of it and hope for the best? (Turn to **326**).

329

You will need to *test your PROWESS* for your rucksack and each ranged weapon you possess, the results of which will determine whether you succeed in throwing each item over the stretch of water!

Note that you do not need to throw close combat weapons or small, water-proof objects: these can remain tucked into your belt (or be carried in your pockets) and will remain unaffected by the water. For your rucksack, however, you must add +1 to the test, to account for the object's size and bulk.

Whenever you pass the test, the item lands safely on the soft soil of the path ahead!

Whenever you fail the test, that item is forever lost in the depths of the swamp, and you must remove it from your *equipment list*! If you lose your rucksack, then everything in it will also be lost...

When you have dealt with your items, you take a deep, calming breath, slip into the water and strike out for the other side.

Turn to **362**.

330

You struggle to pull the spear out of the foot of the canoe where it is stowed and sustain multiple lacerations from the squid while you are distracted!

Lose 4 VITALITY points.

Once you finally have hold of the weapon, you find it almost impossible to use without tipping over the canoe and are almost relieved when a huge Humboldt squid lunges out of the water and tears it from your grip!

Remove the spear from your *equipment list* and prepare to battle the oceanic predators with your oar...

Turn to **166**.

331

The waters to either side of the path seem to grow darker and murkier as you work your way deeper into the swamp. Young, broad-based cypress trees start to rise from the water, their boughs sprouting fine, feathered leaves that gleam and drip with condensation.

So taken are you by the wetland flora, that you almost miss the narrow wooden walkway circling the base of one of the trees. It is supported by a dozen diagonal supports hammered into the trunk and gives access to a rusting iron chain that loops around the cypress before angling off into the depths of the swamp. A thick, mildewed plank acts as a makeshift bridge over a yard of water, connecting the path and the walkway.

Do you wish to venture out onto the walkway and try to see what lays at the end of the chain? If so, turn to **491**.

If you would rather ignore this anomaly and press on through the swamp, turn to **412**.

332

You charge towards the Draconope as the second hunter stands his ground and fires shaft after shaft at the onrushing beast!

He will be permitted THREE shots before the Draconope closes with him, which you must now resolve on his behalf:

DRACONOPE: Prowess - 10; Vitality - 8; Damage - 3; Ranged Defence - 12.

LAZALO THE HUNTER: Prowess - 7; Ballistics - 8; Vitality - 8; Damage - 2/2.

If the Draconope is still alive after these ranged attacks, then both you and the hunter must engage the monster in close combat. Your attack comes first, followed by the Draconope, then Lazalo. All of the monster's attacks will be directed at you! Remember that during Lazalo's bonus attacks, the Draconope will merely be able to fend him off if it rolls a higher *close combat score*.

Note: Lazalo wields a pair of **Toledo steel hunting knives** that give him +1 to his *close combat score*.

If you win, turn to <u>383</u>.

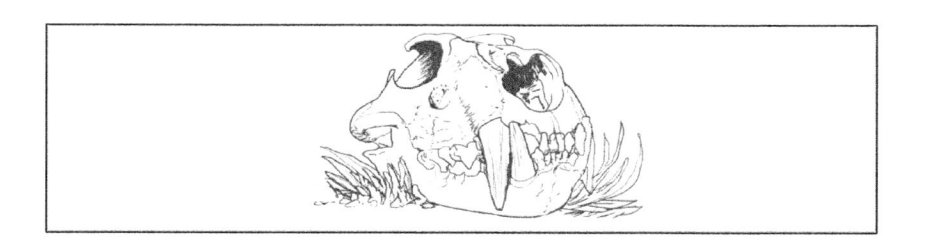

333

Knowing that going drunkenly into the night is tantamount to suicide, you rush past Montgomery and block his way to the door.

'Don't be a fool,' you urge. 'Moreau has just been killed, and your plan is to get drunk with the beast-folk? In such circumstances, even M'ling cannot be trusted - have you forgotten what he truly is?'

'I have not forgotten,' Montgomery retorts, his eye sockets blotches of black under his stubbly eyebrows and a dangerous edge creeping into his voice. 'He is my friend and takes his liquor better than anyone I know. Now get out of the way, my man.'

Will you get out of Montgomery's way?

If so, then you stand aside (turn to <u>53</u>).

If not, turn to <u>541</u>.

334

You begin to tire from the effort of swimming (lose 1 VITALITY point) but spot a piece of rigging hanging over the side of the derelict. It is brown and rotted, but it just might hold your weight!

To try to climb the rigging, turn to **546**.

Alternatively, if you have not already done so, you can strike out for the longboat (turn to **276**)?

Or swim for the dinghy (turn to **127**).

335

To your astonishment, you see about a dozen animal-folk emerging from a fringe of palm trees up ahead. Some are small and stunted, others are huge and musclebound, but all have in common the baleful green-fire stare of the nocturnal hunter, and the unmistakable mark of the beast!

Just as you beginning to think that the creatures are here to cut off your escape, you hear the Dog-man yelping an urgent message to them. This provokes a collective moan of horror from the mob, then yells of outrage. As one raucous mass, the animal-folk charge past you and engulf your pursuers! Wincing at the yelps of pain coming from the Wolf-men, you manage to catch up with your guide.

'Friends of mine,' the Dog-man pants, slowing to a brisk walk. 'They heard the hunting howls and came searching. Now they will punish the wicked ones. They will purify them with pain. It is good!'

After a few more hours' progress along the beach, the pair of you approach a rocky headland that appears impossible. But the Dog-man shows you a frill of rock just below the surface of the ocean that allows you to skirt around the promontory and reach the eastern beach where, by the swiftly spreading light of dawn, you catch sight of the enclosure once more! At the sight of the building your guide grows nervous and passes you a small brass key from his pocket.

'It once belonged to the Master,' he mumbles. 'Return it to him or keep it for yourself. My lord must decide!' (Add the **brass key** to you *equipment list*).

It is daylight by the time you pass the simple jetty harbouring the island boat, and it is with some trepidation that you approach the enclosure. Suddenly, the double gates of the outpost are flung wide, and you see Doctor Moreau, Montgomery and M'ling leading the pack of staghounds out onto the beach. The dogs immediately catch your scent and lurch against their collars in a frenzy of barking and growling. You look around for your Dog-man and are just quick enough to spot him fleeing into the jungle!

Moreau restrains his hounds with a harsh command, stares at you for a few seconds, then leads the animals back into the enclosure, while Montgomery and M'ling advance towards you.

'Where the devil have you been?' Montgomery demands. 'We've been worried sick and were about to set out with the dogs to find you! Now get inside this instant, Moreau will want to have words!'

Your relief at being back among humans sullied by a flicker of dread, you enter the enclosure and let yourself in via the small door leading to your room. It does not take long before you hear the inner door to the courtyard being unlocked, and the doctor strides in...

Turn to 39.

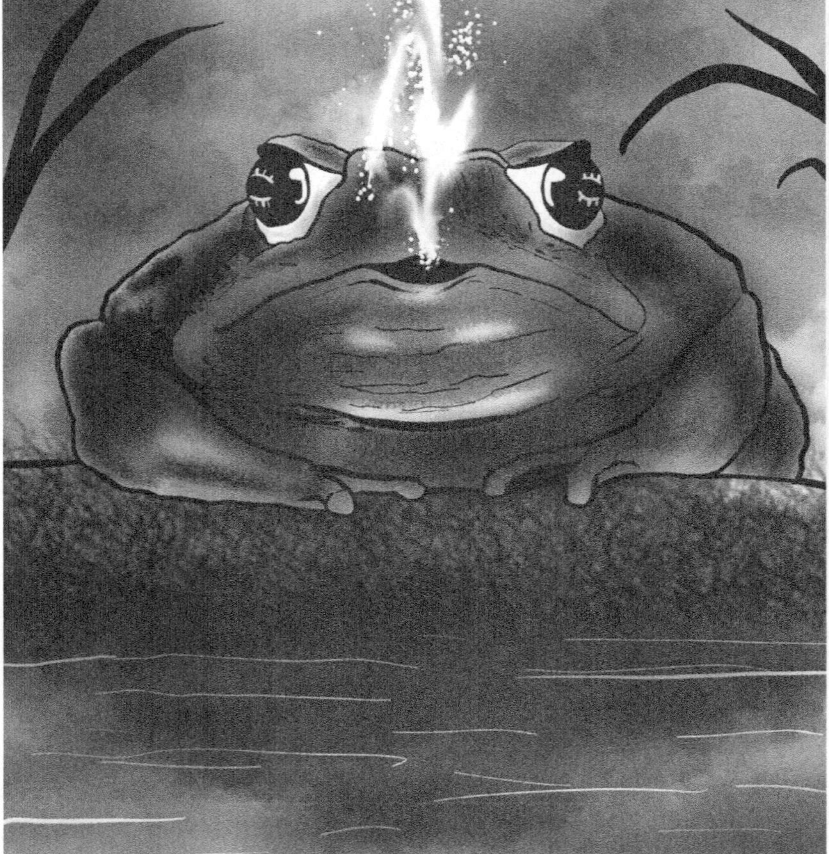

336

As you creep forward, the cane toad fixes you with a baleful, golden-eyed stare, stock still except for a steady working of its throat. Then, the creature puffs a cone of misty fluid into your face!

Immediately, you scramble back and begin to retch and gasp (lose 2 VITALITY points!).

Coating your arrows and weapons in toad poison is going to be more difficult than you thought...

If you wish to press on with your plan to seize hold of the creature, turn to **428**.

If you would rather leave the spitting toad well alone and press on towards the west, turn to **493**.

337

You manage to get your back to a sturdy mahogany tree with a clear field of fire to your front. It is a wise precaution, for the LEOPARD-FOLK HANDLERS release their charges, which you now see are not hunting dogs at all, but a pair of powerful jungle cats. With extraordinary speed, the LEOPARDS and the LEOPARD-MAN you initially spied come bounding into the clearing, their fierce eyes blazing!

You have time for THREE ranged attacks before you must fight these opponents simultaneously:

LEOPARD-MAN: Prowess - 8; Vitality - 7; Ranged Defence - 8; Damage - 2.

First LEOPARD: Prowess - 8; Vitality - 10; Ranged Defence - 9; Damage - 2.

Second LEOPARD: Prowess - 7; Vitality - 9; Ranged Defence - 8; Damage - 2.

If you win, turn to **252**.

338

You lock arms with the Boar-man, your feet ploughing deep furrows in the soil as you are forced back by the power of the creature's charge.

Test your PROWESS!

If you succeed, turn to **268**.

If you fail, turn to **379**.

339

Try as you may, you cannot find the strength to hold on! You plummet the final fifteen yards of the descent, dash your head against the rock face and lose consciousness...

Lose 2 VITALITY points!

Even in your senseless state, you know that you are not safe. From somewhere, a voice screams at you to wake. Is it your inner voice exhorting you to survive? If so, it is unlike any figment of sub-consciousness you have ever known, for it brays and whoops with a bestial, inhuman edge that drags you out of darkness to face the nauseating dizziness from the effects of the fall.

As you come around, you realise that you are being carried deeper into the chasm by a gang of brutish, sharp-fingered, malodorous things whose acrid smell mingles with the wider miasma of the place. Reluctantly, you open your eyes and discern the orange glow of a few dimly-burning torches. They reveal a series of crude, dark dens lining the walls of a narrow lava passage. All around you are chimeric man-beasts, creatures crafted by Doctor Moreau's peerless art.

Other shapes and forms are emerging from the dens. Some are towering and powerful, others are dappled and swift, while a number seem little more than hunched, ill-gotten children. All of them crush together within the narrow confines of the chasm, pressing together until they become an amorphous, shadowy, impossible mass. Your blood turns to ice as twisted hands grasp at you; fetid breath and malodorous bodies accompany sounds of wonder and awe.

'An Other, an Other...!' moan countless discordant voices of shocking singularity and pitch. 'Take it to the Sayer, the Sayer! The Sayer of the Law!'

You are half-dragged and half-carried to the largest of the huts, and unceremoniously shoved within. A hulking brute follows you inside and thrusts you into a dank corner of the abode.

Your heart thumping in your chest, you stare at the shadows within shadows that are waiting in the hut...

Now turn to 350.

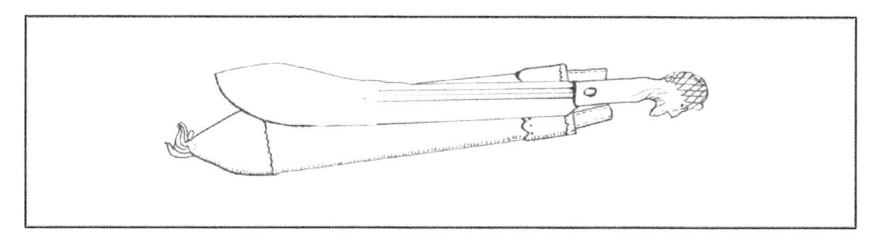

340

You manage to curl both hands over the side of canoe and cling on for dear life. The grip of the quicksand is incredibly strong, but at least you are able to prevent yourself from sinking deeper.

That is, for as long as your strength holds out...

Do you wish to try pulling yourself into the canoe? If so, turn to **10**.

If you would prefer to risk calling out for help, turn to **65**.

341

Have you *won Montgomery's trust?* If so, turn to **167**.

If not, turn to **123**.

342

You conclude that pressing on into this part of the jungle will only waste time and earn you more cuts and bruises, so you decide to head back towards the arena.

Once back in the meadow, you set off into the tree line towards the west.

Turn to **199**.

343

You stare down at the bodies of the two men, scarcely able to believe the ends to which this island has led you.

You may retrieve any items previously lost to the hunters, and take **5** more **arrows** from Lazalo, as well as his extra pair of hunting knives if you wish. As well as this, the camp contains some sun-dried fish, fresh fruit and a large earthenware bowl of some sort of soaked grain. You may eat this and gain 4 VITALITY points and take enough food with you for **5 meals**.

You also find a wooden snuffbox full of a thick **pungent paste** that is for the treatment of wounds (you may use the paste twice to restore 2 VITALITY points at any time other than in combat). Make a note of all these additions to your *equipment list*.

After resting for a little while, you must decide where to go next:

Do you wish to head towards the sea through the copse of trees towards the west? If so, turn to <u>348</u>.

If you would rather head back inland towards the source of the hot springs, turn to <u>261</u>.

344

You strike a death blow and leap back as the Crocodile-man thrashes this way and that. With the last command of its reptilian body, it hooks its claws into the body of the Lizard-man and drags him into the swamp…

You stare at the rippling water, wondering at the source of the hatred that existed between these two beings. Consoled by the thought that you are now free to escape the swamp, you make your way up the muddy trail and enter the jungle once more.

Turn to <u>395</u>.

345

Remembering what the Macaque-man said to you, you take the wind-cutter from your belt and begin to whirl it through the air. The instrument sets forth an extraordinary wailing moan that causes the advancing beast-folk to stop in their tracks. Gaining heart, you vary the speed of revolutions and broadcast a sequence of sounds that resemble other-worldly lamentations. Unnerved, the beast-folk turn tail and slink back into the jungle!

Gain 2 FATE points!

Just as you feel you can whirl the device no longer, the troupe of Macaque-folk - now armed with sharpened sticks - emerge from the tree line to the north. As they approach, their leader scurries forth, raises a bushy eyebrow at your dishevelled state and casts his gimlet eyes over the ashen remains of the enclosure.

When you explain what has happened and your pressing need to find a way off of the island, the Macaque-man nods sagely.

'It was always likely to end thus, though it saddens me to see such aimless devastation,' he says. 'Still, we must have faith that these events were ordained and have their place. Indeed, the arrival of the dead ones in their boat may well have foreshadowed this dire turn of events. Follow us for a little while, young Master, and you will see of what it is I speak...'

At that, the troupe escorts you north and then west along the strip of beach, all the while keeping their spears angled toward the jungle. The Macaque-folk are tireless and in time you find yourself looking up once more towards the steaming and smoking Heart of the island. There, from a tangle of dense vegetation, the creatures pull clear a little schooner with a square flaxen sail.

Within it are the desiccated remains of two dead men, one of whom is tall, red-haired and wearing a white cap. *Captain Davis?* you whisper, before realising that that obnoxious drunk could not have been cast adrift to perish within the few days you have been upon the island. But then you see that the little boat is indeed the one you saw attached to the *Ipecacuanha*...

'They died so that you may live, the victims of shipwreck or mutiny, no doubt,' the Macaque-man leader says, interrupting your growing unease. 'You may take the vessel and begone from this place. But first, we will furnish you with the supplies you need.'

Several of the creatures have already begun the long hike up to the geothermic pools. When they return laden with water-skins, sacks of dried fish and fresh fruit, the other creatures have removed the human remains and buried them in the sand.

Once the boat is loaded, the Macaque-folk carry it into the surf, and you climb aboard. Angling the sail to catch the wind, you steady yourself as the schooner lurches forth, then call your heart-felt thanks to your benefactors.

Soon, you have negotiated the offshore breakers and are heading out into open sea once more...

Turn to **370**.

346

The Lizard-man hisses in approval and its eyes gleam.

'A weapon slaked in the blood of our enemy is a suitable gift,' it says, retrieving the weapon from the ground and passing it to you. 'It is made from the heartwood of the ebony tree; this makes it strong yet pliable. The mouth-knives of the white shark that adorn it are deeply embedded, then reinforced with the resin of the calypso shrub. It will not fail you in battle.'

You heft the weapon, surprised by its weight and reach. The **ebony halberd** is a fearsome close combat weapon that is rather difficult to wield. Hence, every time you perform a successful hit with it, you must roll a dice:

If you roll 2-6, you will cause 4 points of damage, but if you roll a 1, you will cause no damage at all as you overswing! Unusually for a close combat weapon, it will also cause double damage if you roll a double when deciding your *close combat score* (assuming that the total of this value exceeds the total of your opponent's *close combat score*). Thus, it is possible to cause 8 points of damage with the ebony halberd in a single round. A further successful FATE test will take this to 16 points of damage!

'My final gift is...a warning,' the Lizard-man says as you prepare to bid him farewell. 'Leave this island, adventurer, as soon as you may. The Master has unleashed forces he cannot hope to control. Death will come to him sooner than he knows, but you need not share his doom.'

The Lizard-man glances darkly at the broken body of the Crocodile-man, then strides back into the swamp with the monitor lizards scrambling in his wake. You watch the creatures disappear into the mist, then make your way up the trail that leads into the jungle once more.

Turn to **395**.

347

You hear a distant shout from the beach as one of the figures sees you waving; you pray that Montgomery and the white-haired man are not heartless enough to ignore you now that others have seen your plight…

Just as the intensity of the tropical sun begins to burn your skin, you see the island boat launch from the beach and tack towards you. Weeping with relief, you snatch at the rope that is thrown to you and are pulled to the side of the boat where you climb aboard via a rough rope ladder.

You land on the floor of the boat with a thud, and the boat describes a sharp turn to return to the beach.

Gain 1 FATE point and turn to 75.

348

As you pass through the trees, you see a freshly felled palm tree with a **hand axe** buried in its bark.

Take the weapon if you wish (it causes 2 points of *close combat damage*) before advancing onto a stretch of slate-grey beach washed by a gentle surf.

Turn to 473.

349

You pass through the gap in the wall of rubble to find that it surrounds a patch of ground that is covered with a pale sulphurous incrustation that leaks tendrils of acrid white smoke. To your right is a dark tunnel descending steeply into the earth, and to your left is a path leading eastward through the jungle which you guess will lead you back towards the eastern beach from where you first set out.

If you wish to take the jungle path towards the east, turn to 60.

If you would rather explore the tunnel, turn to 476.

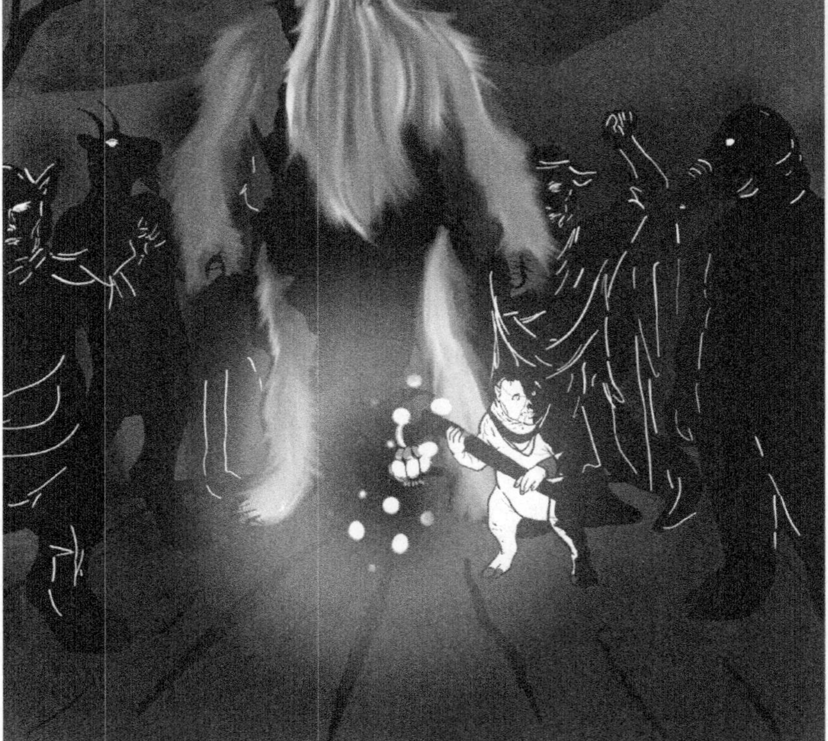

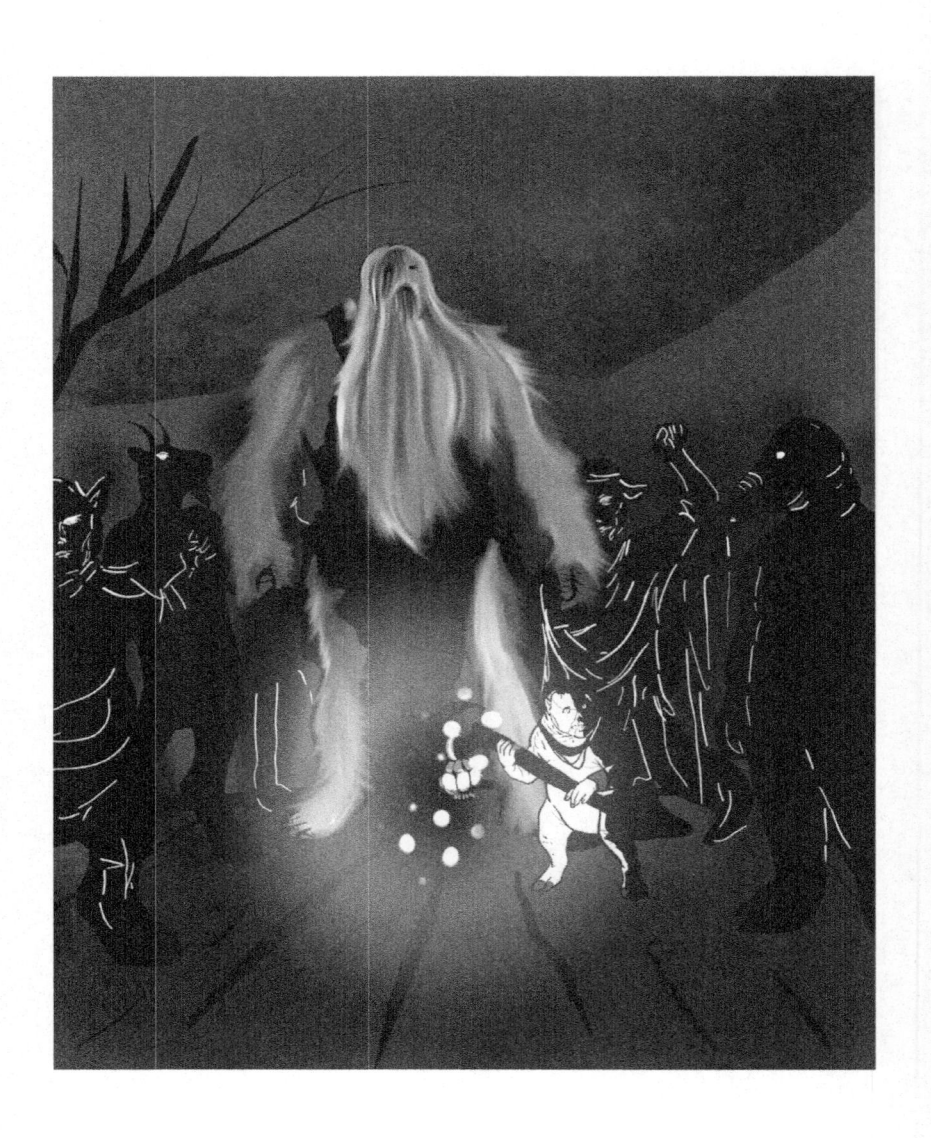

350

As you sit there in the darkness, something cold touches your hand, causing you to start violently.

'It cannot perceive things in the night, you see?' squeaks a voice from beside you. 'Neither scent nor sight will avail it. Just like our five-fingered man, it requires the light of fire to see!'

At these words, a slouching shadow leaves the hut and returns with a lantern that casts an infernal glow on the monstrous forms around you. The thing that spoke is a small, pinkish thing, looking more like a flayed child than anything else in the world. It has the mild but repulsive features of a sloth, but quick, cunning eyes that sparkle with intelligence. There are perhaps another dozen hulking brutes arranged around the semicircular hut - none of them known to you - and a figure opposite that is the size of a large man, yet covered from head to foot in dull grey hair, like a Skye terrier.

'Show me your hands,' it says thickly, leaning forward.

When you oblige, the thing puts out a strangely distorted talon and grips your fingers so that you almost yell in surprise and pain. His face looms closer and you see with disgust that it is neither the face of a man nor beast, but a mere shock of grey hair with three shadowy over-archings to mark the eyes and mouth.

'You have five fingers and little nails,' the grisly creature says. 'It is well, but still you must learn the Law.'

The creature releases you and leans back.

'I am the Sayer of the Law. Here come all that be new, to learn the Law. I sit in darkness and say the Law.'

'None escape,' says one of the beast-folk, glancing around furtively.

'None escape!' come the many blurted responses of the gargoyles around you. 'Evil are the punishments for those who break the Law...none escape!'

'For everyone there is the want that is bad,' continues the Sayer, nodding sagely. 'What you will want, we do not know; but in time, we shall. Some want to follow things that move, some wish to kill and bite, to suck the rich, warm blood; others go tearing with teeth and hands into the roots of things, snuffing into the earth. It is bad.'

'None escape!' come the voices.

'Some go clawing trees, some go scratching at the graves of the dead; some go fighting with heads or teeth or claws; some love uncleanliness.' The Sayer shakes his head sadly. 'Punishment is sharp and sure. Therefore, learn the Law. Therefore, say the words: Not to go on all fours, that is the Law...'

'Say the words!' pipes the little Sloth-man, the figures around you echoing this command in threatening tones.

Do you wish to say the words?

If so, turn to **226**.

If not, turn to **508**.

351

You watch as the white-haired man, Montgomery, his crook-backed assistant and several sailors load the animals into a large boat that lays under the lee of the schooner. Then the boat pushes off, catches the breeze in its sails and moves swiftly away towards the island.

Aboard the *Ipecacuanha*, all hands take to the rigging. The sails flutter, then belly out with the rumble of canvas, and you start to move away from the island.

'Right, boy, you can start off by swabbing the deck of all this filth,' the captain crows, tossing a scrubbing brush in your direction. 'You'll soon learn that I'm king here, and that the rest of my lads are great lords. Obey our every word, and you might live long enough to see our next port!'

Staring down at the vegetable and animal waste smeared all over the deck, you are already beginning to rethink your decision. The animals and crook-backed servant you have seen have piqued your interest, and you know that to remain on the *Ipecacuanha* will bring you tremendous hardship and despair, at best...

Despite these misgivings, do you wish to remain on the schooner? If so, turn to **562**.

If you would rather grab an empty rum barrel and leap over the side of the ship in the hope that you can make it to the island, turn to **480**.

352

The uneven floor of the forest is treacherous in the gloom and your flight is brought to a halt when you twist your ankle and are sent sprawling...!

Lose 2 VITALITY points.

Unable to put your full weight on your left foot, you struggle upright and turn to face the pursuing monster. When the Draconope sees you, it shrieks in delight and lurches towards you...

You may perform THREE ranged attacks before fighting this hideous foe!

DRACONOPE: Prowess - 10; Vitality - 12; Damage - 3; Ranged Defence - 12.

If the Draconope wins three rounds in succession, turn to **456**.

If you are able to defeat the Draconope without losing three successive attack rounds, turn to **411**.

353

You drag the canoe into the sea, seize the paddle and haul yourself into the seat. The vessel is light and extremely maneuverable, and although it takes you a little while to get accustomed to the motion of the sea and the most efficient use of the oar, you are soon paddling along at a steady pace and enjoying the gentle swell.

It is then that you notice the rapidly lengthening shadows and the swift alteration in the tropical light. The day is growing old, and nightfall is less than an hour or two away.

Not too far ahead, you notice a small delta exiting onto the beach. It is issuing from a steep, narrow ravine the banks of which are infested with livid mosses, fungi, and small, twisted trees with claw-like branches tangled with creepers that seem to weep into the narrow channel of water below.

Beyond the ravine the island ascends from a lengthy strip of silver-white sand through layers of lush lowland reeds and deep jungle that is crowned by a rounded summit of fertile meadow punctuated by occasional outcroppings of glassy black rock and jagged iron-grey stone.

Do you wish to come ashore on this delta, drag your canoe into the ravine and prepare to make a camp? If so, turn to 422.

Alternatively, you can press on for a little while before camping out on the beach by turning to 242.

354

There is a stunned silence at your words, then a ripple of throaty growls that swiftly become a dreadful chorus of snarls.

'Gods, man...what have you done?' Montgomery moans, emerging from his stupor. 'The Law alone keeps the beast-folk from indulging the cravings of their animal natures. It alone keeps the meat-eaters ignorant of their taste for blood!'

The circle of creatures closes in, a ring of faces as savage as one might see if hemmed in by a pride of hungry lions or a pack of starving wolves. You realise that you are moments away from being torn to shreds...

Do you possess the **Restored Dragon**? If so, turn to the section that is the same as the number etched on the side of its barrel.

If not, do you possess the **carbine**? If so, turn to the section that is the same as the number etched on the side of its barrel.

If you have neither of these weapons, turn to 458.

355

You cling on grimly until you have choked the hunter into unconsciousness!

Releasing your hold, you use some garments lying around the camp to tie and gag the man, before dragging him into one of the lean-tos where you may retrieve any items previously lost to the hunters. You may also take the hunter's **Toledo steel hunting knives**. These handsome weapons are forged from the finest Spanish steel and will add +1 to your *close combat score*. You may also take the man's **bow** (2 points of ranged damage) and **quiver of arrows** (7).

Gain 2 FATE points for dealing with the hunter in a humane fashion!

As well as these items, the camp contains some sun-dried fish, fresh fruit and a large earthenware bowl of some sort of soaked grain. You may eat this and gain 4 VITALITY points and take enough food with you for **5 meals**. You also find a wooden snuffbox full of a thick **pungent paste** that is for the treatment of wounds. You may use the paste twice to restore 2 VITALITY points at any time other than in combat.

Make a note of all these additions to your *equipment list*, then decide what to do next:

If you wish to head towards the sea through the copse of trees towards the west where the sounds of wood chopping can still be heard, turn to **313**.

If you would rather head back inland towards the source of the hot springs, turn to **261**.

356

As you kick for the furthest bank, you see yet another of the reptilians bearing down on your flank - it is one of the alligator's brood-mates, a little smaller in size but still powerful enough to crush you with a single bite!

You swim madly as the alligator thrashes its tail and puts on a spurt of speed, it jaws gaping in anticipation...

Test your VITALITY with four dice:

If the total is less than or equal to your current vitality, turn to 275.

If the total is greater than your current vitality, turn to 309.

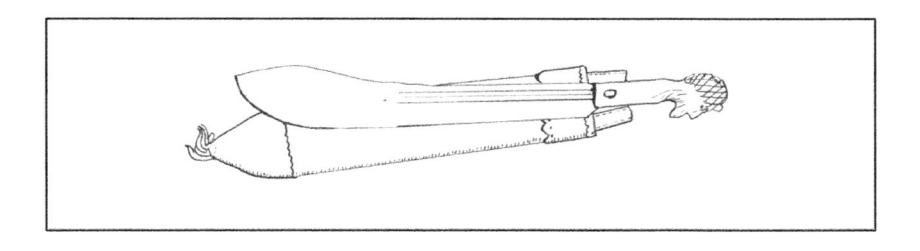

357

Without Moreau's pocketbook, you do not know how to prevent yourself from reverting, but you may have collected the items needed to do so!

Any items associated with numbers may be used to try to stop the reversion. They may be used singly, or in association with other items. Simply turn to the section number associated with the item to see if you have succeeded.

If you wish to use more than one item, then add the values together before turning to the corresponding section.

If the section you turn to makes no sense, then you have failed to stop yourself from reverting. Within an hour the agony becomes unbearable, and you unleash a bestial roar that wakes the entire ship. Within moments, armed sailors storm into your cabin, their faces twisting in horror when they see what you have become. The last thing you see is the barrel of a gun, then a merciful flash...

YOUR LIFE IS OVER!

358

As soon as the thunder of your firearm rends the night, the WOLF-MAN charging you scrabbles to a halt and flees back into the jungle!

Gain 1 FATE point.

You turn to the aid of the Dog-man, but see that his opponent has also fled, leaving the two of you alone in the clearing.

'The Master's wrath is good, the Master's wrath is great!' your guide yelps into the night. 'None escape the fire that breaks and burns - none escape!'

Confident that the Wolf-men will trouble you no more that night, you wait for your companion to finish his vaunting before the pair of you continue on your way.

Turn to **460**.

359

The oar glances painfully off the top of your head (lose 2 VITALITY points), and the sailor raises it for another strike. Thinking better of trying to force your way onto the longboat, you release the rail and watch the vessel pull smoothly away.

You must now consider your other options!

If you wish to swim towards the derelict (if you have not already done so), turn to **86**.

If you would prefer to strike out towards the dinghy, turn to **127**.

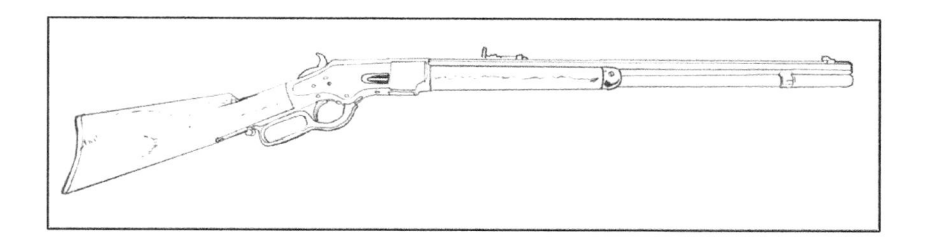

360

You inflict a nasty gash on the Ocelot-man's arm, send his weapon spinning through the air and hack your falchion through his slender neck, killing him instantly.

The crowd roars its approval, storms into the middle of the arena and lifts you into the air where you are paraded around the circle of sand like a great champion. Meanwhile, the bloodied body of the Ocelot-man is kicked and spit upon in a most pitiable and revolting fashion.

'Enough!' bellows the Elephant-man. 'Let our guest down and prepare your victor's gifts!'

The mob do as they are bid and begin to push items into your hands. Most of the gifts are useless baubles, or pieces of grubby sun-dried vegetable matter you would only consider eating in the most desperate of circumstances, but you receive some pieces of fruit and a handful of fresh brazil nuts that are sufficient for **2 meals**. You are also given a serviceable **long-bow** with a quiver of **10 arrows** (this weapon will cause 2 points of ranged damage), a small **iron dagger** (2 points of close combat damage), and a tarnished silver coin from Spain known as a **piece of eight**. You may also keep the **falchion** if you wish.

When this ceremony is done, the Elephant-man drapes the body of the Ocelot-man over one shoulder, proffers you a mocking salute, and leads the hooting mob into the jungle to the south.

'Congratulations on your victory, my lord,' the Fox-woman says with a grotesque curtsey. 'You saw that your opponent would offer you no quarter and gave him none in return, killing him quickly and cleanly. As such, I am feeling generous and will tell you this: go east from here and seek the broken ship. There are objects within that may prove useful.'

With that, the Fox-woman leaves you alone once more.

Next, do you wish to perform a quick search of the area? If so, turn to **87**.

If you would rather leave this place immediately, then you may decide from two directions:

Into the jungle towards the west? Turn to **199**.

Or into the jungle towards the east? Turn to **265**.

361

As soon as you hurl the meal into the water, a large number of the squid converge on it in a wild mass, great parrot-like beaks snapping at the ocean's surface. Remove a single **meal** from you inventory. But you will need to use two more meals for the Humboldts to be sufficiently distracted for you to escape towards the beach...

If you have this many more meals available, and wish to use them in this way, then you throw them out as far as you can (remove 2 more meals from your *equipment list*), before paddling for the safety of the beach. Turn to 82.

If you do not have two meals available, or you do not wish to use them in this way, then you have little choice but to battle the creatures with your oar! Turn to 166.

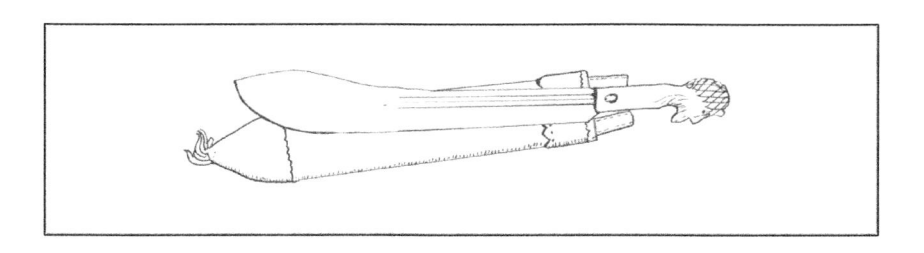

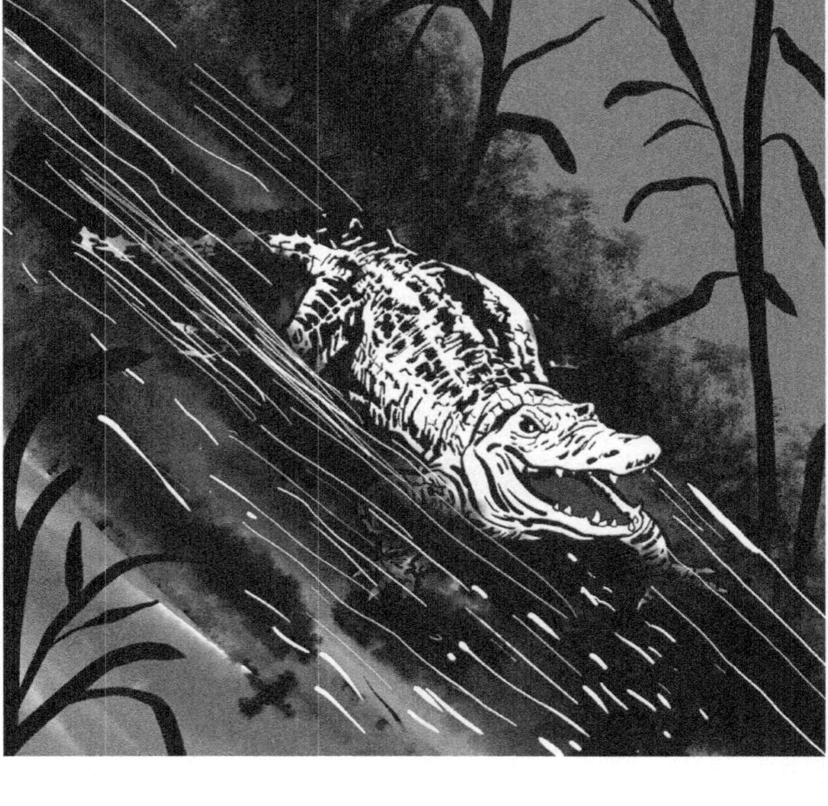

362

As soon as you enter the swamp, you hear a loud splash and see an armoured reptilian creature speeding towards you. The ALLIGATOR must have been waiting for you to enter the water before launching its ambush!

Do you wish to swim hard for the farthest bank? If so, turn to 237.

If you would prefer to immediately haul yourself back out of the swamp, turn to 294.

Alternatively, you can draw a knife or dagger (if you have one) and prepare to fight the creature? To do this, turn to 321.

363

You get to within ten paces of the hunter and aim your ranged weapon at the man's glistening back…

Test your BALLISTICS, adjusting with -4 to represent the ease of the shot.

If you pass, turn to 404.

If you fail, turn to 429.

364

Rung over rung, you haul yourself up about a third of the length of the ladder before the beast-men begin climbing in pursuit. As the creatures stack up beneath you, you realise that the ladder was never meant to sustain this sort of weight!

You hear the fibres begin to snap and unravel, then the ladder breaks...

Fortunately, your fall is somewhat broken by the creatures upon whom you land, but you must still lose 5 VITALITY points from a combination of the impact and the beating the angry animal-folk give you!

Bloodied and bruised, you are dragged back towards the huts where the Sayer of the Law awaits...

Turn to <u>307</u>.

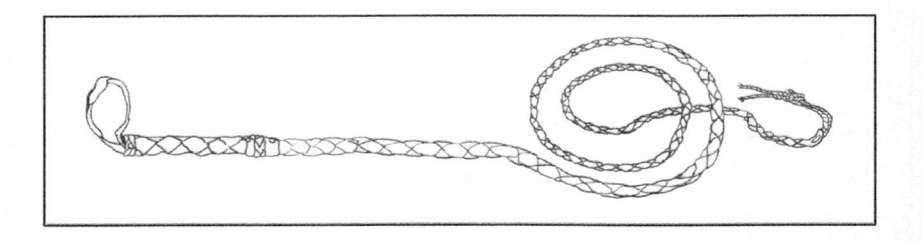

365

The pair of you reach the companionway and climb a ladder into the bright sunlight. There, you find yourself upon a deck that is slimy with scraps of carrot, shreds of vegetable detritus, and indescribable animal filth. Fastened by chains to the mainmast are a number of grisly staghounds with leather muzzles around their jaws, and by the mizzen you see a huge puma cramped in a little iron cage. Further under the starboard bulwark are some hutches containing rabbits, and a single llama lashed down beside them. In a separate section of the deck are a large cheetah, a black bear, and a young stag, all crammed into rusting pens.

Extraordinary as this is, it is not the animals that catch your attention as much as the two men who are running across the aft part of the deck. The one in front is a short, misshapen man with a crooked back, powerful arms, and a head sunken between broad shoulders. His pursuer is a tall, red-headed man wearing a white cap. The misshapen man hesitates as he draws close to the leaping and barking staghounds, which allows the tall man to send him sprawling among the dogs with a thumping blow between the shoulder-blades.

'Steady on there, captain!' cries Montgomery, marching up the deck as the misshapen man howls and rolls about under the worrying of the muzzled staghounds. 'This will not do! You and your deckhands have been hazing my man ever since he came aboard. Have you forgotten that he is a passenger?'

'Go to hell!' slurs Captain Davis drunkenly. 'I do what I like on my ship. My ship was a clean ship. But just look at it now...!'

'You agreed to take the beasts,' Montgomery presses. 'Besides, whoever heard of a spotless menagerie, let alone a spotless one aboard a long distance trader?'

'Filth is filth, and there's more than one kind stinking up my deck!' the captain blares, before leaning in close to Montgomery. 'You speak of agreements, do you? Well, what I bargained was to take a man, his attendant and some livestock from Callao. I never agreed to carry an ugly, mad devil and a silly prideful Sawbones such as you - I'd never have taken such terms if I'd known!'

At the sound of raised voices, several grim-faced sailors appear out of the forecastle and begin to move towards the altercation. The misshapen man scrambles out from under the feet of the staghounds and staggers to Montgomery's side, whose face has grown white with anger.

It is a tense situation which could easily turn ugly!

Do you wish to try to calm Montgomery down? If so, turn to **41**.

If you would rather try to calm Captain Davis down, turn to **258**.

Otherwise, you can stay out of it and wait to see what happens? To do this, turn to **328**.

366

The python is terrifyingly fast, and before you can react it sinks its fangs into your shoulder and begins to coil its body around you in a bone-crushing grip...

Lose 2 VITALITY points, then roll a dice!

If you roll 1-3, turn to **69**.

If you roll 4-6, turn to **193**.

367

You bring the carbine to bear just as one of the frontmost beast-folk - a towering, dappled monster - charges at Montgomery with a heart-stopping roar. M'ling flies at it with a snarl but is smashed aside. A split-second later Montgomery drives in the assailant's head with a shot to the middle of its face. Still the creature ploughs on, gripping

304

Montgomery and landing on top of him, where it thrashes in its death-throes.

Unsure whether either of your companions are alive or dead, you level the carbine and open fire, unleashing devastation all around until your magazine is entirely spent. As the smoke clears, you see that Montgomery has freed his upper body from beneath the slain monster and is staring blankly at the war-torn scene.

Note that you no longer have any ammunition for the carbine, but you may gain 1 FATE point for driving off the ill-intentioned mob!

In the dead silence that follows M'ling staggers to his feet, shaking his head groggily. At your urging, he helps you drag Montgomery free.

'It's a fine thing all three of us made it through in one piece,' Montgomery mutters absently, as he brushes himself down and reloads his revolver with trembling hands.
'After all, it's going to take a grand effort to drag poor old Moreau back to the enclosure. We can't rightly leave him here to have his bones picked, can we...?'

Do you wish to agree that you have to try to return Moreau's body to the enclosure? If so, turn to 223.

If you would rather counsel that you abandon Moreau's body where it lays and return to the enclosure as quickly as possible, turn to 520.

368

You work away at the chain with the hammer and chisel you found in the hull of the wrecked frigate and are pleased when you break the welded link. But upon unravelling the chain, you find that the box possesses a small keyhole in its front and is securely locked.

You hear the dull, heavy clink of metal when you shake the coffer, and note that the edges of the lid fit together so perfectly that whatever lies within has probably remained untouched by the water...

Do you wish to use the hammer and chisel to break into the silver coffer? If so, turn to **302**.

If you would rather refrain from damaging the box, you can stow the item in your rucksack in the hope that you will find the key later. Add the **silver coffer** to your *equipment list* before continuing along the path (turn to **412**).

369

The roars of the Pugnatyr and the babbling shrieks of the Draconope torment your cowardly flight. Then, you hear the battle reaching its final stages...

Roll a dice:

If you roll 1-4, you hear your unfortunate ally give several mournful roars, before all is silent except for the triumphant cries of his killer.

306

You must lose 2 FATE points for abandoning the Pugnatyr to his doom!

If you roll 5-6, you hear the Draconope's shrieks silenced, and the belligerent bellows of the great ape as he proclaims his continued dominance over this part of the island. Though the Pugnatyr has triumphed, you must still lose 1 FATE point for failing to stand with him!

You press on until it is almost dark, then slump to the jungle floor to rest. All is silent now save for the incessant creaking of insects, so you pillow your pack beneath your head and fall into a troubled sleep.

Gain 2 VITALITY points.

When you awake, you realise that you have slept for several hours and that the dawn is not too far away.

It is then that you notice a jungle path just in front of you, bearing on an east-west axis. You are quite sure that heading east will take you in the direction of the enclosure, whereas going west will take you in the direction of the volcanic spring you saw from the beach.

If you wish to head east towards the enclosure, turn to **60**.

If you would rather head west in the direction of the volcanic spring, turn to **450**.

370

As your vessel surges forward under the powers of a brisk wind, the island of Doctor Moreau grows smaller and smaller, the lank spire of smoke at its peak dwindling to a finer and finer line against the hot sunset. The ocean rises up around you, and the dark patch of land is finally hidden from sight.

As the daylight is drawn aside like some luminous curtain, you stare up into that indigo gulf of immensity that the sunshine hides and see the floating hosts of the stars.

Into the night you sail...

If fortune is indifferent to the fates of all living things, then it is by a stroke of incredibly fortuitous possibility that you are picked up on your fifth day by a brig bound for San Francisco from Samoan Apia.

Immediately, you are escorted to the captain and first mate who ask you how you came to be alone in the middle of the south pacific.

Do you wish to tell them the truth about the island? If so, turn to **559**.

If you would rather make up a plausible fiction about what happened to you between the sinking of *The Lady Vain* and now, turn to **248**.

371

At your offer of trade, the MACAQUE-MAN hauls himself out of the pool and throws on a simple belted habit made from coarse brown wool that makes him resemble one of the monks of France you have seen in your travels. As he does so, you marvel at the strangeness of his thick white hair, bushy mutton chops, long arms and crooked bow legs.

'Trade is always welcome, young lord,' he says. 'After all, we see too few visitors to our beloved home and are delighted to meet you.' He then throws open the wicker box and tips its contents out upon the ground.

Most of the weapons and baubles you see are either useless to you or heavily corroded, but you do spot a serviceable **cutlass**, **5 broad-headed battle arrows** and **6 hollow-tip revolver bullets** that have been stored in a watertight oilskin pouch. There is also a corked and wax-sealed **blue phial** that is filled with a mysterious liquid and labelled with the number *148* (make a note of this number if you acquire the phial!).

The **cutlass** is a sharp, heavy close combat weapon that (like a firearm), will automatically cause *twice* the damage when you roll a double for your close combat score.

The **5 battle arrows** will only be of use if you have a bow but will cause 3 points of damage instead of the usual 2.

The **6 hollow-tip revolver bullets** will only be of use if you have the revolver but have been designed to disintegrate on impact with flesh in order to cause maximum injury. They will also cause 3 points of damage, (and 6 points of damage on a double roll!). Remember that a successful FATE test can take the damage from a double up to 12 points!

The Macaque-man knows nothing of the contents of the **blue phial**, but he tells you that coloured phials are of great importance to the Master.

Each of the above items can be traded for the following:

- 3 meals
- A pair of stone necklaces
- 2 leopard skins
- A pair of Toledo steel hunting knives
- A coil of rope
- 1 gold coin
- A bone knife
- A cross-bow

Make your trades, if any, remembering to make the changes to your *equipment list*.

You then thank the Macaque-man, cast a final look at the oblivious bathers, then make your way to the gap in the wall of the volcanic rubble.

Turn to **349**.

372

So intent are you on your grappling match that you hardly have time to register the pair of full-grown LEOPARDS that come bursting out of the undergrowth. Locked in a hold with your chimeric opponent, there is nothing you can do as one of the beasts clamps its jaws around the back of your neck and drags you clear of its master.

You have only moments to see several Leopard-folk staring down at you before the fangs embedded in your flesh sink deep and pierce your spinal cord...

YOUR TIME IS ENDED!

373

The men's blood is vile and salty. Immediately, your stomach rebels and you wretch violently!

Lose 2 VITALITY points!

Cursing your desperate situation, you heave the men's bodies over the side of the dinghy and watch as the patient sharks move in to feed. As night falls, you slip into a morbid sleep, your mouth and throat a torment of thirst. When you awake the next morning, you are unsure whether you are alive or dead, for you see something you can scarcely believe - a set of sails dancing above the horizon! For what seems like an endless period you lay with your head on the thwart, watching the schooner approach, lacking the strength to even cry out.

You are dimly aware of being lifted up onto the ship's gangway, and perceive a large red-headed man with freckles staring down at you over the bulwarks. Then you gain the impression of a dark face with extraordinary eyes close to yours. As some sort of metallic tasting liquid is forced between your teeth, you lose consciousness, unsure whether your rescue is a blessing or a curse...

Turn to 216.

374

You announce to the throng that you are an associate of the doctor, and that he has sent you to test the zeal of the beast-folk dwelling in the chasm.

'You have proven to me that you are loyal supplicants and exponents of the Law,' you tell the Sayer. 'Your Master will be most satisfied when I return to Him and assure Him of your ardour!'

The Sayer stares at you through his veil of grey hair and you feel the sweat breaking on your brow. After an interminable silence, the creature nods slowly.

'It is well that the Master has sent one such as you to view our faith,' the Sayer rumbles. 'I am pleased that we have not failed this inquiry. I ask that you retire for what remains of the night, friend of the Master, so that my people may perform their rites.'

With that, the Sloth-man squeezes between the circle of brutes around you and leads you to a smaller hut that has a small fire burning near its entrance. It also contains several rush-woven mattresses, a jug of water and a pile of fruit piled against the inner rock wall.

Gain 2 FATE points, then turn to **511**.

375

As the figure comes to the edge of the quicksand, the moonlight reveals a lean, lank-haired creature dressed in torn and dirty rags. He has powerfully hunched shoulders, long, strangely jointed legs and an inordinately wide, grinning mouth crammed with teeth. At your entreaty he throws you one end of the rope and pulls you out of the quicksand to the edge of the rocky shore.

You stagger out onto solid land offering your thanks, but the creature stands as still as a statue and glares at you with unblinking green eyes. Then you see movement from the shadows of the ravine and a second figure stalks into the moonlight. He is akin to your rescuer, but his guttural growling and ghastly snarls leave no question as to his intentions. The first man now matches his companion's hostility, his thin lips receding to reveal a pair of glistening lupine fangs…

This pair of WOLF-MEN have not rescued you out of the goodness of their hearts. You may have been saved from the quicksand, but now you must fight these dangerous opponents simultaneously!

If you wish to use a firearm (and have at least one round remaining), turn immediately to **430**.

If you do not wish to use a firearm (or do not possess such a weapon or are out of ammunition), but are using another kind of ranged weapon, you may take TWO shots before engaging in close combat.

First WOLF-MAN: Prowess - 7; Vitality - 7; Damage - 2; Ranged Defence 8.

Second WOLF-MAN: Prowess - 6; Vitality - 7; Damage - 2; Ranged Defence 8.

If you win, you find nothing of use upon the bodies other than a pair of leather necklaces hung with small, drilled stones.

Take the **stone necklaces** if you wish, then proceed into the ravine by turning to 114.

376

You aim your firearm into the middle of the onrushing pack and discharge it with a deafening crack. A spurt of blood erupts from the shoulder of a towering brute and the mob falters, splitting in two as the animal-folk swerve for the cover of the jungle in a disordered rout.

Several smaller creatures are badly trampled and lay writhing upon the meadow, but you have little time to concern yourself with them, for the Fox-woman and Elephant-man are closing in on you with a grim and steely determination!

You must fight these two opponents simultaneously. If you have sufficient ammunition, you have time to perform just ONE ranged attack against one of them before close combat is joined:

FOX-WOMAN: Prowess - 8; Vitality - 6; Damage - 2; Ranged defence - 8.

ELEPHANT-MAN: Prowess - 8; Vitality - 14; Damage - 3; Ranged defence - 10.

If you win, turn to 424.

Realising that the intruder could have fallen on you while you slept, you resist the urge to lash out and sternly demand to know who is there.

'I am your servant, O Rider of the Sea, he who is cast in the image of the Master,' comes a crooning voice. 'At his right hand, you will bring fire and thunder on the wicked and shower rewards upon the faithful!'

'It is well,' you say, regaining your confidence and extending your hand for what you realise is a licking kiss. 'Accompany me into the ravine, so that I may tell you my will.'

Shrugging on your rucksack and gathering up your weapons, you make your way over to the brook where the moonlight reveals your follower to be unlike any creature you have ever seen. Dressed in rags like many of the other islanders, the newcomer has a large protuberant nose, liquid brown eyes, and extraordinarily large, wilting ears positioned high on his head. Everything about him - from the way he glances here and there with his nose held high, to the way he holds his arms awkwardly before him - is highly suggestive of a circus dog that has been taught to walk on its hind legs!

Indeed, he is a DOG-MAN, another of the doctor's bizarre experiments.

Under your scrutiny, the creature shrinks nervously, but when you ask to be shown somewhere safe to spend the rest of the night, his strangely jointed legs quiver with excitement.

'Humans must stay safe at night,' he huffs happily. 'To your home, to my home, I will lead you, yes...yes! But first we must go up, until we reach the white clearing!'

He then bounds up the ravine a little way, pauses and glances over his shoulder expectantly. Feeling that you can trust this earnest little creature, you decide to follow him, but after a short distance your guide stops suddenly, his head cocked as if listening. Then you hear it: a grunting bark echoing faintly through the trees, followed by a dreadful roar.

'My lord, forgive me,' the Dog-man mutters. 'A friend is in need. Follow the brook until you reach the white clearing up on high. If you meet the white-haired ones, then do not disturb their peace for any reason; await to be spoken to if you wish to trade with them!'

Your guide fishes a small **brass key** from out of a pocket, presses it into your hand, then whisks off into the darkness.

Add the key to your *equipment list*, then turn to 496.

378

Exhausted by the combat, you leave the bodies of the lions upon the beach and move back into the jungle. There, you pillow your head on your pack and fall asleep as the night closes in.

Gain 4 VITALITY points from the rest.

When you awake, you realise that the dawn is not too far away. You are about to set off once more along the beach when you notice an animal trail running away inland of where you have been resting.

Examining it closely, you see signs of the recent passage of what appears to be several people. Intrigued, you decide to investigate.

Turn to 503.

379

Though you shift your weight and twist this way and that, you are unable to defeat your opponent's brutish strength. Thrust backwards, you are slammed into the trunk of a tree!

Lose 2 VITALITY points!

Winded, you sink to the ground while the Boar-man backs up in preparation for another charge. You must react quickly!

If you now wish to attempt to mollify the Boar-man with an offering of food, turn to **405**.

If you would rather fight the creature, turn to **502**.

Alternatively, if you simply wish to raise your hands and slowly back away out of the clearing, turn to **483**.

380

As soon as you enter the water, a ravenous squid embraces your legs and pulls you beneath the water. Others of its kind immediately swarm in, lured by the taste of your sweat as it diffuses in the warm salt water. At the first wisp of blood, the creatures' urgency escalates into a feeding frenzy; razor-sharp beaks plunge and snip like so many surgeon's scissors. You do not have time to drown, at least...

YOUR ADVENTURE ENDS HERE!

381

With shaking hands, you break the waxy seal on the phial(s) and drain the elixir(s). Immediately, your fever subsides and the wracking pain becomes a dull ache before fading entirely.

You have prevented yourself from reverting!

Gain 1 FATE point!

Suspecting that the elixir has been laced with tincture of opium, you lay upon your cot and drift into a fitful sleep. When you awake, it is morning, and the captain of the brig is standing in your doorway. You glance at your hands and are relieved to see that they look as human as they always have…

'We've arrived at San Francisco port,' the captain tells you gruffly. 'Be ready to attend an appointment with the Harbour-Master within the hour. Once he is satisfied, you will be free to go, but it shan't be the quiet life for you, at least not at first. Seems there's a fair deal of interest in the sinking of *The Lady Vain*. You're one of only nineteen souls who survived its loss, they say!'

You dress, gather your things, and climb onto the deck to see a harbour crammed with ships. Beyond are the sprawling city and rolling hills of San Francisco. By noon, you have given a vague account of your survival, signed several papers and evaded a number of reporters and photographers.

Anonymous once more, you stroll through the hilly streets of downtown, your heightened senses overawed by the sights and sounds around you.

Have you been exposed to any zoonotic infections?

If not, turn immediately to 570.

If so, you must *test your FATE*!

If you are favoured, turn to 64.

If you are unfavoured, turn to 103.

382

You are making good progress across the delta when you suddenly plunge into quicksand up to your waist!

The viscous matter has you now, and it is just a matter of time before you are drowned. Your only hope is to seize hold of the side of the canoe you were dragging...

Roll a dice!

If you roll 1-2, turn to **534**.

If you roll 3-6, turn to **340**.

383

Leaking from trenchant wounds, the Draconope gives a final death scream before falling silent, its grotesque body twitching and oozing black blood.

Note that you have *killed the Draconope.*

The hunter beside you cleans his knives by thrusting them into the soft soil, before his companion finally arrives, his chest heaving from the sprint. The men are handsome, minimally clad Pacific Islanders with gleaming skin that is the colour of copper and covered with savage tattoos, yet they are wearing sturdy knee-high leather boots of the sort favoured by European explorers. Their bows and beautifully fletched arrows are of indigenous design, and it is with shock and dismay that you find the weapons levelled at your chest!

'Your help, we did not ask,' one of them says coldly. 'Now tell us: who are you and why are you here?'

How will you answer?

If you wish to say that you are a friend of Doctor Moreau, turn to **264**.

If you would rather say that you are an enemy of the doctor, turn to **320**.

Alternatively, you can admit that you are a castaway who has recently accepted the doctor's aid, by turning to **174**.

384

As you negotiate the descent, your foot slips on an extrusion of moss-covered rock and you feel your fingers plucked from the rock face. There is the sudden gut-twisting lurch of falling, a brief rush of air, then blackness...

Roll a dice - this is the amount of damage you take to your VITALITY as you thump into the ravine floor!

If you are still alive, you come to your senses not within the ravine, but in a little den formed in the hollow of a dense press of cane trees. It appears to be the dead of night, but a small candle sheds enough light for you to see the face of the creature you saw earlier in the ravine. It is the DOG-MAN who you turned away!

Startled, you reach for the weapons at your belt, only to see them lying across the den in a pile beside your rucksack.

'Master, did I do well?' the Dog-man inquires eagerly, leaning in. 'Did I pass the test?'

Realising that this creature may well have saved you from discovery by one of the island's more fearsome inhabitants, you swallow your pride and assure him that he has done well. At these words, the Dog-man's eyes light up with delight, while his strangely jointed legs quiver with excitement.

'Humans must rest at night,' the creature pants happily. 'Only beasts are abroad in the dark! When light returns, I will guide you. To your home, to my home - my lord will choose!'

With that, the Dog-man lowers himself to his haunches and sets to devouring some gruel he has wrapped up in banana leaves. When he has eaten his fill, he looks at you with sudden guilt, then offers you one of the meals.

You may eat it now to restore 4 VITALITY points or add the **meal** to your reserve.

Moments later, you hear a blood-curdling howl some distance away, then an answering call that is somewhat closer.

'So, they have come,' the Dog-man whispers. 'Bad men. Beast-men! Savages, not like you and I. We must leave now, my lord, if you will tell me where you wish to go?'

Where will you ask to be led?

To the Dog-man's home? If so, turn to **198**.

Or to 'your' home? (Turn to **475**).

385

The churning of the water as you kick for the beach only encourages the shark. A tremendous blow to your midriff launches you out of the water, and when you return to the surface the oceanic predator bites you almost entirely in half!

Your last sight is of boiling, blood-pinked waters closing over your head. In a day or two, the barrel will wash up on the beach. But of you, not one scrap will remain...

YOUR ADVENTURE ENDS HERE!

386

When you step out from behind the boulder with your hands outstretched, the hunters notch arrows to their bows and stalk towards you from either side. When one of them sees that you have robbed their camp, he spits out a curse and sends an arrow sinking into your shoulder...

Lose 2 VITALITY points!

His companion also fires as you dive back behind the boulder. Resolve ONE ranged attack from the second hunter against you!

LAZALO THE HUNTER: Prowess - 7; Ballistics - 8; Vitality - 8; Ranged Defence - 8; Damage - 2/2

Once you are behind the boulder, you must engage in ONE round of ranged combat with the hunters, but you will gain +2 to your Ranged Defence due to your concealed position. After this (if you are still alive), the two men will engage you in close combat!

VAI THE HUNTER: Prowess - 8; Ballistics - 8; Vitality - 8; Ranged Defence - 8; Damage - 2/2.

Note: Lazalo and Vai both wield pairs of **Toledo steel hunting knives** that give them +1 to their *close combat score*.

If you win, turn to 317.

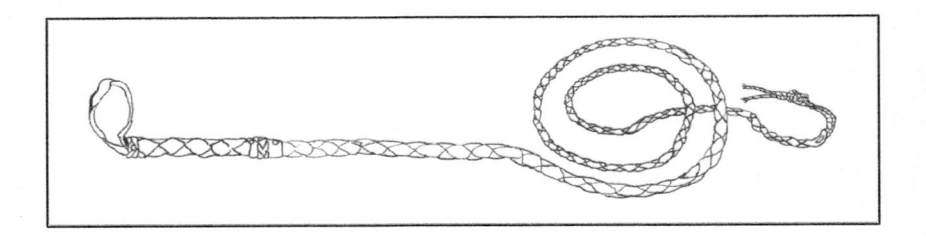

387

Without any firearms to hand, you have little chance against a dozen zealous beast-folk. As such, you are swiftly beaten into submission!

Lose 4 VITALITY points, then turn to <u>307</u>.

388

As you try to climb aboard, you are met with a rain of blows from the other sailors (lose 2 VITALITY points). Even worse, the sailor you swam past has drawn a dagger and stabs you viciously in the back (lose a further dice roll of VITALITY points!).

You slip back into the water and must now defend yourself. If you are unarmed, you must reduce your *close combat score* by 2 for this encounter, as well as a further 2 as a result of fighting in the water.

ANGRY SAILOR: Prowess - 5; Vitality - 6; Damage - 2.

If you win, you see that during the struggle the longboat has pulled too far away for you to reach…

You must now swim towards the derelict merchantman (if you have not already done so). Turn to <u>86</u>.

Or strike out towards the dinghy, by turning to <u>127</u>.

389

The swamp water dilutes some of the Bloodroot venom, but you must still roll a dice and deduct the total from your VITALITY score...!

If you are still alive, you allow the wheezing in your lungs to subside before following the edge of the swamp towards the west.

Turn to 184.

390

You thrust open the door and are instantly struck by the room's generalised disorder. The numerous empty whiskey bottles collecting on a small table and the unmade bed leave little doubt in your mind that this was Montgomery's room.

During a brief spell of frantic searching, the only objects of interest you uncover are **6 revolver rounds** and a **small golden locket** containing a lock of dark hair and a small, faded sepia portrait of a pretty young woman (add these items to your *equipment list*).

Feeling that you have spent enough time in the room, you return to the courtyard.

Turn to 432.

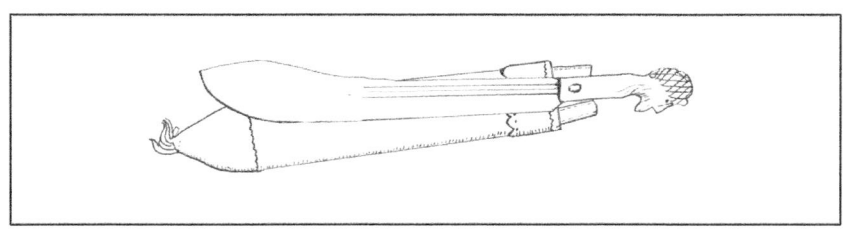

391

Panting heavily, you stand over Montgomery's inert form, trying not to look at the reproachful, half-lidded eyes and the way in which his blood is soaking into his flaxen hair and straw-coloured moustache.

With trembling hands, you retrieve Montgomery's revolver and empty the chamber. You may add **4 revolver rounds** to your *equipment list*.

Suddenly you freeze. There is someone outside, inserting a key in the lock of the small outer door. You just have time to retreat to the doorway of the laboratory when the door flies open, and you find yourself face to face with M'ling!

As soon as the manservant spies his master's limp body, he bares a pair of dagger-like fangs and charges you, his animal eyes alight with rage!

M'LING: Prowess - 8; Vitality; 12; Damage - 3; Ranged Defence - 9.

You have enough space to fire off TWO ranged attacks before you must engage M'ling in close combat.

If you win, turn to **111**.

392

Under the fallen tree you find a simple leather **archer's vambrace** laying amidst a collection of rotting food and scraps of clothing. If ever you obtain a bow and arrow, the vambrace will steady your arm and protect it from becoming bruised from the slap of the bowstring.

As such, it allows you to add +1 to your *ranged attack score* when using a bow.

Pleased with your find, you hasten from the clearing and head deeper into the jungle.

Turn to **436**.

393

The Pugnatyr's den seems to have nothing in it except for piles of branches and leaves that form a rudimentary shelter. You prod around the detritus and are about to move on when you catch sight of the corner of a small, worn, leather-bound book.

Pulling it free, you find that it is a diary that seems to have been written either by a child or an illiterate adult learning to read and write for the first time. It contains simple descriptions and drawings of the island and the sea, the weather, trees, bird-life and different sorts of fruit. But as it goes on, rather than improving the writing and pictures degenerate, becoming little more than mindless scrawls and smears of pencil and pigment. The last dozen pages seem to have been torn out, as if in a fit of sudden rage.

Add the **diary** to your *equipment list*, then decide your next course.

Do you wish to head north through the jungle down a gentle declination? If so, turn to **439**.

Alternatively, you can head westward through the jungle. To do this, turn to **459**.

394

You retort that the Hyena-man's order means nothing to you, and that you would rather give yourself over to a pride of lions!

At these words, the creature snarls and sends a bolt from his crossbow slamming into your shoulder (lose 3 VITALITY points). Meanwhile, his underlings bound towards you!

Immediately, the air turns noxious as the weight of your attackers forces large concentrations of gas to bubble through the water. The unsuspecting Hyena-men start to swoon as they inhale deep lungfuls of the poisoned air, while you hold your breath and attempt to sprint clear of the miasma!

The Hyena-man leader is furious that you have lured his companions into a trap. He is able to shoot ONE more crossbow bolt at you before drawing a bone knife and engaging you in close combat:

HYENA-MAN CHAMPION: Prowess - 9; Ballistics - 8; Vitality - 10; Damage - 2/3.

If you win, turn to **119**.

395

The path leads up into the jungle before fading into the general tangle of thick understory that is populated by feathered ferns, rope-like creepers and the gnarled, moss-infested trunks of mahogany, rubber and brazil nut trees. Everywhere there is the drip and stream of water, as well as the dull hum of diverse insects that swarm about stagnant pools, livid blooms and corrugated fungoid growths.

You ascend towards the island's interior, focussing on the steady cadence of your tread and trying to ignore your mounting discomfort and fatigue. It is only when the rainforest gloom starts to deepen that you realise that night is falling. Making camp in the vicinity of so many blood-sucking mosquitos and gnats is out of the question, so you press on into the darkness, reliant on the shafts of moonlight that begin to find their way through breaches in the jungle canopy.

After several hours, you begin to leave the malarial dankness of the lower band of rainforest behind and enter a section of jungle that is drier and less miasmic. Sweeping moonlit vistas of verdant canopy become apparent beneath you through breaks in the leaves and you spy the island's western beach, an iron-grey thread separating the land from an endless expanse of ocean the gentle swells of which reflect the moonlight in countless silver flashes.

You begin to relax. Here, you might make camp and await first light...

Then you catch a glimpse of a pair of luminous green eyes staring at you from the dense undergrowth dead ahead. This is followed by a furtive rustle to your right, then the flash of a second pair of eyes which is accompanied by a low, menacing growl...

You are being stalked!

If you wish to press on into the jungle in the hope that the creatures will leave you alone, turn to 20.

Alternatively you can hold your ground, prepare your weapon and wait? (Turn to 54).

396

The brothers lead you through the nearby copse of trees so that you find yourself on the extreme north-west corner of the island. Here, a beach of slate-grey sand extends a short distance to your left and right before curving out of view behind the rising land. But it is to the endless horizon that your gaze is drawn, where the sea meets the sky in a dream-like azure haze. You allow your gaze to linger on this scene of tranquility for several moments, then turn your attention to the four canoes drawn up high on the beach.

They are beautifully carved from a warmly-coloured wood, and each canoe has a single, double-sided oar cast within. Though you do not have the seamanship to handle one of them out on the open sea, you feel confident that you could paddle along the island's coast for a fair way and spare your legs a considerable amount of work.

'One of them is yours,' Lazalo says. 'Safe by day but beware of using it by night. When you camp, stay on the beach. Inland there are many dangers - monsters, swamplands and disease. However, try to visit the huts if you can. There, you will learn much of Moreau's power over his creations.'

With that, the brothers bid you farewell and return to their camp.

Glancing up and down the beach, you decide to take a canoe south to explore the westward coast of the island. Turn to **353**.

397

As you attempt to leave the clearing, one of the Thylacine-men darts in and delivers a painful bite to the back of your leg (lose 2 VITALITY points!) and note that you have been *exposed to zoonotic infection*.

You spin around with your weapon at the ready, but the creatures are already escaping into the northward jungle. Limping painfully, you press on through the jungle towards the south...

Turn to 171.

398

The animal-folk seem bemused as you finish reciting the Ten Commandments, but the righteous anger of the Sayer's followers fades.

'We will take the rest of this night to think on what we have heard,' the Sayer tells you. 'For now, I am content if you heed your Law while among us. Let it be known that if you break it, then punishment will be swift and sure!'

With that, the Sloth-man squeezes between the circle of brutes around you and leads you to a smaller hut that has a fire burning near its entrance. It also contains several rush-woven mattresses, a jug of water and a pile of fruit piled against the inner rock wall.

Gain 1 FATE point, then turn to 511.

399

The gap in the wall of rubble gives access to a rocky hillside overlooking a steaming expanse of reeds and marsh. Laid out before you are a series of geothermic pools surging up from deep beneath the earth before overflowing in cascades of heated waterfalls. These energetic waterways rush down the steep inland heights, then grow sluggish and indistinct as they wander over more level ground toward a distant ribbon of sand and silver surf to the north.

The billowing steam in this area reflects the moonlight in a misty haze, but you are able to discern a number of indistinct shapes that seem to be floating in one of the lower pools.

Do you wish to take a closer look at the shapes in the water? If so, turn to **402**.

If you would rather return through the gap in the wall and explore the tunnel, turn to **476**.

400

You crash on through the jungle, but such is your exhaustion from the climb that you are forced to move much slower than you would like. The noise of your own movement and the pounding of the blood in your ears means that you do not hear the sounds of your pursuers closing in. Instead, you *see* them: rangy, hunch-shouldered man-beasts hurtling toward you from either side, their fangs bared and eyes ablaze...

Suddenly, a third shape streaks into sight, slamming into one of the ambushers and bearing it to the ground. The Dog-man has come to your aid!

For a split-second you watch as your ally struggles with his opponent, then you meet the charge of the second attacker, who seizes your arms and gashes your face with a snapping bite!

You must lose 2 VITALITY points before resolving this combat...

WOLF-MAN: Prowess - 7; Vitality - 7; Damage - 2.

If you win, you discover the Dog-man with his teeth sunk into the throat of his quivering enemy. You pull him away from the body, trying to ignore the bloodstains around his jaws as you thank him for his aid. At your words, the creature regains his benevolent countenance and helps you search your attackers. You find nothing apart from a pair of leather necklaces hung with small, drilled stones.

Take the **stone necklaces** if you wish, then turn to **460**.

401

Cursing, the SAILOR pulls out a dagger and stabs at you in a froth of white water! If you are unarmed, you must reduce your *close combat score* by 2 for this encounter, and by another 2 while fighting in the water!

ANGRY SAILOR: Prowess - 5; Vitality - 6; Damage - 2.

If you win, you realise the futility of trying to force your way onto the longboat...

You must now swim towards the derelict merchantman (if you have not already done so), by turning to **86**.

Or you may strike out towards the dinghy (turn to **127**).

402

As you advance through the steam, the indistinct shapes resolve into something entirely unexpected. Before you are a group of creatures that are reclining in the hot mineral waters of the lowest geothermic pool! Like so many of the island's inhabitants the bathers are singular in the extreme, possessing grey-white heads of thick hair, pink high-boned faces, large amber-hued eyes and fine white pelts that undulate and drift with the movements of the water.

Even though it is clear that several of the figures are female, both genders sport thick mutton-chops that are presently lank and beaded with moisture. Around the pool are piles of ragged clothing, and next to one of the bathers you spy a large wicker box.

The creatures seem unperturbed by your presence, though several of them gaze at you sleepily...

What will you do?

If you wish to remove your clothing and join the bathers in the geothermic pool, turn to **434**.

If you would rather make your way over to the wicker box, turn to **467**.

Alternatively, you can leave these creatures to their pleasure and head through the gap in the wall (turn to **349**).

403

When you promise to do what you can to help him, the Sloth-man regains a little of his composure and gives an awkward bow.

'That is more than I could have hoped for, lord,' he sniffles, running the back of a hand across his snub nose. 'In return for your promise, I will bring you some gifts that may prove useful.'

The little creature leaves the hut, returning with a woven basket only when the other beast-folk loitering in the chasm have retired to their dens for the rest of the night. In the basket are random miscellanea of little interest, but you also spot a well-sealed **powder horn**, a pouch holding a quantity of **lead shot**, a number of **oiled rags** and a **green phial** made of thick glass, sealed with a tarred cork and labelled with the number *150* (make a note of this number!).

The powder, shot, and oiled rags will only be useful if you possess the dysfunctional **Blunderbuss pistol**. If you possess this firearm, then you may use the items brought to you by the Sloth-man to clean and recharge it. Doing so will allow you to wield the **Restored Dragon**!

The Restored Dragon is a fearsome firearm. It is unusual insofar that it will allow you to cause one dice worth of damage to one dice worth of enemies in any ranged OR close combat round (thus it will cause 1-6 points of damage to 1-6 ranged or close combat enemies, which can be increased to 12 points of damage with a successful FATE test!). You have enough powder and shot for TWO blasts, but the firearm is so slow to reload that you may only use ONE blast per combat. As you are repairing the dragon, you notice the number *516* etched into the side of its barrel. Make a note of this number!

There is no way of knowing what manner of liquid the **green phial** contains, but you decide to take it anyway.

Make any adjustments to your *equipment list*.

After thanking the Sloth-man for his gifts, the little creature hands you a **sea-polished stone**. He then wishes you luck and leaves you alone within the smoky hut.

You take some time to eat from the store of food (restore 4 VITALITY points) before stretching out on one of the beds and falling into a deep sleep.

Now turn to 19.

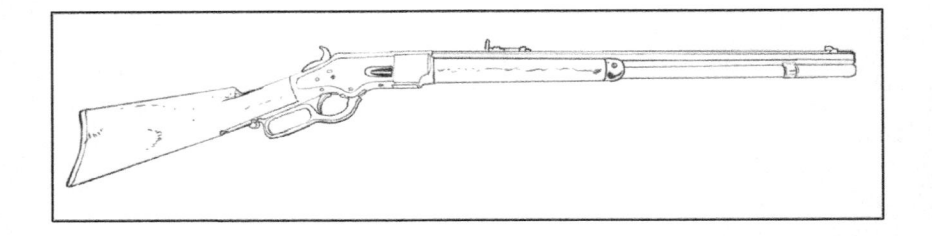

404

Your shot is straight and true!

The hunter arches his back and gives a single cry before crumpling to the forest floor. You may take the man's **hand axe** (2 points of close combat damage), his extra **bow** (2 points of ranged damage) and **quiver of arrows (7)**, as well as his pair of **Toledo Steel hunting knives** (these handsome weapons will add +1 to your *close combat strength*), if you wish.

Now, do you wish to explore the beach? If so, turn to **473**.

If you would rather head back inland towards the source of the hot springs, turn to **261**.

405

You toss some food at the feet of the Boar-man and watch in grim fascination as the creature gulps it down!

Remove a **meal** from your *equipment list*.

Now, do you wish to attack the creature while it is distracted? If so, make a note that you may inflict an automatic wound on your opponent, then turn to **502**.

If you would rather take this chance to leave the clearing immediately, turn to **436**.

406

You are awoken in the early morning by the pattering of bare feet, the sound of heavy objects being thrown about, and the violent creaking and rattling of chains.

You have slept deeply and may restore 4 VITALITY points.

As you come up the ladder, you see the broad back and red hair of the captain, and the terrified puma crouching in the bottom of its cage as it spins on the end of a rope that is rigged to the mizzen boom.

'Overboard with 'em!' bawls the captain, evidently still drunk. 'We'll have a clean ship soon, once we're rid of the whole blasted lot of them!'

He turns to you and stabs his thumb in the direction of the gangway where Montgomery is stood talking to an impressive white-haired man dressed in dirty blue flannels, who has apparently just come aboard from a modest island ship.

If you have *gained Montgomery's resentment*, turn to 123.

If not, but you have *explained your survival* to Montgomery, turn to 167.

If you have done neither of these things, turn to 341.

407

You begin by searching what you realise is Montgomery's room, for it is marked by a generalised disorder, with an unmade bed and numerous empty whiskey bottles collecting on a small table.

The only objects of interest you uncover are **6 revolver rounds** and a **small golden locket** containing a lock of dark hair and a small, faded sepia portrait of a pretty young woman (add these items to your *equipment list*).

Moreau's room is large and well-ordered, with shelf upon shelf of musty books and natural curiosities. In one corner is a simple pallet bed, neatly made up. A selection of large boots are lined up at its foot.

You focus your attention on a large mahogany writing bureau, and during a brief spell of frantic searching discover a **small silver key**.

Do you possess the **silver coffer**? If so, turn to **547**.

If not, you return to the courtyard with the items you have found. Turn to **185**.

408

You plunge your weapon again and again into the Draconope's leathery neck until its burbling roars cease, then fall to your knees in shock. You have truly had a brush with death, and the sight and sound of the Draconope's shrieks of agonised hatred will stay with you as long as you live.

Lose 1 FATE point!

When you have regained your composure, you continue the walk along the northward facing beach, now casting nervous glances both inland and out to sea. To your relief, nothing else comes out of the water and the jungle remains still and silent save for the incessant creaking of insects.

Just as you are beginning to fall asleep on your feet, you catch sight of a glimmer of light in the distance - it is the enclosure! By the time you can make out the distinct stonework of the outer wall, the first light of the new day has come. Your trepidation intensifies when the double gates of the outpost are flung wide open, and you see Doctor Moreau, Montgomery and M'ling leading the pack of staghounds out onto the beach. The dogs immediately catch your scent and lurch against their collars in a frenzy of barking and growling.

Moreau restrains the beasts with a harsh command, stares at you for a few seconds, then leads the staghounds back into the enclosure, while Montgomery and M'ling advance towards you.

'Where the devil have you been?' Montgomery demands. 'We've been worried sick and were about to set out with the dogs to find you! Now get inside this instant, Moreau will want to have words!'

Your relief at being back among humans somewhat sullied by a flicker of dread, you enter the enclosure and let yourself in via the small door leading to the room. It does not take long before you hear the inner door to the courtyard being unlocked, and the doctor strides in...

Turn to 39.

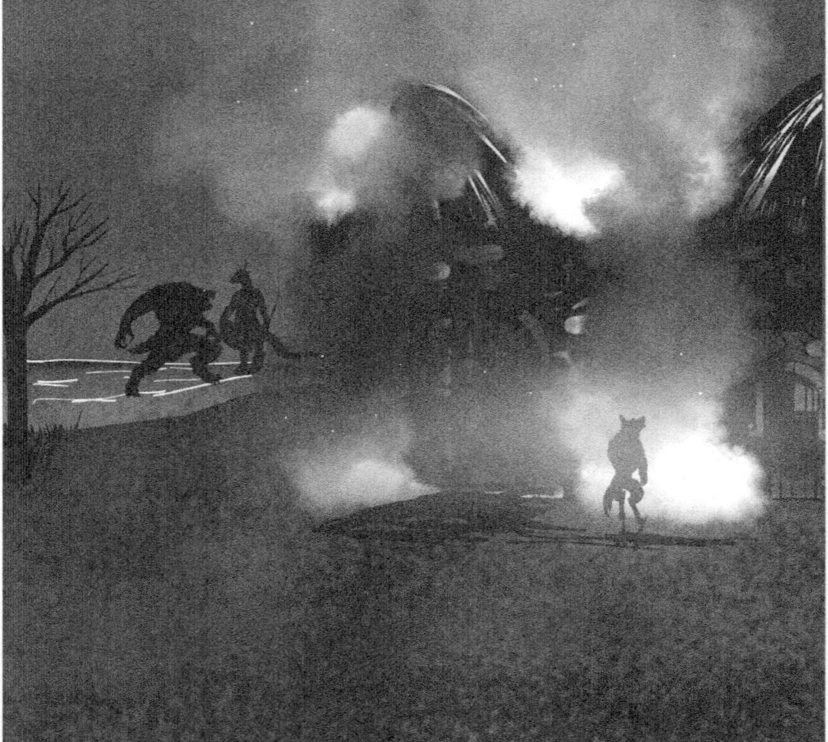

409

You awake at first light, having drifted into a fitful sleep (gain 2 VITALITY points).

The enclosure is now nothing more than a smouldering ruin, and you spy a number of beast-folk advancing from the bushes with hesitating gestures. Alone and without shelter, you are dangerously exposed!

Did you fight and kill Montgomery and M'ling in the enclosure? If so, turn to 4.

If not, turn to 554.

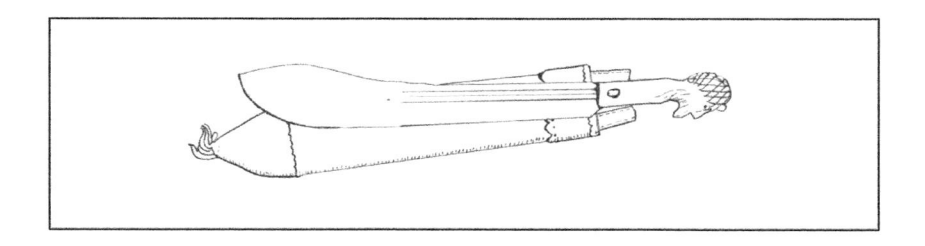

410

You drag the canoe into the sea, seize the paddle and haul yourself into the seat. The canoe is light and extremely maneuverable, and it takes you a little while to get accustomed to the motion of the sea and the most efficient use of the single oar. But you are soon paddling along at a steady pace and enjoying the gentle swell.

Looking up to your right, you see you are passing a steaming, reed-infested marsh that is fed by geothermic springs which are sourced in the loftier middle of the island. Up ahead, the marsh gives way to dense jungle that seems to crowd at the edges of the beach like an invading army.

It is then that you notice the rapidly lengthening shadows and the swift alteration in the tropical light. The day is growing old, and nightfall is approaching...

If you wish to immediately come ashore and scout out the jungle for a suitable camp site, turn to **478**.

If you would prefer to paddle on for a little while before simply camping out on the beach, turn to **254**.

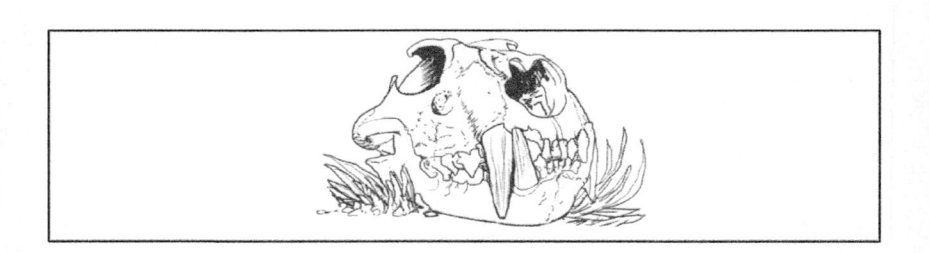

411

You aim attack after attack into the Draconope's leathery neck until its burbling roars cease, then fall to your knees in shock. You have truly had a brush with death, and the sight and sound of the Draconope's shrieks of agonised hatred will stay with you as long as you live.

Lose 1 FATE point!

When you have regained your composure, you move away from the leaking body before choosing a place to rest. Pillowing your pack beneath your head, you fall into a troubled sleep.

Gain 4 VITALITY points.

When you awake, you realise that you have slept for several hours and that the dawn is not too far away. It is then that you notice a jungle path just in front of you, bearing on an east-west axis. You are quite sure that heading east will take you in the direction of the enclosure, whereas west will take you in the direction of the volcanic spring you saw from the beach.

If you wish to head east towards the enclosure, turn to 60.

If you would rather head west, turn to 450.

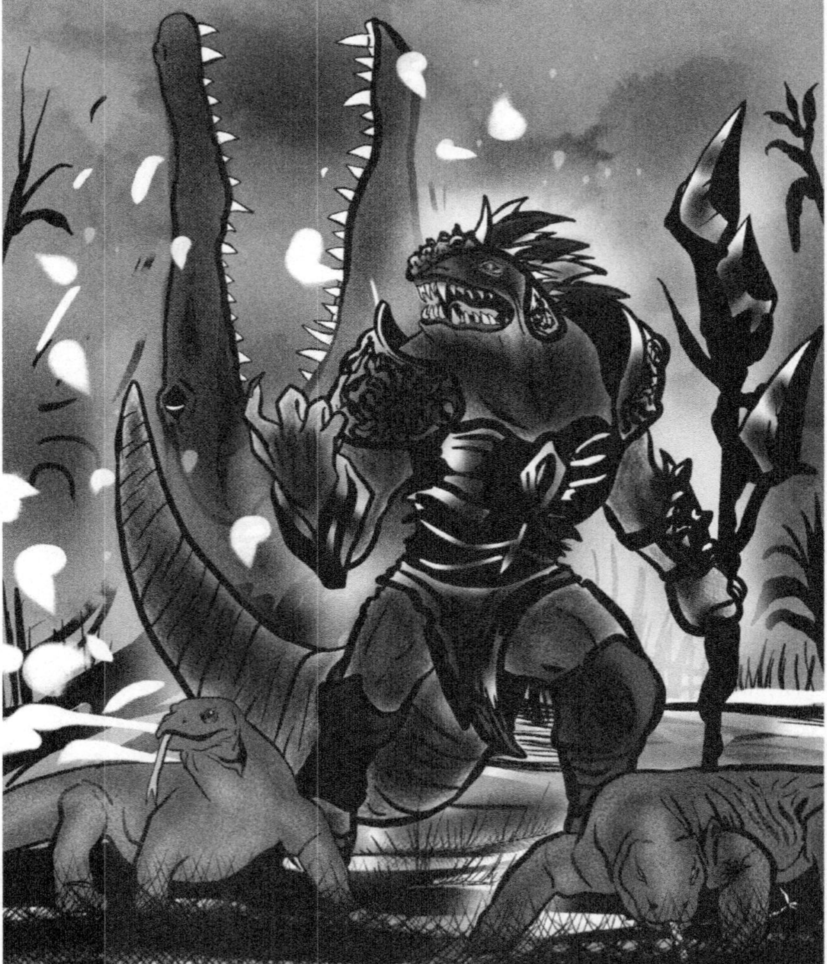

412

As you progress along the path, the fog begins to thin, and you glimpse movement ahead. There is a creature standing guard at the western limits of the swamp. It is clad in some sort of bulky, fibrous armour and wearing a fearsome spiked helmet that appears to be crafted from the dried skin of a pufferfish. In its claws is an immense halberd that reminds you of the ceremonial weapons carried by the Queen's royal guards, except that the polearm is crafted from black wood and is studded with the largest shark's teeth you have ever seen.

But more astonishing is the creature itself. Though its features have been humanised somewhat, it retains slitted nostrils in place of a nose and possesses beady jet-black eyes that are set disconcertingly wide. A lipless gash of a mouth reaches from ear to ear, while its skin is pebbled with a mass of black and grey scales. Behind it a thick, tapering reptilian tail swishes over the path this way and that.

The LIZARD-MAN had been staring into the waters of the swamp, but now it stalks towards you on a pair of black-clawed feet, sniffs the air and makes a strange warbling squawk in the back of its throat. Immediately, two huge MONITOR LIZARDS come scrabbling out of the mist like faithful hunting hounds and take positions on their master's flanks, their pink tongues flickering as they taste the air.

Your hand strays to your weapon as you meet the baleful stares of this trio, but you freeze when a yet more hideous apparition begins to rise out of the swamp behind them; a thing with a vast crocodilian head, hulking shoulders and a pale green torso corded with brawn. Stealthily, it begins to haul itself onto the path, its avid eyes fixated on the three creatures you have just encountered.

Beyond the Lizard-man is a weed-bordered trail leading up into dense rainforest that marks the westernmost limits of the swamp. If the creatures fight, it may give you an easy chance to escape this miserable place. But you feel a pang of guilt for allowing the Lizard-man to be taken by surprise on your account…

Do you wish to shout a warning to the Lizard-man and his pets? If so, turn to **426**.

If you would rather leave the creature to its fate and take advantage of the imminent confrontation, turn to **470**.

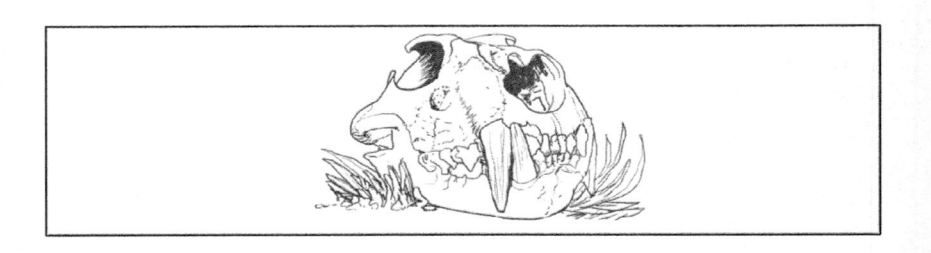

413

Moreau is too distracted by his struggle to notice you approach his back with your weapon raised. Just as you are poised to strike, the puma tears its other arm free, seizes the doctor by the throat and hurls him to the floor once more!

She then snaps the chains on her legs as if they were ribbons and bears you to the cold floor of the laboratory with a springing leap. You glimpse a raw-seamed face and manic lidless eyes inches from yours and fling up an arm to ward off a clawing blow that lands with numbing force…!

Lose 4 VITALITY points, 1 PROWESS point and 1 BALLISTICS point!

Following this assault, the puma bounds over you through the doorway to your room in a flutter of red-stained bandages. You hear the outer door slammed wide open and a parting shriek like that of an angry virago.

Moreau climbs to his feet, glances at you briefly, and snatches a revolver from the countertop. Unhesitatingly, he rushes off in pursuit of the puma, his massive white face all the more terrible for the blood that is trickling from his forehead.

You struggle to your feet to follow but are struck by a sudden agony in your arm and a debilitating wave of nausea…

Turn to 259.

414

You suffer a horrid end; beaten, clawed and savaged to death under a surge of roaring, writhing, malodorous bodies...

YOUR DEATH HAS FINALLY COME!

415

Again, the Thylacine-men wolf down the meal in moments (remove a second meal from your *equipment list!*).

Though you have little doubt that the creatures could devour half a dozen meals between them, they are no longer being driven to distraction by their hunger. One of them immediately turns tail and disappears into the jungle to the north, but the other holds fast for a moment.

'Check the base of the tree, lord,' he says, with some effort, before racing off after his partner.

Do you wish to search the base of the mahogany tree as the creature suggested? If so, turn to **504**.

If you would rather press on through the jungle towards the south, turn to **171**.

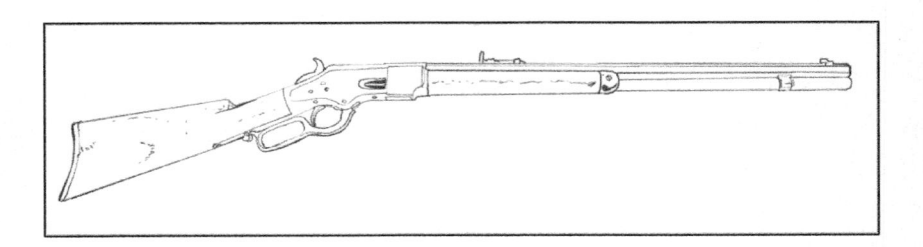

You manage to force your writhing opponent into a deep guillotine choke and snap its neck with a sudden upward surge! As the Leopard-man's body drops to the ground, you see his pride-mates let loose their charges. With horror, you see that they are not hunting dogs at all, but a pair of lithe jungle cats...

Immediately, the fearsome LEOPARDS come bounding towards you, their fierce eyes afire!

First LEOPARD: Prowess - 8; Vitality - 10; Damage - 2.

Second LEOPARD: Prowess - 7; Vitality - 9; Damage - 2.

If you win, turn to 252.

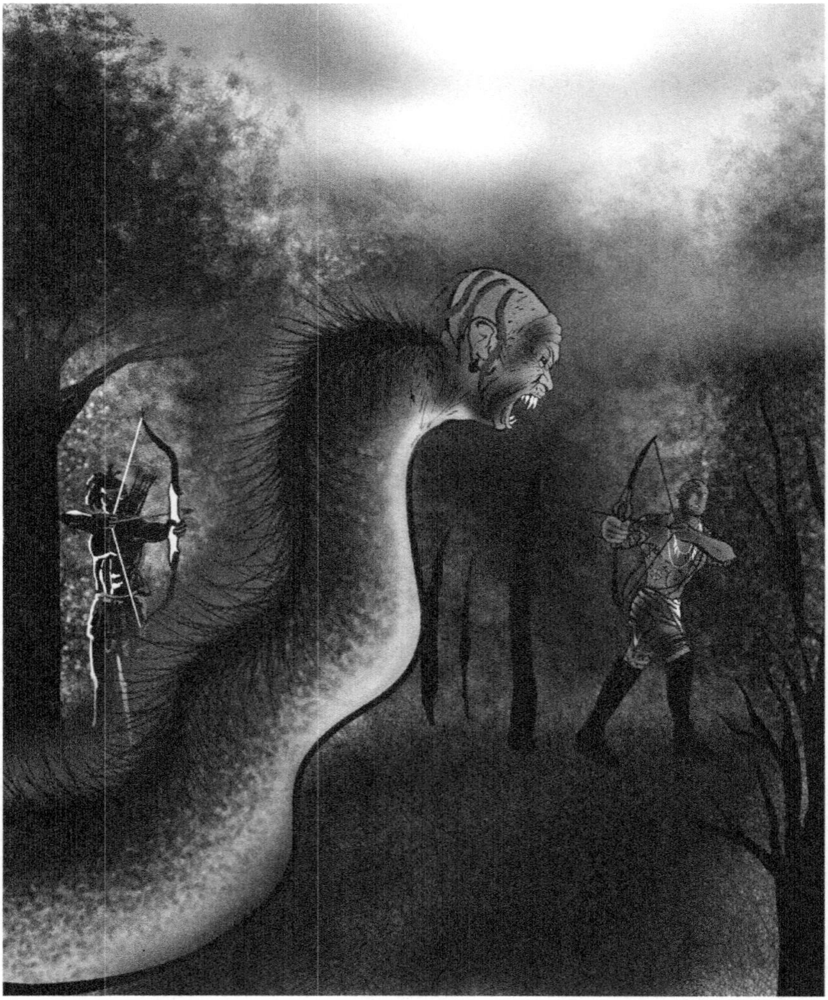

417

You hurry towards the sounds, almost losing one of your boots as you trudge through a section of steaming mire that has spread over the flatter, lower reaches of this side of the island. You find your footing on an area of firmer ground, leap over a meandering streamlet, then pull up in horror as a hideous apparition bursts through a clump of bushes little more than a hundred yards to your fore.

The *thing* before you defies identification, but it resembles a giant, coarsened maggot that is the length of two tall men and the width of nine wine barrels lashed together. Out of its leathery hide protrude black, bristling spines that extrude and retract in rhythm with each bloating breath. These thorny outgrowths sink into the earth and seem to assist the creature's undulating locomotion that is reminiscent of the way that dolphins and whales glide through the water. But by far the most hideous feature of this aberration is its head, for instead of the blind, seeking point of the larva it so resembles, it possesses the huge and twisted face of a man who is in the paroxysms of mortal agony...

It is the DRACONOPE, one of Doctor Moreau's most hellish creations!

Something causes the monster to flop to a halt and bend horribly to peer inland, just as a bow-wielding man breaks out of cover and fires an arrow in the creature's direction. The barb flies high, but it is enough to send the thing into motion once more...this time directly towards you!

In the same moment, a second hunter bursts through a veil of steam to your right, evidently trying to cut off the creature's escape. The Draconope spies him with streaming eyes, roars a wordless challenge and charges the man with a speed that belies its bloated, limbless form. Immediately, you see that the second hunter is in trouble. Though several of his shafts find their mark, the beast shows little sign of slackening its pace.

The first man gives a shout of dismay and begins to race down the marshy declination, but he is too distant to prevent his friend receiving the full impact of the creature's furious charge!

If you have a ranged weapon and wish to shoot at the monster, turn to **477**.

If you do not have a ranged weapon, or do not wish to use it, you may rush in and engage the monster in close combat (turn to **332**).

If you would prefer to leave these men to their sport, retrace your steps to the beach and continue west, turn to **442**.

418

As you recite the biblical prohibitions not to murder, steal, nor commit adultery, the beast-folk cast nervous glances at one another, then turn on you in rage.

'This newcomer's Law is False!' you hear the Sayer roar. 'How dare he set these filthy proclamations above His word, He who wields the lightning and commands the stars above! All those faithful, teach this wretch the purifying power of pain!'

At this, the Sayer's followers knock you to the ground and proceed to subject you to a savage beating...

Roll a dice and remove the total from your VITALITY!

If you are still alive, turn to **307**.

350

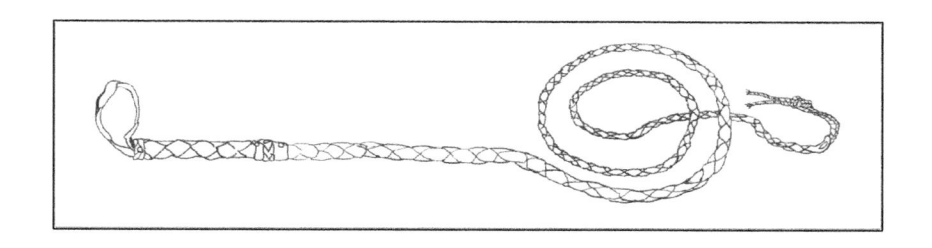

419

Breathing heavily, you push the bodies of the sailor and Helmar into the sea. You may also keep the sailor's **dagger** if you wish (2 points of close combat damage)!

Confident that you have improved your chances of surviving long enough to be rescued, you settle back in the dinghy and try to conserve your strength.

The days pass in a tedium of glassy seas and burning sun, broken only by the sharp chill of the night or the sudden splash of some sea-sleek creature. On the morning of your eighth day adrift, however, you wake to see a set of sails dancing above the horizon!

Thanks to your supplies you are in a fair condition, suffering nothing worse than a mild case of sunburn that causes you to lose 2 VITALITY points. Eager to be rescued, you paddle hard towards the approaching schooner. In your excitement, you take your eye off the sea and are taken unaware by an unusually powerful wave that almost capsises your dinghy. With water sloshing about your little craft, you slip and crack your head upon the thwart, knocking yourself senseless…

Now, turn to 216.

420

Your spirits lift when you see the words '*Webley and Scott - Birmingham*' written on the lid of the small wooden box, for it is the name of one of Britain's leading ammunition manufacturers!

You pry open the tightly-sealed lid and are met with the soft metallic gleam not of gold, but of the bronze tips of 12 tightly-packed **revolver bullets**! Stuffing the rounds into your pockets, you move on to the leather sack. Within, you find a small **iron hammer and chisel** packed in amongst a dozen or so **barbed caltrops**.

Add these items to your *equipment list* and gain 1 FATE point.

Delighted at these finds, you notice that an area of the hull beside the prow of the frigate is so badly rotted that you are able to smash a hole large enough to crawl through. Once outside, you look up to find the Satyr staring down at you. Immediately, his wide nostrils quiver and a nauseated look passes over his ovine face.

'You smell quite bad, my lord,' the little creature grimaces. 'Perhaps I should have warned you about the Rat-wings? Well never mind, what's done is done! If it's any consolation, you should know that those little beasts only anoint those they take a liking to...'

The Satyr frowns and tightens his large mouth in what you are sure is an attempt to conceal his mirth...

'But enough of that!' the creature says with an effort. 'If you care to follow me, lord, I will lead you back to the arena so that you may continue on your way.'

Pausing only to rub yourself over with a number of large leaves, you follow your guide away from the wreck.

Turn to <u>232</u>.

421

As your opponent thrashes in its death-throes, you race to the Dog-man's aid to find him locked in a vicious struggle. You strike at the second Wolf-man, distracting it so that your companion is able to kill it with a crushing bite to the throat!

With both Wolf-men slain, you search the bodies but find nothing of note apart from a pair of identical leather necklaces hung with small, drilled stones.

Take the **stone necklaces** if you wish, then turn to 460.

422

Your canoe grounds onto the delta with a soft whisper and you are startled that the water you leap into is tepid and foul smelling. Worse still, the sand beneath your feet is much softer than you had expected; so soft in fact that you sink down to your ankles, then as deep as your knees!

It is impossible to know which route across the delta will enable you to reach the shore safely. As such, you must trust to chance and *test your FATE!*

If you are favoured, turn to 293.

If you are unfavoured, turn to 382.

423

Unfortunately, the pounding of your feet releases greater concentrations of gas, so that the layer of water around you starts to boil and seethe. Gagging and retching on the poisonous fumes, your legs give out from beneath you, and it is not long before you are utterly overcome...

YOUR ADVENTURE ENDS HERE!

424

You sink to your haunches beside the bodies of these sudden enemies, utterly dismayed by the ferocious unpredictability of Doctor Moreau's creations. Aside from the prone forms of several beast-people that were trampled in the stampede, the arena and meadow are now utterly deserted.

Do you wish to perform a quick search of the area? If so, turn to **87**.

If you would rather leave this place immediately, then you see two directions open to you:

Into the jungle towards the west? Turn to **199**.

Or into the jungle towards the east? Turn to **265**.

425

You listen for a while to the group outside, noting the creeping inspiration of the brandy in the howls and yelps of the beast-folk. Presently, you hear Montgomery's voice shouting 'Right turn! Come on, men!' before the shouts slowly recede into silence.

As the peaceful splendour of the night reasserts, you cannot help but gaze at the body of Doctor Moreau. His massive face is calm even after the violence of his death, while his dead, hard eyes seem to stare at the white moon above. The events of the day leave you little doubt that it is imperative to get away from the island at first light, which entails taking the island ship with as much food and water as you can gather. For Montgomery there is no help; he is in truth half akin to the beast-folk, unfitted for human kindred.

There are many hours till the dawn, and you resolve to make the most of your time. On the side of the courtyard opposite the laboratory there are two rooms that you know to be Montgomery and Moreau's private quarters.

Your eyes also wander to Moreau's pockets - they may contain something useful...

If you wish to search Moreau's pockets, turn to **153**.

Otherwise, you can search Montgomery's and Moreau's private quarters? (Turn to **407**).

426

At your warning, the Lizard-man spins around and is just fast enough to dart to one side as the CROCODILE-MAN'S jaws snap down on thin air! Immediately, the monitor lizards charge the monster. One of them is batted aside by the slash of a short, powerful forelimb, while the second lizard bites down on one of his enemy's broad, scaly shoulders before backing away and hissing fiercely.

The Crocodile-man is the most fearsome of Moreau's creations you have witnessed thus far. At least eight feet tall, its head, neck and limbs seem only marginally altered from the illustrations you have seen of the great amphibious killers that inhabit the large waterways of Africa and Australia, yet its thickly-muscled torso - aside from its pale green hue and the scaly natural armour of its shoulders and back - appears almost human. If such discordances ought to have rendered such an entity sluggish and clumsy, then in practice they appear to have had no ill-effects at all…

Roaring savagely, the Crocodile-man and Lizard-man clash in combat, brute force versus speed and martial skill! It will be a tremendous contest, but you doubt whether the Lizard-man and his charges have the power to defeat so mighty a foe.

Do you wish to aid the Lizard-man and monitor lizards in this fight? If so, turn to **209**.

If you feel you have interfered enough and wish to seize the opportunity to reach the trail leading out of the swamp, turn to **395**.

427

You are roundly ignored as everyone busies themselves with the task of moving the various packages and caged animals. Miserably, you wander to the aft of the ship, where there is nothing to do but stare at the shimmering blue horizon.

When the work is done, Montgomery and his white-haired companion push their boat off the larger schooner and begin to move towards the island without even a backward glance. Meanwhile, Captain Davis and four of his crew move towards you, their faces cold and hard.

'You're being set adrift as before, I tell you,' the captain growls. 'And any laws that be against such an act be damned!'

Glancing desperately over the aft of the ship, you see the little dinghy of *The Lady Vain* that has been towed behind the *Ipecacuanha* ever since your rescue. It still looks to be seaworthy, though it is now half-filled with water, has no oars, and is entirely unvictualled.

Even so, the sailors are planning to abandon you in her once again…!

Do you wish to resist the sailors? If so, turn to 129.

If you feel that you have little choice but go along with their plan, turn to 225.

428

You will have to dodge the cane toad's spitting attack whilst attempting to pin it from behind!

Test your PROWESS with a +1 disadvantage because of the effects of the initial toxic attack.

If you pass, turn to 272.

If you fail, turn to 281.

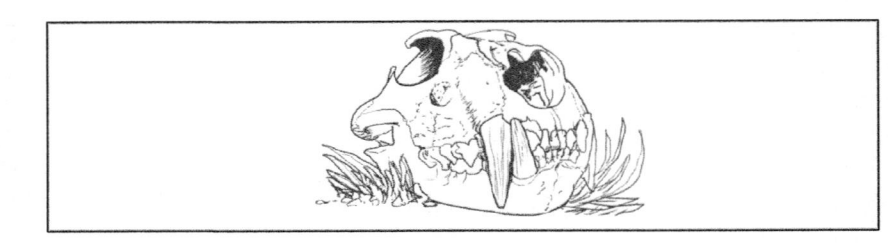

429

Somehow, your shot merely scratches the hunter!

With extraordinary speed, the man spins on his heel and hurls his hand axe at you...

Roll one dice to decide what happens next:

1 - the hand axe hurtles harmlessly past your head.

2 - the hand axe glances from your shoulder, causing you to lose 1 VITALITY point.

3 - the hand axe hits you in the mid-section, but only with the flat of the blade. Lose 2 VITALITY points.

4 - the hand axe gashes your off-arm. Lose 2 VITALITY points and 1 PROWESS point.

5 - the hand axe cuts you on your dominant arm. Lose 2 VITALITY, 2 PROWESS points and 1 BALLISTICS point.

6 - the hand axe thumps into the centre of your chest, cleaving your breastbone in two! You sink to your knees as the hunter draws one of his knives and closes in... YOUR ADVENTURE ENDS HERE!

If you are still alive, the hunter draws a pair of gleaming knives and attacks!

LAZALO THE HUNTER: Prowess - 7; Vitality - 8; Damage - 2.

Note: Lazalo wields a pair of **Toledo steel hunting knives** that give him +1 to his *close combat score*.

If you win, you may take the man's **hand axe** (2 points of close combat damage), **bow** (2 points of ranged damage) and **quiver of arrows (7)**, as well as his pair of **hunting knives**.

Now, do you wish to explore the beach? If so, turn to 473.

If you would prefer to head back inland towards the source of the hot springs, turn to 261.

430

The noise and smoke of your firearm transforms the aggression of these predatory strangers into terror. They flee into the jungle before you can fire off another shot.

Gain 1 FATE point!

Taking a deep sigh of relief and keeping your weapon to hand, you advance into the darkness of the ravine…

Turn to 114.

359

431

When you ask to take ownership of one of the monitor lizards, the Lizard-man's long throat bobs up and down in consternation.

'Many friends have I lost to the dangers of the swamp,' he explains. 'Thus, I will not willingly be parted from the few who are left to me. Instead, allow my gift to be a warning from one warrior to another: leave this island, friend, as soon as you may. The Master has unleashed forces he cannot hope to control. Death will come to him sooner than he knows, but you need not share his doom.'

The Lizard-man glances darkly at the broken body of the Crocodile-man, then strides back into the swamp with the monitor lizards scrambling in his wake. You watch the creatures disappear into the mist, then make your way up the trail that leads into the jungle once more.

Turn to **395**.

432

As you leave the room, you must roll two dice!

If the values of each dice are different, then the beast-folk have not yet found a way into the enclosure. Even so, you dare not linger in the courtyard for fear of becoming trapped and decide to escape to the roof while you can. Turn to **533**.

If you roll a double, then you run headlong into a snarling JAGUAR-MAN who has managed to clamber over the wall and into the courtyard. The creature pulls you close so that you cannot use your firearm, and the two of you fall struggling to the floor. As you fight for your life, you hear the thuds of more beast-folk dropping into the interior of the enclosure. You resist gamely but are hopelessly outnumbered...

YOUR TIME IS FINALLY UP!

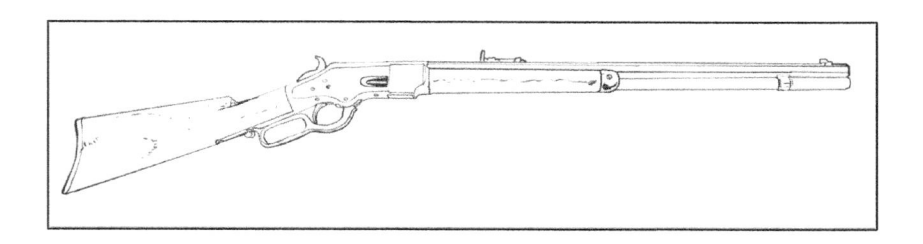

433

Given the proximity of nightfall, you decide that you do not want any of the island's animal-men anywhere near you in the dark, even ones that appear as harmless as this Dog-man.

'Go away!' you warn the creature. 'Do not come near me!'

The Dog-man retreats a little way like a hound being sent home, then stops and looks over his shoulder imploringly.

'May I not come near you?' he calls.

'No. Go away!' you insist, stooping for a stone with which to drive the persistent fellow off. At this threat, the creature slinks back down the ravine and is soon lost to sight in the gathering dusk. Satisfied you are alone once more, you need to decide how you are going to descend into the ravine.

If you possess a rope, turn to __464__.

If you do not possess a rope, turn to __501__.

434

Feeling somewhat self-conscious, you shrug off your rucksack, remove your clothing and ease yourself into the water. Other than casting you diffident glances the creatures do not react, and you content yourself with the sensation of the hot mineral water.

Gain 2 VITALITY points from the soothing powers of the geothermic pool!

As you stare through the steam at the glittering firmament above, your fears and anxieties begin to ease, and you begin to drift towards much needed sleep...

Test your FATE!

If you are favoured, turn to **522**.

If you are unfavoured, turn to **490**.

435

Within seconds of setting off at a run, you hear the hiss and thwack of arrows falling around you. Daring to hope, you swerve this way and that, but you have two highly skilled hunters taking aim at your back...

Roll a dice!

If you roll 1-3, turn to **67**.

If you roll 4-6, turn to **80**.

436

You press on deeper into the jungle, now alert for any further dangers. It seems that M'ling and the white-swathed servants you have seen are milder instances of whatever bizarre phenomenon is at work on Doctor Moreau's island.

Quite how that eminent scientist has created such entities is beyond your understanding, and it is questionable whether what he has done should be condoned or censured. More to the point, you are clearly in no small amount of danger!

Even so, you feel a steely determination to explore the island as thoroughly as possible. In doing so, you may find some answers, make some allies or even find a way to ensure that you are not the doctor's next test subject...

After expending a good deal of effort weaving your way through the jungle, you catch the sound of excited yips and growls coming from ahead. Not wishing to retrace your hard-earned steps, you press on determinedly and break through a screen of vines into a dank clearing...

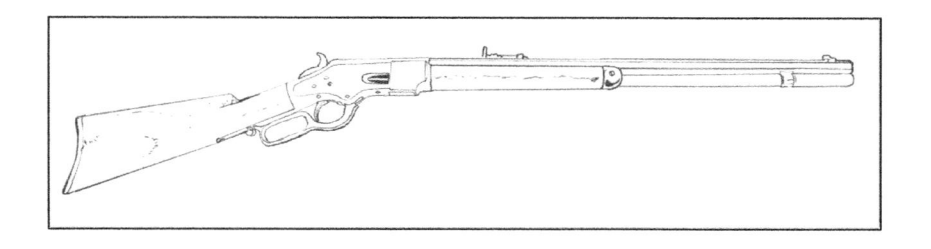

Turn to <u>173</u>.

437

The hunter is so preoccupied with his work that you have no trouble sneaking past him and gaining access to the beach. There, drawn up high on the sand are four beautifully crafted canoes. Each of them is made of a chestnut-coloured wood and has a double-sided oar cast within. Though you do not have the seamanship to handle one of them out on the open sea, you feel confident that you could paddle along the island's coast and spare your legs a considerable amount of work.

You take a moment to orient yourself and realise that heading east will take you back to the enclosure. Not feeling ready to face Moreau and Montgomery yet, you resolve to explore in the opposite direction along the southward beach.

Do you wish to do so in one of the canoes? If so, turn to **353**.

If you would rather ignore the canoes and instead walk towards the south, turn to **285**.

438

Your refusal to make any promises seems to come as no surprise to the Sloth-man.

'It is just as well that you seek to avoid raising my hopes, lord,' the little creature pipes sadly. 'Even so, take this lucky charm as a token of my respect for your courage.'

The Sloth-man hands you a **sea-polished stone**, bids you farewell, then leaves you alone within the smoky hut.

You take some time to eat from the store of food (restore 4 VITALITY points), before stretching out on one of the beds and falling into a troubled sleep.

Now turn to 19.

439

After a few hours heading north you begin to hear the roar of the ocean. When you finally break free of the dense tree line, you smile at the sight of the glimmering emerald expanse before you and raise your sweat-soaked face to a brisk, warm breeze.

In front of you is a beach of gold-grey sand on which foams a playful surf, the tamed remnants of immense breakers that topple onto underwater reefs that lay half a mile out to sea. Pleased at the relief from the claustrophobia of the jungle, you stride out onto the sand and attempt to get your bearings.

You realise that heading eastward will take you back towards the enclosure, so you decide to explore the beach towards the west.

Turn to 485.

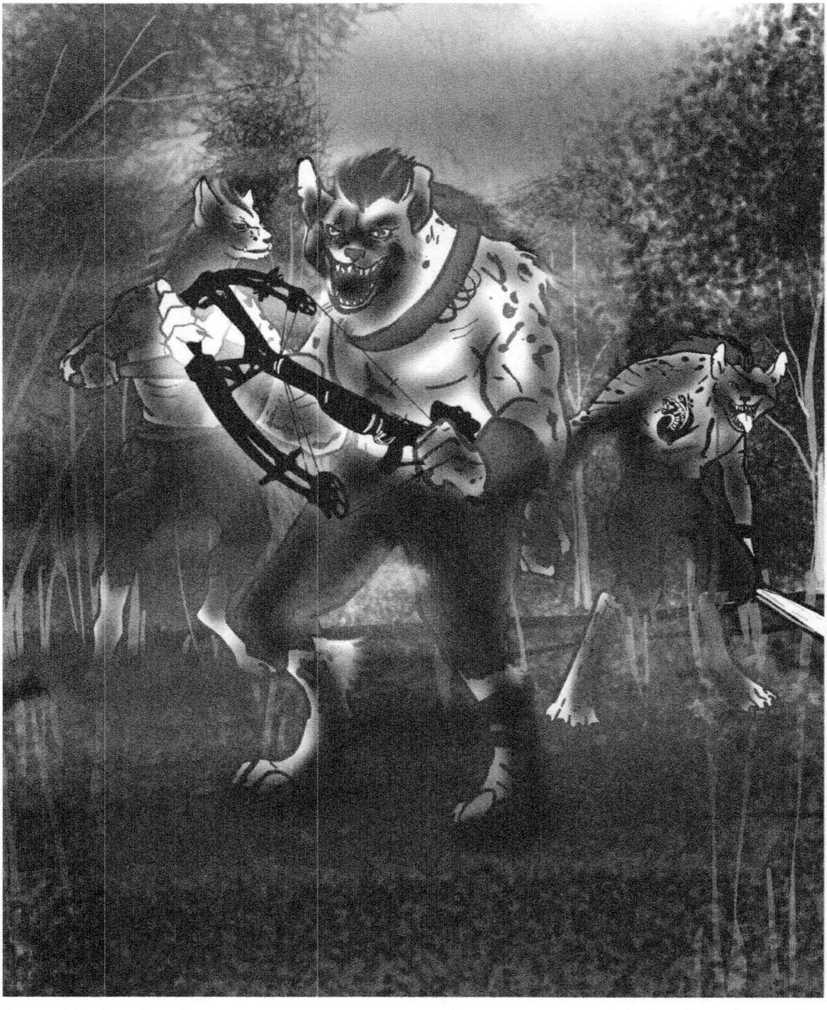

440

You stand very still, your sleeve over your mouth and nose in an attempt to reduce your exposure to the poison gas. Despite your efforts, you must still lose 2 VITALITY points from the hydrogen sulphide's deleterious effects!

With little else to do but wait, you scan your surroundings for anyone who might be able to help. An hour passes before you spy a figure standing at the edge of a line of trees to the south-west. He has a strange, slouching gait, is clad in nothing more than ragged brown trousers, and walks with his head thrust out before him on a long, thick neck. For a moment he straightens up as he sees you, then turns about and vanishes into the tree line. When he returns and starts towards you, there are two companions by his side…

As the party draws nearer, you see that they are running with a skipping gait on short, malformed legs, while their inordinately long necks, arms and torsos are tawny and powerfully muscled. But it is their soulless, jet-black eyes that strike fear into your heart; that and their sinister, giggling vocalisations. Your regret at being seen is confirmed when the largest of the trio stops at ten paces and levels a small crossbow in your direction, while its pack-mates brandish crude wooden clubs menacingly.

'Come forth, come forth, man-thing!' the HYENA-MAN snickers in a voice that reminds you of a violin string being sawn to breaking point. 'Come forth so that we may take you somewhere safe before night-fall...!'

At these words, the other creatures give shrill laughs and grin at you malevolently.

What will you do?

If you wish to taunt the creatures, turn to **394**.

If you wish to charge the creatures, turn to **322**.

If you would prefer to stay still, while trying to explain your predicament, turn to **210**.

441

You hurry into the courtyard and stand before the two doors, trying to ignore the heavy thumps on the double gate and the fierce shouts of the beast-folk. You dare not linger within the enclosure for long, so you must choose ONE room to search before attempting to escape to the roof...

Do you wish to try the door with the rush mattress lying next to it? If so, turn to **390**.

If you would prefer to try the other door, turn to **538**.

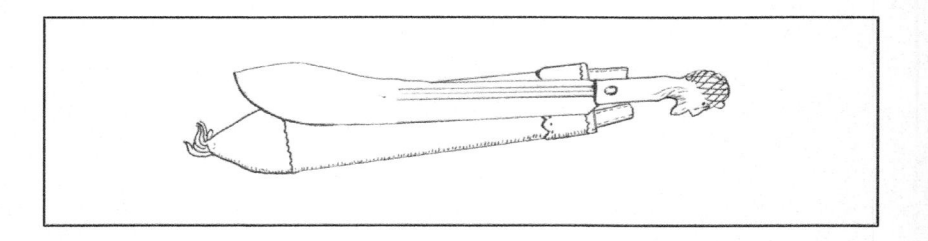

442

As you walk along the beach the jungle reasserts itself landward, while the ocean to your right seems to stretch deeper and deeper into an infinite, cloudless blue. The sound of the gentle surf and the murmuring of the wind lulls you into a reflective state, so that you almost trip over the large objects drawn up high onto the sand.

There is a collection of four canoes before you, resting at a point where the island's coast veers sharply to the south. They are beautifully crafted from a chestnut-coloured wood, and each of them has a single, double-sided oar cast within. Though you do not have the seamanship to handle one of them out on the open sea, you feel confident that you could paddle south along the island's westward coast and spare your legs a considerable amount of work.

368

However, there is also a thick brake of coconut palms inland. Through it runs a path that follows a gentle incline towards the south-east. Following it is likely to give you the greatest chance of finding the owners of the canoes, though you cannot know whether any indigenous islanders you meet will be civilised or savage...

If you wish to take one of the canoes out onto the water and head south, turn to 353.

If you would rather see where the path through the date palms leads, turn to 112.

Alternatively, you can ignore the canoes and the path and continue walking south (turn to 285).

443

Half-blinded by the air-borne toxin and barely able to breathe, you blunder back towards the northern edge of the swamp. As distraught as you are, you have not forgotten about the devil-palms that share this deadly section of jungle.

Even so, you will be fortunate to avoid colliding with one of them!

Test your FATE!

If you are favoured, turn to 234.

If you are unfavoured, turn to 288.

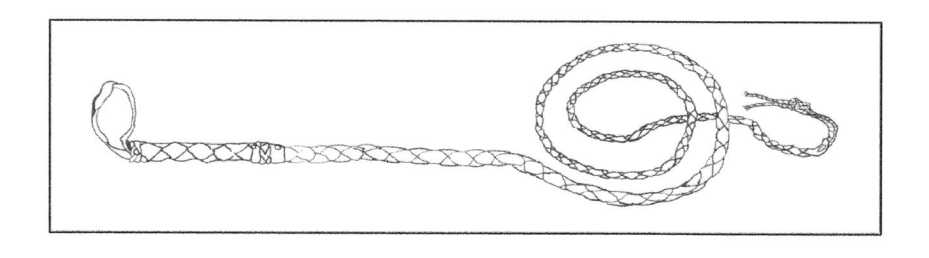

444

You awake in the depths of the night to a sight that makes you think that you must still be dreaming. Clustered around you are a dozen misshapen forms, powerful brutes who are thickly boned and rippling with sinew. Instinctively, your hand strays to your weapon, before you realise the futility of doing so...

Do you have the prickly pear? If so, turn to **482**.

If not, turn to **58**.

445

Feeling like you have little to lose, you try the silver key in the lock of the silver coffer that you found hidden in the swamp. You feel a thrill of excitement when you hear a gentle *click*.

Lifting the lid, you are surprised to find that the interior of the box has been lined with a fine layer of flint. Within is a collection of silver coins and a single velvet bag resting on a deep bed of fine, black powder.

Hurriedly pocketing the coins, you open the bag and find a wax-sealed glass phial inside. It is full of a red liquid and affixed with a label reading *'version 381'* - make a note of this number and add the **silver coins** and the **red phial** to your *equipment list*!

As you do so, you realise the purpose of the black powder. It is gunpowder that would have surely detonated if any thief had tried to break into the coffer with an iron tool!

Pleased with your findings and feeling that you have spent enough time in the room, you return to the courtyard.

Turn to **432**.

446

Due to the narrowness of the steps, you may fight the three ship rats one at a time. If you are unarmed, remember to reduce your *close combat score* by 2 for this fight!

First SHIP RAT: Prowess - 5; Vitality - 4; Damage - 1.

Second SHIP RAT: Prowess - 5; Vitality - 5; Damage - 1.

Third SHIP RAT: Prowess - 5; Vitality - 3; Damage - 1.

If you win, do you wish to head down the steps and search below deck? If so, turn to 49.

If you would rather climb back down the rigging and swim for the dinghy, turn to 127.

447

You train your eyes on the twilit jungle shadows from where you heard the sound, your hackles rising as a hulking shape emerges from the gloom. Only then do you realise that you have wandered once again into the territory of the PUGNATYR, the great gorilla-like creature you communicated with only that morning.

The Pugnatyr's low grunts reassure you of his peaceful intent, but he is clearly agitated by something. He comes to your side, tilts his head in the direction of the beach, and thumps his great fist into the ground.

Danger...!

Just then, a startled rabbit scurries past you and rustles through the undergrowth towards the beach. Moments later, you hear a high-pitched squeal...

Have you killed the Draconope? If so, turn to 297.

If you have not killed the Draconope, turn to 567.

Sadly, none of the friendly beast-folk you have met come to your aid…

Instead, the circle of creatures closes in, a ring of faces as savage as one might see if hemmed in by a pride of hungry lions or a pack of starving wolves. You realise that you are moments away from being torn to shreds!

Do you possess the **Restored Dragon**? If so, go to the section that is the same as the number etched on the side of its barrel.

If not, do you possess the **carbine**? If so, go to the section that is the same as the number etched on the side of its barrel.

If you have neither of these weapons, turn to **458**.

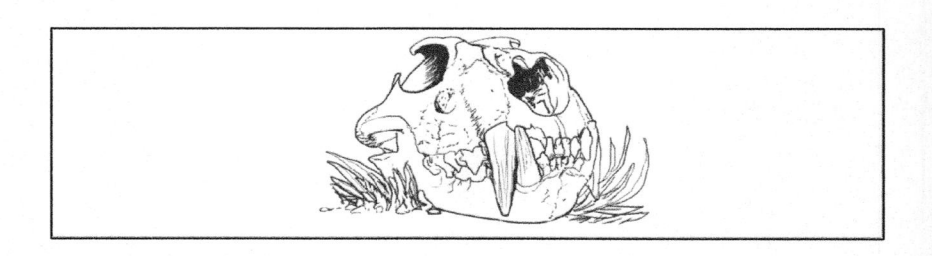

449

You awake to the sound of a raucous tumult coming from outside and see the light of early morning filtering through the gaps in the roof of the hut.

Gain 4 VITALITY points from your sleep.

Any drowsiness is banished when you hear the sharp yelp of a staghound and the unmistakable timbre of human voices. In another moment you are standing outside the hovel, every muscle quivering in dread anticipation. Before you are the clumsy backs of perhaps a score of the beast-folk, their misshapen heads half-hidden by their shoulder blades. They are gesticulating excitedly towards the downhill passage where you see the dark figure and awful white face of Doctor Moreau approaching. He is holding back his pack of leaping hunting dogs and close behind him comes Montgomery, grim-faced and with a revolver in hand.

The beast-folk fall back at the men's advance, their heads bowed and postures slumped. Some of them slink back into their huts, while others flee past you up the chasm. Only the Sayer of the Law and a few of the bolder creatures stand firm, their eyes full of wonder at the sight of their creator. For a moment you too consider flight, but you realise that you would have no hope of escaping the hounds were the doctor to set them loose.

'We have tracked you down for your own good,' says Moreau, coming to a halt before you and eying the huts dubiously. 'As no doubt you have discovered, this island is full of inimical phenomena you've no business being around. You are fortunate that we were able to find you.'

'After you left the enclosure, I expected you would return before nightfall,' Montgomery adds, a little peevishly. 'You've no idea of the worry and trouble you've caused.'

'Nor the time and energy I have wasted chasing after you rather than advancing my work,' says Moreau curtly. 'Now, you will gather your things and accompany us home immediately. Once there, we will talk.'

You do as Moreau bids, and are soon accompanying the two men up the narrow chasm. One or two of the beast-folk attempt to follow but retreat again when Montgomery cracks his whip. Soon, you enter a dark tunnel before emerging into a clearing enclosed by a wall of blackened rubble and scorched trees. There is a ragged gap in the rocks to your left, but Moreau leads you across the clearing onto a gloomy jungle path heading east.

Any attempts by you at conversation are stymied by Montgomery as the three of you advance, and it is not long before your party emerges onto the small sandbank overlooking the beach where you first set out on your exploration of the island. The sun has dispelled any vapours from the dawn, and you see the strong mid-morning light beating down on the walls and roofs of the enclosure.

As is his wont, Moreau leads the staghounds to the main gates of the compound, while Montgomery unlocks the side entrance to allow you access to the room you have been appointed.

'Wait within for the doctor to join you,' he instructs. 'And do not run off anywhere under any circumstances, is that clear?'

Nodding agreement, you enter the room and sink gratefully into the reading chair, your mind racing over recent events. It does not take long before you hear the inner door to the courtyard being unlocked, and the doctor strides in...

Turn to <u>39</u>.

450

You press on west along the moon-silvered path. Presently, the trees lining the route start to blacken, and a pungent scent fills the air. Ahead of you is a clearing covered with a pale, sulphurous encrustation that leaks wisps of white smoke. Around the clearing is a wall of blackened rubble about three yards high through which there are two other exits.

The first is directly across from you, a dark tunnel that plunges into the earth. The second is a ragged gap in the rocks to your right that leads to a hillside wreathed in plumes of steam.

If you wish to try the tunnel opposite, turn to **476**.

If you would rather try the gap in the rocks to investigate the steam-wreathed hillside, turn to **399**.

451

As you follow the streamlet inland, it leads you to the base of a steep spur of dripping granite that is part of the headland located on the south-east corner of the island. The air is still and close, the masses of thickets around you deadening any sound from the enclosure and the beach. Your mind wanders, and you begin to take delight in the flora around you, noticing a peculiar fungus that is branched and corrugated like a foliaceous lichen that deliquesces into slime at your touch.

You are so pre-occupied with your observations that you stop just in time to prevent yourself from emerging unchecked upon a glade made in the forest by the falling of a tree. Seedlings are already starting up to struggle for the vacant space and beyond, the dense growth of stems, twining vines and splashes of fungus and flowers closes in again.

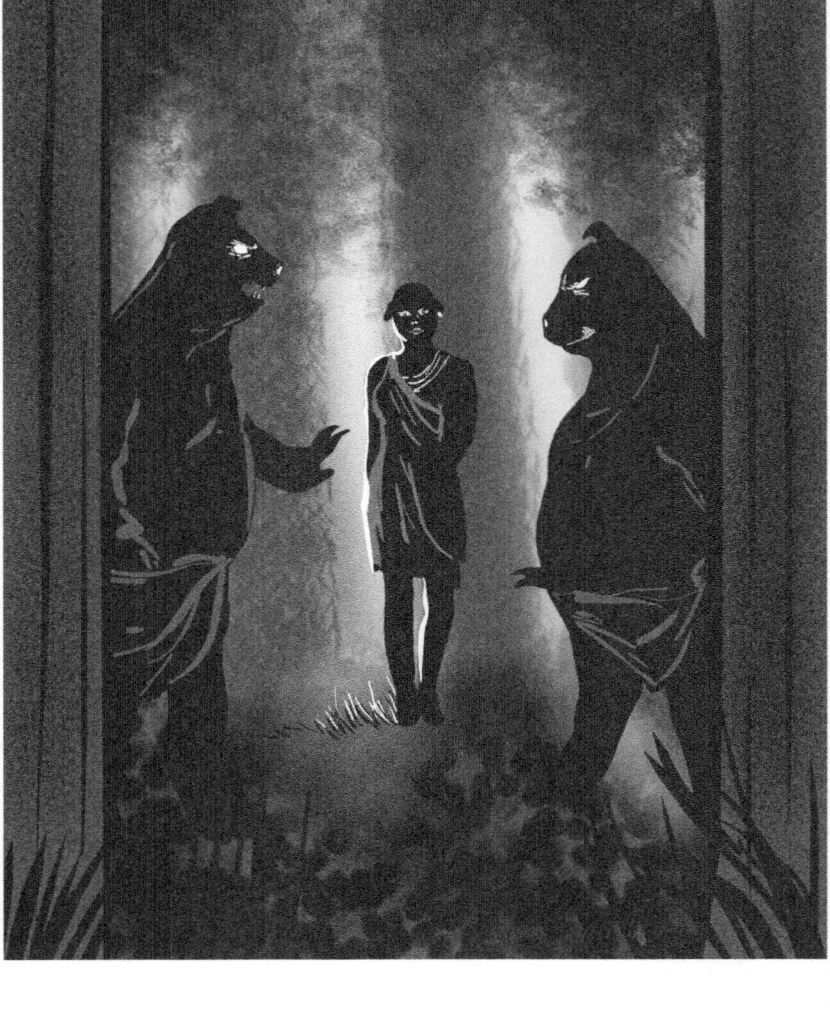

Before you are three grotesque figures standing beside a fallen tree. They are naked apart from swathings of scarlet cloth around their middles, and their skins are of a dull pinkish colour. Two of them are evidently males with inordinately large heads, powerful necks, robust, compact torsos and short, clumsy limbs that end in twisted parodies of hands and feet. The lone female is considerably smaller and more human in appearance, though she shares the heavy chinless face, retreating forehead and prognathous jaw of the males.

With a start, you realise that what offends you about these creatures is the irreconcilable paradox of their structure, form and manner that is caught between utter strangeness and the strangest familiarity. There is woven into their movements, countenance and whole presence the irresistible suggestion of a hog, a swinish taint, the unmistakable mark of the beast!

These creatures are SWINE-FOLK, and true to the nature of wild pigs the males are grunting at one another as they prepare to fight for status and breeding rights. As you watch, the adversaries collide head first, thrashing from side to side and squealing furiously...

Do you wish to stand by and watch the outcome of the contest? If so, turn to 257.

If you would rather attempt to break up the fight, turn to 304.

Alternatively, if you would rather slip by the quarrelling brutes and continue heading west through the jungle, turn to 436.

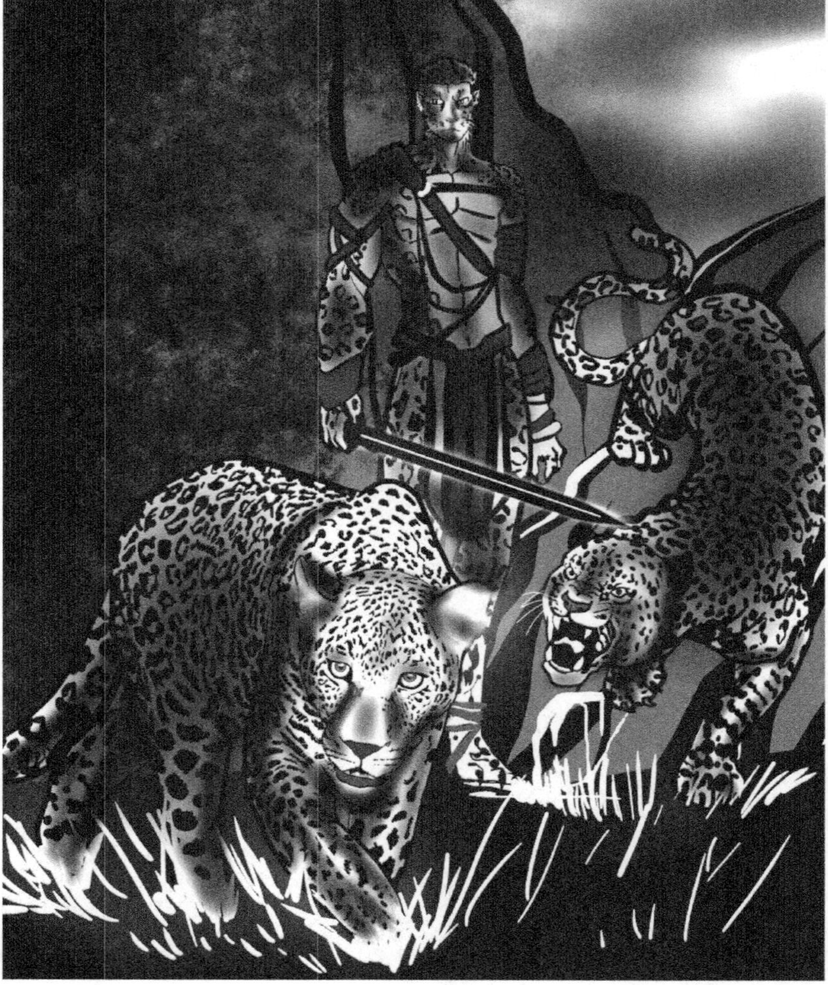

If the creature understands your words, then it has little patience for them. Instead, it snarls a command and its approaching kinsfolk release the beasts they have been restraining. As the bounding forms surge towards you, you realise that they are not hunting dogs at all, but powerful jungle cats!

You will have to fight both LEOPARDS, as well as the LEOPARD-MAN who called them.

You are permitted to perform TWO ranged attacks against targets of your choice, before close combat is joined. You must fight all three opponents simultaneously:

LEOPARD-MAN: Prowess - 8; Vitality - 7; Ranged Defence - 8; Damage - 2.

First LEOPARD: Prowess - 8; Vitality - 10; Ranged Defence - 9; Damage - 2.

Second LEOPARD: Prowess - 7; Vitality - 9; Ranged Defence - 8; Damage - 2.

If you win, turn to 252.

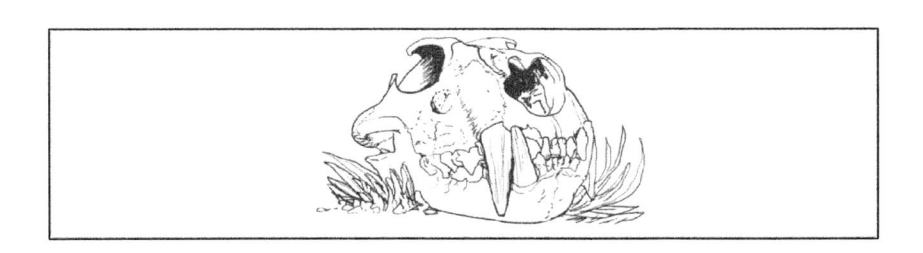

453

What will you say to the white-haired man?

If you wish to say that your family will pay him a handsome reward for offering you sanctuary, turn to **135**.

If you would prefer to tell him that you are a scientist interested in the natural world, turn to **66**.

Alternatively, you can remind the man that helping you is the humane thing to do (turn to **203**).

454

The Thylacine-men begin to drool as you remove the meal from your pack (remove it from your *equipment list*) and devour it within seconds. From the gleam in their eyes, you can see that the creatures are still hungry, though their manner has calmed somewhat now they have eaten something.

Do you wish to offer them one more meal (if you have it)? If so, turn to **415**.

If you do not have any meals remaining (or do not wish to give any away), then you have little choice but to press on towards the south. Turn to **171**.

455

You back away from the beast-folk storming out of the large hut, desperately thinking of a way to avert their wrath. By the time the

Sayer of the Law appears, you have thought of a few ideas to explain why you refused to say the words:

Do you wish to say that you already possess a law known as the Ten Commandments, and that this prohibits you from following any other? If so, turn to 100.

If you would rather tell the Sayer that you have been sent by Doctor Moreau to test the zeal of those dwelling in the chasm, turn to 374.

Otherwise, you can simply tell the Sayer that his Law is a nonsense that has been invented by Doctor Moreau to control them, by turning to 510.

456

With a triumphant shriek, the Draconope snakes around you in a constrictor's grip, its nightmarish face gibbering into yours. You are grateful when your senses blur from the effects of the pressure, and barely register the moment the monster snaps your spine like a wet branch...

YOUR ADVENTURE ENDS HERE!

457

Your final blow sends your opponent crashing to the forest floor, where it kicks spasmodically before falling still. Shaken by the encounter, you take to one knee to regain your breath. The clearing is empty now, and you can only assume that the Swine-woman fled during the fight.

Do you now wish to perform a quick search of the clearing? If so, turn to **392**.

If you would rather leave the clearing immediately, turn to **436**.

458

As the mob closes in, one of the foremost beast-folk - a towering, dappled monster - charges at Montgomery with a heart-stopping roar. M'ling flies at it with a snarl, but is smashed aside, and a split-second later Montgomery drives in the assailant's head with a shot to the middle of its face. Still the creature ploughs on, gripping Montgomery and landing on top of him, where it thrashes in its death throes.

You fire several rounds of your revolver before being overwhelmed and hurled to the ground. You fight bravely, but your attackers are too strong and far too many. Pinned to the ground by gripping claws and tearing jaws, you begin to be eaten alive...

YOUR ADVENTURE IS OVER!

459

After a few hours of toiling through the jungle you break free of the dense cover. To your right is a glimmering expanse of ocean which breaks on offshore reefs before foaming up a slender beach of grey-gold sand.

382

Before you is a geothermal marshland crisscrossed by heated streams that release clouds of vapour. Further uphill and towards the interior of the island are a cluster of geothermic pools that bubble and steam. Beyond them, you can make out a drifting plume of white volcanic smoke seeping from the island's heart.

Here and there, stands of stunted trees have found footholds on areas of firmer, dryer soil. From one of these copses you hear a terrible shriek that freezes your blood. Your reaction is to flee, but then the cry is followed by a different sort of call - that of human voices raised in urgency, excitement and fear!

Emboldened, you advance onto a hillock of firmer ground, from where you see a hideous apparition bursting through a clump of bushes a little more than a hundred yards to your fore.

The *thing* before you defies identification, resembling a giant, coarsened maggot that is eight feet long and as wide as the cabin of a small schooner. Out of its leathery hide protrude bristling spines that extrude and retract with each bloating breath. These thorny outgrowths spike into the earth; they seem to assist the creature's undulating locomotion which is reminiscent of the way a whale moves through the water. But the monster's most hideous feature is its head, for instead of the blind, probing point of the larva it so resembles, it possesses the huge and twisted face of a man that glistens with slime and gibbers incoherently.

It is the DRACONOPE, one of Doctor Moreau's earliest and most hellish creations!

As you stare in horror, a bow-wielding man breaks out of cover from higher up in the marsh and sends an arrow hissing past the lurching creature. In the same moment, a second hunter bursts through a veil of steam to your right, evidently trying to cut off the monster's escape. He marks his quarry with several arrows, but the Draconope shows little sign of slackening its pace.

The first man gives a shout of dismay and begins to race down the marshy declination, but he is too distant to help his friend in this fight!

If you have a ranged weapon and wish to shoot at the monster, turn to **477**.

If you do not have a ranged weapon, or do not wish to use it, you may rush in and engage the monster in close combat, by turning to **332**.

If you would prefer to leave these hunters to their dangerous sport, retreat back to the beach and continue west, turn to **442**.

460

The Dog-man leads you on into the jungle until the pair of you emerge onto the scrubby hillside you saw from the beach. Here, you are led past deep pockets of volcanic soil that have been sown with a wide variety of exotic flowers, plants and fruit trees. Your attention is so arrested by the preponderance of simple agriculture that you are startled when your guide leads you to the edge of a steep chasm that cuts through the hillside and extends into the dense jungle on either side. Descending some thirty to forty yards to the chasm floor is a rough hemp ladder. In the depths of the chasm, you can discern rows of makeshift dens on either side of the chasm floor which are illuminated by a dozen flickering torches.

'Do not be afraid, my lord,' the Dog-man mutters, clambering down the ladder and staring up at you with his large brown eyes. 'Follow me down now, safe to the huts!'

With only the slightest of hesitation, you begin your descent. Though crudely made, the ladder is solid enough and the rough material offers a reassuring grip for hand and foot. The gloom soon retreats before the glow of the torches, and you are struck by an odour that reminds you of a monkey's ill-cleaned cage.

When you arrive on the chasm floor, the Dog-man presses a small brass key into your hand before leading you the largest of the huts (add the **brass key** to your *equipment list*).

'Now you must learn the Law, my lord,' says the Dog-man apologetically.

He leads you into the hut and shows you to a bench in a dim, dank corner. Slipping the key into a pocket, you sit and stare at the shadows within shadows that are waiting in the hut, your heart thumping wildly...

Now turn to 350.

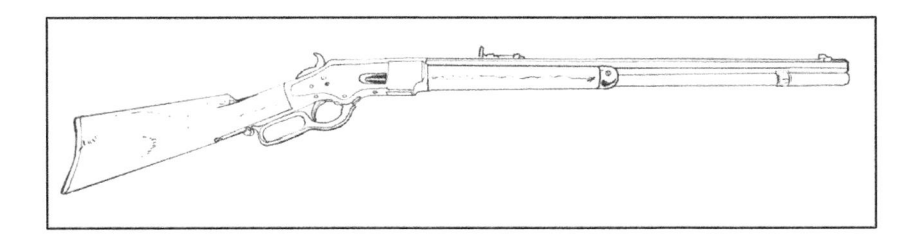

461

You spend a miserable night lashed to the rear railings of the ship. Throughout this torment, Montgomery remains brooding and silent, while his attendant drifts in and out of sleep.

You try to get some rest yourself, and manage to drift into a light slumber.

Gain 2 VITALITY points.

At first light, the deck of the *Ipecacuanha* becomes a hive of activity, and the steersman of the ship approaches your group.

'Seeing as the doctor's on his way and that he's paid decent coin for this journey, the captain's decided to be merciful,' the man says. 'Still, best watch your tone till you've disembarked, if you get my meaning?'

He unties the three of you. As you rub at your bruised wrists and throbbing hands, you see another boat approaching the schooner. It is being piloted by a tall, powerful, white-haired man dressed in dirty blue flannels. Meanwhile, Captain Davis comes up the companionway ladder and gives orders for the puma cage to be rigged for unloading. Soon, the terrified cat is crouching at the bottom of its cage as it spins from a rope tied to the mizzen boom.

'Overboard with 'em!' bawls the captain, warming to the morning and evidently still drunk. 'We'll have a clean ship soon, once we're rid of the whole blasted lot of them, men, beasts, and monsters!'

Moments later, his crew slam down a gangway onto the deck of the island boat, and Montgomery and his attendant walk over to greet the arrival of the white-haired man. You allow them to speak for a few minutes before the captain gestures for you to join them.

If you have *won Montgomery's trust*, turn to 167.

If you have *gained Montgomery's resentment*, turn to 123.

462

You stare down at the bodies of the lions and Pugnatyr, appalled by the loss of life and angry that Doctor Moreau would allow such dangerous predators to roam the island unchecked. Above your grief rises another sensation, however; a sense of pride at having stood firm beside the great ape that gave its life to protect you.

Gain 1 FATE point!

After you have regained your composure, you try to drag the body of the Pugnatyr into the jungle where he may be laid to rest, but the beast is too heavy for you to move. So you leave him beside the lions, hopeful that he would have been glad to know that his death did not go unavenged.

You walk back into the jungle and settle down to rest. Pillowing your pack beneath your head, you soon fall into a troubled sleep.

Gain 3 VITALITY points.

When you awake, you realise that you have slept for several hours and that the dawn is not too far away. It is then that you notice an animal trail running away inland of where you have been resting. Examining it closely, you see signs of the recent passage of many creatures. Intrigued, you decide to investigate.

Turn to 503.

463

Despite your best efforts, you are hurled from the rooftop, where the mob below awaits. After enduring so many hardships, being mauled to death is an ignominious end...

YOUR ADVENTURE IS OVER!

464

You tie the rope to a tree and lower yourself into the ravine without too much difficulty. Fortunately, you are able to shake the rope loose (you may keep it in your *equipment list*).

It is now almost completely dark, but there is already a wan light being cast by the rising moon, which gleams on the wet surface of a crude stairway cut out of the rock in the opposite face of the ravine. Moving towards the steaming brook, you peer through the mist to see that the steps appear to lead up into the dense jungle that crowds the southern bank.

If you wish to take the stairway into the jungle on the other side of the ravine, turn to **36**.

If you would prefer to follow the ravine uphill towards the source of the geothermic brook, turn to **496**.

Alternatively, you can follow the ravine westward towards the sea, by turning to **164**.

465

The white-haired man walks up the beach towards you, regarding you with eyes that are deep set and dark.

'Here is our unanticipated guest,' he announces, withdrawing a bunch of keys from his pocket, inserting one of them into a small door at the corner of the enclosure and unlocking it. 'I apologise in advance if everything here strikes you as a mystery, but you must understand that our establishment here contains a secret or two. Nothing very dreadful to a sane man, you understand, but since we do not know you, Montgomery and I have little choice but to be cautious. You see, this is a biological station, and we - Montgomery and I, at least - are biologists.'

His eyes stray to the strangely jointed, white-swathed men who are awkwardly hauling the puma cage on a set of rollers towards a heavy double gate that serves as the main entrance to the enclosure.

'We can keep you from idleness, if you are willing,' the man adds. 'The alternative is boredom and drudgery, states that are well known to make monsters out of men. It is not as if you can amuse yourself by roaming the island. The wild animals that inhabit it make it entirely unsafe. Also, I'm afraid that I cannot tell you when you'll be able to get away from here. We're off the track to anywhere, and see a ship once every twelve months or so, at best. My name is Moreau, by the way; Doctor Moreau.'

After you return the greeting, the doctor pushes open the small door, then leaves abruptly to unlock the main gate, before shouting instructions to the men pushing the puma's cage.

Montgomery orders his attendant to fetch food, then leads you through the door into a small, sparsely furnished apartment. There is a hammock slung across a corner of the room, a small unglazed window secured by iron bars that looks out over the sea, and a deckchair beneath it beside which is a table piled with books.

There is also an inner door that is slightly ajar and leads to what appears to be a physician's room. Immediately, Montgomery strides over and closes it.

'I will lock it from the other side in a moment,' he explains. 'It's just a precaution, you know, in case of any mishaps. Now if you wait here, my man shouldn't be long bringing the refreshments. His name is M'ling, in case you were wondering.'

With that Montgomery leaves the room by the entrance you have just used. Suddenly, you awake with a start - it seems that you fell asleep for a moment! Your struggle for survival has exhausted you even more than you had realised, and you feel an aching in your limbs that you had not noticed before...

Now, do you wish to examine the pile of books? If so, turn to **31**.

If you would rather investigate the inner door, turn to **109**.

466

Shouting and waving your arms, you succeed in scaring the flying foxes from their roosts. But instead of funnelling out into the daylight, the creatures start flying in a circle around the interior of the frigate, chittering and squealing in a flapping, frenzied mass!

As the colony prepares to leave the safety of their home, they do what many bat species do before an expedition - they void their bowels! A hail of fresh guano rains down around you, and there is nothing to be done but crouch upon the floor of the hull until the storm of excrement has passed.

After what seems like an eternity, the bats find the courage to fly out into the daylight. You are finally left alone, a dripping, reeking mess! You scramble to your feet and stagger to the prow of the frigate, alarmed at how the many cuts and scrapes you have sustained from hacking your way through the jungle have begun to throb hotly.

Make a note that you have been *exposed to zoonotic infection* and lose 1 FATE point!

Cursing your misjudgment and scraping the worst of the muck off on the timbers of the frigate's hull, you are finally able to turn your attention to the items.

Turn to **420**.

467

As soon as you approach the wicker box, the bather closest to it fixes you with his deep-set eyes and - in an astonishingly cultured voice - politely asks you what you think you are doing...!

If you wish to reply that you are taking the contents of the box for yourself, turn to **494**.

If you would prefer to indicate that you are interested in trade, turn to **371**.

Otherwise, you can say that you are lost upon the island and in need of directions, by turning to **296**.

468

You sit down gratefully in the island boat as Montgomery and his white-haired companion assist and direct the sailors in the moving of the crates and cages. Once the boat is fully laden with animals and packages, it shoves off of the larger trader, unfurls a sail and moves ponderously towards the island.

Montgomery keeps his eyes dead ahead; only the white-haired man deigns to raise a hand in farewell to the *Ipecacuanha* and her crew. The crook-backed man begins to mutter something, but Montgomery silences him with a sharp word.

Relieved to be away from Captain Davis, you see that the approaching island is lower than many volcanic outcroppings you have seen and covered in abundant vegetation. From one point deep in its interior a thin white thread of vapour rises slantingly to a great height, before fraying out like a downy feather. The ship is advancing into the embrace of a broad bay fronted by a strip of dull grey sand that slopes up to a ridge set with trees and vegetation. Halfway up the slope is a piebald stone enclosure out of which can be discerned two gently sloping thatched roofs.

Three tall, strange men await you at the water's edge. They are swathed from head to toe in grubby white linen, have lank, black hair, elfin faces, and twisted legs that seem jointed in the wrong place. As you come alongside them, they grow uncomfortable under your curious stare, and you turn your attention elsewhere so as not to offend them. But then the staghounds catch sight of the tall men; this sets off a frenzy of barking, howling, and jangling of chains.

'Come, help me with the hutches!' Montgomery tells you, as the boat settles into a narrow channel that acts as the island's dock and the strange men set about unloading the cargo under the white-haired man's brisk orders.

Together, and with the help of the crook-backed man, you carry several hutches of rabbits onto the beach. There, to your surprise, Montgomery upends them, turning their living, wriggling contents onto the grey sand. He claps his hands, and the little creatures go hopping off up the beach.

'Increase and multiply, my friends,' Montgomery calls. 'Replenish the island! Hitherto we've had a lack of meat here...'

Your stomach grumbles at the thought of a rabbit on a spit, and Montgomery nods in understanding.

'All this manual work and we have not even breakfasted,' he smiles. 'Let's go inside and see if we can remedy that.'

After affirming this fine sentiment, you follow Montgomery and his strange attendant up the beach towards the enclosure.

Now turn to 465.

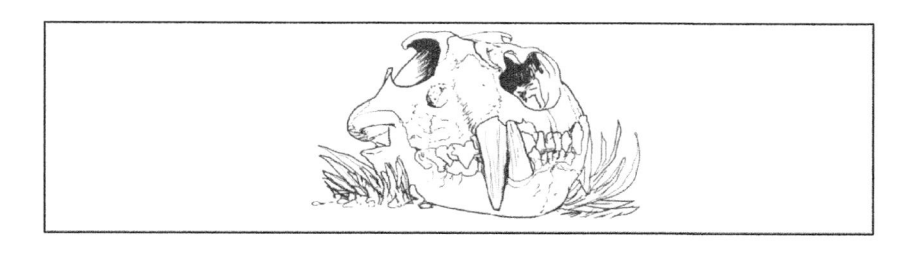

469

You keep the barrel in front of you and stay very still, scanning the water for the oceanic predator. Confused by the stillness, the shark

393

breaks the surface and glides towards you, its huge jaws gaping for a test bite!

Do you wish to thrust the barrel into the shark's jaws? If so, turn to **5**.

If you would rather punch the shark on its nose, turn to **81**.

470

You watch in horror as the CROCODILE-MAN crunches down on the upper half of the Lizard-man, thrashes its victim from side to side, then hauls the twitching body into the swamp...

Lose 1 FATE point for permitting the Lizard-man to suffer such an untimely death!

The monitor lizards stare at the rippling water in confusion, then turn to you with an angry hiss. If they cannot avenge their master against his killer, then you will have to do!

First MONITOR LIZARD: Prowess - 7; Vitality - 8; Damage - 2.

Second MONITOR LIZARD: Prowess - 6; Vitality - 8; Damage - 2.

If you win, there is little left to do but make your way up the trail that leads out of the swamp and into the jungle.

Turn to **395**.

471

Half expecting an alligator or anaconda to come rushing at you from out of the murk, you swim out to the body of the wight and hastily remove its swordbelt and pouch. Upon returning to the bank, you discover that the **short-sword** is too badly rusted to be of any use, while the pouch only contains a handful of **tarnished Dutch copper stuivers** of modest value. Still, you may keep them if you wish!

Upon returning to the bank, you find a number of leeches upon you that have been attracted by the wight's blood. Roll a dice, divide the number by 2 (rounding down) and lose that number of VITALITY points.

Muttering darkly about your misfortune, you pry the parasites from your flesh, crush them beneath your boot heel, and decide where to go next:

Do you wish to continue following the edge of the swamp towards the west? If so, turn to 184.

If you would prefer to head away from the swamp north into the jungle, turn to 211.

472

You look down at the body of the Pugnatyr, your breathing laboured and your arms aching from the effort of slaying the powerful creature. Looking around, you can see no sign of your guide, and can only assume that he ran off when you were charged.

Now, if you wish to search the area of the great ape's den, turn to 393.

If you would rather leave the scene, you can head north through the jungle down a gentle declination (turn to 439).

Alternatively, you can head westward through the jungle, by turning to 459.

473

You find yourself on the extreme north-west corner of the island, the sand extending a short distance to your left and right before curving out of view behind the rising land. But it is to the endless horizon that your gaze is drawn, where the sea meets the sky in a seamless azure haze. You enjoy this scene of tranquility for several moments, then turn your attention to the four canoes drawn up high on the beach.

They are beautifully carved from a chestnut-coloured wood and each craft has a double-sided oar cast within. Though you do not have the seamanship to handle one of them out on the open sea, you feel confident that you could paddle along the island's coast for a fair way on order to spare your legs a considerable amount of work. There is also a sturdy **hunting spear** (2 points of *close combat damage*) leaning up against one of the canoes, which you may take if you wish.

Glancing up and down the beach, you decide to head south to explore the westward-facing coast of the island.

Do you wish to do so by canoe? If so, turn to **353**.

If you would rather ignore the canoes and walk south to explore the westward-facing coast, turn to **285**.

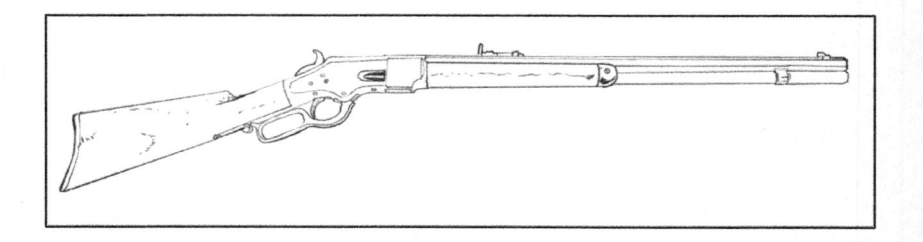

474

You remember that Moreau had written that reversion could be prevented and reversed by taking either the blue, green and purple elixirs all at once, or by taking the red elixir on its own...

If you have the **blue, green** and **purple phials**, then add together the numbers with which each one is labelled and turn to the corresponding section.

If you have the **red phial**, then turn to the section that corresponds to the number with which it is labelled.

If you have all the phials, then choose one of the above options to proceed!

If you do not have the blue, green and purple phials or the red phial, then turn to 143.

475

When you ask to be taken to your home, a worried look creeps over the Dog-man's face, before his eyes light up in sudden hope.

'I know the way,' he pants. 'Along the beach towards the House of Pain. We must keep away from the jungle where man-beasts chase and jump and bite!'

Your guide leads you out onto the trail and hastens towards a break in the cane trees that leads to a slight embankment overlooking the westward-facing beach.

'Run now, my lord, swiftly!' the Dog-man urges, setting off at a trot parallel to the beach. 'Follow me, and do not look back!'

Your guide is fast and tireless, his small feet scampering so lightly that he hardly seems to touch the ground. After the first mile you begin to fall behind. The whisper of sand betrays the fact that you are being followed, and when you glance over your shoulder you are dismayed to see two rangy, hunch-backed creatures with impossibly wide mouths and lolling tongues hot on your heels.

They are WOLF-MEN, one of the doctor's more malevolent creations!

Now *test your FATE!*

If you are favoured, turn to **335**.

If you are unfavoured, turn to **204**.

476

It is extremely dark within the tunnel, but it soon becomes a deep chasm that admits enough moonlight for you to make your way. As you advance, the walls grow steeper and press in on one another, blotches of white and silver playing tricks on your eyes. The scent of sulphur is gradually replaced by something else: an earthy, rotting odour reminiscent of a monkey's ill-cleaned cage. Further on, you catch sight of the faint orange glow of burning torches, then the indistinct shapes of a series of crude, dark dens huddled against either side of the chasm walls. Beyond, you see the rock walls opening up again into dense, tangled jungle.

You hear a whisper of movement behind you and turn to see a small group of creatures following in your wake. The pair at the front are bent double with hunched and crooked backs - they appear to be tracking you in the manner of bloodhounds! The trio standing behind them have eyes of flashing green fire that are fixed on you with terrifying avidity.

And that is not all, for other shapes have begun emerging from the makeshift dens, forming an amorphous, shadowy mass from which come low grunts, growls and squawks. It is a hideous mob of inhumanity that defies clear identification – worse still, you are hopelessly trapped! The creatures press in on all sides, twisted hands pulling you this way and that. The double insult of fetid breath and malodorous flesh causes you to swoon...

'An Other, an Other...!' moan many voices, some deep chested and resonant, others high pitched and childlike. 'Take it to the Sayer, the Sayer! The Sayer of the Law!'

You are dragged into the largest of the huts, and thrust onto a bench in a dim, dank corner. Your heart thumping in your chest, you stare at the shadows within shadows that are waiting in the hut...

Now turn to **350**.

477

You may perform THREE ranged attacks before the Draconope will force you to fight in close combat. The nearest hunter is also able to fire THREE ranged attacks before charging in to assist you (resolve these shots alternately with your own by using the hunter's attributes).

DRACONOPE: Prowess - 10; Vitality - 8; Damage - 3; Ranged Defence - 12.

LAZALO THE HUNTER: Prowess - 7; Ballistics - 8; Vitality - 8; Damage - 2/2.

Note: Lazalo wields a pair of **Toledo steel hunting knives** that give him +1 to his *close combat score*.

If you are forced to fight in close combat, your attack comes first, followed by the Draconope, then Lazalo. Remember that you and your ally can fight the monster simultaneously, while all of the Draconope's attacks will be directed at you!

If you win, turn to <u>383</u>.

478

Thinking it wise to give yourself a little daylight to find a suitable camp for the night, you drag the canoe onto the beach, shoulder your rucksack and enter the jungle. The canopy is so thick that it takes a few moments for your eyes to adjust to the gloom, but at least the ground here is relatively dry. You are about to settle down when you hear a furtive rustle coming from deeper into the trees...

If you have killed the PUGNATYR or have not encountered it, turn to <u>14</u>.

If you possess the diary AND the Pugnatyr is still alive, turn to <u>447</u>.

479

Montgomery sees you darting out of the enclosure and shouts for you to stop. When you start to scramble up the slope overlooking the beach you hear him give a sharp order. Moments later, you are hit hard from behind and dragged to the ground!

Lose 1 VITALITY point!

You are rolled over by powerful arms and find yourself staring into M'ling's bestial face. He gives a deep-throated growl and for a moment you fear that he is about to tear out your throat with teeth that are long and pointed like those of a wild beast...

'Easy, my boy, easy!' Montgomery warns, approaching the pair of you with the tray of food still in his hands, the revolvers still tucked into his belt. 'You may release our guest now, M'ling.'

As you regain your feet and brush yourself down, Montgomery stares at you with his watery grey eyes.

'M'ling is faster than any man I've ever known,' he says. 'Let alone one in such a weakened state as you. I cannot begin to imagine what possessed you to run off like that. Now, shall we stop this silly nonsense and take some breakfast or not?'

If you wish to reconsider your position and join Montgomery for breakfast, then the three of you return to the room. Turn immediately to 301.

If you refuse to go with Montgomery and M'ling, turn to 118.

480

The *Ipecacuanha* is going at a good clip, and you hit the water with blinding force...

Deduct 1 VITALITY point from the impact!

Coming to the choppy surface, you see the barrel bobbing in the swell and pull it in close. Even with the aid of its buoyancy, it is a long swim to the island, and you are still weak from your ordeal aboard the dinghy.

You catch a glimpse of Captain Davis mocking you from the taffrail of his ship but are relieved that he does not seem interested in bringing the schooner around. Soon, the *Ipecacuanha* is lost to sight and you are left alone upon the roiling sea. You begin to kick towards the island, hoping that the current is in your favour.

Test your current VITALITY by rolling four dice!

If the total rolled is greater than your current vitality, turn to **214**.

If the total rolled in less than or equal to your current vitality, turn to **240**.

481

When you insist that you do not require a reward, the Lizard-man stares at you intently, before shrugging off his armour and laying his halberd before you.

'Abstinence and courage are rare confidants,' the creature hisses. 'I see that there is more to you than meets the eye, adventurer. As such, I must insist that you accept these gifts. The cuirass is Kiribati armour, that which is woven from many layers of coconut fibre in the manner of old.

'The halberd is made from the heartwood of the ebony tree; this makes it strong yet pliable. The mouth-knives of the white shark that adorn it are deeply embedded, then reinforced with the resin of the calypso shrub. It will not fail you in battle.'

The Lizard-man helps you don the armour, which is surprisingly light and flexible. While you are wearing the **Kiribati armour**, you may subtract 1 point of any damage received on a roll of 5-6!

Next you heft the pole-arm and are surprised by its weight and reach. The **ebony halberd** is a fearsome close combat weapon that is rather difficult to control. Hence, every time you perform a successful hit with it, you must roll a dice. If you roll 2-6, you will cause 4 points of damage, but if you roll a 1, you will cause no damage as you overswing! Unusually for a close combat weapon, the ebony halberd will also cause double damage on a double roll (assuming that your *close combat score* is higher than your opponent's!).

'My final gift is...a warning,' the Lizard-man says as you prepare to bid him farewell. 'Leave this island, friend, as soon as you may. The Master has unleashed forces he cannot hope to control. Death will come to him sooner than he knows, but you need not share his doom.'

The Lizard-man glances darkly at the broken body of the Crocodile-man, then strides back into the swamp with the monitor lizards scrambling in his wake. You watch the creatures disappear into the mist, then make your way up the trail that leads into the jungle once more.

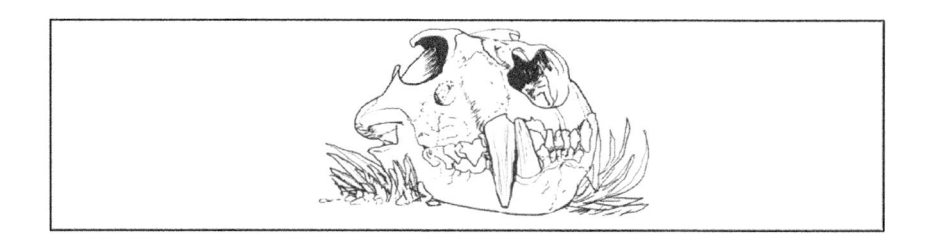

Turn to <u>395</u>.

482

To your relief, the familiar figure of the Ape-man pushes his way to the front of the small crowd.

'Come with us now, five-fingered man,' he mutters, eying you up and down as if seeing you for the first time. 'Come home...to the huts...to safety...to eat man's food!'

The other creatures crowd in, eager to hear your reply...

Will you accept the invitation? (Turn to **12**).

Or decline the invitation? (Turn to **141**).

483

As you begin to back away out of the clearing, the Boar-man gives an ear-piercing shriek and charges!

If you wish to fight, turn to **502**.

If you would rather try and escape, turn to **550**.

484

You dive away from the snake and plummet towards the jungle floor!

Roll a dice, divide it by 2 (rounding up) and deduct the total from your VITALITY due to the serious fall.

Are the Thylacine-men waiting for you? If so, turn to **132**.

If not, you decide to leave the clearing while you still can and press on towards the south. Turn to 171.

485

As you walk west along the beach, the inland jungle starts to thin and be replaced by an expanse of tall reeds and stunted trees. Cutting through this region are a number of steaming geothermal brooks that run down to the island's shore or create areas of fenland on the more level areas of ground.

Several miles into the interior of the island and at a considerable elevation are a cluster of large geothermic pools that feed the streams. Beyond them, you can make out a steady, drifting plume of white volcanic smoke coming from the island's heart.

Here and there, broad stands of stunted trees have found footholds on areas of firmer, dryer soil, and it is from one of these copses that you hear a terrible shriek. Your reaction is to flee, but then you hear a different sort of call - that of human voices raised in urgency, excitement and fear!

Rendered stock-still by indecision, you spy a cluster of trees quivering as something large blunders against them...

Do you wish to head inland to investigate the sources of these sounds? If so, turn to 417.

Or would you prefer to press on along the beach in order to avoid this commotion? Turn to 442.

486

Recalling climbs you have completed in order to study geological sites in the north-east of England, you keep most of your weight on your legs, using your arms only as secondary points of support. Painstakingly, you descend the face, and are relieved when you are able to drop the last few yards onto the floor of the ravine.

It is now almost completely dark, but there is a wan light being cast by the rising moon, which gleams on the wet surface of a crude stairway cut out of the rock in the opposite face of the ravine. Moving towards the steaming brook, you peer through the mist to see that the steps lead up into the dense jungle that crowds the southward bank.

If you wish to take the stairway into the jungle on the other side of the ravine, turn to **36**.

If you would prefer to follow the ravine uphill towards the source of the geothermic brook, turn to **496**.

Alternatively, you can follow the ravine westward towards the sea, by turning to **164**.

487

The thought of dying in this thicket of carnivorous flora drives you on through paroxysms of agony as your skin blisters and your lungs congest with each wheezing breath. With what remains of your strength, you burst through a screen of leaves, only to slam into a sheer cliff face!

The granite wall rises into a tangle of foliage and vanishes on either side into a mass of Bloodroot plants. The blossoms' perfume is now like mustard gas in your lungs; tears stream down your face as you lose your vision. You are trapped and unable to escape! Your body will sustain many generations of this deadly floral species, but for you...

ONLY DEATH AWAITS!

488

Suddenly, two of the friendly creatures you have met on your adventure push their way to the front of the mob.

'The Law is great, the Law is good!' they proclaim, standing side by side in the face of the encroaching predators. 'We must honour the Master by upholding His Law! The Others with the thunder-makers will lead us, the Others with the thunder-makers will guide us. We were made, but they have always been - their blood, *our blood* must not be spilt!'

At these words, the mob wavers...

Test your FATE!

If you are favoured, turn to 74.

If you are unfavoured, turn to 530.

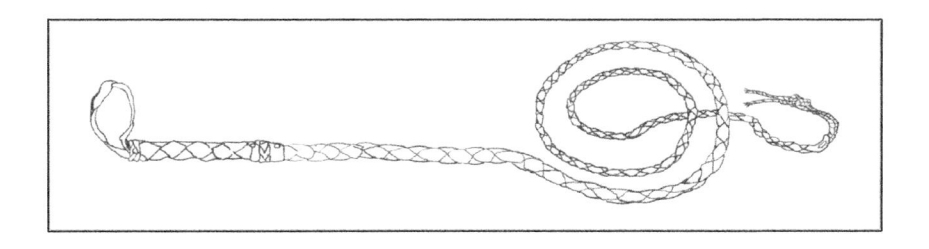

489

The Satyr seems surprised at your eagerness to be away, but readily agrees to your request and leads you back into the jungle.

Turn to **232**.

490

Unfortunately, you are unable to resist the temptation to fall asleep!

When you awake, you see that one of the bathers has left the pool. Suddenly alert, you see that even though your boots and clothing have been left untouched, your rucksack and equipment have been taken! Then you see one of the erstwhile bathers carrying your possessions towards the edge of the jungle...

Do you wish to shout at the thief to stop? If so, turn to **311**.

If you would rather take the time to throw on your clothes before chasing the thief, turn to **537**.

Alternatively, you may set out in immediate pursuit of the thief without bothering to get dressed, by turning to **101**.

491

The plank holds firm under your weight, and you edge out onto the walkway. The chain yields to a determined tug and you are delighted when a **small silver coffer** emerges from the dark waters!

Surprised by the item's weight, you carry the box back to the path and settle it upon the ground to study. It is clear that the owner did not want the coffer removed from the swamp, for the iron chain is wrapped around it three times and has been arc-welded in upon itself. The rust has caused some weakening of the links, but you will need the right tool if you wish to liberate the coffer.

Do you have an iron hammer and chisel?

If so, turn to **368**.

If not, you have no choice but to leave the coffer behind and continue along the path (turn to **412**).

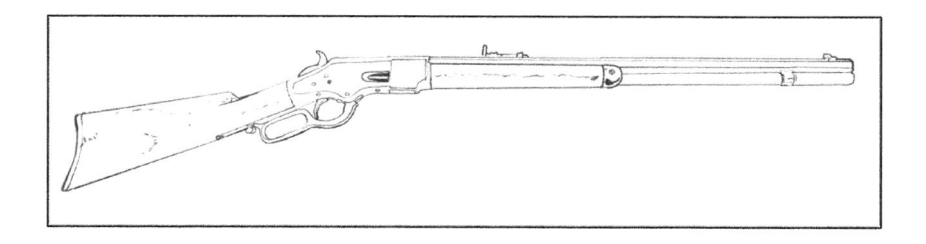

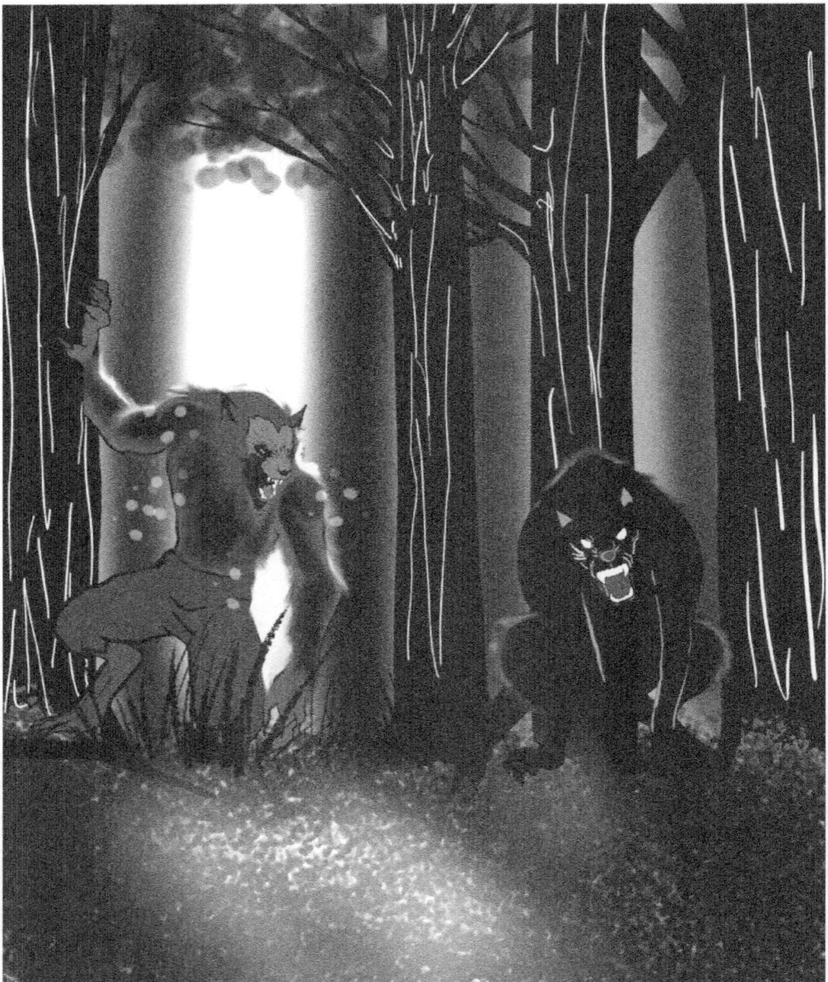

The Dog-man gives a slight whine when you make clear your intention to stand and fight, but he comes to your side and makes no further complaint.

You prepare your weapons and scan the moon-lit tree line, your senses alert to sounds and movement. Nothing! Then, just as you start to relax, the Dog-man gives a low growl. Suddenly, two rangy, hunch-shouldered man-beasts come hurtling out of the trees, their fangs bared and eyes ablaze...

As swift as lightning, the Dog-man rushes to meet one of the attackers, leaving you to face a single opponent!

WOLF-MAN: Prowess - 7; Vitality - 7; Damage - 2; Ranged Defence - 8.

If you are using a firearm (and have at least one bullet for it), turn immediately to 358.

If you are using a silent ranged weapon, then you have time for ONE shot before close combat is joined!

If you win, turn to 421.

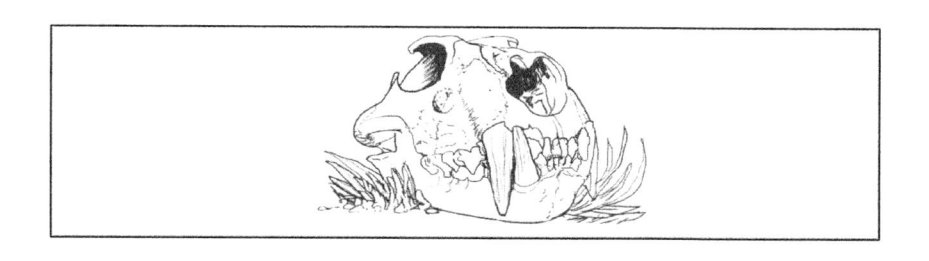

493

You follow the southern edge of the swamp towards the west without incident. In time, you spy a ridge of jungle ahead that seems to border the westernmost limits of the swamp.

Cutting up through the jungle is a red-soiled, weed-choked trail. It appears to be the best way to advance into the heart of the island, so you elect to follow it.

Turn to **395**.

494

When you tell the MACAQUE-MAN that you intend to take the box for yourself, he hauls himself out of the pool and looks you up and down critically.

'You will attempt to prosecute the laws of the jungle, eh?' he replies cordially. 'Though I admit that such an approach fits our setting, I fear that you may have bitten off more than you can chew, my man. As you can see, you are hopelessly outnumbered...'

He inclines his head towards the other seven bathers who are beginning to clamber out of the pool. Though they all possess lank arms, crooked bow legs and are all much smaller than you, you see that they are lean and robust beneath their soaking pelts. Moreover, there is the telltale glint of fanaticism in their amber-coloured eyes...

Do you wish to fight these creatures for the contents of the wicker box? If so, turn to **180**.

If you would rather back down from the confrontation, turn to **27**.

495

Unfortunately, none of the distant figures upon the beach seem to notice you, and the island boat shows no sign of turning about. With a strong current threatening to pull you even further from the island and the dinghy half-filled with water, you now have little choice but to attempt to paddle towards the beach!

Roll three dice and compare them to your current VITALITY score.

If the result is less than your current vitality, then you are able to paddle close to the beach before the dinghy is swamped by a wave. As the little rowing boat founders, you swim for the shore! Turn to **240**.

If the result is equal or greater than your current vitality, then you are still a long way from the beach when the dinghy is swamped. You are left floating in deep, cool water. Turn to **303**.

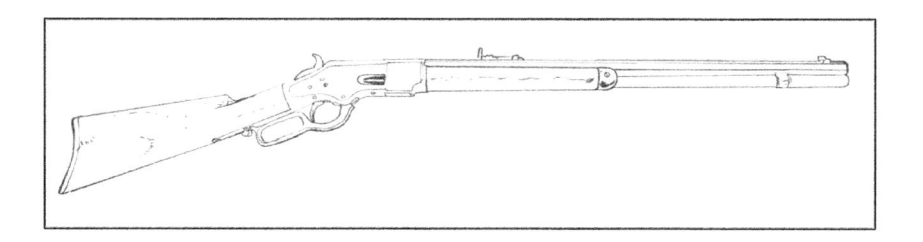

496

The ravine narrows until it reaches a small, scalding-hot waterfall that sends plumes of steam into your face. Fortunately, the rocky sides of the ravine are less steep here, and you are able to climb out onto a hillside overlooking a steaming expanse of reeds and marsh.

Laid out before you are a dozen or so geothermic pools which feed numerous cascading streamlets. These narrow waterways bubble energetically down the steep decline from this high point of the island, until they become sluggish and indistinct as they reach gentler slopes that lay towards a distant ribbon of beach and silver surf to the north. Close by to your right, there is a circular rampart of volcanic rubble emerging from the jungle.

The thick steam in this area reflects the moonlight in a silver haze, but as you advance you are able to spy a gap in the wall of rubble. There are also indistinct shapes floating in some of the lower geothermic pools that capture your attention.

Do you wish to make straight for the gap in the wall? If so, turn to **349**.

If you would rather take a closer look at the shapes in the water, turn to **402**.

497

A ripple of discontent passes through the mob as you make your objections to the impending bloodshed known.

'I understand, young Master, I understand,' the Fox-woman croons. 'Your nature allows you to care for the lives of others...it is well!' Her smile widens horribly, and you cannot help but feel that you have fallen into some sort of trap. 'But a pledge of blood cannot be reversed. Unless you would be willing to put yourself forward as a contestant? Then - if you triumph - you may exercise your right of mercy, so that no life need be lost this day...?'

Will you agree to stand as a combatant so that you might have the chance to exercise mercy? If so, turn to **72**.

If you are unwilling to fight in the arena, turn to **560**.

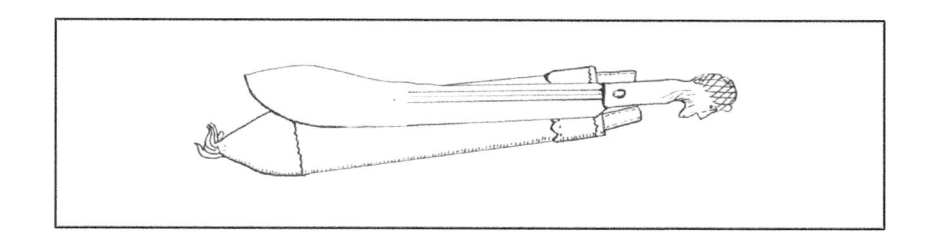

498

As you walk along the long, straight beach, you notice that the day is growing old and that you will soon need to make camp for the night. Scanning inland for a suitable site, you see little more than a steaming, reed-infested marsh above which are a series of geothermic springs. Further ahead, the marsh yields to dense jungle, but you do not think you can reach that area before dark.

On the beach, at least, there is a freshening onshore breeze, the sounds of the sea and the light of the moon and stars. Easing off your rucksack, you lay back to watch the last of a crimson sunset retreat before the emerging stars. Lulled by the sighing of the sea and bone weary from the day's exertions, you drift off into a deep, restorative sleep...

Have you killed the Draconope?

If so, turn to 444.

If not, turn to 555.

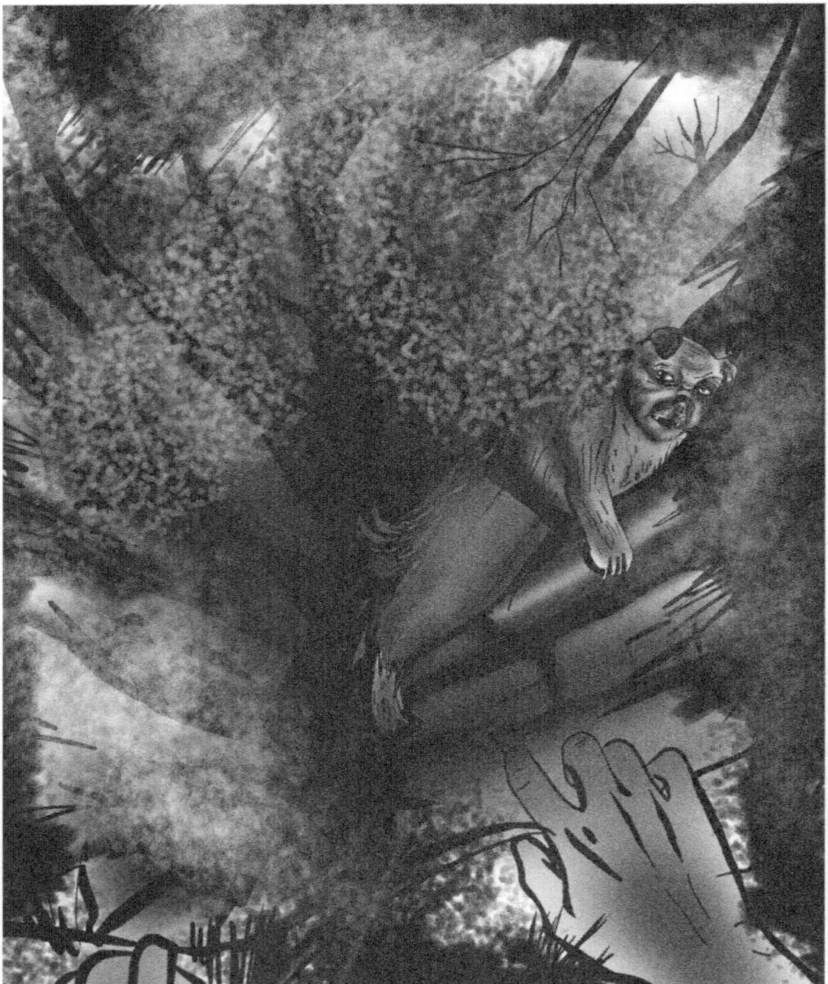

499

As you advance deeper into the trees, you see that they conceal a steep, narrow ravine about twenty yards deep that cuts across your path from east to west. A whispering geothermic brook runs down its middle, while its opposite bank is thick with moss-covered palms trees choked with thorny creepers and hanging vines.

Climbing down into the ravine will not be a straightforward matter, for its sides are steep and slick with moisture. To complicate matters further, you estimate that nightfall is only an hour or two away.

As you are considering your options, you notice a ragged figure working its way up the ravine towards you. As it draws closer, you see that it is a creature of an oddly benign countenance, possessing a large, protuberant nose, liquid brown eyes and extraordinarily large and mobile ears located high up on its head. You stare for several moments before the realisation strikes you that everything about this creature - from the way he glances here and there with his nose held high, to the way he holds his arms awkwardly before him - is highly suggestive of a humanised circus dog.

Indeed, it is a DOG-MAN, another of Moreau's bizarre experiments!

Under your scrutiny, the creature comes to a halt and smiles uncertainly.

Do you wish to ask the Dog-man to find a way to help you down the side of the ravine? If so, turn to 63.

If you would rather order him to leave you alone, turn to 433.

500

The sound of the firearm discharging is like a thunderclap in the stillness of the jungle (remove a round of ammunition). The creature nearest you flees from its hiding place behind the bush. As it flashes through the foliage on feet no larger than a small child's, you see that the creature possesses bizarre backward hinged legs that are long and powerful in their upper parts, but short and bone-thin where the calf ought to be.

Neither does the LEOPARD-MAN retreat far. Instead, it settles behind the trunk of tree, peering out at you while two more of its kind arrive. Alarmingly, these newcomers appear to be restraining a pair of harnessed hunting dogs!

Worried that you may be surrounded, you decide to withdraw deeper into the jungle...

Turn to **337**.

501

You take a deep breath and ease yourself over the edge of the precipice, the tips of your worn boots scraping on the rock face. Panic flares as you begin to slip down the near vertical surface, but you find a pair of finger holds just in time to arrest a fall.

Falteringly, you continue your descent...

Test your PROWESS!

If you pass, turn to **486**.

If you fail, turn to **384**.

502

The Boar-man is a fierce and stubborn opponent who loves little more than a fight to the death!

You may perform ONE ranged attack before close combat is joined:

BOAR-MAN: Prowess - 7; Vitality; 9; damage - 2; Ranged Defence - 8.

Note: whenever your opponent hits you, roll a dice. On the roll of a 6 you suffer 4 points of damage (instead of the standard 2 points of damage) from the Boar-man's flashing tusks!

If you win, turn to 457.

503

You follow the trail until it emerges onto a rocky hillside overlooking a steaming expanse of reeds and marsh. Laid out before you are a series of geothermic pools surging up from deep beneath the earth before overflowing in cascades of super-heated waterfalls. These energetic waterways rush down the steep inland heights, then grow sluggish and indistinct as they wander over more level ground towards a distant ribbon of sand and silver surf to the north.

The billowing steam in this area reflects the moonlight in a misty haze, but you are able to discern a number of indistinct shapes that seem to be floating in one of the lower pools.

There is also a curving wall of rubble on the other side of the pools that appears to offer entry via a jagged gap in its north face.

If you wish to take a closer look at the shapes in the water, turn to **402**.

If you would prefer to give the shapes a wide berth and head through the gap in the wall of rubble, turn to **349**.

504

At the base of the tree you discover a small hollow. After prodding around with a stick to ensure that no snakes or spiders have made it their home, you pull out a small oilskin pouch in which you find two beautiful **gold coins**!

Add these items to your *equipment list*.

After thanking the Thylacine-man, you press on through the jungle to the south.

Turn to **171**.

505

You kneel by the edge of the swamp and splash water over your face, almost weeping at the immediate relief.

Have you slain the Water Wight?

If so, turn to **389**.

If not, turn to **526**.

506

Though the cane toad's transformation is alarming, you recognise the behaviour for what it is: a final defence this species employs to render itself as difficult as possible to swallow!

Smiling at the notion that anything might consider eating such a repulsive thing, you set about coating your arrows (if you have any) and close combat weapons in the thick, viscous fluid leaking from the glands in the toad's back.

Make a note that any arrows and close combat weapons you currently possess have been *envenomed*. This means that when you successfully wound a target with a treated weapon, then they will be killed instantly on the roll of a 6! Even if you do not roll a 6, then the target will suffer 1 dice of extra damage, divided by 2 (rounding down). Naturally, this effect will only work against individuals, not groups of creatures who are treated as a single opponent...

However, the venom will only be effective for 2 successful hits per weapon (arrows will be expended after a single use, as usual). After this, the venom has rubbed off!

Pleased by your increased deadliness, you release the cane toad and back away. The creature rapidly deflates, gives a reproachful croak and hops into the swamp with a loud splash. Now there is nothing to do but continue west along the edge of the swamp.

Turn to **493**.

507

The roars of the Pugnatyr and the lions torment your cowardly flight. Then, you hear the battle reaching its final stages...

Roll a dice!

If you roll 1-3, you hear your unfortunate ally give several mournful roars, before all is silent except for the growls of his killers. You must lose 2 FATE points for abandoning the Pugnatyr to his doom!

If you roll 4-6, you hear a sudden silence followed by the belligerent roars of the great ape as he proclaims his continued dominance over this part of the island. Though the Pugnatyr has triumphed, you must still lose 1 FATE point for failing to stand with him!

Miserably, you press on into the darkness, then slump to the jungle floor to rest. All is silent now save for the incessant creaking of insects, so you pillow your pack beneath your head and fall into a deep sleep.

Gain 4 VITALITY points.

When you awake, you realise that you have slept for several hours and that the dawn is not too far away.

It is then that you notice a jungle path just in front of you, bearing on an east-west axis. You are quite sure that heading east will take you in the direction of the enclosure, whereas going west will take you in the direction of the volcanic spring you saw from the beach.

If you wish to head east towards the enclosure, turn to **60**.

If you would rather head west in the direction of the volcanic spring, turn to **450**.

508

When you refuse to say the words there is a stunned silence that is quickly followed by howls of outrage. One of the beast-folk strikes you a stinging blow across the face with the back of its hand, while the others crowd in, jostling and bawling, punching and kicking.

You must lose 2 VITALITY points from the assault!

Falling to your knees with your arms over your head, you hear the booming voice of the Sayer rising above the tumult:

'Punishment is swift and sure for those who refuse to say the Law. Punish him with pain, my followers! Beat and bloody him so that all may know his crime!'

Fearing for your life, you begin to crawl towards the entrance of the hut, glad that the dwelling's narrowness is causing the towering brutes around you to get in one another's way. You make it outside, scramble to your feet and blanch at the dense press of creatures that stand clustered around the large hut. Their eyes are wide and confused, but there is no hostility from them yet.

Then the brutes from within the Sayer's hut begin to rush outside after you...

Do you wish to flee? If so, turn to 267.

If you would rather try to fight the creatures from the Sayer's hut, turn to 387.

If you would prefer to attempt to reason with them, turn to 455.

509

Your pursuers are hindered by the narrowness of the chasm and you gain a good deal of ground on them, your arms and legs pumping. As your muscles begin to burn and tire, you enter a dark tunnel before bursting out into a clearing covered with a pale encrustation which smoulders with wisps of acrid smoke. At the edge of the clearing the charcoaled trunks and twisted limbs of trees poke through heaps of blackened rubble that rise to the height of your head.

To the left of the clearing is a ragged gap in the rocks, while ahead of you is a path leading through the jungle.

Orienting yourself by the light of the sinking moon, you realise that the jungle path will take you towards the eastward beach and Doctor Moreau's enclosure, so you decide to follow it before the Sayer's followers catch up with you.

Gain 1 FATE point, then turn to <u>60</u>.

510

There is a stunned silence at your words, then a cacophony of outraged howls.

'Heresy!' roars the Sayer. 'The newcomer is a liar and a deceiver! All those faithful, teach this wretch the purifying power of pain!'

At this, the Sayer's followers knock you to the ground and proceed to punish you with a savage beating...

Roll a dice and remove the total from your VITALITY!

If you are still alive, turn to <u>307</u>.

511

Once you are in the hut, the Sloth-man stares up at you in awe.

'None have ever had the courage to refuse to say the words!' he squeaks. 'There are others - many others - who profess to believe the Law but follow it only when it is convenient to do so. Some have already rejected the Law's prohibitions; they roam the island in the dark, chasing and biting, doing what they will. When others of my kindred weaken and do the same, what am I to do?'

Tears begin to run down the Sloth-man's cheeks, which he wipes away with the backs of his twisted hands.

'One day, a stalking shape will seize me or one of my swifter cousins will chase me down and devour me,' he weeps. 'Tell me, my lord, is there anything you can do to help?'

If you wish to promise the Sloth-man that you will do what you can to help him, turn to 403.

If you do not wish to promise anything to the Sloth-man, turn to 438.

512

You rush to the side of the operating table opposite Moreau just as the puma tears its other arm free and clamps a claw around your throat. Even as you struggle to break the iron grip and begin to choke, you cannot help but marvel at the creature's strength and the fact that its hand seems as well-formed as that of any man's. Then, the puma hauls you in close to its raw-seamed face and lidless eyes before launching you across the laboratory, where you smash into a glass-fronted cabinet and slump to the floor in a cascade of glinting shards.

Lose 2 VITALITY points!

Stunned, you watch as the creature struggles briefly with the doctor before hurling him to the floor once more, snaps the chains on its legs as if they were ribbons, then flees through the doorway to your room in a flutter of red-stained bandages. You hear the outer door slammed aside and a parting shriek from the puma that is like that of an angry virago.

Moreau climbs to his feet, glances at you briefly, and rushes off in pursuit of the puma, his massive white face all the more terrible for the blood that is trickling from his forehead. You struggle to your feet to follow but are struck by a debilitating dizziness and nausea…

Turn to **259**.

513

'Very good,' Montgomery says. 'If any of the beast-folk come within fifty yards of the building, do what you must to deter them. I do not plan to be gone for long.'

If you do not possess a **revolver**, then Montgomery will give you his spare from the belt of his trousers. If you do possess a revolver, then he will give you an extra **6 rounds** of ammunition before following Moreau's boot prints along the beach and vanishing into the fringe of jungle.

Even in Montgomery's absence, there is a restless contagion in the air, and you pace up and down nervously. The morning is as still as death. Not a whisper of wind is stirring, the sea is like polished glass, the sky empty, the beach desolate. You find yourself in a half-excited, half-feverish state where the stillness of your surroundings are oppressive.

In time you are arrested by the distant voice of Montgomery bawling 'Coo-ee...Mor-eau! Coo-eeee!'

Your shadow grows shorter, then begins to lengthen again, when you hear a single, distant pistol shot. This is followed by a long silence that is finally broken by a series of rapid shots. Then nothing. As the evening wears on, you hear raucous shouts drawing closer and a mob of perhaps forty beast-folk emerges from the jungle's edge.

They are parading three objects above their heads, passing them to and fro so that they resemble insects being carried by a swarm of soldier ants. But then you see that they are not objects at all, but bodies - the bloodied, broken, mauled remains of Moreau, Montgomery and M'ling...

Sagging to the ground, you are forced to watch as the mob surges towards the boathouse, throws the corpses into the sand and begins to demolish the island boat with rusted axes and hammers. They cast the broken timbers onto a mounting pyre in the middle of the beach, drag the bodies of your erstwhile acquaintances atop it, and thrust burning brands into the wood. It does not take long for the bodies to be engulfed in smoke and flame...

The mob cavorts around the fire for a little while as the day dies, then - one by one - they turn their green-fire glares upon the enclosure, the hated seat of their overthrown lord where they were born into suffering and pain. You shrink back under their regard and retreat to the doorway as a dreadful silence falls. With the falling night, fire glow of the human pyre, and countless horrid faces turned your way, you feel like you have already entered hell.

Then the mob starts to scream. It advances. Slow at first but gathering speed. They intend to tear the enclosure apart, as well as anything living still within!

Now turn to <u>528</u>.

514

As soon as you leave the path you seem to enter another world - one of dappled light, muffled sounds, and rampant vegetation. Taking this route means that progress will be slow, but at least you have the benefit of concealment. Indeed, you doubt that even the finest bloodhound could track you through the rich earthen and decomposition scents that permeate the air.

Wide eyed at this rich and unfamiliar environment, you press on towards the north, alert for strangling snakes or poison spiders that might lurk in the humid gloom.

Turn to <u>439</u>.

515

Seeing how things lay with the beast-folk, you lift up your voice.

'Children of the Law! The Master is not dead, but he has changed his form!'

A profound hush falls and M'ling turns his sharp eyes on you.

'He has changed his shape,' you go on, gathering confidence. 'For a time you will not see him. He is...there...' You point upwards.

428

'Where he can watch you. You cannot see him, but he can see you. Fear the Law!'

Some of the foremost predators flinch.

'He is great, he is good!' jabbers a voice from within the crowd.

'Do not surrender to the want that is bad!' pipes another. 'That is the Law, that is the Law! Are we not men?'

The mob wavers with uncertainty. Many of the meat-eaters slink away into the jungle, while the more placid creatures crowd in to gawp at the bodies of the doctor and puma.

Regaining his composure, Montgomery singles out a pair of strong Bull-men to help you carry Moreau's body back to the enclosure. The powerful creatures are evidently still afraid of the doctor, but they lift him gingerly and begin to follow you back to the beach. Progress is slow, for Moreau was a heavy man, and there are still flurries of sudden movement on the edges of sight and nearby roars that have your party reaching for their weapons. Montgomery says nothing the entire journey back, while M'ling ranges around your group, his eyes and ears alert for further danger.

Finally, as dusk is falling, you reach the enclosure, where the Bull-men eagerly depart. Montgomery opens the double gates and the three of you lay Moreau's body upon a pile of brushwood in the courtyard. Seeming to be drawn by something, M'ling then ventures out into the deepening darkness, while you and Montgomery lock yourselves in, then slump to the floor in grief.

Gain 1 FATE point for retrieving Moreau's body, then turn to 525.

516

You are pulling the blunderbuss from your belt just as one of the foremost beast-folk - a towering, dappled monster - charges at Montgomery with a heart-stopping roar. M'ling flies at it with a snarl, but is smashed aside, and a split-second later Montgomery drives in the assailant's head with a shot to the middle of its face. Still the creature ploughs on, gripping Montgomery and landing on top of him, where it thrashes in its death throes.

Unsure whether either of your companions are alive or dead, you level the dragon and unleash a blast!

Decide whether you wish to spend any FATE points to increase your result, then roll a dice...

If you roll 1-3, turn to **24**.

If you roll 4-6, turn to **40**.

517

You manage to clamber over the wall of volcanic rubble without injury, landing in a rocky clearing where wisps of acrid smoke leak through a pale incrustation of sulphur oxides. There is a ragged gap in the rocks in the north wall of the clearing, while there is another gap to the east where a path leads into dense jungle.

Orienting yourself by the light of the sinking moon, you realise that the path will take you towards the eastward beach where Doctor Moreau's enclosure can be found. Only then do you notice the tunnel entrance plunging into the earth in a south-westerly direction...

If you wish to take the jungle path towards the eastward beach and Moreau's enclosure, turn to 60.

If you wish to try the gap in the north wall of the clearing, turn to 122.

If you would rather enter the tunnel, turn to 476.

518

As soon as you leap from the path, you see a pair of immense jaws break the surface of the swamp. Horrified, you realise your mistake. The alligator you attracted further down the path was not the creature you first encountered, but merely one of its brood-mates. It is the last thought you will have before the reptilian predator drags you into the depths to drown...

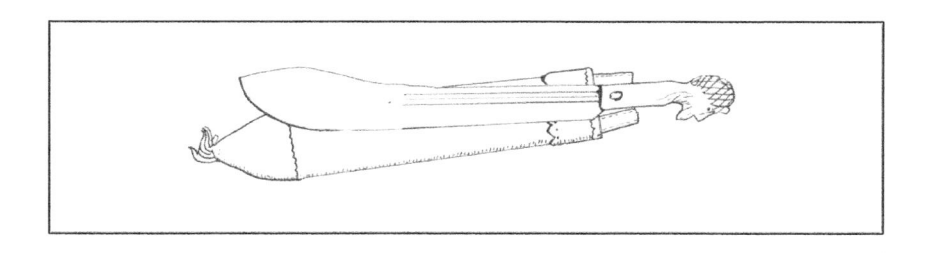

YOU HAVE DIED!

519

You fire into the water until the Water Wight sinks beneath the churning surface in a bloom of swirling blood!

Do you wish to enter the swamp once again to claim the creature's short sword and leather pouch? If so, turn to **471**.

If you would rather not risk it, you can follow the edge of the marsh towards the west (turn to **184**), or head north into the jungle (turn to **211**).

520

At first, Montgomery resists your suggestion, but then a terrible shriek carries through the jungle before being abruptly cut off.

'Damnation!' Montgomery spits, holding his head in his hands. 'What does it matter whether we leave Moreau or not? He is dead, isn't he? Dead and beyond caring. It is not as if we can offer him a decent Christian burial - he would be dug out and defiled within hours! Even if we can get him back home, we'll be forced to burn him or cast him into the sea, like any other savage who has roamed these islands since time immemorial. Whether we leave him or not matters nothing at all!'

So decided, the three of you begin to hurry back to the enclosure, but your progress is slowed by constant interruptions by beast-folk howling and shrieking this way and that. Your little party is not attacked again, although Montgomery does - a little wantonly, you feel - gun down an undersized Felid-man who dares to stray too close.

When you finally make it back to the enclosure, M'ling seems to catch the scent of something on the air and - without a word - ambles off along the beach. You and Montgomery do not have the energy to question him, and instead lock yourselves in the small guest room. From there, Montgomery unlocks the inner door to the laboratory, leading you into the open-air courtyard where you can better hear the approach of any beast-folk. Utterly exhausted in body and soul, you both slump to the floor in grief. Silently, you watch the day turn to night...

Lose 1 FATE point for failing to retrieve Moreau's body, then turn to **525**.

521

Through the window you see that a bonfire is burning upon the beach, and around it a mass of perhaps a dozen black figures are struggling. The pink tongue of Montgomery's revolver licks out, close to the ground. Somewhere, you hear the furious snarls of M'ling. Fearsome at first, these vocalisations grow weaker before falling silent with abrupt finality. Moments later there is a final flash and report of the gun, before a collective shout of triumph from the beast-folk rolls forth. Two limp bodies, unmistakably those of Montgomery and M'ling, begin to be flung about and dragged in circles upon the sand...

You sag against the wall of the room - the last of your acquaintances are dead! But the beast-folk care nothing for your grief. Manically, they hurl more wood upon the fire, and only then do you notice that the island boat and dinghy that had been drawn up on the beach beside the boathouse have vanished. Understanding strikes you like a thunder flash: before his death, Montgomery oversaw the demolition and burning of the vessels, in order to prevent your return to humanity!

Your fury at this betrayal is swiftly forgotten as the beast-folk toss the bodies of your erstwhile companions atop the pyre. There they burn with a black, oily smoke that drifts across the island and makes you feel sick to your soul. Drawn by the stench, more creatures slink out of the jungle until a mob of perhaps fifty creatures has formed.

433

They cavort around the fire for a time, yelling their delight at the demise of their oppressors until - one by one - they turn their green-fire glares upon the enclosure, the hated seat of their overthrown lord where they were born into suffering and pain...

You shrink back under their regard but find the vision before you oddly compelling. With the fire glow of the human pyre and the countless horrid faces turned your way, you feel like you have already begun to enter hell. How many living men have seen such a sight?!

Then the mob starts to scream. It advances. Slow at first but gathering speed. The beast-folk intend to tear the enclosure apart, as well as anything living still within!

Your heart hammering, you brace a chair against the handle of the outer door, then reel backwards as a body slams against the wood and a rhythmic pounding shakes the timber in its frame. A ravening face appears at the barred window, dashing its shoulders against the stonework as it tries, madly, to gain entry through a space the size and shape of a large book. Impulsively you raise your revolver, take a pace forwards, and blow out the creature's brains (remove **1 round** from your revolver ammunition)!

The thumping coming from the double gate leading into the courtyard does not concern you too much, for you took the opportunity to bar the entrance with its heavy crossbar upon returning to the building. The door to your room also looks like it can withstand a good deal of punishment. Your main concern is the open-air courtyard and the hatch to the roof you saw in the laboratory when accompanying Moreau to view the puma. The walls of the courtyard are fifteen yards high and the apex of the buildings taller still, but if any of the beast-folk are able to scale them, they will find easy ingress...

You realise that your best defence will be to use the stepladder in the corner of the laboratory to access the hatch and climb out onto the spine of the gently-sloping thatch of the main building. From this highest point of the enclosure you can mount a rigourous defence. If the courtyard is overrun, you will at least have an escape route along the beach or into the jungle!

Now turn to 533.

522

Somehow, you are able to resist the urge to sleep! After an exceptionally fine soak, you climb out of the pool, get dressed and consider your next move.

Do you now wish to make your way over to the wicker box? If so, turn to 467.

If you would prefer to leave these creatures to their pleasure and head through the gap in the wall, turn to 349.

523

'I don't want no blasted castaways on my ship!' Captain Davis yells in reply to your appeal. 'You're bound to bring the same ill fortune on us as that which sank you in the first place - now that's my final word!'

Now (if you have not already done so), do you wish to appeal to the large, white-haired man? If so, turn to 453.

If you have already tried to appeal to the white-haired man, or if you would rather simply accept your fate and do nothing, turn to 427.

435

524

At your words, there is a puzzled silence as the beast-folk grapple with the notion of a law that might survive the death of its creator...

'If the Master is dead, then the Law is dead!' one hulking Wolf-Bear suddenly booms, its bright eyes swivelling to Moreau's corpse.

'If the Master can bleed and die, then the Others with the whips and thunder-makers can bleed and die!' adds another crouching, predatory beast.

'Lies, so many lies...' hisses another, its dark lips drawing back from dagger-like incisors.

The mood is turning ugly, so you scan the mob for any beast-folk who might support your assertion and help turn the opinion of the mob.

During your adventure, you may have come across the following items: the **prickly pear**, the **brass key**, and the **sea-polished stone**.

If you possess just one of these items, turn to 448.

If you possess two of these items, turn to 488.

If you possess all three of these items, turn to 531.

525

After a period of hopeless silence you light some oil lamps, while Montgomery reaches for a bottle of brandy and begins to drink himself into a garrulous misery, muttering bitterly to himself. It is only now that you realise how greatly under Moreau's influence he had been, and that it had not occurred to him that the doctor might actually be killed.

When you try to discuss how the two of you are going to escape the island, Montgomery peers at you irritably.

'What's the good of getting away?' he says. 'I'm an outcast. Where am I to go? It's all very well for you. Besides, what will become of the better part of the beast-folk? As you will have seen for yourself, not all of them are silly asses. Now will you stop being such a solemn prig and take a drink with me? Or will you insist on playing the logic-chopping, chalky-faced son of an atheist?'

Knowing that you will need to keep your wits sharp this night, you refuse.

'I'll be damned!' Montgomery says, staggering to his feet as if with a sudden inspiration. 'M'ling at least will take a drink with me! Of all the creatures in the world, he is the only one who has ever cared for me. Perhaps some liquor will even tame one or two of the wilder beast-folk out there. They couldn't rightly offer worse company than I'm cursed with in here!'

With that, Montgomery marches through the laboratory and makes for the small outer door to the guest room.

Do you wish to try and stop him? If so, turn to 333.

If you would rather let him do what he wants, turn to 53.

526

The swamp water dilutes some of the Bloodroot venom on your face and arms, but you are taken by surprise when something explodes from the surface of the swamp. You perceive a grinning face with piercing blue eyes and flailing blonde hair, before a pair of strong hands drags you into the water and holds you fast until you inhale the fetid waters!

Until your flesh degrades and becomes one with the swamp, you will make an excellent plaything for the WATER WIGHT…

YOUR ADVENTURE HAS COME TO AN END!

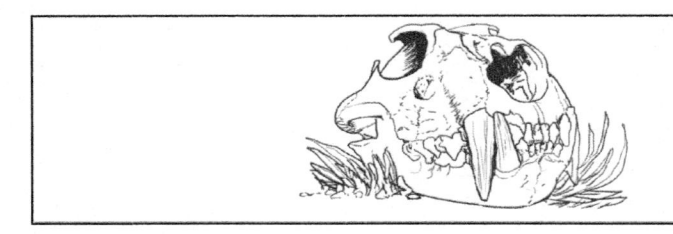

527

You have drawn the longest straw! Now Helmar must take his turn... Roll one dice for him:

If you roll 1-3, turn to **18**.

If you roll 4-6, turn to **160**.

528

Your heart hammering, you slam shut the outer door to the room, lock it and brace a chair against the handle. Moments later you reel backwards as a body slams against the wood and a rhythmic pounding shakes the timber in its frame. A ravening face appears at the window and dashes its shoulders against the stonework as it tries, madly, to gain entry through a barred space the size and shape of a large book. Impulsively, you raise your revolver, take a pace forwards, and blow out the creature's brains (remove **1 round** from your revolver ammunition)!

The thumping coming from the double gate leading into the courtyard does not concern you too much, for you took the opportunity to bar the entrance with its heavy crossbar upon returning to the building. The door to your room also looks like it can withstand a good deal of punishment. Your main concern is the open-air courtyard and the hatch to the roof you saw in the laboratory when accompanying Moreau to view the puma. The walls of the courtyard are fifteen yards high and the apex of the buildings taller still, but if any of the beast-folk are able to scale them, they will find easy ingress...

You realise that your best defence will be to use the stepladder in the corner of the laboratory to access the hatch and climb out onto the spine of the gently-sloping thatch of the main building. From this highest point of the enclosure you can mount a rigourous defence, and if the courtyard is overrun you will at least have an escape route along the beach or into the jungle!

Your thoughts stray to the two locked doors across the courtyard from the laboratory that lead to the private quarters of Montgomery and Moreau. Even though each moment spent in the enclosure runs the risk of beast-folk dropping into the courtyard and trapping you inside with nowhere to run, there may be items of use therein...

Do you wish to risk breaking into one of the rooms?

If so, turn to **441**.

If you would rather access the roof immediately to begin your defence of the enclosure, turn to **533**.

529

Fortunately, you avoid the full force of the blast. Even so, your torso is peppered with splinters of silver and your hands and face are blackened and singed.

Lose 4 VITALITY points, 1 PROWESS and 1 BALLISTICS point!

439

If you are still alive, you sit upon the path as your smarting eyes and ringing ears return to some semblance of normality. There is little you can do about the splinters of metal lodged in your body – you will have to hope that your wounds do not become infected and that you can receive a physician's attention in the near future.

Of the silver coffer, there is little left apart from a single, blackened corner laying upon the path. Neither is there any sign of the silver coins and velvet pouch that you glimpsed resting within the box! The hammer and chisel, however, have remained intact (retain the tool in your *equipment list*).

Shaking your head at the wicked ingenuity of the maker of the flint-spark trap, you press on into the swamp along the path.

Turn to **412**.

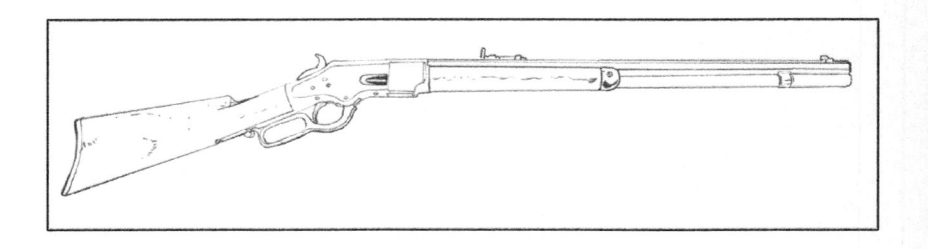

530

Unfortunately, your allies are unable to placate the mob. Instead, they are met by a tirade of slurs and insults, before being hauled back into the crowd and savagely beaten.

You protest loudly, but the circle of creatures closes in, a ring of faces as savage as one might see if hemmed in by a pride of hungry lions or a pack of starving wolves. You realise that you are moments away from being torn to shreds...

Do you possess the **Restored Dragon**? If so, turn to the section that is the same as the number etched on the side of its barrel.

If not, do you possess the **carbine**? If so, turn to the section that is the same as the number etched on the side of its barrel.

If you have neither of these weapons, turn to **458**.

531

To your astonishment, the Ape-man, Dog-man and Sloth-man push their way to the front of the mob, having apparently formed some sort of loyalist alliance.

'The Law is great, the Law is good!' jabbers the Ape-man, pacing up and down with his peculiar gait and holding the glares of the towering beast-men before him. 'We must honour the Master and five-fingered men by upholding His Law!'

'We must serve the Others with the thunder-makers,' yelps the Dog-man, his legs quivering with excitement. 'Only through service, sacrifice and love of the Law can we become great!'

The Sloth-man too creeps around the circle, clutching knees and gazing up into feral faces. 'Do not surrender to the want that is bad!' he pipes. 'That is the Law, that is the Law. Are we not men?'

At these entreaties, the mob wavers. Many of the meat-eaters slink away into the jungle, while the more placid creatures crowd in to gawp at the bodies of the doctor and puma.

The Ape-man singles out a pair of strong Bull-men to help you carry Moreau's body back to the enclosure, bids you a jabbered farewell, then ushers what remains of the mob westward towards the village of the beasts. The Dog-man bounds to your side, licks your proffered hand, then scurries out of sight, while the little Sloth-man gives a slow wave and starts to inch his way up a nearby tree.

You turn your attention to the pair of Bull-men. The powerful creatures are evidently still afraid of the doctor, but at your instruction they lift him gingerly and follow you back to the enclosure. Progress is slow, for Moreau was a heavy man, and there are still flurries of sudden movement on the edges of sight and nearby roars that have your party reaching for their weapons. Montgomery says nothing the entire journey back, while M'ling ranges around your group, his eyes and ears alert for further danger.

Finally, as dusk is falling, you reach the enclosure, where the Bull-men eagerly depart. Montgomery opens the double gates and the three of you lay Moreau's body upon a pile of brushwood in the courtyard. Seeming to be drawn by something, M'ling then ventures out into the deepening darkness, while you and Montgomery lock yourselves in, then slump to the floor in grief.

Gain 1 FATE point for retrieving Moreau's body, then turn to **525**.

532

Gritting your teeth and holding the collar of your jacket over your nose, you begin to pick your way through the guano, grateful for your sturdy leather boots and doing your utmost to avoid stepping on the corpses. As you reach the middle of the colony, one of the bats hooks its foreclaws into a rotting timber, unfolds a pair of surprisingly long hind legs, and begins to urinate in a thin yellow stream a few inches to your left. Appalled, you watch as several of its roost mates begin to do the same – one of which is directly above you!

Do you wish to continue moving with care, despite the risk of being hit by these animals' bodily waste? If so, turn to 189.

If you would rather put your head down and make a dash for the prow of the ship, turn to 565.

Alternatively, you can try to scare the bats away from their roost so that you have the frigate to yourself, by turning to 466.

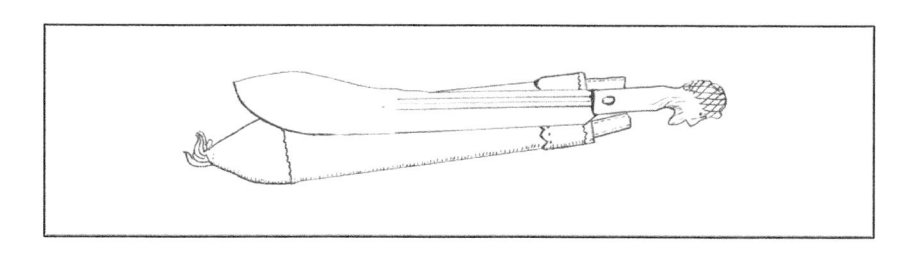

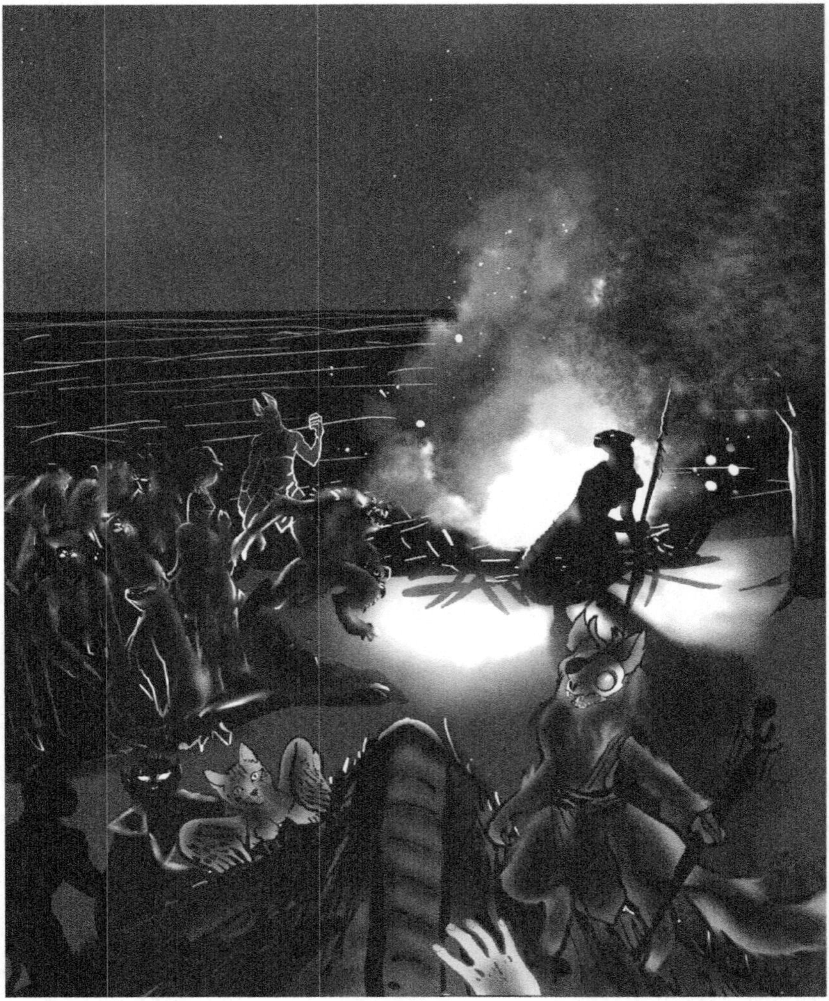

533

You rush into the laboratory, use the stepladder to reach the skylight and haul yourself onto the roof. Once outside, you inch up onto the spine of this section of the building, come to one knee and stare down into the milling beast-folk.

Though you have started to become habituated to the sight of these creatures, the flickering light from the fire on the beach lends the beast-folk an even greater impression of sinister grotesqueness. Worst still, they are animated by murderous energies that you do not doubt have been released by the death of the one man whose proclamations had bounded their imaginations.

Quite simply, the denizens of the island had been hypnotised by an intellect far greater than their own. Moreau had been their creator, judge, tormentor, and executioner. Above all, he had been their God. These chimeras had been told that certain things were impossible, that certain things were not to be done. Such prohibitions had been woven into the texture of their minds beyond any possibility of disobedience or dispute. Or so Moreau had thought....

With the doctor's death, the beast-folk have been freed from the shackles of humanity. They are at liberty to indulge their animal hates, at liberty to engage in whatever brief, hot struggles their natural animosities dictate; at liberty to kill and be killed in turn. For countless millennia, monsters have preyed on humanity. This night once again…

You have become little more than prey!

A great howl goes up, many pairs of flashing eyes affix upon you. You hear scrabbling sounds as the mob tries to scale the enclosure's walls. Some of the more agile beast-folk, finding purchase between the stones with unsheathing claws, start to reach the edges of the roof. Smaller predatory creatures tumble through the air to land flailing upon the thatch - the stronger beast-folk are hurling them up onto the roof!

You are under siege and face a vicious battle for survival!

BEAST-FOLK MOB: Prowess - n/a; Vitality - 15; Damage - n/a; Ranged Defence - 7.

In this fight, you must rely on any ranged weapons you possess, for if you are engaged in close combat, you will lose your balance and tumble to the ground where you will certainly be killed!

If you run out of ammunition, or as soon as you miss three shots, turn to **463**.

If you reduce the mob's VITALITY to 0 without running out of ammunition or missing three shots, turn to **138**.

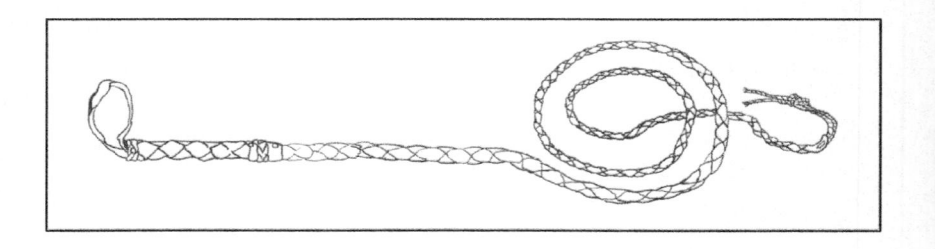

534

Try as you may, the canoe is just out of reach and your efforts cause you to sink all the faster. You take a final look up at the darkening sky before the quicksand sucks you into its depths...

YOUR STRUGGLES END HERE!

535

The Ape-man is able to move through the trees faster than you can tear through the undergrowth, but you spy a narrow path that heads in the direction he is going. By following it, you just might be able to keep up...

Test your VITALITY by rolling four dice!

If you pass the test, turn to 15.

If you fail, turn to 77.

536

You work your way into the gully and enter the rotting hull by way of a gaping hole in the centre of its bow. Unsurprisingly, the wooden planks and beams that comprised the inner decks and cabins of the ship have been entirely removed by scavengers, so that the interior of the ship is a single gloomy cavity that reeks of dampness and decay. Gnawed and split bones of indeterminate origin crunch beneath your boots; the imaginary snarls and grunts of the wild beasts that have lived here over the years putting you ill at ease.

The broken deck of the frigate at least allows the ingress of a tentative light. This wan illumination reveals a leather sack and a small wooden box lying in the furthest reaches of the prow. Between you and the items, however, are hundreds of twitching shapes suspended head first from the planking of the deck. The creatures before you are roughly the size of large cats and are wreathed in vascular, gleaming membranes above which stare chattering, eye-bulging, vulpine faces.

You have discovered a colony of PACIFIC FLYING FOXES at roost!

For now, the bats seem unperturbed by your presence. This is just as well, for you will be forced to walk beneath them to reach the items. Unfortunately, the floor of the hull lies several inches deep in rich, pungent guano. Worse still, there are a dozen or so Flying Fox corpses embedded in the waste which are emitting the most horrid, putrescent stink.

Do you wish to try and walk through this noxious mess and reach the items? If so, turn to **532**.

If you would rather leave this place well alone and return to the Satyr, turn to **489**.

537

By the time you have thrown on your clothes and pulled on your boots, the thief has disappeared into the darkness of the jungle!

Lose 2 FATE points and make a note that you have lost all of your weapons and anything that may have been in your rucksack! You may keep anything that was small enough to fit into your pockets, however (such as coins, keys, or phials).

Cursing your tardiness and misfortune, you cast a bitter look at the oblivious bathers before making for the gap in the wall of rubble.

Turn to **349**.

538

The room within is large and well-ordered, with shelf upon shelf of musty books and natural curiosities. In one corner is a simple pallet bed, neatly made up with a selection of sturdy boots lined up at its base that you recognise must have belonged to Moreau.

You focus your attention on a large mahogany writing bureau, and during a brief spell of frantic searching discover a **small silver key**.

Do you possess the **silver coffer**? If so, turn to 445.

If not, you return to the courtyard (turn to 432).

539

Test your PROWESS to see if you are able to sneak past the creatures unnoticed!

If you pass, the creatures remain fixated on the tree, allowing you to press on unnoticed into the jungle towards the south. Turn to 171.

If you fail, then the creatures spin around, their eyes widening in excitement and surprise. Turn to 238.

540

Identifying the sailor as the stronger opponent, you take him by surprise by striking him hard in the face. Snarling, he pulls a slender dagger from his boot and leaps on you. Meanwhile, Helmar tries to assist him by tackling your legs!

If you are unarmed, remember to deduct 2 from your *close combat score* for this fight.

SAILOR: Prowess - 6; Vitality - 6; Damage - 2.

HELMAR: Prowess - 5; Vitality - 6; Damage - 1.

If at any time you lose an attack round, turn to 178.

If you win without losing an attack round, turn to 419.

450

541

At your refusal to move, Montgomery whips out his revolver and points it at your chest.

'GET...OUT OF THE WAY!' he roars.

In his inebriated and grief-stricken state, you have little doubt that Montgomery is quite capable of killing you on the spot. Charging him would be foolhardy, but there are other tactics you might employ, for his own good if nothing else...

Do you wish to feign compliance, then attack Montgomery as he passes? If so, turn to **548**.

If you would rather let Montgomery go, turn to **53**.

542

The great ape is upon you with such speed that you may perform only ONE ranged attack before close combat is joined!

PUGNATYR: Prowess - 9; Vitality - 12; Damage - 3; Ranged Defence: 8

If you win, turn to **472**.

543

You listen for a while to the group outside, noting the creeping inspiration of the brandy in the howls and yelps of the beast-folk. Presently, you hear Montgomery's voice shouting 'Right turn! Come on, men!' before the tumult slowly recedes into silence.

The events of the day leave you little doubt that you have to get off of the island at first light, which entails taking the island ship with as much food and water as you can gather. For Montgomery there is no help; he is in truth half akin to the beast-folk, unfitted for human kindred.

There are many hours till the dawn, and you resolve to make the most of your time. On the side of the courtyard opposite the laboratory there are two rooms that you know to be Montgomery and Moreau's private quarters.

Do you wish to search Montgomery and Moreau's private quarters? If so, turn to **407**.

If you would rather leave them alone, turn to **185**.

544

You wake up next to the reeking corpse of the Draconope, your mouth dry and your head pounding. You probe the lump behind your right ear where you were struck, and groan when you realise that you have been robbed!

Note that you have lost everything from your *equipment list*!

By scanning the immediate area, it is clear that the hunters headed across the soft ground toward the north-west. Though you may not have much of a chance against two well-armed men, their treatment of you and the loss of your possessions is difficult to accept.

Do you wish to pursue your assailants towards the north-west? If so, turn to **92**.

Alternatively, you can cut your losses and head further into the interior of the island (turn to **261**).

545

The Lizard-man bobs its head in approval.

'Your flesh and hide are soft and smooth,' it hisses. 'You are wise to seek the protection of Kiribati armour, which is woven from many layers of coconut fibre in the manner of old.'

The creature removes its cuirass and pufferfish skin helm, makes some adjustments to the strings and straps, then helps you try them on. Immediately, you are taken by the lightness and flexibility of the harness. While you are wearing **Kiribati armour**, you may subtract 1 point of any damage received on a dice roll of 5-6!

'My final gift is...a warning,' the Lizard-man says as you prepare to bid him farewell. 'Leave this island, adventurer, as soon as you may. The Master has unleashed forces he cannot hope to control. Death will come to him sooner than he knows, but you need not share his doom.'

The Lizard-man glances darkly at the broken body of the Crocodile-man, then strides back into the swamp with the monitor lizards scrambling in his wake. You watch the creatures disappear into the mist, then make your way up the trail that leads into the jungle once more.

Turn to **395**.

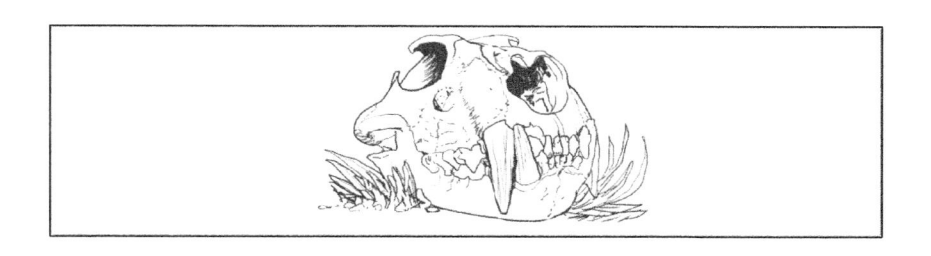

546

The rigging creaks alarmingly as you climb, and you hear several fibres snap under your weight...

Roll a dice!

If you roll 1-3, turn to **120**.

If you roll 4-6, turn to **222**.

547

Feeling like you have little to lose, you try the silver key in the lock of the silver coffer that you found hidden in the swamp. You feel a thrill of excitement when you hear a gentle *click*. Lifting the lid, you are surprised to find that the interior of the box has been lined with a fine layer of flint, but your attention is drawn to the collection of **silver coins** and the single velvet bag laying within, which rests on a deep bed of fine, black powder.

Hurriedly pocketing the coins, you open the bag and find a glass phial containing a red liquid inside. It is affixed with a label reading '*version 381*' - make a note of this number and add the coins and the **red phial** to your *equipment list*. As you do so, the reason for the black powder becomes clear. It is gunpowder that would have surely detonated if any thief had tried to break into the coffer with an iron tool!

Feeling that you have spent enough time in the room, you return to the courtyard.

Turn to **185**.

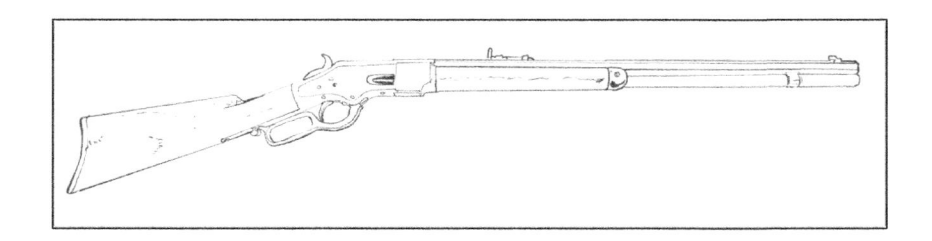

548

You hold up your hands and step to one side, then rush at Montgomery as he tries to leave!

Your surprise attack takes Montgomery completely off guard, and the two of you go crashing into the table and chair by the small window. As the pair of you fall to the floor, you seize Montgomery's wrist and twist it away from you as two rapid shots are discharged. With a further twist, Montgomery's revolver is sent spinning out of reach. You pull your own firearm out of your belt, but Montgomery swiftly knocks it out of your hand.

'Swine!' he hisses. 'Your presence here has ruined everything. You are to blame for all this death. You, I say...!'

With that, Montgomery draws a knife and attacks! Your attempt to help him has become a fight to the death...

If you have a dagger or a knife, you may use it in this fight. If not, you cannot reach any larger close combat weapons you may possess and must fight unarmed with -2 to your *close combat score*.

MONTGOMERY: Prowess - 10; Ballistics – 9; Vitality - 8; Damage - 2; Ranged Defence - 9.

If you win, turn to **391**.

549

As a naturalist you should have known better - running away from the charge of a great ape is one of the worse things you can do! You manage a mere five paces of flight before the powerful creature runs you down and thunders its massive fists repeatedly onto your back!

Roll a dice and remove this number of points from your VITALITY!

After this outburst, the Pugnatyr seems unsure of what to do with you. It grabs one of your legs, swishes you left and right across the jungle floor, then seems to lose interest before retreating to its den. The next thing you know, the Ape-man is tugging at your shoulder.

'You must go now!' he gabbles. 'The beast is displeased! You may go north to the sea. Or west towards the marshes, but here I must stay!'

Before you leave, the Ape-man gives you a **prickly pear**. Add it to your *equipment list* if you wish.

Now, do you wish to head north through the jungle towards the sea? If so, turn to **439**.

If you would prefer to head west through the jungle towards the marshes, turn to **459**.

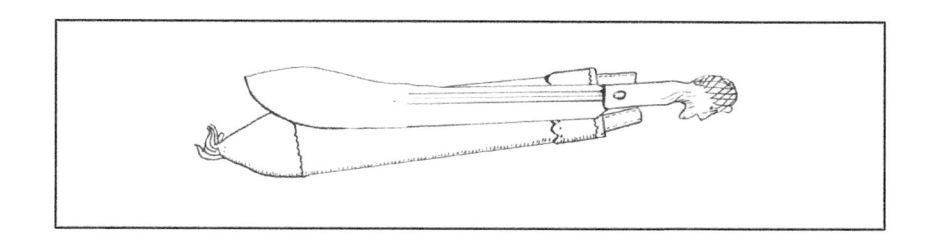

550

You sprint for the edge of the clearing, swerving to avoid the fury of the Boar-man's charge!

Test your FATE!

If you are favoured, you are able to evade the creature's attack.

If you are unfavoured, then the rampaging creature butts you in the rump and sends you flying into the undergrowth (lose 2 VITALITY points)!

Once you are ejected from the clearing, the Boar-man loses interest and returns to his sow, leaving you to continue your journey through the jungle.

Turn to **436**.

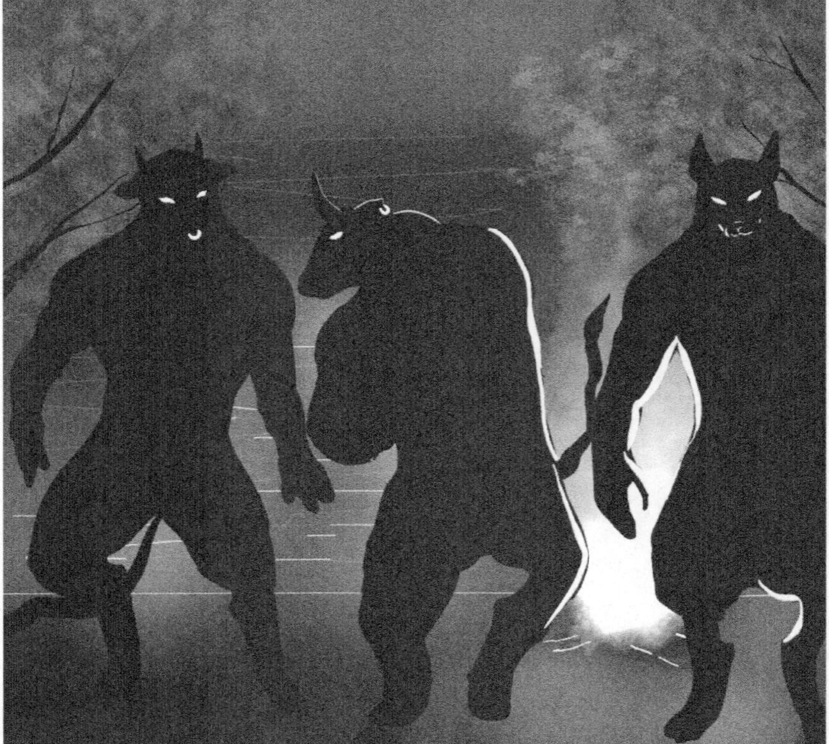

551

As you rush through the laboratory and small room to the outer door, you hear some of the packing cases behind you smash to the floor of the courtyard. Heedless, you unlock the door and throw it open.

Upon the beach a bonfire is burning, and around it a mass of perhaps a dozen black figures are struggling. Montgomery calls your name and you run towards the fire, weapon in hand. The pink tongue of Montgomery's revolver licks out, close to the ground. Somewhere, you hear the furious snarls of M'ling.

You shout with all your strength to create a distraction and come to a halt as three beast-folk take the bait. In the flickering firelight, you see that one of them is a leering WOLF-BRUTE, while the others are horned and powerful BULL-MEN.

Their faculties might have been dulled by the liquor they have consumed, but so has any fear they might have had of you...

You are permitted to perform TWO ranged attacks against any of your opponents before close combat is joined. You must fight these enemies simultaneously!

DRUNKEN WOLF-BRUTE: Prowess - 6; Vitality - 8; Damage - 2.

First DRUNKEN BULL-MAN: Prowess - 6; Vitality - 10; Damage - 3.

Second DRUNKEN BULL-MAN: Prowess - 7; Vitality - 8; Damage - 3.

If you win, turn to **201**.

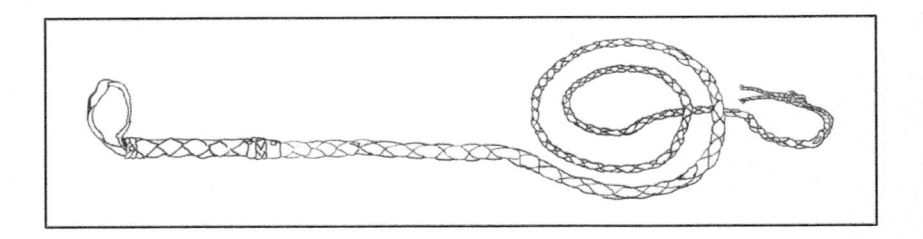

552

The volcanic rock is extremely sharp. A fall or slip could be both painful and dangerous!

Roll a dice.

If you roll 1-2, turn to **325**.

If you roll 3-6, turn to **517**.

553

To your relief, the man takes pity on you!

'Alongside all the other allegations levelled at me, I do not wish to add that of being an accessory to murder,' he says. 'Besides, you speak like an educated man and may be of some use to me on the island. You may cross the gangplank and rest in our boat, if you wish, while we bring aboard our stock.'

Not wishing to spend a moment longer aboard the *Ipecacuanha* and her bully of a captain, you thank the white-haired man before crossing over into the island boat.

Gain 2 FATE points, then turn to **468**.

554

With the destruction of the island boat, you are trapped upon the island with nowhere to run. You prepare your weapons and watch the beast-folk advance, keen to give a good account of yourself...

Do you possess the blood leaves? If so, turn to 224.

If not, do you possess the wind-cutter? (Turn to 345).

If you possess neither of these items, turn to 558.

555

You jolt awake as if disturbed by a nightmare. Sitting up, you hear the swirl of water and see something large angling through the water towards the beach. At first you think it might be a whale, for it is a mottled grey colour and swims with a vertical rolling motion, but then you see a hideously twisted human face gasping for air before disappearing beneath the surf.

Within moments a monster surges out of the shallows – a *thing* resembling a gigantic maggot fused with the hideously twisted head of a giant man. It fixes you with streaming eyes, licks its lips, then lurches up the beach with an ear-piercing shriek of agony and rage!

The DRACONOPE is one of Doctor Moreau's earliest and most reprehensible experiments. Tormented by unrelenting pain, it is a gibbering, shrieking monstrosity that lives only to unleash its rage upon the world. It is deadliest within the water but is also a terrible adversary upon the land.

For a moment you are transfixed by the sight and sound of this abomination, but then you scramble to your feet and prepare your weapons!

You may perform THREE ranged attacks before entering close combat!

DRACONOPE: Prowess - 10; Vitality - 12; Damage - 3; Ranged Defence - 12.

If the Draconope wins three rounds in succession, turn to **456**.

If you are able to defeat the Draconope without losing three successive rounds, turn to **408**.

556

The moment the Lizard-man falls, the monitor lizards scrabble back into the depths of the swamp, leaving you to finish the fight!

CROCODILE-MAN: Prowess - 9; Damage - 3.

If you are able to finish the monster off, turn to **344**.

557

A disturbance from the main gates distracts the two men for a moment. You are able to duck behind the corner of the building before they see you!

Turn to **188**.

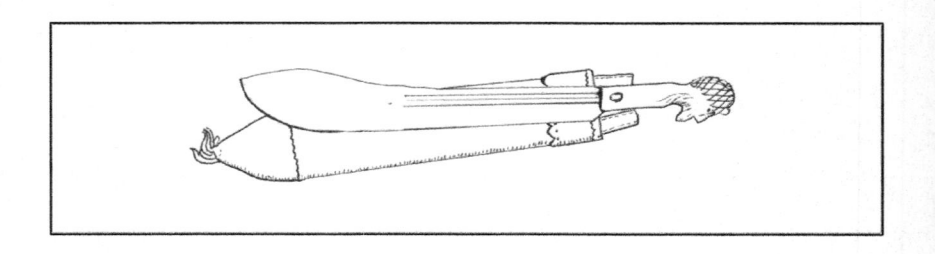

462

558

Whether or not you are able to dissuade the beast-folk on the beach from attacking you, there is no longer any place upon the island where you can secure food, rest and sleep. The deaths of Moreau and Montgomery have shown the predatory chimeras that men are mortal and physically weak. Worst still, you recall Moreau's words to you upon your arrival on the beach:

'We're off the track to anywhere, and see a ship once every twelve months or so, at best.'

It is unlikely that you will last that long...

YOUR ADVENTURE ENDS HERE!

559

The captain and first mate listen intently to your talk of Doctor Moreau, vivisection and beast-folk. Halfway through your account, the mate excuses himself on the grounds of fetching you a tot of rum. Instead, he returns with three burly sailors.

'It will be for the best if you spend your time with us secure below decks,' the captain explains, pulling out a small silver pistol and pointing it at your chest. 'We will keep you fed and you will not be mistreated, but I would be a fool to leave a madman to roam my ship at will, no?'

You cannot fight the entire crew, so allow yourself to be escorted to a small cabin near the forecastle. There you are disarmed, imprisoned, and deprived of your possessions. The sailors are not unkind, however, and they allow you on deck for an hour each day. The captain even lends you one or two of his books when he establishes that you are not an immediate danger. But you are securely locked in your cabin each night.

The weeks pass easily enough, and you begin to think about what you will do when you reach San Francisco...

Turn to **319**.

560

At your refusal to fight, the Fox-woman's smile falters.

'Then one of the creatures you see before you will soon die,' she says coldly. 'And you must tell me which of them you favour. You are our guest, and these are our rules.'

Feeling the eyes of the mob upon you and the sting of shame from refusing to fight, you decide to go along with this barbaric game.

Make a note once again of which contestant you favour, then turn to **187**.

561

Realising that further movement will only cause the gas pocket to discharge more rapidly, you stay very still. As you suspected, the bubbling immediately subsides. Your weight alone continues to compress the pocket of gas, however, and the air remains tainted. All you can do for the time being is to wait until the hydrogen sulphide steadily depletes. Only then will it be safe to move!

Turn to **440**.

562

Alas, menial labour and servitude under the tyranny of Captain Davis and his crew were not your idea of adventure when you boarded *The Lady Vain* out of El Salvador! Even if you do enough to survive the journey to Hawaii, you will forever wonder what was afoot on that mysterious island...

YOUR ADVENTURE ENDS HERE!

563

You fall to your knees, rummaging through your equipment for anything that may be of help. Your hands have become coarse and clumsy; you do not have much time!

Do you possess Moreau's pocketbook? If so, turn to 474.

If not, turn to 357.

564

The dinghy has been taken by a strong current and you realise that you do not have the endurance to reach it. Desperately you turn back towards the derelict, but a thick bank of fog rolls in, disorienting you. When it finally clears, neither the derelict nor the dinghy are anywhere in sight, just an endless expanse of rolling sea. As cramps begin to wrack your legs, you realise that the battle is lost. Even so, it is nearly dark by the time you finally slip beneath the waves...

YOUR DAYS ARE AT AN END!

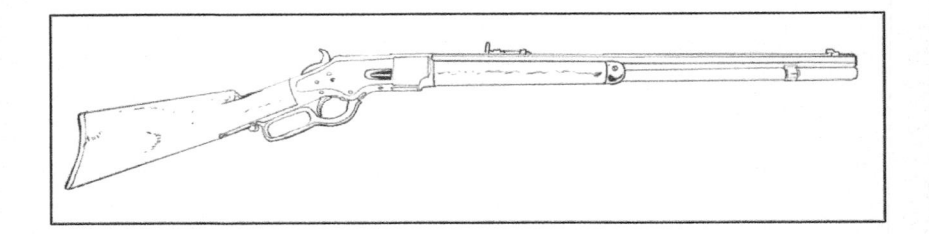

565

You begin to rush clear of the urinating bats. Immediately, you begin to slip and slide in the guano...

Test your PROWESS!

If you pass, turn to **243**.

If you fail, turn to **305**.

566

The jungle is cool, still, and garnished with splashes of white and crimson that you recognise as the blooms of trailing epiphytes. For some time you wander on, keeping parallel to the beach so as not to lose your way. Then, your eyes are drawn to something upon the forest floor. It is the ragged mess of a dead rabbit - still warm - with its head torn off...

Your hackles rise as you hear a rustle from the ground-level thickets and catch sight of the flash of a pair of emerald, half-luminous eyes staring at you from behind a screen of twisting tropical flora. The creature shies away from your gaze and you discern a deep-chested brute with tawny skin and an unmistakably feline face. Impelled by natural curiosity you stride forth, only to be halted by a savage, throaty snarl. This is no placid, curious native of the sort you have encountered on other expeditions.

Then you catch sight of two others of its kind slinking through the jungle toward you. Worse still, each of the newcomers are restraining some sort of large, dappled hunting dog by means of leather harnesses that are twisted around their wrists. If you stay where you are, then the three creatures and their charges will surely surround you...

Do you wish to attempt to speak to the nearest creature? If so, turn to 452.

If you would prefer to charge the nearest creature in the hope of scaring it away, turn to 290.

If you would rather back away towards a more open area so that you can more easily attack any creature that might attempt to come too close, turn to 337.

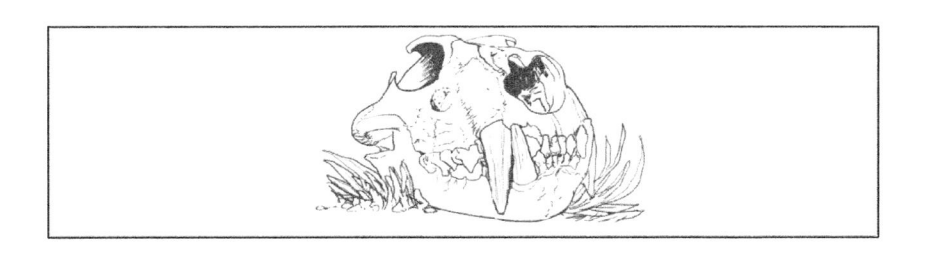

567

Alarmed, you move in the direction of the beach and peer through the trees. Standing halfway up the beach is a creature out of your nightmares. It resembles a gigantic grey maggot that is eight feet long and as wide around its middle as four wine barrels lashed

467

together. But instead of the blind, tapering head of a larva, the bloated body is somehow fused with the hideously twisted head of a giant man that is slick, dripping with mucus and in the process of swallowing the unfortunate rabbit whole. Once the pair of trembling hind legs has disappeared into its gullet, the monster smacks its lips and turns its streaming eyes on you...

The DRACONOPE is one of Doctor Moreau's most reprehensible experiments. Tormented by unrelenting hunger and pain, it is a gibbering, shrieking monstrosity that lives only to unleash its rage upon the world. It is deadliest within the water, but also a terrible adversary upon the land. With a gnashing of its teeth, the monster breaks towards you with an undulating charge!

Immediately, the Pugnatyr thunders past you with a deafening roar. It intercepts the Draconope before it reaches the tree line, holding its snapping jaws at bay with one hand while pounding its face and body with a mallet-sized fist. The great ape is incredibly strong, but you fear that even he will not be able to withstand the Draconope's thrashing body...

If you wish to leave the creatures to their battle and flee deeper into the jungle, turn immediately to **369**.

If you wish to help the Pugnatyr, then you may fire at the Draconope for as many combat rounds as you possess ammunition (and in this instance you may switch ranged weapons at any time), before engaging in close combat. If you cannot or do not wish to use a ranged weapon, then simply join the fight in close combat!

PUGNATYR: Prowess - 9; Vitality - 12; Damage - 3.

DRACONOPE: Prowess - 10; Vitality - 12; Damage - 3; Ranged Defence - 12.

Note: the Draconope will focus entirely on the Pugnatyr in this fight. You will be able to attack it, but if the Draconope rolls a higher *close combat score*, then it has simply fended off your blow.

If the Pugnatyr is killed, then you must continue to fight the Draconope in close combat, unto death!

If you win, and the Pugnatyr is still alive, turn to **17**.

If you win, but the Pugnatyr has been killed, turn to **150**.

If the Pugnatyr is killed and the Draconope is able to win three consecutive rounds against you, turn to **456**.

568

Now that he is unable to escape into the trees, the creature defends himself with sudden ferocity, wrapping you up in his lank arms and prehensile legs. All the while he sends up a shrieking alarm call!

You must fight the APE-MAN:

APE-MAN: Prowess - 6; Vitality - 7; Damage - 2.

After two combat rounds, turn to **133**.

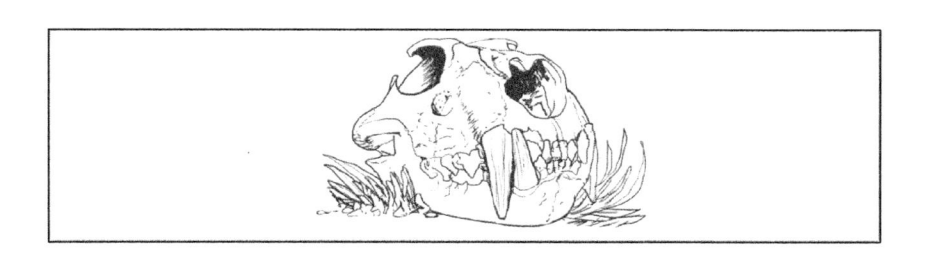

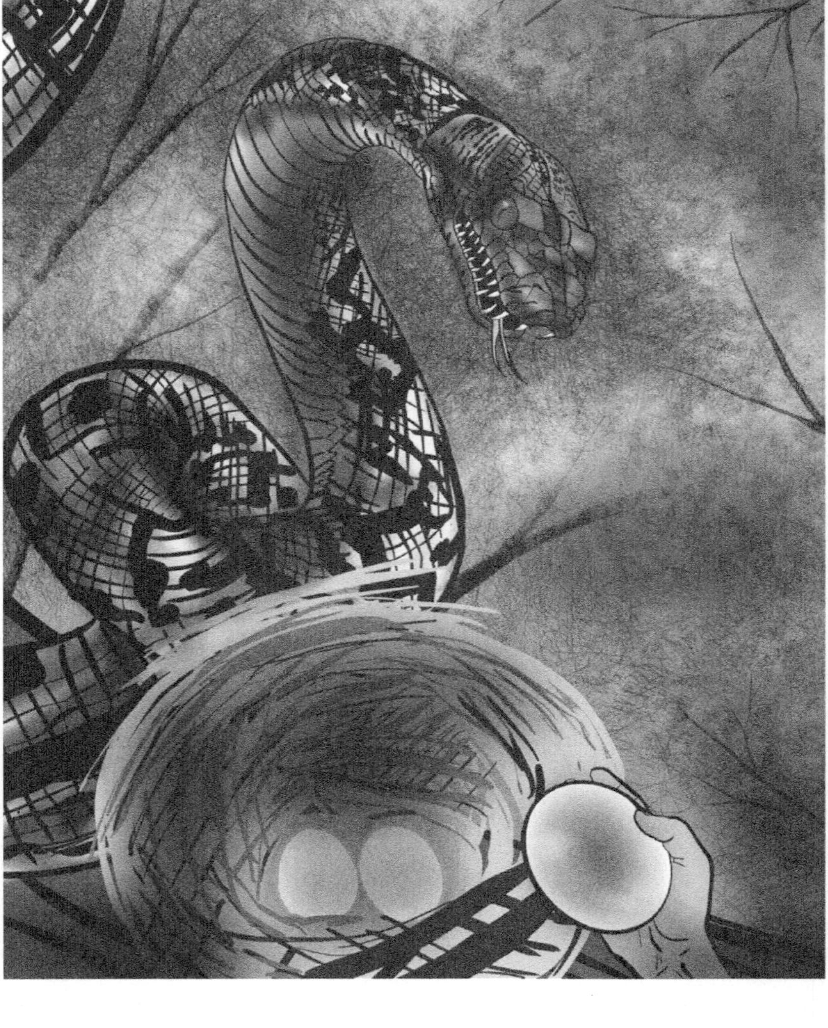

With an invigorating thrill, you climb high enough to see a clutch of five large pale blue eggs within the nest. Crawling out onto the limb, you begin to place the eggs into your pockets and down the front of your shirt. Just as you are reaching for the last few eggs, you catch a flicker of movement from a bough above you. It is fast and fleeting, like a long, forked worm lashing out of a burrow in the wood...

Too late you spot the cold, dead eyes behind the movement, then the rounded, glistening snout perfectly adapted to detecting the heat of active, warm-blooded life.

The GIANT PYTHON has been waiting for the adult birds to return to the nest. It is almost invisible thanks to its red and black-striped hide, and its patience is formidable. More to the point, it is always on the lookout for larger, juicier prey...

With blinding speed, the snake strikes!

Do you wish to hurl yourself off the branch and risk a fall to the ground in order to escape the predator? If so, turn to **484**.

If you wish to try to fight off the snake from where you are, turn to **366**.

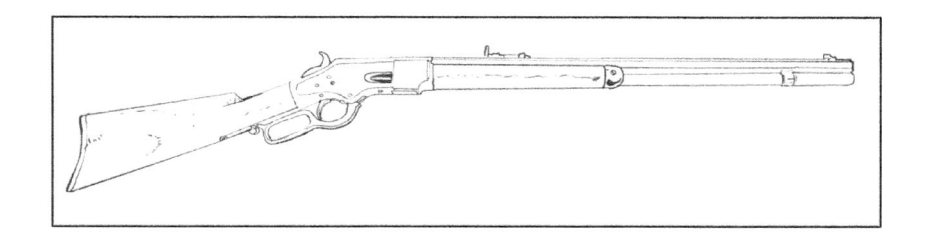

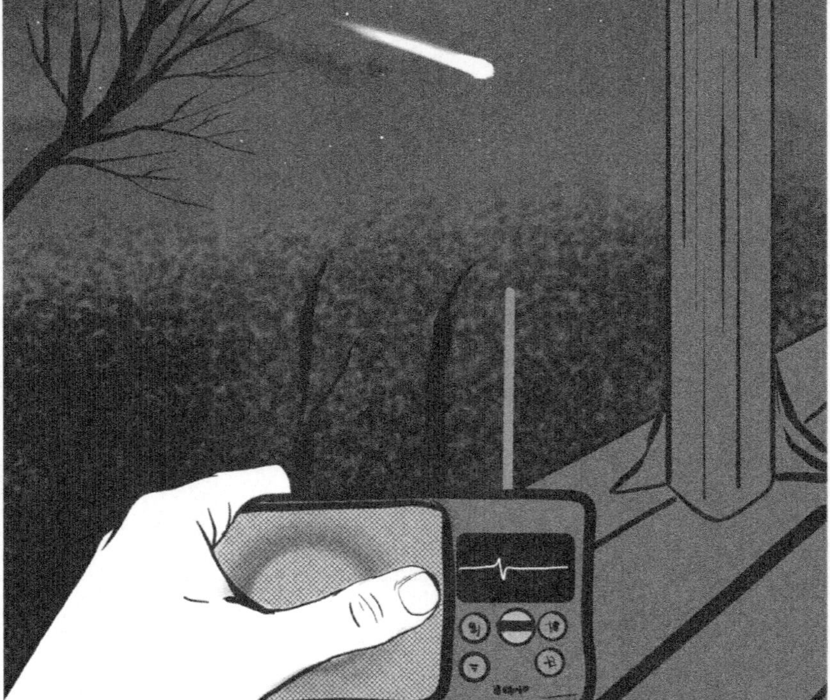

570

After a few weeks of rest in San Francisco, you head out into the American wilderness as you have always done.

It is a relief to escape the city, for - in spite of what you thought - you have gained little in the way of confidence and sympathy from living amongst men and women once again.

It is not so much that you are aware of what you have become - in truth, you are inclined to do your utmost to discredit what happened to you in the brig as some sort of malaria-induced delirium - but that the terror of the Island of Doctor Moreau is never far from your thoughts.

Somehow, you are unable to persuade yourself that the people you meet are not well-crafted beast-people, mere animals half wrought into the outward image of human souls. Your ever-present fear is that the multitudes will presently begin to revert, to show first this bestial mark then that before attempting to tear you to pieces...

You also fear that the effect of the elixirs the doctor crafted are impermanent, and that you may begin to hunch, twist and devolve into a slavering, merciless thing that will be captured and subjected to experiments as vicious as any Doctor Moreau ever conducted.

But it is people who unnerve you most. When amongst them, you see faces keen and bright, others dull or dangerous, others unsteady and insincere; none that have the calm authority of a reasonable soul. This apprehension is worsened by the fact that your senses have become heightened, whether from terror or from the beasts with which you have been spliced. You see and hear things that a human could not possibly discern, you *smell* things that the human nose could not know. Your reflexes are swift, and your strength is beyond that of a person of your modest frame.

As the years pass and you retain your outward humanity, you take passage from New York back to London on a fancy to see the place of your birth once more. Upon arrival in that dank metropolis, you swiftly realise that it is a place far worse for one such as you than ever the large, dispersed American cities could be.

Wherever you go in the foggy streets, prowling women mew at you, furtive men glance jealously, pale and weary workers go coughing by, old folk pass murmuring to themselves, and everywhere there are ragged packs of gibing children with the wildness of the beast glinting in their eyes.

Thus dismayed - and with the last of your money - you withdraw to a modest home upon the English South Downs, devoting your days to reading and to experiments in chemistry, while you give a good part of the night to the study of astronomy. In the glittering hosts of heaven you find a sense of infinite peace and protection. Mars the Red Planet compels you, for you have read learned articles speculating that there is intelligent, technological life there.

One night you see flashes of light emanating from that planetary body. They persist for several nights. Then, you see the flash of a shooting star near your home, and begin to hear strange reports from the wireless...

YOU HAVE SURVIVED **THE ISLAND OF DOCTOR MOREAU** - WELL PLAYED!

BUT A FAR GREATER THREAT REMAINS...

Look out for the second book in KJ Shadmand's *Great Literature Gamebooks* series,

War of the Worlds - An Interactive Adventure

Coming soon...

Note from KJ Shadmand

If you enjoyed *The Island of Doctor Moreau - An Interactive Adventure*, leaving a positive review on Amazon and/or Goodreads will really show your support for any future *Great Literature Gamebooks*. Positive feedback lets independent authors like me know that we are doing something right. You don't need to write much, just a sentence or two. Of course, if you would like to leave a more detailed review then that is excellent as well!

As well as leaving a review, consider acquiring a copy of my highly-acclaimed debut fantasy book, *Children of Anshar*, also available on Amazon:

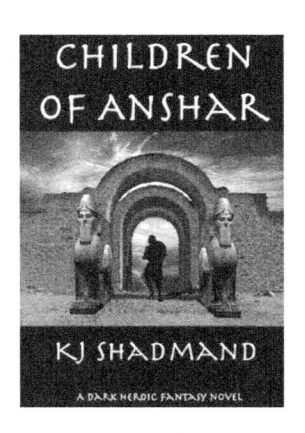

About the Author

KJ Shadmand is an avid reader of fantasy novels and gamebooks. Originally from Southampton, England, he studied modern history at the University of Oxford, and has lived in the UK, Ireland, South Korea, and Japan.

KJ is also Founder of OtherWorldsLearning, a company that provides fantasy roleplaying games for corporate team building and English language learning.

The Island of Doctor Moreau – An Interactive Adventure is KJ Shadmand's debut gamebook; look out for more works to come under Great Literature Gamebooks.

To learn more, you can find KJ on the following platforms:

LinkedIn: Kurosh James Shadmand

Twitter: @KShadmand

Website: Otherworldslearning.com

Email: support@otherworldslearning.com

476

To Helmar and the Unknown Sailor, consigned to a watery grave…